Jason Queen meets with Way in Devon, forming them half way round the has an unusual and sign father that gains him admittance to Mr James Passendale of the East India Company, and an appointment as apprentice midshipman. He is introduced to Margaret, the very appealing daughter of Mr Passendale, and the romance that starts between these two is somehow inevitable and almost pre-destined, but the ominous threat to their future is the consuming desire of Jason to sail as deck officer on a tall ship . . . a desire that will take him away to sea for long years. He serves as midshipman on an early East Indiaman, a ship superstitiously damned from inception and which suffers from recurring trouble and bad luck. Jason Queen is an idealistic youth who, after many adventures, proves himself as a leader of men, one who can command unusual devotion and loyalty from his crew. Then he has to come face to face with the barbarity of the human animal, and his ideals are torn asunder, leaving him bitter and with a blood lust for retribution, born of affection for a native Princess, and nurtured under a hanging tree on an Indonesian island. He captures a formidable pirate ship and, after assuming command, takes his ship back into the South China Sea on a personal vendetta . . . a vendetta that ends in piracy and brutal murder. Command! Power! The lust for absolute power dominates Jason Queen; this is a legacy from his father who own lust for command eventually drives his sweetheart into another man's arms. Is Jason about to do the same? All his life he has found great difficulty in letting go of treasured possessions. He can't let go! Of his ship . . . his comrades . . . his faithful crew, and most of all . . . of his Maggie?

Maggie tells him that there has to be a compromise somewhere, butr compromise is a double-edge sword that must cut both ways: or it will surely sever them!

About the Author

Born Salford, Lancashire. Educated C of E primary school and Salford College of Technology. Served three years in the Royal Navy. Rank Petty Officer, Electric Articifer. During which time developed a love of the sea that was carried on into private sail boats and after taking a sabbatical to sail full time for six months my wife and I moved to Devon where I sold my previous, smaller yacht to buy a thirty four foot sloop which we moored at, and sailed from, Dittisham on the River Dart. The association with the sea and sailing was my incentive, even my compulsion to write, but of the old-time square-riggers. The romance of sail! Because I feel very strongly that the tall ships were among the loveliest creations ever designed by man.

My wife and I live at Providence in the parish of Throwleigh, Dartmoor. This must be one of the smallest hamlets on Dartmoor with just five dwellings and, of course, the Gospel Chapel that was the first to be built here, and brought with it the name Providence. It is remote, rural, and an ideal situation for creative writing. While enjoying much time in writing, I have kept solvent with my occupation as your friendly neighbourhood builder. Dartmoor seems far removed from the coast yet I have returned to the sea and the sailing ships with "Jason Queen" in which I invite the reader to sign on in a passenger berth aboard an early East Indiaman, outward bound, and I am confident that all readers will find much to enjoy in this epic story of adventure: and romance!

Other titles by the same author

MONTAINGE BARTON
ASK ME TO STAY WITH YOU
PAVANE FOR A DEAD SEAMAN
JOKER

The Coming to Manhood of
Jason Queen

Frank Smith

To Brian

With Regards

Frank Smith

Higher Providence Publishers

This novel is entirely a work of fiction. The names, characters, localities and incidents portrayed in it are the work of the author's imagination. Any resemblance to actual persons, living or dead, or events is entirely coincidental.

© Frank Smith 2005

First published in Great Britain 2005 by
Higher Providence Publishers.

All rights reserved. No part of this publication can be reproduced. Stored in a retrieval system, or transmitted in any form or by any means without the prior permission in writing of the publisher, nor be otherwise circulated in any form of binding or cover other than that in which it is published and without a similar condition, including this condition, being imposed on the subsequent purchaser.

ISBN 0-9541211-2-0

Printed and bound in Great Britain by
Short Run Press Ltd, Sowton Industrail Estate,
Exeter, Devon.

Cover design by David Ashby, Orchard Cottage,
Throwleigh, Devon.

Higher Providence Publishers, Providence, Throwleigh, Devon.
E-mail: frank@smit55.freeserve.co.uk

Dedication

As always . . . To my wife, Eunice.
For the belief and confidence that
keeps me writing.

Mariners Way

Buried in the obscure mist of ancient legend and local belief handed down through the generations are many stories about the bridle paths and right of way across the County of Devon, in particular across the vast area of the exposed, bleak and rugged high ground known as Dartmoor.

There is a strong tradition on the eastern side of the Moor that there once existed a route used by seafarers travelling overland between the port of Bideford on the formidable northern seaboard, and the snug port of Dartmouth on the southern. Why seamen should choose to travel this distance is open to conjecture, though substance to the old legend can be found among the dusty papers of Gidleigh village 15th century church, in which payments of alms given to such landlocked sailors are recorded.

One of the stories, to which the legibility of proof is difficult to find, suggests the track was signposted with huge stones on which the markings were ships' anchors chiselled in the weathered granite, and it is further related that old fashioned tobacco pipes with distinctive small bowls, have been picked up along the lines of the track.

Sufficient it is to suppose that the route wends south from Bideford by way of the Torridge valley and Great Torrington. On through Merton and Exbourne to the diminutive villages of Sticklepath and Throwleigh and possibly crossing Forder and Chapple farms to the lovely old church at Gidleigh. Then up through Yardworthy and Jurston and ever south-eastward over the Moor . . . finishing the trek along the Dart valley and so to Dartmouth by way of Buckfast and Totnes.

Reporting in *c*1706, William Simpson, surveying for the Duchy on the possibility of developing farming and mining on Dartmoor wrote, "that within the last twenty years there was only three or four very blind roads across the Moor insomuch that going over the Moor in winter was always considered not only as an arduous, but as a really dangerous undertaking: and the many lives lost in the undertaking are too notorious to be doubted."

The distance from Bideford to Dartmouth is some sixty miles by the kindest of calculation and, by any yardstick: is a long walk.

Part One

Chapter One

Mid-Summer *c*1720
The bridle path was hard going, mud clutching at his boots and slowing his rangy stride. The village of Sticklepath was almost two hours behind him now and he thought his destination of Gidleigh must be close because he had caught a glimpse of a church bell tower. Coming out of the shadow of the trees, the going was immediately easier where the earth had been dried by exposure to wind, and sunshine. Pausing to scrub his boots with a handful of long grass, then stepping out again with renewed energy and the fields flowed by in sweet-smelling, disoriented patterns of shading green. He had encountered barely a soul since the last village but now ahead he could see figures and movement in a cleared area under the spreading branches of a great oak tree, and a wisp of smoke curling from a log fire in front of a lean-to shack. As he drew nearer, he realised this was just a roof of woven twigs supported on the corners by cut down branches of trees. Three men

were gathered around the fire on which spit roasted the carcass of a large rabbit, or hare. Dressed in seafarers' rig they viewed the newcomer with open curiosity. Sitting with his back against one of the corner posts, a fourth man appeared to be dozing then one eye opened.

'Take the weight of your legs, boy,' he said in friendly greeting, 'sit down and enjoy the last of the sunshine.' As the youth eased the pack of his shoulders with a grunt of relief, the speaker enquired. 'Travelling south? You a seaman?'

Nodding to the initial question. 'I'm going to be a sailor, sir, ' said the newcomer.

'Just like that, eh?' Shrewd eyes scrutinising the youth who sat cross-legged beside him, noting the stout boots and the woollen hose pulled up over tough looking Devon trousers his voice held a note of indulgent humour as he stated. 'That's a good rig for walking the Moor but I somehow fancy you haven't long been away from home. How old are you, eighteen?'

'Going on twenty, sir.' The voice conveyed a sense of assurance. Respectful, but in no way subservient and he smiled easily at the man before him.

This man was quite young himself, probably in his late twenties. Dark hair, that swept down to form luxurious side whiskers and a full moustache and beard. His cheeks were the colour of tanned leather, and his eyes were clearest blue and diamond sharp. He wore a faded fisherman-type smock and tan coloured sailcloth trousers, well frayed at the leg bottom. He was smoking a clay pipe with a curving stem and a small tobacco bowl. Scratching his head with the mouthpiece he then placed it back in his mouth. A manoeuvre watched with fascination by the new arrival.

'What's your name, lad?'

'Jason Queen.'

'And I, young Jason, am Daniel Vinderman, seaman extraordinary.' He had a flowing way of speaking and his apparent lack of modesty brought a grin to Queen's face. 'Call me Vindo,' said Vinderman, 'everyone does. Got a berth waiting at Dartmouth?'

'No, sir.'

'Any experience?'

'My father taught me to sail, in small boats in and around the estuary of Bideford and Instow.'

'Hardly deep sea stuff,' scoffed Vinderman, 'you won't find it easy to be taken on by the hard-headed ship masters at Dartmouth.'

'Only need a berth as far as London.'

'Why London?'

'I have an introduction to a shareholder in the East India Company and hope to secure a post as apprentice deck officer.'

'Seems a roundabout way to get there?'

'It's a long walk from Bideford to London,' said Queen in explanation, 'and I thought a few weeks experience at sea might be to advantage.'

'Ship I'm joining is paying off in the Pool of

London, but not until she's traded the French coast up from Bordeaux.' His eyes were speculative and so was his voice as he mused. 'East Indiamen, eh, wouldn't mind a crack at that myself?' The thought seemed provocative and he said in thoughtful tone. 'Might be able to talk the skipper into taking you along for the ride. No guarantees mind, and you won't get paid more than a few shillings and your keep.'

'I'll work for nothing to get to London.'

'The fool kind of sentiment that keeps seamen poor,' snapped Vinderman in angry retort, 'and you remember that fact, Jason Queen. When you work for a living, expect to get paid or you might just as well sit here and sleep in the sunshine with your back against yonder tree stump. You've a lot to learn, lad,' he said in quieter tone. 'Ship owners are a tight-fisted breed who would exploit someone as green and landlubberly as you for their own miserable profit.' Allowing a moment for this to sink in, he queried. 'You had schooling?'

'Yes, sir.'

'Stop calling me sir! The name's Vindo, and I've been at sea since I was eleven years old. Perhaps I don't read too well but I can sure find my way across a chart and work wind and tide like no man ever did before, aye, then feel the ship home through fog thick as seagoing green pea soup.' Vinderman in full rhetoric was worth hearing, and Queen listened with growing respect as he went on to state. 'That was my schooling, hardest classrooms of them all. Salt water and ships and of men as hard and tough as the ships they sail in. Some mean and some miserable but sometimes . . . just sometimes,' he added with feeling, 'you meet one in whose hand you can put your own. Men whose lives cross for but a brief moment of time and then sever for always, but the memory of such men lingers on to enrich your own life.' Eyes calculating on the attentive face of his young listener, he mused as if to himself. 'What kind of a man are you going to be, Jason Queen?' As he spoke the name, a thought occurred to furrow lines on his brow. 'Are you any relation to the Mr John Queen who was harbour pilot at Bideford?'.

'My father.'

'Sorry, lad,' said Vinderman. 'Time I learned to keep my mouth shut.'

'It was a long time ago.'

No emotion evident in the words and Vinderman seemed to approve of his reticence. 'Stick with me across the Moor and on to Dartmouth,' he promised, 'I'll get us both to your East India Company.'

'We're about ready here, Vindo,' called one of the men at the fire.

'Got anything to eat, Jason?'

'Some bread and cheese.'

'Save that for tomorrow, come over to the fire and share what we have.'

They sat round the fire and the man in charge of cooking doled out portions of meat. There was also a huge pan of potatoes, steaming hot and still in their jackets. The men ate quickly and with hunger apparent, while Queen wondered about the origin of the potatoes, but kept prudent silence. They were a rough but cheery bunch and he was soon at ease in their company. During the mealtime conversation he learned that this was the recognised resting place for such as them and that all utensils in use were to be left in the shack, just as they had been found, for the benefit of other seamen walking the route. As the youngest, Queen was detailed for washing up, using the cool-running water of a nearby stream for this, and for his own brief toilet.

Cool of evening, sitting round the glowing embers. 'How about a tune, Vindo?' asked a drowsy seaman.

Vinderman nodded, and from his pack produced a musical instrument, strangely small and with an awkward turn to the shape of its body. Wriggling it into position between upper thigh and arm, he returned Queen's look of amused interest with a grin.

'Queer little thing, is it not? Picked it up on the Spanish seaboard some years ago.' Cradling the instrument as he said, 'Where I go, so goes my lute.' Thumbing the strings and, satisfied with the tuning, he began to strum. Sang a few melodies. His voice was a rich baritone and strangely moving in the quiet of that woodland glade and Queen fell asleep with the music soothing his tired mind.

He had the dream again! And woke with a start to find Vinderman looking at him, and querying, 'Nightmare?'

'Not really.' Eyes closing in sleep. Vinderman tucked his jacket around the youth's shoulders.

Next morning, all up and about and preparing to move off: Vinderman and Queen striding away together leaving the others trailing behind.

Along a leafy lane and across sloping meadows, climbing over stone steps built into the hedges and following the faint track up the early slopes through the hamlet of Jurston and then ever upward. The gradient was much steeper now and they paused in the early morning sunshine to ease off their packs and drink from a fast flowing stream. Ice cold and refreshing, so they rested awhile before again hoisting their packs and striding along the path winding ahead in clear view. The moorland began to open out and reveal something of its vast ruggedness. They would reach a summit thinking this indeed must be the top only to find there was another, and yet another slope ahead. Bright sunlight, casting a glow over contrasting colours . . . away in the distance could be seen the dense and darker green of a wooded area stretching for miles. The scenery was breathtaking and as Queen stopped to gaze on the raw splendour, Vinderman sat on a clump of rock. 'Thought you'd never take a rest,' he grumbled, 'beginning to wish I'd stayed with the others and let you rush off on your own.'

The morose tone brought a smile from Queen. 'This Moor seems to go on forever and I can hardly take it all in.' Sitting alongside Vinderman, he jested. 'Anyway, you said you had been this way often.'

'Said before, not often. The less I see of Dartmoor the better as far as I'm concerned. May be a lovely sight today but just wait until you have to do this walk in foul weather. Was across only once in winter. Never again! I'd rather die of hunger in Bideford than freeze to death in this God forsaken place.' Cramming tobacco into his pipe he said emphatically, 'The Moor is better left to the sheep and wild ponies that roam here, it's no place for a sailing man to get run ashore on.'

They slept rough that night at Widecombe and the next close to Totnes. The following day saw them walking the banks of the river Dart where the sleepy villages of Tuckenhay and Cornworthy meandered by the water's edge while the rising tide made over mud and shingle. Up a wooded slope into clear view and the upper reaches of the Dart opened out before them. Sunshine fired the river into blue silver that dazzled the eyes and the hills dropped in a curving wooded pattern of green, which seemed to dip into the water. Brown sail moving downstream and making slow progress against the tide and the distance making everything appear in miniature.

Queen was spellbound at the beauty of the valley and, sharing the moment of appreciation, Vinderman stated with conviction rife in his voice, 'Really something, isn't it, no matter where you travel in this world, Jason lad, you will find few places to equal this. What better haven could a seafaring man wish for when his time comes ... to sit quietly in the sun and watch the waters flow by? This is where I'll finally drop the anchor and finish my days.' Not a man to brood on such thoughts he said with a grin. 'But not yet, eh Jase. Not yet! Time enough for the rocking chair when the blood stops running hot. When the last jug of wine's been drunk and when every pretty girl has been loved: and left.' Pounding Queen on the shoulder he boldly declared. 'Time is on our side and a whole world is out there somewhere: with fame and fortune beckoning.' His exuberance was infectious and he finished with a cry of:

'So let's be at it then, mate!'

Chapter Two

Leadenhall St. A multitude of pedestrian's . . . the roadway bustling with horse-drawn traffic. Covered wagons rumbled behind pairs of great shire horses and rattling delivery carts hindered smart carriages and brought impatient gestures from their drivers. Among the melee walked a young man. Though bewildered by the sight and sound and the incredible haste his eyes never ceased from scrutiny and came to focus on a tall and prominently-structured facade, the curved apex of which hosted the statue of a seafarer in a jaunty pose and, just below, the upper story portrayed an imposing mural of a tall ship under all plain sail.

As he waited a chance to cross in safety a smart coach came to a halt in front of the building and a be-wigged footman sprang forward to assist three occupants to alight. The men were fashionably dressed and hurried through the double doors of the entrance as if they were late arriving. The driver urged away his team of four and, as the footman regained his position by the entrance, the young man confronted him. 'Excuse me, sir,' he asked politely, 'is this the office of the East India Company?'

The footman looked suspiciously at him and the haversack on his back. 'Thought everyone knew that.' A big man, thick bodied and heavy in the shoulder, he said, not unkindly, 'Move on. No one's allowed to loiter in front of the East India office.'

The stranger stood his ground but his voice reflected extreme nervous tension as he said, 'Is it possible to see Mr James Passendale?'

'Mr James,' echoed the footman, 'soon to be Sir James if the rumour's true.' Standing solid in the doorway, he repeated in hard tone. 'Now move on! Mr Passendale is too important to be concerned with the likes of you.'

'I have come a long way to see him.' Holding out his hand to disclose a small coin. 'If you show him this he might find time for me?'

The footman refused to even look at the coin. 'This is the great John Company,' he snapped, 'casual strangers are not allowed in. Now beat it! Before I have you arrested for loitering, and if you ever get into one of those prison 'ell 'oles you'll probably end up in one of them new colonies and thousand of miles away.' Adding as an afterthought, 'If they don't hang you?'

A tall, stoop-shouldered man had approached from dusty Leadenhall St. He wore a shiny top hat and, curious at the truculent manner of the footman, he paused at the entrance, then said, 'Trouble, Johnstone?'

'Good morning, Mr Smethurst, sir,' said the footman, knuckling his forehead. 'This man thinks he can just wander in to see Mr Passendale, he has brought a coin that he claims will gain him admittance.'

'What kind of a coin?'

'Show him,' commanded Johnstone.

The youth opened his hand to disclose a tiny, crescent-shaped piece of gold with a hole drilled through the centre. Looking at it, Smethurst seemed intrigued as he queried, 'Why should Mr Passendale be interested in such a coin?'

''Old memories perhaps, it was given to me by my mother, she said it would gain me admittance to Mr Passendale of the East India Company.'

'What is your name?'

'Queen, sir: Jason, John Queen.'

Smethurst's jaw dropped. 'Queen,' he blurted. 'Your name is John Queen?'

Queen nodded, taken aback at this reaction. Smethurst held out his hand. 'Let me have the coin,' smiling at the reluctance greeting this request he added, 'not to worry, Jason John Queen, I'll not be after stealing your little curio.'

Looking at him in a calculating manner Queen handed over the coin. Slipping it into his vest pocket, Smethurst instructed, 'Bring him inside; he can wait in the foyer while I look into this mystery. Is Mr Passendale in his office this morning?'

'Came in about an hour ago.'

The foyer was a wide hallway revealing a depth of building unimaginable from outside. Long corridors branching off, they were cool and polished with numerous doors of light oak displaying engraved nameplates. A wide stairway at the end curving in grand style up and on to a broad landing and as he stood alone increasing tension made him begin to wish he hadn't come at all, then from the landing, a bulky figure raced down the stairway with Smethurst just behind. Gaining the foyer, the first man stared around then asked breathlessly, 'Where is he?'

Smethurst pointed. Queen held his breath.

'You are John Queen?' Face registering a blend of surprise and disappointment, he advanced towards the youth, whose resolve was fading fast before this formidable man, his throat was dry and his tongue immovable as Passendale's eyes bored into him with curiosity rampant. 'For a moment, I hoped . . .' muttering the words, breaking off before he had finished. Slightly shorter in height he had to look up as he said in demanding tone. 'Asked you a question?' His voice was brusque, and only his eyes showed signs of agitation.

'Jason John Queen, sir.' Hesitant, with nerves tingling, he found it very difficult to be at ease within these cloistered halls.

'Jason, eh?' Appraising him, Passendale noted

the wide spread of his shoulders and the lean waist and the long straight legs outlined in tight hose. 'Got his build, at least.' Murmuring the words as if to himself then, glancing around. 'Come up to my rooms, we can't have any kind of private conversation down here.' An understatement. The presence of Mr Passendale in animated dialogue was creating a good deal of interest among the staff bustling through the hallway and many curious glances were directed at them as he led up the stairs.

Mr Passendale's office was warm and well appointed with a long, table-like desk adorned only by a single sheaf of papers held down by a paperweight of solid silver, moulded in the shape of a cannon. The chairs were of leather with rich Indian cushions and to further accentuate the Eastern influence a luxurious square of Oriental rug covered the centre of the polished hardwood floor. 'Would you order coffee,' said Passendale to Smethurst, 'and then kindly leave us?' Smethurst disappeared, closing the door behind him. Seating himself behind the desk, Passendale asked. 'Where is your father, Jason?'

'Both my parents are dead.'

Slumping down in his chair, Passendale's eyes were sad and suddenly darker as he murmured, 'How long have you been on your own?' Kindness softening his tone and helping to ease Queen's dry-mouthed nervousness:

'Father died when I was aged ten,' he said, 'but

my mother only recently.' He offered no explanation and Passendale did not pursue the obviously painful matter but the embarrassment was relieved by the arrival of a manservant bearing a mahogany tray with a silver coffee pot and two huge cups big as soup bowls. Placing his tray on the table he poured two steaming cups then after an enquiring look, moved out of the office.

Queen was glad of the coffee, which had been liberally laced with cream and sugar. The cup gave his hand something to do, and his thoughts time to absorb the turmoil of the last few minutes. Passendale couldn't keep his hands off the coin and the look on his face was one engrossed in sentiment and remembrance then he reached into an inside pocket of his waistcoat to produce a similar piece and placed them both on the desk. They were identical apart from the tiny hole pierced in the one brought by the newcomer.

'Mother wore it round her neck,' Queen said in explanation. 'That's why she had the hole drilled, but only after my father died, I always knew there was another coin exactly the same.'

'Do you know how we got them?'

A far away look of reminiscence had appeared on Passendale's face and Queen's eyes lit up. 'He would tell me such stories. Used to listen for hours-on-end when he was talking.'

'Did he tell you how we fought the Portugese man of war to a standstill? How we boarded her in the pale light of dawn off the coast of Sumatra and how we fought hand to hand until they finally surrendered?'

'My favourite story, wanted him to tell me that one over and over again.' Unable to restrain himself and taking up the narrative, Queen excitedly stated. 'This is where you got the coins. Taking one each and making a vow that if ever one of you was in need the sight of this coin would bring the other running: without question and with no regard for cost or personal danger.'

'We took them . . . stole them, if you like, from one of the passengers, a man of noble rank from the style of his dress.' Visibly shaken by the memory, Passendale cried out. 'Oh, God! When the world was young, and so were we!' He then said with great sadness. 'John Queen: where have you been all these years?'

Warming to this man, who was so obviously moved by the memory of his father, Queen's apprehension faded. 'You and he must have been real comrades,' he said

This statement caused Passendale to glance down for a moment. Then, raising his head, he declared, 'There was never again a man such as John Queen. This was a man upon whom you could stake your life.' Pausing for reflection, before adding, 'And I did, on more than one occasion.' Eyes riveting on Queen's face. 'Did he ever speak of me?'

'Not a word apart from the story of the coins,

and then I always had to plea with him.'

'Even John Queen could not completely shut out the memory of those early years.' Tone hardening, and Queen began to sense conflict in the relationship between these two as Passendale asked. 'How old are you, Jason?'

'Nineteen, sir.'

'How the wheel turns full circle.' Nostalgia rife in his voice, looking at Queen as he demanded. 'And what brings you to East India House with a coin that restores the fire of old battles to this battered frame. What need has a John Queen that he has to beg assistance from one such as me?'

Gaining his feet in one swift move he reached for his cap and his shoulders tensed and he seemed to grow inches taller and his nostrils flared. 'Thank you for your time, sir,' he snapped, 'but I am in no way a beggar and stand here only to fulfil a pledge made to my mother before she died. That I would seek out Mr Passendale of the East India Company and lay before him this gold coin.' Reaching for his coin, he said as if in conclusion. 'This much have I done.'

Passendale's hand fastened on his wrist and held tight. Then, with sardonic amusement in his tone, he declared, 'I'd almost forgotten how fiery runs the Queen blood. You might not look much like him but you certainly inherit his temper and pride.' Mood of amusement subsiding, Passendale came from behind the desk. 'I have so many questions I don't know where to start. Will you come and stay at my home until we have discussed more fully just what we are going to do with you?' Grasping him by the arm he said with quiet assurance. 'Please believe, Jason, I'm overjoyed to have you here and I think your mother was a very shrewd and sensible lady.' Throwing papers into a top drawer he snapped it shut. 'No work today,' he announced. 'First we'll get some food down that lean body of yours, then a tour of London and home to what has the makings of a very enjoyable evening.'

Hesitating, Mr Passendale looking at him with a puzzled glance, then Queen smiled, and, picking up the coins from the desk, handed one to his host. Threading a fine chain of gold through the hole in his own he hung it round his neck:

'I'm ready now, sir.'

Chapter Three

The Passendale home was situated high on the sloping meadows at Richmond and far removed from the teeming streets of London. A large, imposing residence set way back in extensive grounds, it was reached only after the carriage had driven through double wrought iron gates and up a long driveway where trees on either side formed an appealing arch of green.

The room into which he had been ushered looked out over meadow and river. It was cool and comfortable, with a huge four-poster bed monopolising the room. A quiet knock on the door and in response to his invitation to enter a manservant appeared with a request for him to attend Mr Passendale in the study. He had washed and tidied up in readiness and now joined his host in the study, which was a lofty, ornamental-ceiling room amply provided with armchairs of dark leather. Bookshelves lined two walls and under the window was positioned a sideboard on which were numerous decanters of cut glass, their prisms reflecting the colour of the contents. 'Come and sit down,' greeted Passendale warmly, 'don't suppose you drink strong liquor yet but perhaps you'll join me in a glass of claret?' Pouring wine into a goblet, rich and ruby red. Sipping the wine, Queen found it rough on his tongue, but not unpleasant. After he was seated comfortably, Passendale said to him. 'Tell me about your family, Jason lad, live somewhere in Devon you said?'

'Just to the west of Bideford and about five miles inland.'

'Could never understand why an all-action man like your father would bury himself out in the wilds?'

'Don't know of his reasons, but my mother was a native of the area. I think they met when my father's ship put into Bideford for repair.'

'Did he leave the sea at that time?'

'For a short period, then he was offered the post of pilot to the Port and when there was no shipping to be brought over the bar he would work on the farm that had been left to my mother.'

'Sounds a busy life.'

'Never heard him complain and he seemed at his happiest working the land.' Sadness reflecting in his voice as he went on. 'But I have only childhood memories now and can't really know how he felt.'

In quiet unobtrusive tone, Passendale asked the question uppermost in his mind:

'How did he die, Jason?'

'Went out to a ship in distress one terrible stormy day. He and his crew reached the vessel safely but she broke up crossing the bar and they were all drowned.' His voice trembled, then recovered as he explained. 'He knew they were taking enormous risk because he was heard to say that the Master must be a fool running for the estuary in those conditions and that he would have been safer staying out in deep water.' The look of anguish devastated the listener, then Queen proudly declared. 'It was his job! And he knew the men aboard the ship had no chance at all without local knowledge. They brought the bodies ashore the next day and after the service we buried them in the chapel graveyard overlooking the sea.' Shrugging away the melancholy that always seemed to shadow him when he thought of his parents, he then stated. 'My mother cried for days after the funeral. Then one day, when the sun was shining, we went up to the little graveyard and planted daffodils on the mound of earth, after which she turned to me and said, "We'll dry the tears now, Jason. Your father was John Queen. He died as he lived. Bravely and well: and we'll not shame his memory with everlasting sorrow."'

'You've had more than your share of sadness in such a tender life, young Jason,' said Passendale with evident compassion. Intrigued by the narrative and wanting to learn more, he asked. 'What happened to the farm after your father died?'

'Mother let it go back to the brothers in the family because she maintained that if we were to go on living and working at the farm I would spend all my time working and not getting any learning. Said my future was too important to her. So we moved into Bideford and I went back to school and mother found jobs of work enough to just keep us.' Adding with a smile. 'She came from a large family and there was plenty of food on the table from the farm and other places about.'

Gulping wine. Trying to hide the emotion that threatened composure. 'Your mother seems a very wise woman and a devoted wife to John,' said Passendale.

'She always told me how happy her life had been but I don't think she ever got over losing him in such a way.' The expression on his face belied his tender years. It was a look of understanding and inner strength and his eyes were deep and clear as crystal and a note of infinite tenderness crept into his voice as he explained. 'She was so sad that she had nothing to leave when her time had come. Asked me to forgive them both for leaving me without material needs or anything of value.' Eyes closing as if in pain, he murmured, 'I loved her so very much.' He had more to say but only secret words and only to himself. If only he could tell her now? His parents had no cause for regret, for his childhood had been filled with a content that had always been more than enough. He came back from private sorrow to find Passendale placing an arm round his shoulder.

'Will you take me to see their grave one day?' he asked quietly.

Wiping the back of his hand across his eyes to close out the tears, suddenly glad to have the warmth and hospitality of this man whom he hardly knew. His host was dressed in a dark-blue frock coat and there was lace at his neck and wrists and his silver-coloured hair swept back from a keen, hawkish face and as their eyes met Passendale returned Queen's look of curiosity. 'Can't understand why my father never spoke of you?' asked Queen in wondering tone.

Passendale seemed reluctant to reply. The expression on the young face was typical John Queen and as the past reached out to stir the blue-veiled and misty banks of memory he couldn't sit still and gained his feet to momentarily lean against the oak lintel that spanned the open-hearth fireplace. Then he straightened and said in a voice that was somehow far away and melancholy. 'John Queen and James Passendale, apprentices together and from the very first our friendship was such as few men have ever known. For two years we served on the same ship, the little *Argo*.' As he spoke the name, a thought occurred that brought a flush of pleasure to his face and he pulled across a chair to sit close and eagerly declare. 'He didn't forget after all, even John Queen could not so easily close his mind, for where else do you think you got the name of Jason?' Allowing a moment for this to register, he then resumed his reminiscence. 'We sat together for our Master's ticket. The East India Company needed ships' Masters, and liked them young and eager. Only then would we accept that we had to be split up and posted onto separate ships, but we always sailed in convoy and sought each other in foreign ports.' Draining his glass and pouring another as if needing time to collect thought and memory into coherent speech, he said at last. 'The world was young and beautiful, and there were great opportunities for men like us.' Smiting a hard fist on the arm of his chair he cried. 'John Queen could have been a wealthy man if he had not been so proud and so pig-headedly obstinate! And just when we were beginning to see reward for our early years of hardship.'

The way he said this bordered on self-criticism, causing Queen to look at him. 'Something desperate must have happened for him to leave the service of the Company,' he said curiously.

'Another story: and one that I'm not prepared to divulge. Sufficient is it that I am given the chance to build the name of Queen to its former glory and respect. So trust in me, lad, for the memory of John Queen. Aye,' he added with feeling, 'and for the love I had for him.'

The door opened and a young woman swept in, stopping in her tracks as she sensed the emotion lingering in the study. She was dressed elegantly in a gown of royal blue, with a full, hooped skirt. Her hair was dark. She was so petite she looked almost fragile but great vitality reflected in the sparkle of almond coloured eyes and in the softness of a lovely mouth.

'Father,' she said in dismay, 'have I come at a bad moment?'

'There are no bad moments when you are around, darling. Your timing is perfect so come and meet the son of a very old friend.' Passendale then said with a smile. 'Jason John Queen, allow me to introduce my daughter, Margaret.'

She curtsied in brief formality. He had no idea what to do or what to say, more flustered than ever before in his lifetime. The sight of this lovely young woman had further shattered his already exposed emotions and he found great difficulty in getting his mouth under control enough to say anything and Passendale raised an eyebrow at the sudden silence. His usually loquacious daughter seemed speechless and her eyes were like huge saucers as she looked into the face of the young man before her. A shudder ran through her, and with the shudder came the strangest feeling that she had met him before. He gave her a shy smile. It was a revealing flash of even teeth in a face coloured by exposure to wind and salt water and framed by the long and unkempt hair that swept down his face and neck and she had to step back a pace to free her from confusion. 'Queen,' she finally managed to say, 'that name has a familiar sound?' Looking enquiringly at her father as she said this.

'No doubt you have heard your dear departed mother tell of John Queen,' said Passendale. He appeared a little anxious in the atmosphere that had developed but the tension was relieved by the appearance of a manservant announcing that supper was ready.

Always hungry, Queen acquitted himself well at the table and there was little in the way of conversation whilst they were eating, but he was uncomfortably aware of the attractive girl sitting opposite. She ate very little and every time he looked up from his plate he found her eyes upon him. Mostly she would glance demurely away and make pretence at eating but once her eyes held on his and he noted the expression of perplexity and the fine lines furrowing her brow.

Lighting up a long-stemmed pipe, Passendale poured brandy and looked at Queen, who shook his head in negation. He had that evening drunk more wine than he should and was even then a trifle heady. Passendale looked with meaning at his daughter. 'Please may I stay, father,' she immediately retorted, 'we so rarely have guests of my own age.'

Margaret knew how to obtain from her father most things in life she desired and contrived to look very sad, but he towered over her to say with a frown, 'Young ladies are not allowed to stay after supper when men are smoking and have important matters to discuss.' Looking across, he asked. 'What do you think, Jason?'

Queen looked at her and her eyes were huge, and appealing.

'Perhaps we can make an exception, sir,' he said, 'just this once.' He was rewarded with the full blast of her smile and the tingling touch of her feet brushing his under the table.

Pulling on his pipe, pouring more brandy into his glass, his mood growing ever more expansive, Passendale said, 'Now then, young Jason, just what are we going to do here. You say that you have had a thorough schooling?' Taking silence for assent, he stated. 'I can place you in the service of the Company as a writer.' Finding this amusing he couldn't restrain a chuckle and giving no time for reply hurried on with. 'There are tremendous opportunities for a man with education and many a young writer has risen to a position of great esteem, and made a considerable fortune along the way.' Having delivered this statement, he glared at Queen.

'I think you tease me, Sir.'

'The post of writer does not appeal?'

'No.'

'What exactly do you envisage for yourself?'

'What you and my father have done, sail as deck officer on a square rigger.'

Margaret was no longer unable to restrain impatience. 'Is it your ambition to spend all your life at sea,' she scorned, 'you surely must realise those voyages to the Far East and back can take as long as three years?'

'Margaret,' admonished her father, 'this is men's talk and I'll thank you to keep your silence.' Thoughtful now, he said to Queen. 'She's right though, it's much more comfortable in Leadenhall St. than spending long years back and forth to India and places.'

'I'm not looking for comfort.'

'Never thought you would be, and I cannot imagine the son of John Queen being happy behind a desk. Know what I was doing at your age, and assure you that the Company needs capable men to run its ships and keep the goods of commerce returning to England.' Concentrating on more practical matters, he queried. 'Any sea going experience?'

'Only about two months on a trading smack from Dartmouth to Bordeaux and back to London, paid off in the Pool just two days ago.'

'Hardly qualify you for deck officer. The best I can offer is a berth as apprentice but you must realise that an apprentice post is not to be recommended and once at sea you will be on your own and far removed from any influence of mine.'

'Seek no further favour, sir, and I'm grateful for your kindness.'

His calm determination impressed and Passendale nodded in approval. 'Tomorrow we go to East India dock to fix a berth. There is no ship sailing for several weeks and this is good because it will give us time to know you better and also to kit you out for seagoing.' Sudden enthusiasm brought him surging from his chair to look at Queen. 'Wish to God I was going with you,' he said excitedly, 'me and John were among the first adventurers and I can still revel in the glory of it.'

Queen looked at him and, noting the speculation on his face, Passendale's excitement subsided. 'Was there something else?' he queried.

'Have a friend who also needs a berth.' Shaking his head emphatically at the question in Passendale's sharp glance, he added quickly, 'Not as an apprentice. Fancy he is a little too old for such an appointment and would probably be offended at the thought, but he's a first rate seaman and has helped me so much I wonder if you can find him a berth aboard the same ship as myself.'

'No problem...what name?'

'Daniel Vinderman: they call him Vindo.'

Entering the dining room the butler placed a small, silver tray before Mr Passendale who glanced at the note contained thereon. 'Please excuse me,' he said rising to his feet, 'I have a business matter to attend.' Addressing his daughter, he suggested. 'Perhaps you will entertain Mr Queen for a while. Maybe a stroll on the terrace while there is daylight still remaining.' Tongue in cheek as he added, 'I'll send in Mrs Bronson if you need a chaperone.'

'In our own home, father?' Then, with a sweet smile. 'Think Mr Queen is more afraid of me than I of him. You might send in a chaperone for him. He needs one.'

Shrugging his shoulders in a gesture of resignation, Passendale went out of the room trailed by the butler. Queen's chair screeched back as she rose from the table. His feet were suddenly like lead and twice their normal size and she greeted his clumsy posture with a teasing smile. 'Would you care to take a turn around the terrace?' she asked. Moving away without waiting for a reply and he hesitantly followed through the French window on to a stone-paved patio. The evening was warm, daylight lingering and the sky was brilliant blue with no cloud in view and a crescent moon hung suspended with just one solitary star in attendance.

Pausing close to an ornamental wrought iron balustrade fronting the terrace, her delicate perfume invaded his senses and her smile devastated and her eyes were deep and lustrous as she gazed at him with interrogation apparent, and unavoidable. She was so right: he was afraid! He had never encountered such a composed and bewildering young woman. She could only be about eighteen, he estimated, but her bearing seemed altogether more controlled than his own. His tonsils were glued to the back of his throat then their eyes met and suddenly came wonderful communion between them. Her uplifted face was a picture of appealing youth and he felt his stomach muscles contract in the breathless and perplexing contact.

'How strange it all is,' she said, 'from the first moment I saw you in the study I have had this sensation of somehow recognising, as if I have known you before but in some other, long ago world?' Turning away with her thoughts and facing out towards the dim lights of the city, she went on to state in mystic tone. 'This is the time I like most, when the day is done and when dreams and realities merge into each other,' hesitating, as if unsure of his reaction and as if fearing ridicule, before composing herself to conclude, 'and when descending dusk allows a confidence to be shared without risk of embarrassment.' The way she said this, and the coy manner in which she said it, seemed to be inviting him to share in some deep secret and he found himself yielding to the strangeness of it all. Standing close beside her, with his hands reaching as though to touch only to fall away and be clasped together in the small of his back. They had met only this evening but already there was a definite sense of harmony between them. But he had never been at ease with girls, of any age. Always clumsy and with nothing to say, like now, and his reticence brought disappointment. 'Have you no hidden thoughts, Mr Queen,' she asked pertly, 'no fantasies of your own to rhapsodise upon?'

Again this wonderful sense of attraction, he couldn't resist the encompassing need to confide in her. If only he dare? Deeply embarrassed, his face burning and the wine perhaps making him more susceptible he somehow found voice to reply:

'My only fantasy is a strange recurring dream. One I have had since childhood and which has kept me awake on many a dark night.'

'Please. Do go on.'

'It's a dream in which I'm constantly pursued by a laughing, reckless girl,' speaking made it easier and he added more calmly, 'always ends up with me falling into space with her laughter echoing round me.'

'Does the dream frighten?' A whisper, that he could hardly hear. Turning to face him and her eyes were bright with consuming wonder. 'What does this dream girl look like?'

Somehow their searching hands came together and her fingers were cool but tight, almost demanding. 'That is the strangest part of it all,' he huskily said. 'Never at any time do I feel afraid yet I am always running the other way.'

'What does this dream girl look like?' she repeated insistently.

'Can't tell you because I never saw her face, just this dark swirling skirt and a pair of little red boots with pearl buttons up the inside.'

'Do you believe in fate, Jason Queen?'

'My father used to tell me that things happen only when they are made to happen.'

'Was our meeting tonight made to happen, or this strange sensation of knowing you?' He made no answer and his brow furrowed with lines of uncertainty. Removing her hands from his grasp she turned away from him and, as if far away in thought, asked. 'Why do you find your dream so disconcerting?'

'Because even though I have the dream so often I can never understand what it is all about.'

'Never mind then, Mr Queen, one day it will make sense.' She spoke in casual tone. Her eyes were dark and mysterious in the fading light and she placed her hand on his arm. 'Papa will be out soon, he's a stickler for propriety and won't leave us alone for long.' Her voice took on a note of mischief and devilry. 'Lest you pick me up in those strong arms and carry me off into the night.' Her eyes sparked fire at the thought, and he laughed out loud and the sound echoed mockingly around the terrace. 'What's so funny?' she asked haughtily.

'You are.'

'Glad the idea gives you cause for amusement,' she said with a toss of her head.

He had no experience of such bewildering conversation and couldn't cope with her changing moods and his laughter faded. 'The thought was provocative,' he said very uncomfortably, 'but I know you were only teasing.'

He had gone too quiet and she tried to make amends. 'Why so serious, Mr Queen? Liked it better when you were laughing at me.'

He didn't know what to say, and said nothing. They had strolled to the end of the terrace and had to turn back. Her hand had fallen away and he made a gallant arm. Laying her hand on his forearm with mock formality and again he knew the impact of penetrating eyes and a mouth curving into a smile of breathtaking warmth and vitality. He had no defence against her capricious changes of attack and, fumbling for words, blurted, 'Do you have to call me Mr? My name is Jason, and we have been formally introduced.'

'I'll drop the courtesy titles if you will,' she instantly replied. 'I'm Margaret: but you can call me Maggie.'

He had the dream again that night. But this time it was different.

The girl had a face!

A westerly wind gusted around the sweep of the East India dock at Blackwall, bringing the warmth of the countryside down the Thames valley, but not, alas, the fragrance. The stench of London's dock land had long since overpowered any breath of country air with its stench of stagnant salt water and seaweed and with the racket of workmen . . . shipwrights and riggers and dock labourers toiling on the mass of shipping that lay along the wharf side and outlying arms of the tidal jetty.

But around the dock that was the haven of the East India Company hovered an exciting aroma of exotic spice as a towering merchantman disgorged its cargo on to the stone-cobbled jetty and his nostrils twitched in appreciation and his senses revelled in the adventure and the suggestion of faraway, romantic places. The ship had recently docked. Stevedores hurling bulky sacks from ship to shore, derricks creaking under the strain of swinging nets loaded with boxes and crates, sailors leaving with packs a-shoulder. Many were gathered in the waist of the vessel and a fiddle played a lively tune and sailors and dockside women danced and made uncaring love in close embrace.

Entranced by the colour and spontaneous air of gaiety he turned to Mr Passendale, who had just finished instructing the coachman who had driven them from Leadenhall St.

'Looks as if they are having a celebration?'

'When you've been at sea as long as they, just being back home is reason enough to celebrate.' Shrugging, as if the scene was normal occurrence but at the same time sharing the boyish enthusiasm, 'Although in this case they have good cause because they have just made the second-fastest round trip in the history of the Company. Eighteen months from London to Bombay and back A record only once bettered and who else but John Queen would get his ship home in less time.' His mood changing even as he spoke, Passendale said in sombre tone. 'Being a good seaman isn't always enough. You need a great deal of luck in the shape of fair winds, and John would be the first to admit that his record making passage met with more than its share of good fortune.' Breaking off as he observed a man in the uniform of ship's Captain striding down the boarding platform.

Square shoulders ... medium height and stocky build and securing his hat over his forehead against the threatening lift of wind. His eyes were set deep in a sunburned face. He was clean-shaven except for the greying side-whiskers that lent his face an ecclesiastic look. With an air of genuine pleasure Passendale greeted the Captain and they clasped hands: warmly.

'Good of you to come down and meet me, James.'

He had a deep, resonant voice that penetrated above the incredible clamour, and Passendale responded fervently. 'Had to congratulate you personally, Fitz, we had a rider up from Gravesend to tell of your arrival. A wonderful run home and the directors are planning a big party for you and the officers of *Pandora*.'

'How about the crew?'

'Looks as if they are having a hornpipe of their own,' retorted Passendale, then, remembering his companion. 'I have a young man here who wants to serve as apprentice,' he said, 'and thought you might take him on.' Beckoning Queen forward. 'I would like to introduce you to Captain Fitzroy Probus, late of the *Pandora*.'

Looking sharply up at this statement, the Captain then gave courteous attention to the young man standing before him, taking in the broad shoulders and lean waist and hipline and the sturdy legs placed astride with the weight balanced agilely and as if poised for action.

Fitz,' said Passendale with anticipation apparent. 'Meet with Jason Queen.'

The Captain looked at Passendale, and his look was one of shock and speculation. 'Queen,' he repeated, adding incredulously, 'any relation?'

'Son and heir.'

He took Probus aside for a brief explanation, after which the Captain confronted Queen. 'Glad to have you serve with me.' Appraising the supple frame, he stated. 'Certainly got the build for it, lad.' Though intrigued at this encounter his thoughts were elsewhere and he accosted Passendale with a frown. 'Late of *Pandora*,' he snorted. 'Trying to retire me, James?'

'After a trip like this one, not bloody likely! Thought you may like a change of ship.' Hurrying on to explain. 'You've driven her hard for more than five years and she's due for a refit.' Glancing at Probus he said slyly. 'Can't afford you the same privilege.' Taking him by the arm he hurried along the dock and Queen followed, keeping discreet distance, realising he had no part in the business between the two. Passendale was speaking animatedly as they walked, then both speech and pace slowed as they came abreast of the stern of a sleek, tall-masted ship. The windows of the great aft stateroom towered over them but Probus had eyes only for the lines of the black and yellow painted hull. The ship swarmed with men hammering and sawing. Craftsmen were working on the dock alongside a number of long, slender tree trunks already stripped of their bark and now being shaped into yardarms with skilfully wielded adzes and chips of wood were flying high in steady progression. They slowly walked the length of the hull taking in every fascinating detail.

At the bow soared the figurehead of a bewigged statesman carved in oak with a scroll of parchment clasped in his fist. The statesman-figurehead was at once distinguished and commanding. Not for the Honourable John Company the voluptuous-breasted figure beloved of lesser mortals, and high on a staging erected at the bow a bearded man in a paint-smudged smock brushed final touches to the gilt lettering adorning the bow, *Earl of Rothesay*, painted boldly in a flowing hand, the artist seemed justly pleased with his work.

'What do you think of her, Fitz?'

'If she sails as good as she looks she'll be unbeatable.'

'First of her class! Designed and built to our own specification and then hired out to us.' Explaining in more detail, Passendale went on to state. 'The directors have known for some time that our vessels are too slow and unwieldy. We need a fleet that can sail faster and closer to the wind as well as run before them, we must get our convoys home more quickly.'

'You didn't bring me down here to waste time talking about fair winds,' questioned Probus, 'and you did say late of *Pandora*?'

'She's all yours. A new command.' Passendale was enjoying this and gesticulated at the row of gun ports along the hull. 'Twenty-four guns,' he stated, 'mounted twelve either side and with bow and stern chasers in addition. Yet the important thing is the fact that she is capable of out-sailing most ships you are liable to encounter.' Smiling at the look on the Captain's face, he said fondly. 'Our finest ship deserves our most capable Captain, and,' as an afterthought, 'keen and willing midshipmen to train as future Captains. By God, Fitz! This is the beginning of the finest fleet ever to sail the Seven Seas. I envy you. How I wish I could shed my responsibilities and sail with you, be Master again: of a proud ship.' Including Queen in the dialogue he now exclaimed. 'And here could be one of our future Masters. But make no mistake, Jason, this is no easy course I set. Opportunity is here and the time to grasp it is now, and only dedication and hard work will determine whether you are man enough to stay the distance because once you step aboard you'll be on your own to fight your way up to the officer's deck, for my influence stops here on the cobblestones of this dockside.' Staying his narrative to observe for reaction but Queen's eyes were level on his and clear and unafraid and his shoulders were set proud and, at that moment, he looked eager to get to work on rope and sail and steering wheel.

'I won't let you down, sir,' he said, 'always assuming the Captain will take me on.'

'I'll take you; if for no other reason than you are the son of John Queen. But I must warn you; this name you bear is going to be your hardest taskmaster. You have a great deal to live up to for the name of John Queen is respected in the memory of those who knew, and sailed with him, and you will inevitably be judged by his own formidable standards.' Looking at him as he said this and liking what he saw, he added, 'I reckon you will not be found wanting.' Shrugging away the trend of his thoughts, Probus looked at Passendale. 'When do I take over?'

'Patience, Fitz, she won't be ready for some weeks. Spend some time at home. We are holding a commissioning party at East India House in two weeks time to get together the officers.' Glancing at Queen to add, 'Maybe even apprentices, by which time we will be in a position to make definite plans.' Probus relaxed at this and

Passendale led him away. 'Come on. Fitz,' he said exuberantly, 'we'll share our midday meal and perhaps a glass or two?' Looking at Queen, who was away on thoughts of his own and his thoughts were proudly of his father and of the awe that everyone seemed to hold of him. Coming down to earth, he stammered hastily:

'Not really hungry, sir: may I go aboard?'

'You'll see more than enough when you get to sea.' Sensing disappointment, Passendale said with a shrug, 'As you wish, but don't get in the way and make a nuisance of yourself asking damn fool questions. I'll pick you up at four o'clock at the dock office. Is that understood?'

'Thank you, sir.' Leaving them standing he ran up one of the many broad planks bridging ship to shore.

'A fresh-faced likeable lad, James,' said the Captain, 'were we once like that?'

' Too long ago.' Passendale was in a philosophical mood. 'The world waits for the young men,' he said, 'and I reckon Jason Queen will make out just fine.'

Chapter Four

Lying in bed prematurely awake with so many conflicting thoughts churning over and over he couldn't get back to sleep. As he threw back the blankets and scrambled out of bed, dawn's early light through the window revealed the green of the woodland sloping down to the river and on an impulse he pulled on his clothes and a warm jacket then with boots under his arm stole quietly down the stairs and out the back door. The morning air struck chill and he hunched into his coat and strode out for the water's edge fully awake now and more able to deal with the turmoil of his mind.

He had been at the Passendale home for almost a month and now, with the ship ready for commissioning, he was increasingly aware that his sense of fulfilment was coupled with regret. A feeling almost of needing something more or, he conceded ruefully, someone else? His mind focussing on the laughing-eyed girl of whom he had grown so fond. Maggie! What a damn fool name for such an accomplished young lady. Yet how it suited her personality and ever-changing moods. During the long days waiting for the *Earl* to be made ready they had constantly been together in a wonderful harmony counter-balanced by sadness in the knowledge of impending departure.

This was a source of frustration to her and an irritant much in evidence on the night of the Ball given by the shareholders of the Company to celebrate the inception of the new ship.

"The Grand Ball"! Mind mirroring in retrospect the brilliance of the banquet hall he heard again the measured tones of the Duty Officer announcing the arrivals.

'Mr James Passendale, Miss Margaret Passendale, Midshipman Jason, John Queen.' Shaking hands with the Lord Mayor of London and his bejewelled lady and with a long line of dignitaries and, lastly, with Captain Probus.

Splendid in dress uniform with epaulettes of gold gleaming at his shoulders the Captain exuded good-natured authority. Looking at Queen in his newly tailored uniform, he said, 'Make the most of tonight, Jason lad, you won't get many chances to wear that rig once we go to sea.'

'Will it be soon, sir?'

'Soon enough, when we reach open water you might wish you hadn't been so eager.' The exchange received a snap of exasperation from

Margaret as she swept impatiently by. 'You are dismissed, Jason,' said the Captain, 'don't waste time with me when there are lovely young maids lying in wait for you,' adding with a stern-faced, 'but behave with proper decorum, my officers are in the hall keeping a keen eye out for any misbehaviour.'

Margaret had disappeared with her father into the crowded ballroom with the bustling figure of Mrs Bronson in close proximity. Hesitating on the fringe of the great hall. The scene was formidable ... full of colour and animation with the brilliance of the ladies gowns dazzling in splendour. Uncomfortable and feeling despondently out of his depth he followed in the wake of Mrs Bronson, knowing she would find Margaret with the instincts of a homing pigeon, and eased through the throng to a long table laden with dainty and appetising dishes of food. Bottles and decanters on trays at both ends, the centre dominated by a huge bowl of ruby-coloured punch and everywhere swarmed serving maids and bewigged footmen to cater for every need. He caught a glimpse of dark hair before she was hidden from view among a press of men and he heard her laughingly protest. 'Steady now, gentlemen. One at a time please!'

Easing out of a conversing quartet, Passendale said to Queen, 'You won't see much of Margaret for a while, her dance card fills very quickly.' With a speculative look he added, 'You have been much in each other's company these past weeks and I've been pleased to see you getting on so well together.' Appearing to have something on his mind and frowning as if having difficulty assembling speech, he said in thoughtful tone. 'You see, Jason, since her mother died there have been many times when life has been lonely for Margaret and I have tried to compensate with evenings such as this. With music and young people, in fact, all the good things I can afford to lavish on her.' Allowing this to register he then went on to explain. 'This is her kind of world ... heritage if you like, and even though she is so young and impressionable I don't think she would wish to have it changed?'

Wondering where this conversation was leading, and suspecting there was more to come. 'Are you trying to tell me something, sir?'

'If I am,' replied Passendale, 'then it is something I myself am not sure about, I just have this ominous feeling when I see you so close together.' Hawkish eyes probing as he stated. 'You must realise that the life you have chosen can without doubt be very rewarding, but which also,' he said in a tone that held the conviction of experience, 'is a hard and lonely one keeping you at sea and away from England for countless years. I would hate to see my daughter wasting her precious years of youth in waiting for promises that may never be fulfilled: or to see a capacity for love such as hers be desolated in a life of frustration and loneliness.' Waiting for reaction but none was forthcoming so he asked. 'Do you understand what I'm trying to say?'

'Indeed I do, sir. But looking at the many elegant men surrounding her I think perhaps you read more into the situation then you need, for it is obvious that I cannot compete with company such as this. Tonight I seem completely forgotten by her.'

Looking long at this young man in midshipmen's uniform, at the classic line of forehead and of nose and mouth and proud, erect carriage. 'You are a good-looking devil,' said Passendale fondly, 'but you know nothing of the whims and fancies of capricious girls. Margaret plays this kind of situation with an instinct old as life itself so beware, young Jason, you are sailing in very deep and disturbed water tonight.' The look of dismay that greeted this summary statement brought humour to replace the sense of foreboding and, gripping his arm in intimate gesture, Passendale concluded with. 'Thank you for listening so courteously and for honouring a father's concern.'

Queen had great respect for this man. 'I'll try not to let you down, sir.'.

Music suddenly flooded the hall and brought a flurry of couples leading on to the dance floor. She gave Queen a snide glance as she promenaded by on the arm of a fashionably dressed partner, and seeing the forlorn look on his face Passendale drew him to the buffet table.

'You'll feel more at ease with a glass in your hand,' he said with a smile. Serving from the punch bowl he excused himself and went back to his friends. Queen took a hearty drink; the liquid was warm and fruity but too sweet for his taste.

'Put that rubbish down,' said a familiar voice in his ear, 'I'll serve you a proper drink.'

Vinderman's face was the only feature recognisable. Scarlet coat of the footmen, silver wig shining brilliant and incongruous against the close-cropped beard and side-whiskers and Queen recovered from shock to look him over. 'Where the hell did you come from,' he blurted, 'if the crew of the *Dartmouth Trader* could only see you now.' Unbelieving, he stopped laughing long enough to ask. 'Just tell me one thing, Vindo. How?'

Inclining his head in the direction of a full-figured woman busy serving plates of delicacies, Vinderman said, 'Nice to have a friend in high places, and I wasn't going to miss out on a free-for-all like this.'

Not having seen him for a while, Queen asked, 'Did you get fixed up alright on the *Earl of Rothesay*?'

'Aye: already got most of my gear aboard. Look out for yourself among these bleedin' toffs, Jase, they ain't real people!' With which words of advice Vinderman hefted a tray of empty glasses and moved away.

Looking after him in wry approval. Vinderman seemed able to adapt to any situation and was a constant revelation to Queen. Glancing idly about he perceived a youth nearby who was dressed in identical uniform. His look was received with equal frankness and on an impulse he held out his hand. 'Jason Queen,' he said, 'apprentice on the *Earl of Rothesay*.'

His hand was gripped warmly and a grin spread over the other's mouth. 'Billie McFie,' he said in rolling Scotch accents. 'Hello, shipmate.'

Five voluble minutes later they had established themselves as fellow apprentices: and friends. McFie was eighteen years of age and explained that his father was a draper and a recent shareholder in the Company, whose sponsorship had secured the post for his son. . 'Come and meet my family,' he said invitingly.

Billie's father and mother were a complete contrast in appearance. Robert McFie was a stoop-shouldered cadaverous man with a pale complexion and thinning hair while his wife, Flora, was small and stout with a round, laughing face. Pleased and impressed with their son's new acquaintance they introduced their daughter Jeannie.

Jeannie McFie was charming. Tall like her father and yet the full-faced roundness of her mother, and with a most pleasing figure. She was strikingly dressed in a ball gown of flame-red sparkling with a multitude of sequins and Queen hastily averted his eyes from the creamy neck and curvaceous breasts that the off-shoulder gown seemed unable to contain.

'She's dying for someone to ask her to dance,' prompted Billie, 'she refused me in case she missed her chance with one of these other dashing society blades.'

Anticipating her embarrassment, Queen asked, 'Miss Jeannie, may I have the honour?'

Looking at him in a worried manner but reassured by his smile and complete courtesy, she took his arm and they threaded into the progressing line of dancers. As they stepped out, she said uncomfortably, 'I'll kill that Billie McFie one day.'

Glancing into deep chestnut eyes, his arm around her yielding waist they suddenly joined in conspiratorial laughter and so immersed in each other that he missed the indignant glare of Margaret Passendale as she whirled by. The dance over, they rejoined the family where Queen excused himself but not before exacting a promise from Jeannie that they would dance together again soon.

Maggie displayed coolness as he approached and said to her, 'Scarcely seen you since we arrived.'

She was dressed in a flowing evening gown of royal blue cut low off the shoulder to expose a creamy neck adorned by a double row of pearls like a choker chain of lustre. Her dark hair was unclipped and flowing free about her lovely, oval cheek face, and shrugging in apparent disdain, she said, 'So many young men seek my attention that my time is practically all spoken for.' She was trying to sound casual but her eyes flashed danger signals and he thought he was in some kind of trouble but meeting up with Vinderman again had stimulated, and restored confidence.

'Thought you were keeping out of my way because you've heard how badly I dance,' he said boldly. With this he took the dance card from her unsuspecting fingers. The first half had no empty places so he tucked it into an inside pocket. 'Now you have no excuse for not spending the rest of the evening with me.'

His manner, as unexpected as it was unusual, had her eyes opening wide. Disdain was fast vanishing but she gave him a haughty look. 'I presume this sudden assurance has something to do with your new uniform.' She appeared to relish this manner of approach and her eyes softened and she said in mischievous voice. 'If you dance so badly it seems I must prepare for a very dull evening, are you asking me to waste this lovely Ball and all the music by sitting down quietly, you and me and Mrs Bronson?'

As she said this, he could sense the gaze of Maggie's chaperone probing from where she sat with the other matrons on a chaise lounge. Mrs Bronson took her duties very seriously, and he felt somewhat exposed. 'Looks that way,' he said, 'otherwise you will have to put up with my clumsy feet and dance with me.'

'Are you asking: or telling?'

'Anyway you like.'

Just then the music struck up with provocative rhythm and she looked up at him. 'I'll risk it, if you will.'

Clasping her hand he led out with an exuberant step and proceeded to whirl her around at measured but ever-increasing pace. This was the first time he had held her in his arms and the close-ness of her body aroused new and strange sensations. She was soft and light as thistledown and they moulded together as one and he looked down into eyes of veiled mystery and a face flushed rose-petal and devastatingly lovely. Her lips parted in a half-smile and their eyes met in wonderful communion. She was breathless, and not just with dance exertion when he returned her to Mrs Bronson.

'Said you didn't know how,' remonstrated Maggie.

'Going too fast for you?' Jest fading as he looked at her and softly said, 'Maggie.'

'I know, Jason,' she murmured, 'felt it too.'

He had a desperate need to touch, and to hold her again. Reaching for her hand their fingers entwined, the happiness shining in her eyes inspired boldness and he whispered in her ear, 'How about us sneaking out on the balcony?' Her eyebrows raised and he added quickly, 'Just for a moment or two.'

'What are you asking of me, sir?' said Maggie coyly.

'That we might share a few minutes alone, in fresh air away from this heat and all the people,' assurance growing as he added, 'and because I have no intention of letting you out of my sight for a single moment.'

'I'd love to,' she responded with devilment, 'but this next dance is reserved for a very special person.'

'Who,' he growled in deflated tone.

'Me! I'm exercising rank on you so better get used to the idea.' Fitzroy Probus made a gallant arm and she gave Queen her most dazzling smile as she skipped away with the Captain.

'Cheer up, Mr Queen, the night is still young.' Mrs Bronson was dressed in a gown of demure grey, her hair was the colour of bright silver, cropped short, and severe about a face that seemed permanently set in a stern mould. Her eyes were darkest brown and worldly shrewd, and very perceptive as she then said, 'You must not think me unobservant, for I see the light that shines in you both, you and Margaret are so perfect together,' voice secretive as she went on to state with feeling, 'only once before have I seen two people so obviously meant for each other. Jason, lad, don't waste what the Good Lord has given. Such a smile as He has bestowed on you is all too rare and should not be regarded lightly.'

Queen realised that his first impression was misleading, there was more to Mrs Bronson than just a mere chaperone; he hadn't suspected she was such a romantic and he looked at her in a conspiratorial manner. 'Then you won't mind if I sometimes ask you to look the other way.'

Scrutinising him severely, she replied, 'Can recognise true gentleness when I see it but never forget, young Jason Queen, I will carry out my duties as I see fit and without any improper suggestions . . . if you don't mind?'

As she rejoined the matrons his searching gaze focussed on Billie McFie amidst a group of richly attired men, and there was heat in the face of his new friend. Then one of the men jerked his head towards a nearby doorway and led off with McFie and the others close behind. The definite lack of cordiality in this exchange aroused curiosity so he followed them, significantly catching the eye of Daniel Vinderman who stood with arms folded by the buffet table. Acknowledging the gesture and, after a careful glance around, Vinderman sidled behind through the partly open door.

The room they entered was deserted but heated discourse could be heard from outside so they moved to the entrance of a courtyard and stood silently observing while McFie angrily confronted the five assembled men, the centre one of which drawled in languid tone, 'She's just a draper's daughter . . . can't really imagine what the company is coming to allowing in these trades people?'

'Has the wine gone to his head or something,' simpered another, 'who is he anyway, Bonham-Jones?'

'Hanged if I know. A snotty midshipman from his dress.' Tall and slim, burgundy velvet tailored jacket with high collar, vest-waistcoat of matching, upholstered velvet with the cravat at his throat secured by a conspicuous gold and diamond pin. His breeches were white silk and his high-heeled shoes were of soft black leather with silver buckles. Thin faced and aristocratic-handsome, Jasper Bonham-Jones then said with an arrogant sneer. 'Though I wouldn't mind getting into bed with his sister.'

Struggling out of his coat in haste to get to grips with him McFie shouted at top voice. 'You rich bastard's are all alike, but you won't insult my sister and get away with it!'

He was half out of his uniform jacket when a powerful-shouldered man stepped behind and trapped his arms in the sleeves. Bonham-Jones came forward and slapped the pinioned McFie hard across the face back and forth in quick succession, then drawled as if bored to tears, 'Must teach these trades people to behave like gentlemen.'

Queen and Vinderman emerged from the shadows and obviously in support of McFie.

Vinderman had a look of anticipation on his face and spat into the palms of his hands.

'My Gawd!' said one eyeing Queen's uniform, 'more of them: how the working classes do stick together?' After which derogatory comment he brought his fists up in educated boxing stance.

Lip curling,, teeth showing white in an evil grin at this classic pose Vinderman kicked the man in the balls and clubbed a fist into his face as he jack-knifed and the stylist went down with his shattered nose spurting blood over his mouth and down the spotless white neckband. Queen grabbed Jasper in a crushing bear hug with his eyes boring into a face no longer arrogant but suffused with alarm. A leg hooked round Queen trying for a trip and throw, Jasper was wiry and, twisting with strength born of panic, rasped his hand under Queen's chin and clawed for the eyes but was thrown away with a force that sent him sprawling then Queen left him lying and turned to deal with the muscular man endeavouring to contain the frantic McFie. Free of his jacket at last McFie hurled into the fray and going without hesitation for the retreating Bonham-Jones. Hands slapping with venom across his face and all the while shouting in manic fashion he chased Jasper all round the courtyard heedless of the blows he was taking in return. Then, smashing him down he hurled across the prostrate man and straddled either side with his hands fastened in

Jasper's long hair and preceded to batter his head on the cobblestones to a rhythmic accompaniment of obscenity. It took the two of them to wrestle him away. McFie wouldn't be contained and, struggling to get back at Jasper, swung out in blind temper. Yanking his head back by the hair, Queen forced the raging midshipman to look into his face. McFie's eyes widened as he realised who was holding him and he gave up struggling and glared around. Vinderman and Queen had dealt efficiently with the aristocrats. Two of the five were flat out and the remaining three squatted in postures of injured dejection.

'Is it over,' growled McFie, 'I could have handled them.' Looking at the footman's coat that graced the husky figure of Vinderman. Uncomprehending. 'Who the hell are you?'

'Another shipmate,' replied Queen as he dusted him down, 'and be grateful he's on our side.'

Grinning at this, Vinderman said to McFie, 'Bit of a tiger when you get steamed up. Reckon you'd have killed poor Jasper if we hadn't pulled you off.'

'One dance with my sister and he couldn't keep his hands off her.' Glaring at Jasper as if he wanted to hit him again. 'Perhaps the next girl he dances with might receive more careful treatment?'

'He won't be dancing again tonight,' said Queen as he straightened his own dress. Apart from a reddening bruise on his face he felt little the worst for the encounter and well satisfied with the outcome. Moving across to lift one of the recumbent figures to his feet. 'You going to be alright?' he asked.

Grimacing affirmative, the man tottered with exaggerated care to one of his companions.

'Shall we rejoin the party?' said Queen with a grin.

This Ball isn't so dull after all thought Vinderman as he took up his former position at the buffet table. Looking around. The incident had passed off apparently unnoticed. He gave a crafty glance at the row of decanters, could do with a belt of hard liquor, rejecting the thought. He'd already stashed away a couple of bottles.

Margaret Passendale was not waiting around for Queen and was on the floor in a formation of dancers. McFie came to him pulling behind a flushed and very embarrassed Jeannie. McFie seemed pleased with himself as Queen enquired, 'Miss Jeannie, I hope you are not too distressed?'

'Trust Billie McFie to make an issue out of something so trivial, that temper of his will get him in real trouble one day.' Her breasts swelled indignantly as she declared. 'Perhaps when he finally goes off to sea I will find a young gentleman to pay me some attention without having to fistfight my brother for the privilege.'

'You might be considered lucky to have such a

champion.' With a wry smile, he added, 'Would he be offended if I asked you to dance?'

Grinning at the thought, McFie said, 'Like the look of your friend, is he really sailing with us on the *Earl*?'

'Hope so. He's something special.' Offering his arm to Jeannie, as they turned for the dance floor, McFie pulled a derisive face as she said forcibly:

'And for goodness sake keep out of any further trouble!'

'I'll have to keep a watchful eye on McFie,' stated Queen. Falling in step with the music, she lost her worried look and clinging tight to him for a moment, murmured:

'But who, my gallant Jason Queen, is going to keep an eye on you?'

A blackbird rhapsodising above brought him back from the night of the Ball. The early morning bird chorus was at once melodious and cheerful, allowing no mood of melancholy and with an appreciative smile he slung his jacket over his shoulder and broke into a trot back to the house.

Chapter Five

Due to report aboard ship on the following Monday, Queen had all weekend to pack and prepare for seagoing. He spent Saturday alone for Mr Passendale had business to attend at Leadenhall St. and Margaret elected to accompany her father to the city as if she was deliberately ignoring him and he couldn't figure her out and thought she was mad at him for some reason and he was in a disconsolate mood: and who needed girls anyway. Coming downstairs on Sunday morning he found them both at breakfast and the frigid atmosphere as he sat down made him wish he could join ship this very day.

Looking up from behind a sheaf of papers, Passendale focused pointedly on the bruise on Queen's face. 'I hear there was a little excitement on the night of the Company Ball,' he said, 'and that a number of guests had to be taken home early?' Suddenly alert and interested Margaret regarded her father curiously as he went on to state. 'It appears that two of our apprentices were involved and also that friend of yours, Vinderman, the one you asked me to take on aboard the *Earl*.' Thinking about this, he asked. 'How did he manage to get into the banqueting hall?'

'Needed the pay,' replied Queen guardedly, 'Vindo seems to find his way into any situation that pays a wage.'

'He could well have lost the chance of a situation aboard ship because the Bonham-Jones family have great influence in the Company and are determined to punish those responsible for rough handling their beloved Jasper.'

'Is that why you deserted me,' asked Maggie with dangerous quiet, 'to go off with your friend Vinderman looking for trouble?'

'No, it wasn't!' At this abrupt but convincing retort, Passendale put down his paperwork and leaned tentatively forward as Queen looked appealingly at her to explain. 'Bonham-Jones behaved abominably towards Jeannie McFie and her brother took him to task over his behaviour.'

'Why did you become involved?' asked Passendale.

'Because he was a shipmate and because they outnumbered him five to one.'

'Figured it for something of that nature. The Bonham-Jones are very much infused with a sense of grandeur, pity their behaviour doesn't match the family pride.' Unable to hold back a smile, he asked. 'Did you have to knock them about so much?'

'Seemed the thing to do at the time.' Realising he had gained Mr Passendale's approval he gave a return smile before appealing. 'Please don't blame Vindo, he only came in support of me.'

'No cause to worry, they wouldn't wish the reason for this incident to be made public.' Passendale's appreciation was obvious as he stated. 'Been looking for a chance to deflate their ego, I'll be down at Blackwall tomorrow to make sure Vinderman is listed among the crew.' Looking sternly at his daughter, he said with authority. 'Now enough of your foul mood, this is Jason's last day with us and it will do you good to get out of the house for a few hours and have done with this brooding. Take a picnic lunch and drive down by the river. The day appears most pleasant and some sunshine might return the smile to that glum face.' His tone didn't allow of refusal as he concluded. 'I'll instruct Mrs Bronson accordingly.'

Making a face at his retreating back, she grumbled, 'Always Mrs Bronson.' Glancing at him with guarded eyes. 'Perhaps I misjudged you, for when you disappeared that way I assumed you were seeking the company of Miss McFie.'

'How contrary you are, all the evening dancing with anyone but me yet you persist in giving this cold, outrageous treatment just because I spent a few minutes with Jeannie.' Always sensitive when uncomfortable, his face flushed at the name, and she looked at his red face and thought he liked

Jeannie McFie more than he was telling. Though normally a poised young woman, for once her tender years betrayed and she seemed on the brink of tears.

'What was I supposed to think?' she said dolefully, 'one moment you were monopolising me and insisting I spend the rest of the evening only with you and then you rushed off leaving me alone to suspect the worst: especially when I saw you dancing again with your precious Jeannie.'

'Oh, Maggie, forget that dismal night. Let's just enjoy ourselves today.'

Responding to his fervent appeal, her eyes began to clear. Relief and enthusiasm brought a smile and quick movement. 'I'll get ready,' she said, 'just give me half an hour. I know a lovely spot for a picnic.'

The river Thames was wide at this point and flowed with stately passage around a sweeping bend where wooded areas fringed the riverbank on either side. Strolling along the lush green with the late morning sun warming, Queen had shed his jacket and unbuttoned his shirt at the neck, the crisp white linen in colourful contrast to the cherry striped poplin dress Maggie wore, a dress that cut away from the waist to show off a pretty, quilted petticoat. Her face was pink-flushed and lovely under a bonnet of stiffened white muslin tied on with black ribbon and he looked down at her in complete approval as he said, 'This last month has been something to remember. I owe a great deal to your father and only hope I can justify the trust he has placed in me.'

Linking arms, she replied, 'He has taken more pleasure from your presence than you realise. I have thought more and more of late that he has been doing these things for himself, almost as if he was making up for something he thought was owing to you.'

'What could he possibly owe to a complete stranger?'

'Perhaps the debt is to the memory of your own father. You surely must have realised their relationship was special and that you being here has brought new life to Papa. Nostalgic perhaps, but I haven't seen him so alive since my mother passed away.'

They began to retrace their steps, anxious not to impose on the indulgence of Mrs Bronson who was busy laying out food at the picnic site. But her words had aroused curiosity and he looked at her with interest. 'I have wondered,' he said, 'if they were so very close why had they no communication all these years?'

'It was a long time ago, and perhaps we will never know.' Smiling in secret manner she then said, 'Tell me again about your dream.'

'Haven't had it lately?'

'Not at all?'

'Only once, but this time it was different.'

'In what way?'

He felt more than a little uncomfortable, reluctant to explain, and she clung to his arm and her voice pressured. 'Tell me, Jason,' she insisted, 'was I in your dream?'

'If you must know, yes,' he blurted, 'it was the same girl in the same red boots but with your face!' Acutely embarrassed, face coloured red and causing extreme discomfort but, willing him to look at her, she queried:

'Are these the boots that run through this dream of yours?' Raising the hem of her skirt to expose her ankles and feet that were encased in tiny bootees of cracked red leather with pearl buttons up the side.

Staring in dumbfounded amazement. These were indeed the tiny feet, which had pursued him on countless nights, and he heard again but now at first hand the merry laughter that had echoed round his sleepy mind. Speechless. Gaping mouth. But caught up in a magic wonderland all her own Maggie's eyes were shining and her mouth was soft and full. 'These boots were my mother's,' she explained, 'found them among her belongings after she died and I sometimes wore them in the quiet of my room and pretended she was still alive.' The words hung between them for an awesome moment, then she said in musing voice. 'How strange it all is and yet how wonderful is this feeling between us, this closeness that seems to belong not to us but to a man and woman from another time and place.'

Maggie had matured in these last few minutes, as though certain now of something that had tormented her and her hand trembled inside his own while the other wove enchanted patterns. He could sense her striving to communicate. To ensnare him in wonderful emotion and he knew again the panic of those pursuing feet just as in his dream but he couldn't break free from the spell this witch of a girl was weaving over and around. Her eyes were moist and they were like cascading waterfalls and he was drowning in them and in the sight and sound and scent of her. Her voice came as if from a great distance but penetrating his befogged mind. 'I'm sure now,' she said, 'that you and I have been together in a past life with a love so great and so compelling that it could not pass into oblivion but has just been waiting for the time when it could be revived: brought back to life in the form of us two.' Darkly intense as the revelation overpowered her, she said in hushed tone. 'I believe you and I are destined to live our lives together because we are the incarnation of two people who were so desperately in love. But this must have been a love never consummated and so became a sort of spirit that has just been waiting. Oh, Jason, like I too have been waiting, for such a long time.'

She was suddenly a child again. So easily broken. Her lovely face rose to look at him and her eyes beseeched. His own emotions were out of control and the need to touch and hold this exquisite, so desirable girl proved beyond restraint and his arms moved of their own accord around her waist. 'What would you do,' he whispered in her ear, 'if I picked you up in my strong arms and ran off with you into the woods?'

Her own words and she smiled in retrospect then with her eyelids lowered, she said demurely, 'How could I hope to prevail against such strength and impetuosity, but I think the screams of Mrs Bronson would be heard even unto Leadenhall St.'

He tucked his arm inside hers again. 'Perhaps,' he then said, 'yet I happen to know that your Mrs Bronson is not without sympathy for you and me.' Adding with a grin. 'Although she must be getting somewhat restive wondering when the picnic is going to start.' His stride lengthened at the thought and she skipped happily along at his side. The emotion that had almost overwhelmed them still simmered but the warning voice of Mr. Passendale intruded to remind him that his chosen way of life had to be totally dedicated if he was to succeed. Almost, if he could face the fact, be brutal in its selfishness with little room for the sentiments that moved him in such contrary manner when he was close to the enchanting Maggie. His withdrawal went unnoticed because, still immersed in the magic, she was too happy and content in the wonder of the communion they had shared to concern herself about the spectre of impending departure.

The promise of a fine morning was misleading and the picnic came to a premature end in a flurry of cool, driving rain that had them hastily clearing the site and running for the shelter of the carriage.

Chapter Six

A cheerful seaman took his baggage as he came up the boarding plank on to the main deck then proceeded aft to the midshipman's cabin. About twelve feet square, dark and bare, smell of paint and tar and the wonderful, tangy aroma of sawn oak. Breathing it all in. This is where he wanted to be, as if he had come home! Looking around this mess-room cum cabin that would be his quarters during the long months ahead and which he would have to share with the other apprentice midshipmen.

Overhead ran massive beams of shaped oak heavily reinforced at the joint of ship's side and deck. He could just pass under without cracking his skull but at the sides and corners the downward curve of the deck head lowered the height and gave much less headroom as if lying in wait for the unwary. Heavy section table amidships with one matching stool, the only other items of furniture were two folding chairs with canvas seats and a deep-fiddled book shelving arrangement that took up one bulkhead, and the whole aspect of the cabin was Spartan in the extreme. A sea chest bearing the initials T.B.J. lay on the floor close to the table and the owner had already slung his hammock, staking his claim to the best position by the solitary porthole.

A clatter of feet announced the arrival of Billie McFie followed closely by a pallid-faced youth and a seaman staggering under the weight of a huge, leather bound chest. 'Won't be long now,' said Billie as he dropped his sea bag on the cabin sole. The other youth introduced himself as Abraham Verber. Quiet voiced and shy, he obviously wished to appear friendly and, after shaking hands all round, they proceeded to allocate the remaining space among the three of them. There was a locker each available but otherwise they were going to have to learn to live out of their sea chests.

They set about slinging their hammocks and it was apparent that the first hammock had been fixed in a position that monopolised the limited space and, though uncertain, after a short discussion they agreed to re-sling it, still close to the porthole but in a manner that allowed all a fair share of the available light and area. Interrupted in this action by the arrival of the offending hammock's owner, Queen stepped forward with hand outstretched to introduce him. The new arrival said in reply, 'Toby Bonham-Jones.' The accent was exaggerated and the handshake a mere touch of fingers.

'Any relation to Jasper?' asked Queen.

'My cousin, you know him?'

'Met at the commissioning Ball held by the Company.'

'I was up country and couldn't attend.' Bonham Jones words were suddenly guarded as he stated. 'Heard he was jumped by a crowd of ruffians.'

A derisive snort came from McFie, he didn't easily forget the indignity suffered by his sister, and Queen stepped in quickly. 'Come and shake hands, Billie,' he said, 'we have a long way to go together and might just as well get acquainted.' The handshake was brief with Bonham-Jones very much aloof and looking as if all this was beneath his dignity.

Abraham Verber stepped forward reluctantly, sensing unease in this tiny room and wanting no part of it. He was unhappy about being aboard in the first place, having led a sheltered life as the fifth son of a wealthy dealer in precious stones and metal, and felt more than a little resentful that of all the sons in the family he was the only one not offered a post in the business. He suspected that he had been driven to sea because they didn't know what else to do with him.

Looking right through him Bonham-Jones snapped, 'Who moved my hammock?' A demanding tone that brought silence.

'There are four of us,' said Queen apologetically, 'we allocated the space more evenly.'

'You should have consulted me before touching any of my gear,' anger in the tone of his voice as he added, 'I was here first and you might as well realise that as senior apprentice I have prior claim.' Allowing this information to register he then snapped. 'I'll let it go this time but don't ever touch my gear without permission.'

'Fair comment.' Queen then asked with interest. 'You've been to sea before?'

'One round trip to India, I'll be sitting for my officer's ticket when we return this time.' He spoke in a languid but confident tone and McFie and Verber were eyeing the bulky Bonham-Jones warily. A scrutiny returned in equal measure then he gave a hard look at the hammock lashed alongside his own. Brand-new sea coat slung over it with a name tab prominent. With a grimace of distaste he started to untie the hammock from its fixing on the deck head.

'That's my hammock,' said Verber, 'have I lashed it wrongly or something?'

'It's lashed in the wrong place. Don't want a stinking Jew alongside me!'

Verber's eyes flared, for a moment he looked as if he would hurl at Bonham-Jones then pulled up short, shrugged as if he had heard it all before and began to let down his hammock. Delighted at the lack of resistance, Bonham-Jones unsheathed a knife from his belt. 'I'll help you.' Raising his arm to slash at the rope.

'Leave it, Jonesy!'

Queen's voice, rasping across the cabin, challenging, and the lack of respect for his seniority infuriated Bonham-Jones who stayed his move and turned on him. 'The name is Bonham-Jones,' he said in a haughty and commanding tone. Coming at Queen with menace apparent, he sheathed his knife. Anger in his voice and in his stance as he threatened. 'Give me one good reason why I shouldn't knock you down?'

'Give you two! I'm fitter than you and, I fancy, a hell of a lot dirtier in a fight.' Seafaring with Vinderman had toughened Queen and he faced the threat with confidence and Bonham-Jones stopped short. The coolness of Jason Queen had him suddenly unsure but Verber came to stand between them.

'Please,' he entreated, 'I'll move my hammock rather than cause trouble.'

'I'll second that,' said McFie with a cheeky grin, 'only because I'd hate to see such aristocratic blood all over our brand new living quarters. Although, as I remember, cousin Jasper's blood wasn't really so blue.'

Bonham-Jones drew back from conflict. Feeling outnumbered, he took the way out offered by Verber but not without trying to reassert authority. 'The sooner you lot learn who is senior officer here,' he threatened, 'the easier it will be on you!' His threat had little effect, especially on McFie but the tension was relieved by the interruption of a smartly dressed seaman clattering down the companionway to state.

'Cap'n wants you on the poop deck, at the double!'

Tapping Verber on the shoulder as they proceeded to the hatchway, Queen suggested, 'Better wear your hat.'

Verber was a slightly built young man of medium height and while his uniform was well tailored it didn't sit easily on him, he seemed ill at ease, much removed from his normal environment and obviously wishing he wasn't here. Confused and worried and most unhappy, Verber jammed on his hat. 'Must think I need a nursemaid?'

'We are all new on board and have much to learn together.'

Verber's first smile since he boarded lit up his eyes and turned up the corners of his mouth yet he was very pensive as he replied, 'Some more than others.' Racing up the companionway onto the poop deck they formed a hasty line before the assembled officers.

'When I send for you,' snapped Captain Probus as he eyed each of them in turn, 'I expect you here fast!' Introducing his three officers, no handshaking, just a friendly nod from the First Officer, Mr Sethman, a tall and ruddy-faced man with mutton-chop, greying side whiskers who they quickly named Seth, behind his back of course. Second Officer Gaywood regarded them with brusque interest. He looked a hard case, and, as they were soon to find out, was very ambitious. His Christian name was Michael but they referred to him only as Mr Gaywood, he was much too forbidding for trivial thought. The Third Officer was a young man who had trouble repressing a welcoming smile. David Ashbury had only recently completed his own apprenticeship and his sympathies were with the newcomers.

'We sail on the early tide tomorrow,' said the Captain, 'no-one to leave the ship tonight. Organise them in watches, Mr Sethman, starting at eight bells. I want duty watches continued through the night and all hands on deck at first light.' This was a vastly different Probus from the one Queen had met on the quay side by the old *Pandora*. He was a Captain demanding respect, discipline his way of life, to himself and all who sailed with him. He had a unique way of making it clear from the start that he would not suffer fools gladly. 'Mr Bonham-Jones,' he now said, 'as senior midshipman I hold you responsible for the conduct of your apprentices. When on deck you will be properly dressed and at all times be expected to look and behave as gentlemen and future officers.' Holding them in cold scrutiny he stated. 'Last visitors will be coming on board this evening. You'll find it easier if you make your goodbyes brief. Take them in hand, Mr Ashbury, I expect them to know their way around every corner of the ship by the time we reach open water.'

He strode away with his officers and, now alone with the midshipmen, Ashbury shook hands with each of them. 'Call me David,' he said, 'but never when we are on watch or if the other officers are about.' Lowering his voice he took a crafty look around. 'Take a word of advice and watch out for Gaywood, he's an out-and-out bastard!' Ashbury was a stocky young man broad in the shoulder with lean waist and hips. He had an outdoor-rugged face and his eyes were clearest grey under fine-lined eyebrows and wisps of unruly blond hair had escaped from under his hat. He was friendly and welcoming and the new midshipmen were immediately at ease with him, turning to Queen he casually asked. 'Believe you have spent much of your life on a farm?' Nodding, Queen wondered what was coming next, with due cause because the smile on the face of the Third Officer was fast becoming out of control. 'Under the circumstances,' he declared, 'I have the ideal job for you.'

Later in the day, perspiring and dishevelled, the midshipman was regretting his admission. Animals of incredible variety were being herded aboard, chickens in crates, frightened sheep and pigs grunting and scattering out of control in the waist, or galley deck. Their squeals were voluble and indignant as cursing seamen pursued them. Some of the men were rough and heavy handed with this lively cargo.

'Gently now!' His voice held stern authority and a burly sailor hastily lowered the rope's end with which he was about to belabour a struggling pig. Every variety of farm animals was hoisted aboard to be properly stowed, even the ship's longboats were pressed into service as all available deck space filled to capacity and soon a bewildering press of sheep and pigs were pinioned in readily constructed pens. Among the confusion came a pair of goats, stubborn and uncooperative, Abraham Verber doing his best to tether one of these, only to be on the receiving end of a sharp-horned head in the backside from the other just as he was bending down. A great roar of laughter came from the crew as Verber went sprawling over a nearby crate but taking it in good humour he scrambled up and made a dive for the stubborn goat.

'Got you!' Grabbing the head rope and rubbing his backside he ruefully threatened. 'You won't be so cocky when it's your turn for the pot!'

It was customary aboard the early sailing ships to carry meat on the hoof. Only in such a way could a prudent Master keep his crew efficient and minimise the dreaded scourge of scurvy and other diseases brought on by a monotonous diet and lack of fresh food. It was common, once a sea going routine had been established, for such livestock to be given their freedom and in fair weather allowed to roam the deck and soon treated as family pets and looked upon with affection. Still laughing at Verber's downfall, Queen said, 'I don't think we'll get to eat the goats. They're here to provide fresh milk so I beg you not to upset our little friends, we might need them more than they will us.'

Holding on to the head rope Verber said in wry tone, 'Thought I was here to learn the arts of sailing and navigation and now I find myself on a bleedin' Noah's Ark playing farm hand to a bunch of bleedin' wild animals.'

Probus had strolled up to check on the loading, shaking his head at the chaos. 'You calling me Noah, Mr Verber?' he asked calmly.

'No, sir,' stammered Verber. He sprang erect in salute and the goat escaped again.

'Then get a grip on the goat.' The Captain found difficulty in maintaining a calm expression as he enquired with great innocence. 'Trouble, Mr Queen?'

'No more than you might expect, sir.'

'Seen it done better,' preparing to move off, he added, 'but I have also seen it done much worse.'

While realising this was praise, of a sort, he couldn't resist making a face at the ramrod straight back of his Captain.

'Get on with it, Mr Queen.' The Captain's

voice came back at him, jerking him sober-faced and wondering if Probus really did have eyes in the back of his head.

With all animals finally stowed the decks were washed down and order restored. The midshipmen's uniforms were in a sorry state and Ashbury excused them further duties until their evening watch. Back in their cabin they shed their dishevelled clothing. Tea was served in their quarters and in the peace and quiet that followed Queen had time on his hands and realised that he felt more than a little forlorn. Perhaps it was the thought of tomorrow and imminent departure. He wished his mother were still alive so he could write and tell her some of the things he had never said, or ever thought needed saying. Remembering her face. Understanding. Serene, and he had a quick comforting sense that perhaps words weren't really necessary. What a wonderful legacy of love and comfort she had left him, worth infinitely more than the material wealth she never had to bestow. His melancholy trains of thought continued then brought Maggie to mind. He sat at the table. There was someone to whom he could write. Hand poising over the page. It would be a long time before he had a chance for communication with her, but the words wouldn't come. Forcing his quill to paper, he started to write.

Miss Margaret Passendale,
Dearest Margaret,
Tomorrow we sail. Down the river and out into the wide oceans. Yet I sit here chewing the end of my quill wondering just what I can say to reach out and touch you across the great distance that must separate us by the time this letter is in your hand. Why does it sound so stilted . . . so formal? Miss Margaret indeed! When I know you only as Maggie, the laughing-eyed girl who has so completely filled my world these last, fleeting weeks? My mind reels at the thought of you and yet so desperately when I think of the time that will have to pass before you and I can again meet and, dare I hope, know again the unending joy of being together.

It has already been pointed out, and by someone for whom I have great respect, that a sailor's life has to be considered very carefully. For years at sea are long and lonely and that such a way of life is not easily shared, nor is one that I could reasonably expect to be shared. What am I saying? Wish I knew. The thoughts revolve but my fingers refuse to write the words. Oh. Maggie! Dare I ask? Will you sometimes come to me in my dreams? Again pursue me through the night in those silly, adorable red boots? Questions.

Questions. The words come easier now and I wonder why I have always found difficulty in saying such things to your face. What a coward I am, hiding behind these pages. My mind surges with the thought of you and the need for you and I suddenly have to wonder whether I still want to go away. If this need to sail the great oceans is just make-belief and that the real fulfilment is closer to home: and you!

These are riddles into which I dare not probe, because my course is already charted. But perchance, when I return to England, you will allow me to call on you again. To pursue these thoughts together, always with the terrible assumption that you care enough to wait. Will it be too long? The dread is real and almost unbearable and yet I again remember the fascinating threads that seems to join us from a distant past, an association which makes me want to accept, albeit with a hesitant sort of confidence, that what will be: will be?

Dearest Maggie, I will think of you. When the harvest moon hangs high in the heavens: and again on the darkest night.

I will think of you.
Jason Queen.

Sitting in contemplation, he sealed his envelope. Then found to his surprise that he was alone in the cabin. So immersed in his writing that he hadn't noticed the departure of Abraham Verber. Then McFie came flying in. 'Quick, Jase, my family is just about to leave and wish to say goodbye to you.'

The evening was upon them. His letter had taken a long time to write. Pulling on his uniform coat, he slipped the letter into his pocket. 'Lead on, McFie.'

They were pleased to see him, sensing the friendship developing between the two and taking comfort from the fact that their darling Billie was not alone onboard ship. Jeannie McFie was lovely in a dress of dark blue, with a short riding coat and a pretty bonnet sporting a red ribbon around the crown. Smiling a welcome, then hastily averting her face as Billie said teasingly:

'What a coincidence it all is? Would you believe, Jase, that the impetuous Jasper has been round to see father and apologise for his atrocious behaviour, and even had the flaming cheek to ask for the favour of calling on Jeannie?'

He certainly knew how to embarrass his sister, for her face was a delicate shade of pink so Queen took her arm and eased her away from McFie's unsubtle humour and she looked at him with discomfort apparent. 'Do me a favour, Jason?' she murmured.

'Anything.'

'Drop that brother of mine overboard in the deepest ocean you can find.'

Laughing out loud, he jested, 'You know he would die for you, but not quite in that way and I'd hate to lose my best friend so soon.'

'He doesn't deserve such good fortune.'

Hesitating, she asked. 'Hope he hasn't fought again with the Bonham-Jones family?'

'Not so far, but I wouldn't bet on it. Toby is a little overbearing.'

Smiling at this she said, 'Jasper is quite charming really, and trying so hard to prove he can be a gentleman.' She looked at him with enquiring eyes. 'Rather hoped I might see you again,' she said shyly, 'or is that not a ladylike comment?'

He felt at ease with Jeannie McFie and nothing like the tongue-tied fool he always seemed with Maggie and he smiled back at her. 'We had better rejoin your folks,' he said, 'now that Billie has stopped laughing.' He was saved the need to make further response by the voice of Abraham Verber calling to him and he turned to observe Abraham standing with an elderly couple. The man was small and portly and clad in a dark greatcoat with the collar upturned against the breeze. His mother was slim and darkly attractive and he realised the source of Abraham's sensitive eyes and mouth. Bidding goodbye to the McFie's, he moved to greet the Verbers.

'It's so reassuring to know that Abraham has such nice shipmates.' Mrs Verber was warm voiced and voluble and her un-gloved hands waved expressively as she spoke and the flash of gold and diamonds from the profusion of rings suggested great wealth. Joining them in conversation Abraham seemed glad of Queen's company, for he needed support before the abrasive power of his father.

'Abraham has always been delicate,' explained Mrs Verber. Her rings sparkled, mesmerising Queen as they waved in emphasis. Then she said in a worried manner. 'I'm still not sure we are doing the right thing in allowing him to go to sea this way and him just a boy but Mr Verber thinks it will put new life back into him.'

Intrigued by the formal way she spoke of her husband Queen thought Mr Verber was held in due respect by all the members of his family and he wondered if Abraham's own wishes had been considered before making the decision because he seemed a most unlikely looking sailor. Mrs Verber started an instructive discussion with her offspring and after regarding Queen in shrewd observation Mr Verber drew him aside.

'I'd take it as a considerable kindness if you would keep your eye on him.' Looking up at the lofty spread of masts and rigging he shuddered as if with real fear. 'I'd no idea these ships were so small or the masts so dangerous. Does your apprenticeship mean having to go aloft like common sailors?'

'The rule is one hand for the ship and one for yourself.'

Mr. Verber looked sick and Queen suppressed a grin. 'Try not to worry, sir,' he said, 'we apprentices will stick together all the way.'

'Thank you for that small comfort, and I wish

we could spare the time to know you a little better.' Looking at his watch as he said this. 'Isabelle,' he then called loudly, 'we must go!'

They watched them tread gingerly down the boarding plank. 'That's my father all over,' said Abraham, 'too busy making money to have time for anything else.' In contemplative mood he then stated. 'Now I look back on it all, perhaps I prefer the idea of becoming a sailing officer and my old man may have done me a greater service than he realises.' With a sardonic tone evident in his voice he added, 'Or else he wouldn't have done it.'

As Abraham's parents drove away in a highly polished coach drawn by a pair of gleaming black horses and driven by a formally dressed coachman Queen remembered too late the letter he had intended to ask them to take ashore for posting. Then Officer Gaywood approached. 'Captain wants you in his cabin, Mr Queen,' he said in commanding officer voice, 'after which you and Verber are watch on deck until midnight. Nobody to leave or board ship after the last visitor has departed.' Finishing with a snapped. 'Is that clear?'

'Aye, sir.' Making his way aft, he passed close to where Toby Bonham-Jones was in earnest conversation with a silver wigged man of distinguished appearance. Toby looked right through Queen and turned his back in cold rebuff.

'Good to see you, Jason,' greeted James Passendale as Queen entered the stateroom.

These were spacious quarters occupying the full width of the stern with great aft windows overlooking the sprawl of Blackwall Dock. The furniture was rich hardwood and there was a square of Oriental rug in the centre of the cabin sole. Two cannons mounted on trunnions facing closed gun port's leant an air of forbidding reality to the luxurious interior.

Probus and Passendale were sitting at a table of polished oak that hosted a decanter and wine glasses. Queen declined the offer of a glass of claret; his eyes had gone to where Margaret Passendale stood looking out the stern window. Turning, she said with a smile, 'Captain Probus has been entertaining us with the story of your expertise in handling livestock.'

Managing a grin to cover his confusion and, with thoughts of the letter in his pocket, he said in a tone that conveyed both pleasure and embarrassment, 'Didn't realise you were coming down to the ship again?'

'Don't sound so disappointed,' she replied disdainfully, 'how could we allow you to sail without a last goodbye?'

He had made his farewells at the Passendale home that morning, an experience both protracted and painful. But now he was glad to see Maggie because he wanted to leave her with a picture of himself and the ship in her mind. Regarding him from the comfort of leather upholstered dining chair, Passendale sipped from his glass. 'How are you settling in to shipboard life?' he asked.

'Already had some lighter moments.' Careful, revealing words that brought smiles all round.

'And your accommodation?' queried Passendale.

Probus raised a bushy eyebrow. Queen said hastily, 'Er – adequate, sir.'

'I can visualise the confinement, but when at sea you'll be working watches about with only two of you below at a time and then conditions won't be so cramped.' Looking at him, then at Maggie, he said to Probus. 'I would like to take a turn around the ship now she's in sea going trim.'

Nodding in compliance and as though he understood, Probus then instructed, 'Mr Queen, I leave you to entertain Miss Passendale for a few minutes.' Following his guest, he closed the door behind him.

Joining her on the thwart under the window. Her eyes meeting his, tawny like a cat's and flecked with hazel. Her bonnet lay on the window seat and her hair was gathered at the nape of her neck and she stood motionless as he reached with gentle fingers to release the silver comb and allow her hair to cascade, dark and luxurious and so fragrant. She just stared at him with huge eyes and his stomach muscles fluttered and contracted and his hands rose of their own volition to unbutton her topcoat. Offering no resistance, she came easily into his embrace, soft and so very fragile. His arms tightened and she responded with a fierce, possessive grip round his waist.

'Maggie, Maggie,' he murmured, 'you have been in my mind all day, driving me frantic with the thought that I wouldn't see you again.'

'I know, Jason.' Face raising to reveal a moistening of her eyes, she said in desperate voice. 'Don't say anything about leaving. Just keep your arms round me. Hold me as if you will never let me go.' Sad, desolate words that tore into him and brought indecision and turmoil and love: and longing.

'I'm going to kiss you, Maggie.' Breathing the words as if asking permission then his mouth touched hers, cool at first, then searching and a flood of emotion bursting free and tearing down the last barriers of restraint as her lips parted for him and so tremulous and demanding and they clung to each other in wondrous ecstasy. She finally pulled away, gasping for breath and with eyes aflame. 'Why, Jason,' she cried, 'why have you waited so long, until it was almost too late? You would have sailed away without a sign that you cared the way I do.' Breathless words and a minute nerve pulsed in the slender column of her neck and she seemed almost indignant as she declared. 'I knew right from the beginning how it would be with us but never at any time did you speak or show that my feelings were shared. I had to persuade my father to bring me down to the dock aboard your all-consuming *Earl of Rothesay* just to see you once more.' Concluding in sad voice. 'You would have sailed without a second thought.'

'Wrong again, Maggie.' Reaching into his pocket and her eyes opened wide at the sight of the long envelope bearing her name. She made a grab for it but he held on to her fluttering hands and waved the envelope before her face and, with his face flushing crimson, muttered. 'Only if you promise not to read it before you return home.'

'Why, Mr Queen,' she said with coy humour, 'I believe you are embarrassed?'

He certainly was, and made as if to replace the letter back in his pocket.

'Promise!' Urgent now, and he gave the letter into her eager hands but with a reluctance which had just cause, for she straightaway began to tear open the envelope then, relenting at his look of dismay she tucked the missive up the sleeve of her coat. 'Promised, didn't I. What does it say?'

'You are a tormenting devil, Maggie.' He had no defence against her ever capricious moods, and discomfort was evident as he strove for words, then stated in a tone that reflected acute longing. 'It tries to describe feelings of which I was hardly aware until this very day.'

He couldn't keep his hands from her and their bodies came together and her face lifted and her mouth was close and so inviting. 'I've never been kissed like that,' she whispered. 'Do it again.'

Immediate response. He crushed her to him with a breathtaking need and with growing awareness. Physical desire brought fervour to an embrace that had them reeling in the exquisite magic and mystery of first love then the sound of footsteps in the companionway outside caused them to spring apart in immature reflex. Passendale entering, eyes quickly assessing, but the happiness of his daughter was plain to see and he said wryly, 'So much for explanation and good intentions.'

Queen's face was on fire but Maggie answered for them both.

'We couldn't help ourselves, Papa.'

She spoke as a child and her father inclined his head. 'I know the difficulties involved,' he stated, 'and can remember the feelings only too well. We'll talk about this at a future date, when time and distance has given the opportunity for a less emotive discussion.'

Maggie looked back at the ship from the moving landau. Queen could just see her face as he stood by the boarding plank in the fading light of evening ... a tall figure in dress uniform touching his hat in farewell salute, and she turned away and sagged into her father as if for support. Passendale looking at her with mournful eyes, the very situation he had sought so desperately to avoid and he wished with all his heart that he could have found a way to resist her plea to see

Jason once more before the ship sailed. Thoughts sombre and self effacing as he said inwardly:

'Curse the sea! And the call of the lonely ocean which beckons men off into the dangers of the deep and, most of all,' placing a protective arm around her, 'for the heartbreak of a young girl who has the misfortune to fall in love with a good-looking fool of a midshipman!'

The night was dark, it needed but a further half hour to midnight Lamp flickering above, Queen and Verber standing out the remaining minutes of their lonely vigil by the boarding plank. The ship shrouded in quiet, a time for whispers, when the slightest noise carried clearly across the silent water of the dock basin. Distant sound intruding, jerking the two into alertness ... someone singing a shanty, one Queen knew well. 'Vindo,' he said joyfully, 'wondered where the devil you were?' No sign of him all day and he had reluctantly begun to accept that his friend had decided against joining the *Earl*. Big smile on his face as the melodious voice came nearer. Shadows emerged from the gloom and he realised that Vinderman had his arm around the shoulders of a young woman who appeared to be holding him upright. Staggering on the edge of the dock, she hauled him back from the brink. Regaining balance, he took up his inebriated chant.

'Who is it?' queried Verber.

'The one and only, Daniel Vinderman,' said

Queen, 'and, to use his own immodest words, seaman extraordinary.'

'If the First Mate sees him,' said Verber with conviction, 'he won't be seaman anything.'

'Look out for me,' said Queen as he took off down the boarding platform. Vinderman and his companion had made their precarious way along the water's edge and now tottered directly below them. Vindo with a bag carried on his back, lady friend carrying his lute.

'Where the hell have you been, Vindo?'

''Tis the Capt'n himself come to greet me in the shape of me old shipmate, Jason Queen.' Shaking free of his companion, he said to her. 'Polly, me-darlin', 'tis yourself has to be leavin' now.'

Vinderman's natural accent was pure Devon and his attempt at mock Irish not very convincing and Queen couldn't repress a grin. 'If Mr Gaywood sees you in this condition,' he said, 'you'll both be leaving.' Taking hold of the bulky sea bag, trying to urge him up the gangplank but Vinderman jerked away and reached for his lute then he grabbed Polly and kissed her. She seemed as drunk as he was and they nearly fell over in close embrace. Planting luscious lips on him she kissed him hard and laughed out loud and cupped his face in both hands.

'Come and see me when you get back, Danny boy, haven't had such a good time in years.' Digging a playful fist in his ribs and nearly knocking him over so he reached for Polly again but Queen grabbed his arm and steered him away and up the steep slope of the gangplank. With the heavy bag on his shoulder and the weight of Vinderman pulling behind his feet were sluggish and resounding on the wooden boards. Verber came to assist and together they yanked Vinderman inboard.

'Has she gone?' He was transformed, sober and coherent. Grinning at their confusion he said, 'It's easy to forget promises made under the influence of strong liquor. Mistress Polly there had ideas for us getting hitched.' Peering after his departing lady love as he declared. 'A good time is one thing, but marriage? Anyway, I'm far too young to be getting tied down.'

'Do us all a service, Vindo, and get below before someone sees you.'

Chapter Seven

The shrill call of the Bosun's pipe pierced the early morning quiet and brought a horde of seamen rushing on deck, a confusion of all shapes and colours in their heavy shirts and wide bottomed trousers. Most of them wearing no shoes, and bare feet slapped the deck as they ran to station. Queen and Verber were already on deck, having worked the morning watch from four a.m. Bonham-Jones and McFie had shared the middle watch from midnight to four and now came running, tousled but bright-eyed. The Captain and his Officers assembled and Mr Gaywood beckoned to Queen and Verber. 'Come forward you two and try not to get in the way.'

The wind had got up in the night and now channelled across the deck, making the rigging vibrate and slap against the masts with a resonant rattle. The commissioning pennant at the centre topmast stood straight as a board and a hairy coir fender groaned protest as it took the weight of the ship and was flattened against the stone dock wall. Bonham-Jones working with a small crew on the quarterdeck, while David Ashbury, with McFie in attendance was on the high poop deck with his crew at the ready. A bustling crowd of dock labourers were busy taking off the massive ropes tethering the ship and soon all were coiled away except for a single bow and stern line and a midships breast rope, ready to warp the ship into the lock that formed the entrance and gateway into the tidal Thames. A procedure that meant virtually pulling the ship forward, manually with ropes, and also mechanically with the giant winches on the lock gates. Laborious work, but a well-found ship rode easily on the water and eventually responded to a concerted heave-ho.

As the last three ropes were taken off the shore bollards, a flurry of wind pressed hard against the masts and rigging causing the ship to move a few yards away from the wall. Instant commands ringing out from bow and stern and the men on shore leaned into their ropes to check the surge. The breast rope had been neglected and a loop had formed and lay loose and unnoticed on deck. Among the milling crew a slightly built seaman inadvertently placed his foot in this loop at the same moment the dock labourers took up the strain. The rope tightened round his ankle and before he could shake loose the men ashore gave a mighty heave in unison and the noose closed and held him in a vicelike grip then dragged him forcibly up and over the side bulwark to plunge head first into the dark, dirty water of the dock.

Men crowded the rail, finding humour in their shipmate's mishap as he splashed about below, apparently unharmed. The surface was about six feet below road level and he began to swim toward an iron ladder channelled in the dock wall. There seemed no danger but Vinderman came flying aft with a length of rope in his hand, an urgent sight that brought immediate reaction from Captain Probus and a shout of alarm from Bonham-Jones who had a clear sight from the quarterdeck. The strength of the dock labourers heaving on their ropes had reversed the movement of the *Earl* and she was returning, slowly but inexorably towards the side of the dock, and closing the gap! The seaman in the water now realised his danger and thrashed in panic for the safety of the dockside ladder not heeding the rope that came spiralling down from Vinderman.

The wind, contrary as ever, stayed its gust and hundreds of tons of ship closed on the dock wall. The seaman had nowhere to hide and turned in terror, grabbing too late for Vinderman's safety rope. The *Earl* towered over him and his terrified scream of fear and pain as he was crushed between ship and stone hung over the dock like a shroud.

'Heave away, men!' Came the sad command. Unnecessary, for the whole company were pushing the ship away from the wall. With bare hands, spare yards and oars, anything that could be used as a purchase. She moved, ponderous, gap of a few feet appearing and a hundred eyes scanning the narrow void and, as the body came into view, 'There he is!' Four men jumping in, and sturdy pieces of timber were quickly lashed to the ship's side to prevent her closing once again on the men below. The dockside was crowded with hushed onlookers as the stricken man was brought up and laid on deck. Unmarked except for a trickle of blood from his nose and mouth: but with limpness about his body that told its own story of broken bone and crushed tissue. A brief examination confirmed their worst fears. They wrapped him in sailcloth, covered over by the ship's ensign.

Now deathly quiet, the crew huddled together in frightened posture. Danger at sea they understood and accepted but this simple accident had exposed all the age-old superstition because such a tragedy before the ship had even started on her maiden voyage was an omen of bad luck and a warning that the ship was forever damned. To a man, they wanted only one thing: to get off fast as they could.

Fitzroy Probus knew what was going on in the minds of his men, many of who had sailed with him on previous occasions and were familiar faces and names, and his own thoughts were far from happy. 'Get them moving, Mr Sethman,' he snapped, 'I don't intend to miss our fair tide down river. Keep every man jack of them so fully stretched they'll have no time to think about young Peters there. Transfer his body ashore and prepare to enter the lock immediately.' Pointing at Vinderman. 'Bring that man aft.'

Sethman snapped into action. Striding down the length of the ship. Barking commands to the junior officers. As the shrouded body was lifted ashore the sullen and reluctant crew took up position once more. The ship was winched and warped forward. The great, worn oak gates of the lock ground shut behind them under the combined efforts of the dock labourers and the clicking cogwheels of the winch mechanism. Front sluice already allowing water to flood into the lock and the muddy waters of the Thames surged around the black and yellow hull.

'What's your name?' asked the Captain.

'Daniel Vinderman, sir.' He almost added his usual embellishment but decided instead that discretion was more suited to the gravity of the occasion and Probus looked him briefly over. The Captain was meticulous in addressing his officers in the formal mode of address but took much satisfaction from knowing the crew by first name, establishing a degree of personal contact that was unique in these early days of sail.

'Vinderman,' he said, 'Mr Passendale mentioned that name. Friend of one of our midshipmen I believe?' Thoughtful for a moment, he stated. 'I was impressed with the speed of your reaction back there. You saw the danger before any of us and acted on your own initiative.' Eyes boring into Vinderman and taking in every detail. 'We just lost our chief helmsman, think you can handle the job?'

'Yes, sir.'

No false modesty about Vinderman and Probus nodded approval. 'Stand by the helm, then,' he commanded, 'but if we take so much as a sliver of paint from our topsides when we leave the lock you'll be straight back in the fo'c'sle.'

Vinderman took a quick glance along the ship as she lay dominating the lock. Men already aloft on the yardarms and two seamen legs astride on the bowsprit ready to set the forward sails.

'Let go aft! Set lower topsails! Back forward yards!' The topsails dropped from their bunt lines and were sheeted tight. Forward yards braided round by a seeming confusion of halliard ropes leading down to deck level. Sails filling. The backed forward topsails balanced much of the drive of the working topsails, and she moved, but slowly, assisted in this by the shore men along the bank with long warps.

Vinderman was wishing he hadn't been so forthcoming. It was a hell of a responsibility to helm a ship of this size in such a confined space. 'Give me sea room anytime,' he muttered to himself. But Probus observed all things. He was not about to risk damage to his ship.

'Steady the helm.' The Captain's confidence was reassuring as he moved to the rail and watched the gap between ship and lock. The *Earl* responded to the pull of wind in her lower topsails. Vinderman felt the wheel stir in his hands. Now the backed topsail brought her head round. She slowly cleared the rounded corners of the lock entrance and he breathed a sigh of relief as the river opened out before them. He thought his Captain had done this before.

'Starboard a half point.'

'Starboard a half point.' He spun the wheel, repeating, 'Starboard a half point on, sir.'

'Haul forward yards and set main courses.' The forward topsails were hauled round, The jib sails flapped free for a moment, then set with a thump. She came out from under the lee of the gaunt warehouse buildings, freeing the wind which was blowing direct across the larboard side and she smoothed forward under the press of her topsails and a rhythmic chant started from the leadsman in the chains forward.

'By the mark, six,' and the ship nosed a careful way into the deep water of the main channel. The *Earl* had a laden draught of sixteen feet and the shallow, ever shifting underwater banks could swiftly grip such a deep keel, so great care and precision were needed, especially on a falling tide when a ship could soon be stranded high and dry.

From this point the River Thames Pilot took control and the voice of Captain Probus stilled as he relinquished command to the grey-bearded man who had come aboard early that morning.

The River Pilot was to steer them through the intricate channels and would then be replaced by the Channel Pilot when they were safely in the lower reaches.

Now the bottom sails, or main courses were set to draw, and as the channel wound its tortuous route into deep water so were the crew kept at full stretch pulling on rope and bracing yards to get maximum drive from the wind. Soon, the ebb began to run in their favour and the great ship slipped without fuss down the widening river.

'We'll anchor just past Tilbury and spend the night,' said Probus to Sethman, 'give us a chance to change Pilot's and wait for our fair tide tomorrow.' Looking at his First Officer. 'How is the crew settling down?'

'Just as you'd expect, too damn quiet. Haven't seen a smile or heard a single cheerful word since we left dock?' His own voice seemed far from cheerful as he went on to state. 'Mr Gaywood and Mr Ashbury have kept them hard at work all day and they should be glad of a peaceful night at anchor.'

'Drop the hook well out in midstream and double the guard on deck, don't want anyone diving over the side and making a swim for shore.' The morning's tragedy brought a note of melancholy. 'Keep your ear's open, Alan, anyone grumbling unduly I want brought before me in the morning.'

With Tilbury abeam, the ship's head was

brought up into wind . . . anchor splashing down from the bow. With all sail furled, peace descended and the hands were piped to supper. The lower reaches were quiet that evening. A small collier drifting by, Curlew calling from the distance and a dog barked somewhere ashore and the sound carried clearly across the darkening water and brought a grunt from a feeding pig.

Queen, on the quarterdeck, he had the first watch again and his fellow watch keeper Abraham was on station by the anchor cable. The men had finished the evening meal and silence reigned supreme, a fact commented on by Mr Gaywood as he strode the deck.

'Nice to have it quiet instead of the usual topside din or some fool scraping a fiddle and singing out of tune.'

'You don't like the crew cheerful, sir?' asked Queen.

Not caring for the insinuation, Gaywood glared at him. 'Neither do I want slackness and lack of discipline,' he said, 'and I reckon some of the idiots will be after jumping ship, either here or when we pick up passengers at Spithead.'

'Passengers?'

'Company personnel to the base at Surat, but only about six or seven.'

'They could have boarded more easily when we were alongside the dock.'

Allowing himself a rare smile, Gaywood said in contemptuous tone, 'Poor sods don't fancy the thought of a first few days beating down Channel and prefer to take the stage direct to Portsmouth. Anyway,' he went on, 'we have to wait at Spithead until the other ships join us. We usually sail in convoy with three or four Company ships. Sometimes a Navy frigate as far as Cape Town, or even India.'

Queen had learned much about the Honourable East India Company in the preceding weeks. How, for instance, the ships were heavily armed and carried a detachment of their own marines in case they should encounter trouble from foreign ships or even from pirates operating out of the many ports bordering the Indian Ocean.

'Do you anticipate trouble, sir?' he asked.

'Never know. It's possible to start a voyage in time of peace and then find out half way across the ocean when a ship fires on you that the war is on again. So we face the fact that situations change and that supposed friends have become enemies and for obvious reasons the more ships to sail in company the better for all.' Allowing this to register, Gaywood then added, 'Starting together is no guarantee because a fierce storm can scatter ships and the most precise of Master's before journey's end.' Terse and instructive tones, giving the distinct impression that it was below his dignity to explain such things to a mere apprentice. Gaywood was formally dressed; his figure must have been a delight to his London bespoke tailor. Just over medium height, square shoulders wedging down to a fine column of waist and stomach, what he lacked in physical size was more than compensated for in the commanding, whip-like snap of his voice, and sharp as a sabre thrust! His face was equally forbidding, thin and sallow and clean shaven, yet with a blue haze that the razor could never seem to erase. He seemed well poised and always in control with a forbidding air of authority that was evident in the hard, almost cruel set to his mouth and in the narrowing of always contemptuous, steely-grey eyes. Preparing to move off he ordered. 'Remember what I told you about deserters, and don't hesitate to call out the Duty Officer if you notice anything suspicious.'

'Aye, aye, sir.'

With the ending of daylight the breeze died away to a gentle zephyr. The tide swirled against the ship and set up little whirlpools at the stern. The moon peeped a shy face from behind a bank of drifting cloud and lit the upper deck with a soft glow. Taking a turn round the galley deck, checking that the livestock were securely tethered. The animals were mostly asleep. A sheep stirred and opened an uneasy eye at his approach; otherwise all seemed peaceful then the cook emerged from the galley carrying a bucket of slops. Of indeterminate age and skinny thin he wore a dour expression of long-suffering contempt for the motley crew he had to feed. In turn, the crew were suspicious of a lean cook because they suspected he was too concerned about the quality of the food he dished up to ever eat any himself . . . so a constant state of ribaldry existed between galley and fo'c'sle.

'Careful with your bucket, Mr Cook,' suggested Queen politely, 'the slightest splash tonight will bring the duty guard on the run.'

One thing the cook disliked more than a grumbling able seaman was a jumped-up midshipman but the controlled air of authority on this one stilled his instinctive desire for retort. Casting a sideways glance, he contented himself with the doleful comment, 'Have to clear away after supper, Mr Queen. Never knew a crew so off their food as this lot.'

'I'm sure the reason is not in your cooking.' Thick pea soup and boiled leg of pork had been served and he knew it was first class.

Stumping across the deck the cook lowered his bucket of slops over the side then stumped back again. He had one leg shorter than the other and walked with an uneven gait and the crew had immediately nicknamed him Gimpy. He went from sight and Queen continued his tour of the upper deck. A light flared and the glow lit up the bearded face of Vinderman and as fragrant tobacco smoke drifted back he moved close to say, 'You seemed to be finding favour with the Captain today, Vindo.'

'Aye: reckon he knows a good hand when he sees one.'

The cocky reply brought a smile. 'Gimpy was just complaining about the crew not eating his fine supper.'

'All the more for the animals.'

Vindo seemed withdrawn and his disgruntled tone of voice caused Queen to look closely at him. 'What's on, Vindo?' he asked.

'Nothing for you to be concerned with, though I suggest you keep clear of the foredeck tonight. There's talk of jumping ship and I wouldn't like to see you in the way and perhaps getting hurt.'

'Can't you talk sense into them? They surely know the officers are armed and expecting deserters. They'll never reach shore alive.'

'Not my concern and I've already said too much,' countered Vinderman, 'don't blame them wanting to get off after today's accident.' Relighting his pipe, he looked at Queen and said in positive tone. 'A death on board before a ship starts on her maiden voyage is more than they can handle or overlook. They know worse will happen before this trip is over.'

'Do you believe it too?'

'No doubt about it.' As he made reply, his eyes ranged over the ship. 'Damned shame,' he said, 'she really is a beauty, but she'll have a bad name for as long as she sails.'

'Captain Probus will prove you all wrong,' defended Queen hotly.

Vinderman was of the same mind as the crew and if it wasn't for a sense of commitment to his friend and shipmate, would have been long gone by now. He said in dour tone, 'Probus knows the score, just as we all do.'

He prepared to move off, but Queen held out a detaining hand. 'Will you do something for me?' Vinderman looked on with foreboding as Queen suggested. 'It's a lovely warm evening, play the lute and sing a few of your bawdy songs out here on deck. Your music might bring some cheer back aboard the *Earl*.'

'Not tonight, haven't the feeling for it.'

'It might be the way to prevent more disaster,' insisted Queen.

'Sorry, Jase, you ask more of me than I have to give.' After these words Vinderman disappeared from view behind a mass of standing rigging.

Queen slumped regretfully then made his way aft to the poop deck where reflection from the great stern window cast soft light on the water swirling down stream. The wind sighed a soft lament in the rigging and the moon disappeared behind a cloud, as if it too wanted no part in the gloom below. His head suddenly cocked and his face broke into a wide grin and he could hardly restrain himself from running forward as he heard the plaintive strum of Vinderman's lute. The preparatory tune-up was followed by a short silence, then his melodious baritone rang out. He was singing a song heard several times on board the *Dartmouth Trader*, both at sea and during quiet evenings in the ports along the French Atlantic seaboard. A melancholy, moving song that brought many a tear to the eyes of sailors far from home in a foreign port, and there came a furtive movement from the shadows as men emerged from below and came on deck to gather around the musician. Pipes were lit up; a lantern suffused the scene with a kindly glow. Seamen the world over love nothing better than music on a calm night and the strains of the melody died away to murmurs of appreciation from the growing assembly.

Queen's eyes were smarting unashamedly. Vindo had an audience and nothing would stop him now. A long, shimmering chord, then Vinderman's voice came boldly, unaccompanied.

'I have a pretty coloured gal, her name is Mary Lou,

And everywhere that I did go, you know she'd be there too.

She wanted us to marry, said we should settle down.

But like a fool I sailed away, and left my girl in Spanish Town.'

Lute strumming. The song was well known and popular, a few reluctant voices taking up the chorus line.

'Like a fool I sailed away.'

'Louder!'

'Like a fool I sailed away.' Chorus swelling . . . Vinderman insisting. 'Can't hear you?'

'Like a fool I sailed a-way!' Full throated roar developing.

'And again!' Cried the music maker.

The chorus bellowed round the main deck.

'Like a fool I sailed a-way! . . . and left my girl in Spanish Town.'

The verses went on and on growing more ribald and greeted with hoots of laughter yet always came a great roaring chorus, howling round the main deck and transforming the ship into a vibrant, living thing.

Queen resisted the urge to join in with difficulty and regret. This was the place of the crew, he would not be welcome and as the singing grew in volume he was joined by officers and fellow midshipmen, then finally, Probus made an appearance. Focusing, he queried, 'Vinderman again?' Queen's eyes were still streaming and Probus looked at him intuitively and gripped his shoulder. 'Well done, lad,' he said with feeling, 'and thank God for music, and that voice of Vinderman's.' Foot tapping the chorus rhythm. 'Makes me want to go down there and join in. Hanson,' he called to his cabin steward, 'break open a cask of rum. Pour a measure for every man on deck, and make Vinderman's a double!' Smashing a fist into the palm of his other hand, he exuberantly declared. 'By the Grace of God we will yet have a happy ship!'

The music and singing went on until the early hours, the sound carrying far across the patient River Thames and not one member of the crew attempted the long swim ashore.

Chapter Eight

Spithead in a gale force wind and incessant, driving rain is the loneliest place on earth. Some small shelter from the southwesterly was afforded by the sprawl of the Isle of Wight but the gale buffeted without restraint and tunnelled down the Solent between the Island and the low-lying Hampshire coastline. Four East India ships anchored in the Roads. Bucking and snubbing to their anchor chains and causing a round-the-clock anchor watch for fear the ship might drag. The *Earl* had two anchors down and a third ready on deck should a cable part to place the ship in jeopardy. The fleet of tenders that would normally be doing brisk business between ship and shore were lying snug in harbour, for only a foolhardy skipper would risk life and boat in such weather.

Three male passengers had boarded on the previous afternoon before the wind force increased to severe gale. A platoon of twenty marines in charge of a sickly looking Lieutenant had also managed to scramble aboard with their gear and weapons. These new arrivals all disappeared below decks and had not been in evidence since, although two of the passengers made a brief appearance at tea before retiring in obvious discomfort to the privacy of their cabins. These were situated aft, running either side of the ship and along the main assembly and mess deck where they were to associate and dine with the Captain and his officers. The cabins were equipped with the personal furnishings of the passengers concerned and in some cases fitted out most luxuriously. On a voyage that could take an indeterminate length of time to complete it was considered proper to travel in a style more in keeping with shore standards. Many of these fixtures and furnishings were sold off at journeys' end to travellers returning home, and in such manners made several repeat voyages. The general feeling among these reluctant sea goers was one of making the best of a bad situation.

Dawn broke wild and wet with no sign of a let up in the foul weather. Work on deck reduced to a bare minimum and the duty watch went about their duties heavily garbed and unrecognisable, amid scenes of acute desolation. The waves came at them in fierce progression. Short and steep, crests curling and blown off by the wind and smashing against the topsides sending spray and foam high and stinging cold over the foredeck, and still the rain lashed down in torrential, driving sheets and the deck ran wild with water torrents gushing out of the scuppers.

The anchorage was crowded with ships taking shelter. A normal summer gale in the English Channel tends to blow itself out after a few hours but this storm seemed unrelenting and was the climax to an increasing wind that had headed the *Earl* from the moment they rounded the North Foreland and then for four, endless days and nights, had tacked and beat their way down Channel to reach Spithead.

The normally philosophical Fitzroy Probus had grown gloomier during this time. Pacing the quarterdeck with a dark scowl as tack after tack seemed to gain hardly any distance over the ground. Only when the tide turned in their favour was any appreciable gain apparent but even this advance was paid for in extreme discomfort as the head wind worked against the tide flow to heap up short and steep seas that smashed against the plunging bow and kept the ship in perpetual, rolling motion.

He found no fault with the ship. Quick to the helm she responded bravely to the challenging wave and he knew that given any kind of a fair wind the *Earl* would pick up her skirts and dance her way over the restless sea. But such a fair wind was denied them and a weary ship's company brought her head up for the last time and heard the welcome sound of the anchor splashing down into the dirty brown, disturbed waters of Spithead Roads.

Stalking the quarterdeck in the cold light of morning. It was his custom to take exercise at this hour and he counted the turns religiously; time for contemplation and solitary thought. Even Mr Sethman was loath to break into his constitutional and everything except matters of urgency awaited the Captain's pleasure.

Raising a hand to secure his hat as the wind buffeted, lifting the tails of his cape and rain slashed his white cotton hose and his legs were chilled to the bone and water dripped from cape to shoes and his feet were squelching wet in the soggy leather. Peering in vain for a break in the sky but the dark rain clouds hovered and the gale shrieked with demoniac fury through halliards and standing rigging. Swearing out loud. Probus needed to get his crew away! Out into the open sea where his ship had freedom of movement and the men could settle into the rhythm of sailing a fine ship. Again the thought nagged: urgent! For his crew had retreated into a shell of reluctance and melancholy hinting of dark discontent with every minor setback seized upon as a sign that the ship was jinxed, and he could foresee real trouble if they didn't soon get away from land. But he had to accept the fact that until the wind stayed its force from the very direction in which they were to leave the Solent: there wasn't a damn thing he could do! Looking despairingly across the water . . . between him and shore was the Royal Navy frigate that was to accompany the East Indiamen to Cape Town. He judged it to be of thirty-eight guns, fifth rater and commanded by a Post Captain or even a Commodore. A powerful vessel, much bigger than the *Earl* yet he knew a flush of pride for his own command; she too was well armed and capable and his crew included many who were well trained in defence. Like himself, his First Officer had experience of danger and both had taken a ship into action. Among his prizemen was one Mr Jancy, master gunner, who had served in the Royal Navy before being badly wounded and seeking a quieter life in the merchant service. There was also the newly boarded platoon of the Company's own marines, hand picked for their marksmanship and, all things considered, Probus was optimistic that after a few weeks at sea they would develop into a very capable force.

'Blast this foul wind!' Out at sea they could take it in their stride but in these confining waters it couldn't be more hopeless. A spate of torrential rain sent him scurrying for shelter and swearing like a trooper all the way.

The atmosphere in the forward mess deck was even gloomier! Watch below had finished breakfast and all was cleaned away and tidy and the mess deck wreathed with tobacco smoke. The men's state of foreboding was betrayed by an ominous quiet as a thin faced, sardonic looking man held court.

'I tell you again,' he said in a doom-laden voice, 'the ship is a Jonah and the ghost of Colin Peters is aboard,' an experienced orator and rabble-rouser he made every word count.

'What a load of superstitious rubbish,' scorned Vinderman, 'look at the way she beat down Channel right into the teeth of this westerly with hardly a drop of green water inboard.' Challenge in his voice and several of the men nodded assent as he went on to claim. 'Trouble with you, Arnie, is that you are too busy being a prophet of doom instead of thanking your lucky stars for a stout deck under your feet and a bloody fine skipper like Probus.'

'Easy for you to talk,' retorted Arnold Waugh, 'you being Probus's blue-eyed boy an' all. Didn't take you long to find a comfortable berth.' Scowling into the bearded face of Vinderman he said accusingly. 'Suppose you'll be taking your gear back aft before long?'

Eye-balling him for a moment, Vinderman said in contemptuous tone, 'Rather my hands are on the helm than yours, Arnie, and you might have cause to remember that one day when you're aloft with the wind blowing cold up your arse and the yardarm shakin' fit to knock you off into the sea and the only person between you and a watery grave is the man at the helm. When one wrong turn of the wheel brings her head up and the footrope you're stood on starts to jump all over the place. Aye, that's the time you'll be glad it's Vinderman back there and not some cunt of a sea lawyer like you.'

Many of the men grinned approval. They had all seen shipmates torn from precarious hold on a foot rope, and when a ship is sailing close to the wind the safety of men aloft so often depended on the sound judgement of the man at the wheel.

Arnie Waugh loved a good argument. He had no intention of losing control over his captive audience and, glancing round for support, said in derisive voice, 'How the hell would you know? From what I hear you've never been out of the English Channel. You know nothing about the great oceans. Better stick to sailing a boat on the duck ponds you're used to.'

Grinning at the jibe, Vinderman tapped his head with the curved stem of his pipe. 'What I know is in here and I don't need to shout it about.' Assured, confident words delivered without any pretence of modesty and although the crew had yet to settle in to know each other it was obvious that most of them approved of Vinderman and they listened without interruption as he continued. 'Old Probus might be hard but no more than any Capt'n worth his salt. Handles the *Earl* well enough though and I reckon he'll show us a fair shake if we give him the chance.'

Waugh shook his head in dismissive gesture. 'She drew blood from one of her crew before she had set a single stitch of canvas. No matter what the Old Man tries to do, he can't wash away that stain. Another thing,' he added as if in challenge, 'have you ever known a gale this strong in summer and lastin' for days on end. Just listen to it?'

Wind gusting with venom, the fo'c'sle lurched and the anchor cable snubbed with a noise like a roll of thunder. Vinderman grabbed for a nearby post as he lost balance. He reluctantly had to agree, for he had never experienced such a prolonged blow. His eyes were sombre, but still he persisted. 'That's no reason to talk of Jonahs' or other such omens. Give the ship and Probus a chance and you could start by being thankful we are anchored here snug and safe instead of being out there at sea.'

Waugh had made his point and was determined to drive it home. 'No good you talkin' that way, reckon the message is clear and simple and if we don't take heed we're a bunch of fools.' Eyes narrowing in emphasis as he added, 'Give me half a chance and I'm for the shore.'

The crew were in accord with this and murmured approval and one hulking brute turned on Vinderman. 'If it hadn't been for you,' he snarled, 'I'd have been ashore at Tilbury and back in Old London by now.'

'All I wanted was a quiet tune before turning in,' countered Vinderman, 'who invited you? Anyway, Jacko Abbot, anyone going over the side that night would have been feeding the fish. The deck officers would have shot you under as a mutineer.'

'Suppose your friend Jason Queen warned you, I saw you on deck with him.' Abbot leered at Vinderman. 'Must be cosy to have a nice soft-arse midshipman to keep you happy on a long passage?' Thrusting his face forward, he goaded. 'Perhaps you'll lend him to me some dark night?'

Vinderman's fist exploded into the bloated face. Following Abbot as he staggered backwards from the force of the strike, he pumped a crippling knee into his stomach. Abbot was a hard man. Shaking his head with a snarl of rage, he started to regain balance. Vinderman let him come up almost to his feet and then leaned almost lazily into a looping uppercut that clubbed Abbot on the side of his unshaven jaw. Head flying back, Abbot's body brought up hard against a bulkhead and he slid down in an untidy heap. Vinderman's mouth was set in a hard line as he turned on the crew. 'Anyone else got ideas about Mr Queen?'

Nobody moved. The beating had been brutal and over in seconds. Up spoke a grey-bearded seaman. 'Reckon not. We ain't too sorry for Jacko, he was askin' for trouble.' Looking appraisingly at Vinderman he suggested. 'But if I was you I'd look to my back for a day or two, he ain't used to being bested in a scrap and won't forget too quickly.'

The fight had changed the mood and a sudden cheerfulness had even appeared. The show of violence had been a welcome diversion and served to relieve and lighten gloom and shed a few forebodings: if only for a short while.

No signs of despondency in the midshipmen's cabin, because of the conditions all four were down below. Abraham Verber had not been well on the passage to Spithead and was still feeling decidedly queasy, which caused great amusement to Bonham-Jones who took great delight in teasing the Jewish boy.

Sitting on one of the collapsible stools by the table, McFie was trying to write a letter. Pushing away with a grunt of despair as the ship lurched and his quill scratched ink across the page. Queen lay in his hammock, hands behind his head and listening to the storm. His own passage had brought seasickness. The long, slow roll of the *Earl* was very different to the lively movement of the much smaller *Dartmouth Packet* and he was taking longer to adjust. He had sympathy for Abraham and also admiration for the manful way he had stood his watch on deck.

'How the devil can you be expected to write with the ship jumping all over the place?' Tearing up the page with a degree of enthusiasm, McFie grinned all over his face. 'That's my excuse, anyway.' Billie was blessed with the supreme gift of laughter, nothing seemed to trouble him, he was tough as old boots. Dressed in a blue and white striped shirt and baggy matelot trousers his shoulders were wide and his arms bulged with muscle. His forehead was broad beneath a fringe of chestnut hair and his square chin had a cleft that altered shape when he laughed, which was most of the time. McFie never took anything seriously except the Captain: and Mr Gaywood. Practical jokes were his constant source of entertainment and they soon learned to give a rapid search to their hammocks before climbing in. The others spent many hours figuring some way to catch the irrepressible McFie. But without success . . . he was too crafty to allow the tables to be turned on himself.

Bonham-Jones had already come across McFie's rude justice. They shared the larboard watch and the senior apprentice had gradually inched his hammock over to the porthole where he could lie and read, but effectively shielding the daylight from any other occupant. McFie watched all this without comment but, one afternoon when the ship was driving hard and spray was flying, he waited for his watch mate to fall asleep then quietly opened the porthole.

Bonham-Jones had a nightmare: in which he was adrift in the open sea and threshing for his life. Waking with a shout of panic he found himself shivering cold and wet with his hammock soaked from the spray spurting in from the open porthole. Nothing was said, but life on watch was made miserable because as senior apprentice, Bonham-Jones had the authority to find McFie all manner of demeaning tasks that he carried out in his inimitable, carefree manner. Harmony was eventually restored but never again was the hammock slung across the porthole.

Queen cast a wary eye at McFie who had come across to where he was lying, and just now stood close to the rope-securing hammock to deck head. He knew that an idle Billie was the one to be on guard against.

'I'm watching you, McFie.'

'Why's that, Jase?' Hand hovering on the quick release knot,

'Because I don't bloody trust you!'

With a look of innocence, McFie said woefully, 'Just thought you might like to write to my folks, I'm hopeless at letter writing.'

'Write your own letters.'

A short length of rope appeared in McFie's hand. Queen started to scramble up but the rope was already over and around him and trapping him in the restrictive hammock, which began to swing from side to side. 'Did I hear you say you would love to write to my folks?'

Struggling frantically, but a banana-shaped hammock isn't easy to get out of, especially with several turns of rope around the middle.

'Didn't quite hear what you said, Jase?' As he spoke, McFie eased the hammock down until the curve touched the cabin sole at the bottom of its swing and Queen's rear end just scraped the floor. Now McFie pushed gently and the hammock gyrated from side to side. Queen's bottom thumped every time the hammock centred.

'I'll get you for this,' he threatened in a voice high pitched with laughter.

Thump! Thump! Swinging with gusto . . . Queen alternating between bumping his head on the deck head and his bottom on the cabin sole.

'What was that, Jase?' He was having a great time. Thump! Thump! No let up in pace.

'Alright, you monster,' cried Queen, 'I'll write your letter!'

'How many pages?'

'Two.'

Thump! Thump!

'Four!'

'Promise?' Thump! Thump!

'Promise!' Hysteria making the words almost inaudible.

The hammock stayed its descent, caught in the sure hand of McFie. 'Wish I'd gone for six,' he said with a grin as he released the rope so Queen made a grab for him but he was away lightening fast but only as far as the table where he where he posed in a provocative stance, then offered the quill and said, 'I like a man who keeps his word.'

Toby Bonham-Jones had watched this performance with amusement and, he admitted, a little envy. There were times when he wished he could join in the fun, but on reflection, he was the senior and consoled himself with the thought that his breeding and pedigree were a cut above the others, especially McFie, who had already shown a distinct lack of respect for seniority. The Jew, Abraham, didn't appear to have much spirit yet, after a slow beginning, was fitting in well with the other two in a comradeship that omitted Toby and gave him cause to regret his earlier, derogatory comment. As for Jason Queen, looking thoughtfully at the tall youth, he knew a sudden longing to make friends. His judgement was also prejudiced by the fact that Queen had found favour with the Captain. Dismissing the thoughts with a shrug. On a long passage there would be lots of time to cultivate friendships. Toby had led a cloistered childhood. Educated at the best public schools he had known only affluence and took every arrogant opportunity to make this evident. His face was floridly handsome. His eyes were like blue steel under bushy eyebrows and his hair was jet black, brushed severely back from a low widows peak and, when at sea, tied in a bun at the back of his head in a stylish, coiffured manner. A tall figure, indulgently overweight, he was dressed in casual off duty clothing, dark blue Guernsey-type jumper, and white, stovepipe trousers . . . he had no liking for tight fitting breeches for they showed off his bulky thighs to disadvantage and he wore them only when circumstance necessitated.

Hammering on the door. Third Officer David Ashbury entering. 'Captain is planning to entertain the passengers in his stateroom this evening,' he stated, 'and orders you all to attend. Full dress uniform, pre-dinner drinks at six but take my advice and accept only claret, and little enough of that. The Captain will not welcome any exhibitionism.' Looking straight at McFie. 'None of your tricks . . . try just for once to be serious.'

Billie saluted and his face was a picture of indignation. 'Hope the ship doesn't roll too much, Mr David, sir,' grin appearing as he added, 'or we might find we have nobody to entertain?'

Trying hard not to smile, difficult when McFie was about, Ashbury explained, 'Captain is anticipating the wind to veer and ease off, enough for us to take the tide out through the Needles early tomorrow. Concluding with a strict. 'So be very careful. Any indulgence tonight will be paid for dearly when we get out into rough water.'

As the day progressed so did the Captain's intuition prove correct? The wind veered northerly and abated in strength, easing from severe gale to little more than a fresh breeze. The rain clouds dispersed to allow an intermittent sight of sunshine and blue sky.

Queen took his watch on deck in the early afternoon, his post being the entry port in the ship's side. This was merely a gun port that had been cut larger to allow headroom and outboard of which was slung a platform staging. At this point of entry the boarding ladder consisted of a series of steps built in to the curving side of the hull, twelve in number and rising up to the intricately carved entry port.

The anchorage had undergone a transformation. With the easing of wind began to appear scores of little craft. Portsmouth wherries plying back and forth, square-sailed luggers and naval whalers moving briskly under oar and sail from ship to shore. Sails of all shape and size were busying around the anchored merchantmen and the towering man-o-war.

'Ahoy, *Rothesay*!' A wherry coming alongside under sail, her mainsail came down at a run and the boat wallowed beneath the entry port. Queen was admiring the skill of her crew when he realised with consternation that two of the three passengers were women. The wherry rose and fell with abandon as the heavy seas lifted her high then dropped her back into the trough. The crew had their hands full keeping their fragile craft from pounding against the *Earl*.

'Lively now, Mr Queen,' snapped Gaywood.

Looking at the women's clothing in dismay ... climbing on these narrow steps from a boat rising and falling a good six feet called for considerable agility and the wide hooped skirts they were wearing seemed most unlikely to allow such freedom. To complicate things further they both had on large-brimmed bonnets with black lace at the crown. Swinging out and down on the knotted rope strategically placed for such purchase he hovered over the wherry with his foot on the lower step and the women eyed this apparition with alarm akin to panic. The little craft rose like a buoyant eggshell then dropped away again. The male passenger clutched his stovepipe hat and the two crewmen steadied the wherry as best as they could.

'Take my hand, ma'am, on the next rise,' suggested Queen to the elder of the two women, 'place one foot on the step and hold on to me.'

Mr Gaywood appeared at the entry port and he gestured to the two seamen on boarding watch to take position on the platform. 'For God's sake, Martha,' called the man in exasperated voice, 'do as the officer tells you!'

The wherry came up, Martha made a wild grab for Queen, and missed, nearly losing balance before one of the wherry's crew managed to support her with a well-placed hand.

'Easy now, ma'am,' cautioned Queen, 'just reach up your hand and take mine.'

Her eyes were wide and staring, with fear evident. Up surged the wherry and she felt her wrist taken in a confident grip yanking her up and on to the steps where the two seamen straightaway grabbed her and pulled her unceremoniously inboard. Looking down with horror at the little craft rolling gunwales-under she scuttled for safety. Preparing to assist the other woman Queen was shocked to find the man preparing to board. Momentarily taken aback about such lack of gallantry he yanked him forcibly inboard, swung back out and said with a smile. 'Next, please,' the little boat crashed against the hull, bringing a curse from its skipper:

'Hurry, sir, or I'll have no boat left!'

The wherry rose on a crest. His hand was gripped firmly and eyes of deepest brown confronted him. He even had time to notice the tiny wrinkles that spread from each corner to hint of easy laughter then, as he brought her safely through the entry port her bonnet took off in the wind. Catching it in mid air he thrust the bonnet between his teeth and swung inboard where Martha took it and returned it to the young woman who coloured slightly but said nothing, being too busy controlling her hair long enough to jam the wayward bonnet back on her head.

'Next time, Trudy,' said Martha, 'do as I tell you and pin it properly.'

'Don't stand about, Mr Queen,' broke in Gaywood harshly, 'get the baggage aboard.'

The baggage consisted of four huge trunks and a small valise inscribed with the initials T.M. that he guessed belonged to the girl Trudy. With the luggage netted and aboard the wherry dropped astern and was soon under way back to Portsmouth. A squad of seamen manhandled the luggage and Queen preceded them along the quarterdeck to the passenger's cabins.

'In here,' called a dry voice, and as the trunks were bundled into the cabin Queen looked around with interest. This suite was luxurious with two comfortable looking berths snug against the side under a porthole each. A small annexe was situated off the main cabin and he caught a glimpse of the dark-eyed Trudy before he found himself abruptly dismissed. As he closed the door on his way out, he heard a whispered:

'You might have thanked him, Ernest.'

'For goodness sake, Martha,' came the short reply, 'he was only doing what he's paid for doing!'

Promptly at six o'clock four immaculate midshipmen presented themselves at the Captain's stateroom and were ushered in by the cabin steward. They stood stiffly in line, caps under their arm. Probus was conversing in a group of five including the ship's surgeon, a latecomer, and an impeccably uniformed Lieutenant of Marines. Officers Sethman and Gaywood sat either side of Martha who was dressed to kill in a classic gown of white, bordered with silken cherry coloured ribbon and cut daringly low to display creamy shoulders and a lovely neck adorned with a double row of pearls. Her face was high-cheeked and oval under well-coiffured ash-blond hair and her eyes sparkled like diamonds as she regaled them with the horrific story of her arrival inboard. No sign of the young woman and Queen began to suspect that she was a servant to the Harpers, a thought that made him remember the ungracious manner she had been left to the last when boarding. The steward brought over a tray and the four each took a glass of wine. Then Mr Sethman escorted Martha across and after regarding them in brief scrutiny, thought indulgently, not such a bad bunch after all. Bit harum-scarum perhaps. Especially McFie! Yet they certainly looked good tonight. Blue uniform jackets, sturdy legs in spotless hose, even the buckles on their shoes were shining bright. Introducing them in turn, Martha repeating, 'Bonham-Jones? Are you related to Sir Jasper?' She seemed impressed as Toby nodded assent, then she suggested. 'We must get together for a little chat.' Smiling as she said this and Toby thought she was a hell of a good-looking woman and was well pleased with the reference to his illustrious family. After a friendly word with McFie and Verber she confronted Queen. 'And you, of course, are the young man who pulled us all aboard in such virile manner.' Appraising the wide-shouldered midshipman for a covert moment. 'I must say that the only time I felt safe in that wretched little boat was when I felt you take hold of me.' Holding out her arm to expose a dark blue bruise on her forearm. 'And I have the mark to prove it.'

His face burned as he stammered, 'Sorry I had to be so rough.'

'No need to apologise, young Mr Queen,' said Martha with a smile, 'I haven't been handled so splendidly brutal for many years, and now that it's all over I think I quite enjoyed myself.' Her eyes had sudden fire then she waved a languid hand and said with studied petulance. 'Your Captain is displeased with my husband because we delayed coming out to the ship. But how could I be expected to brave that terrible wind, and anyway, what difference can one day make?' She delivered this with a sideways glance at Probus just as the steward came to request their presence at dinner.

The Captain's table was radiant with silver cutlery and cut crystal glassware, and the midshipmen exchanged glances as they compared this luxury with their own, sparse accommodation. The meal was superb and taken at a leisurely pace, giving the four youths a chance to make acquaintance with the passengers who had boarded two days before. They had the sallow complexions of men who spent long working hours behind a desk passing documents to and fro. John Simmons, Warrington-Smythe and Francis Warr were writers hoping to find fame and fortune. It had been so done on many occasions and they were looking forward to a new and financially rewarding future and all three were bound for India to take up administrative posts. The Company policy was to send out young men who had shown promise. One of the main reasons was in the rather short life expectancy on the Indian station for it was rapidly becoming evident that the inherent risks were formidable. With disease rampant, and hazards such as the too easy addiction to opium and other loose ways of living that could endanger the moral fibre of a lonely and homesick writer. But they had ambition: and optimism. They could in no way foresee any problems ahead and the conversation inevitably turned to the commencement of the voyage and to the long passage ahead. The midshipmen were engrossed in the details, for up to now they had only acquired such knowledge as was freely distributed over the "scuttlebutt".

Probus was speaking and all were attentive. 'Our first, and only port of call,' he said, 'will be Table Bay, Cape Town. Then we sail around the Cape and, hopefully, up the eastern seaboard of Africa following the route of Vasco da Gama which takes us across the Indian Ocean and Sea of Arabia to our destination of Surat.'

'Why do you say hopeful,' queried Mr Harper, 'surely this is the shortest route?'

'Shortest is not always the quickest. Everything depends on timing and if we can find a fair wind across the Indian Ocean. I have known occasions when the only way to make India from the Cape is to stand boldly out on a southerly course until the westerlies are gained, then run before them almost clear of Australia. Only then has the wind been fair enough to allow a ship to alter course and head north-west for the Indian continent.' Focussing with meaning on Mrs Harper as he concluded. 'This is why every hour must be counted and why we must keep to schedule where humanly possible.'

Martha's pearls glowed in the candlelight and she smiled sweetly at the Captain. Finding much pleasure in being the only woman amidst this colourful assembly she wasn't the least put out by his pointed remark.

'And when you leave us at Surat?' asked Francis Warr.

'We sail south for a cargo of spices from the Islands of Indonesia.' Probus frowned as he added thoughtfully. 'Not so easy as it sounds because the Dutch are well entrenched and have no intention of sharing the spice trade.'

The midshipmen were enthralled but the officers had heard all this before and Mr Gaywood looked bored to tears. He wished this dinner party would end so he could get on with preparing for sea, and his impatient manner brought rebuff from Harper.

'You are of course aware, Mr Gaywood, that my wife and I intend to make the round trip.' Allowing this to register he then brusquely explained. 'We have commissioned this ship for the sole purpose of reviving our dismal record of trade with the Spice Islands and, Dutch reluctance or not, I intend to return with a profitable cargo.'

'Really, Ernest,' remonstrated his wife, 'wish you wouldn't make it sound so dangerous.'

Appealing to Probus, she asked. 'Do you anticipate hostility?'

'The South Seas are a long way from Portsmouth,' reassured Probus, 'and there will be plenty of time for worry when we are a little nearer. We neither anticipate nor invite trouble but are prepared for anything.' Rising from the table he announced. 'I expect to sail at first light, and regretfully ask you to retire so that my officers may prepare the ship for sea.'

Chapter Nine

The night was cold but clear . . . every star in view and glowing brilliant against a backdrop of dark velvet. Navigation lamps flickering, otherwise the only light visible was the subdued pink illumination of the compass binnacle. Wind steady from the east and the great square-rigger reached with purpose along her course. A yardarm creaked with the stately roll as she ploughed through the water under night canvas. Four o'clock in the morning: watch keepers relieved. As Queen came on deck the helmsman gave up the wheel. Chalking course and progress on the slate-board register able seaman Jack Dooley said as Vinderman took over. 'Due south.'

'Due south, I have her, Jack.'

'She's going well,' said Dooley, 'think I'll sling my hammock topsides . . . too damn nice to go below.' Stamping circulation back into his legs he then left the steering position.

The fresh, early morning air sent a shiver

through Vinderman. Hunching into his sea coat, he cast a speculative glance at the young officer of the watch. Apart from his lack of shoes and the hat carried in his hand, Queen was formally dressed. His hair had grown long and swept back from forehead and temples and his face was coloured by exposure to wind and spray.

'Reckon you've looked better this last day or so,' said Vinderman slyly.

The observation brought a wry smile. 'There was a time back there,' replied Queen, 'when I was so sick I wished I was dead. Crossing Biscay in that storm was an experience I could well do without.' Looking at Vinderman as he countered. 'You were a bit green around the gills yourself.'

'Must admit, it was a fair blow and surely whipped up some big seas? Not much like the short chop we are used too in the Channel but at least the ship rode it all in great style and proved more seaworthy than some of the younger members of the crew.' Laughing at Queen's discomfort he then complimented. 'No matter, lad, stood your trick well enough.'

'Less gossip, helmsman!' Second Officer Gaywood strode aft to look over the stern as he spoke but the wake was straight and true and bubbling phosphorescent and he could find no cause for complaint. Gaywood allowed no idle chatter on deck. His first trip with a mate's ticket and he was determined to stamp his authority on the entire ship's company.

'Go aloft, Mr Queen,' he ordered, 'main top platform. Keep a strict lookout and I'll have you relieved in one hour: and wear your hat when on duty!'

Jamming his hat on. Hurrying forward to mount the rigging up to the main top. She rolled to larboard as he wedged in a safe position. His favourite place! The quietest watch since leaving Spithead, peaceful, and soothing to an unsettled stomach. Soon would come the dawn, and at last perhaps, a fine day. Content with his thoughts. Feeling good. Seasickness over: he hoped. Looking down on the graceful lines of the ship he was aware of a sense of belonging, and yet? Mind reaching back to London: to the enchanting girl of whom he had grown so fond. Maggie! What a fool name for such an accomplished young lady, but how it suited her personality and joyous nature and her ever-changing moods. Remembering the strange harmony they found in each other. Walking arm in arm along the river at Richmond, her face lovely and mysterious as she revealed those tiny red boots. Which reminded him of his dream and brought the realisation that she would be tucked up in bed at this time, cosy and warm. Provocative thought, interrupted by Abraham who came rattling up to inform. 'You're excused, Jase, we have to take an early breakfast. Seth wants us on deck for our first lesson in navigation.'

* * *

Five days out from Spithead, southerly latitude with the sun appearing in a cloudless sky bringing a warmth that transformed the ship's company. Such a welcome change from the misery so far. Of days grey and forbidding when the wind cut through outer layers of clothing and the watch on deck quickly chilled to the marrow. When comfort was found only in the warmth of a hammock and a woollen blanket. Rain and spray continually washing the deck leaving rimes of salt over man and rigging and when a four-hour trick at the helm was more than any man could sustain, so the wheel needed two pairs of hands to control the surging ship.

But advantage could be found in the most adverse conditions and the strong-to-gale force wind drove the ship speedily on her way south into warmer climes. During this time the Captain had nothing but praise for the two hundred and fifty miles that was the noon-to-noon recorded run for these hectic first days. Then, with clearer weather came an easing in wind strength as the strong easterly reduced to a gentle breeze. Ghosting over calm water. Every scrap of canvas set to draw. The sun shone fire through the towering press of sail and the main deck was crowded with men soaking up the glorious warmth.

These conditions continued and the *Earl* was a picture of grace and efficiency in the freedom of a wind that blew from just abaft the beam. A true soldiers wind! So called because, as seamen mockingly acknowledged, even an ignorant "sojer" could sail a boat in a wind such as this. Speed reduced to less than seven knots she sailed almost level, the motion was barely noticeable and one by one the passengers appeared on deck and eventually the Harpers made their presence, with Mrs Harper always in company with Trudy Manson.

The afternoon was magnificent. Noon observation placed the ship exactly on the line of the Tropic of Cancer and though the sun blazed down the breeze kept the deck area reasonably cool.

'Good day, Mr Queen.' He came from deep reverie as the strident voice intruded and brought him upright from his lounging stance on the beam rail

'Nice to see you on deck, ladies.' Greeting them in courteous tone, his off-duty mode of dress had reduced considerably these last days and was merely a faded black shirt open at the neck and chest and with sleeves cut back to the shoulder, and cotton breeches shortened and tied just below the knee. His beard now grew too quickly to ignore and while shaving regularly he had allowed his moustache to lengthen into a bushy, luxurious growth hiding his upper lip.

Martha regarded him in covert appraisal. 'You begin to look like a buccaneer,' she said, 'all you need to complete the picture is a gold earring.'

He grinned at the idea. A matching smile

spread Trudy's mouth as Martha delicately fanned her face. 'These conditions in which men seem to flourish, it's either so rough and miserable we have to be confined to our cabins or else unbearably hot whether above or below decks. We ladies, you know, are but fragile creatures and cannot be expected to behave as robustly as you sailors.' He didn't see Mrs Harper as a fragile creature but remained the model of politeness and attention as she continued her good-natured grumble. 'And what are we supposed to do all day long on your very dull ship? The hours are endless and all we have to do is to just wait around for mealtimes with the only civilised moment being found in a glass of wine before supper.'

'I find it difficult to imagine a state of boredom,' just then the sun appeared from behind the after royals to lend conviction to his voice as he announced, 'have you ever seen anything so magnificent as those sails, or the sunshine over the sea?' The water dazzled in reflected brilliance, almost painful on the eye, and he said in quiet tone. 'I spend hours, particularly in the evening, stood at the rail wondering just where we are on the surface of this great ocean.'

She was intrigued with this unsuspected eloquence. 'Why, Mr Queen,' she murmured, 'I believe you are a romantic.' Eyes contemplative on the colourful midshipman she said in an inviting tone. 'Perhaps you will join us this evening so we can be further tutored in this mystic of the sea?' The depth in her voice had him embarrassed and he thought he was getting in the deep end here, but his excuse was immediate and truthful.

'I have the first watch tonight and don't imagine Mr Gaywood would approve of my entertaining the passengers instead of being about my duties.' A thought occurred and he suggested. 'But if you would care to accompany me to the foredeck I'll show you something that might alleviate your boredom.'

Peering along the undulating deck. 'Doubt if I can endure such a walk;' she said with a shudder.

'How about you, Miss Trudy?'

Eyes shining at the invitation, she replied, 'I would love to.'

'Really, Trudy,' admonished Martha, 'you know Mr Harper wouldn't approve of you wandering about un-chaperoned.'

The snappy comment deflated Trudy and Queen thought she needed support against the formidable Martha. 'Promise to bring her back within the hour,' he said. Not waiting for further remonstrance he grasped her arm and proceeded to lead her down the short companionway. He sensed a distinct lack of confidence but his maintained pressure sustained momentum and resisted her move to turn back.

'Mrs Harper will not be pleased,' said Trudy in sotto voice.

'Think she'll report me to the Captain?' His apparent unconcern was rewarded by a flashing smile, one that encouraged him to ask. 'Just what is your position with the Harpers?'

'More like a poor relation,' she said frankly. 'Mrs Harper is my aunt and took me in when my mother died. I owe them a great deal and try to repay in anyway I can. My aunt is really very nice but has to keep proper decorum when Mr Harper is about.' She wore her chiffon bonnet and an ankle length dress of blue silk and most becoming but hardly suited to tropic heat. Glancing enviously at his bare feet. 'This decking is so very hot,' she said uncomfortably.

Halting at the base of the stairway leading to the forepeak he sat her down on a hatch cover. 'No one's looking,' he said, 'slip off your shoes and leave them for me.'

Smiling in delightful compliance, her feet wriggled under the dress then she rose to move up the stairway. Retrieving the slippers, he followed after her. A familiar aroma of tobacco hovered and he looked up to see a broad grin on Vinderman's face.

'Nicely done, Mr Queen.' Lowering one eyelid in a significant wink as he moved away.

The unusual sight of a woman forward brought speculative interest from several lounging seamen and as he shepherded Trudy through coils of rope and around the giant capstan into the fore peak he noted with surprise that Francis Warr was sitting outboard astride the bowsprit with his feet tucked into a foot rope and with a sketch pad in his hand. Though seemingly engrossed, he stopped work at their approach and his gaze focussed appreciatively on Trudy. Taking her arm Queen brought her to the rail. Responding to his gesture she looked over and down into the frothing bow wave and her face registered immediate astonishment and delight. A school of porpoise swam in company with the ship and their sleek, grey shapes were clearly visible through the translucent water. Her mouth formed a round, soft looking circle of enchantment and she leaned further over for better view and her eyes sparkled. 'How truly wonderful,' she said in delight.

Her pleasure was rewarding but her position precarious and he had to keep tight hold. 'I brought you to see the porpoise, not join them,' he jested.

Enjoying the spectacle for a long minute, she turned back inboard. 'I begin to understand your interest and enthusiasm, Mr Queen, are the porpoise always with us?' By this time Francis Warr had clambered inboard to regard Trudy with open admiration before answering the question himself.

'They've been alongside for several days.' His face had shed its former office pallor and glowed with healthy colour. His hair was long and bleached by the sun and brushed back behind rather large ears and a few weeks at sea had considerably changed the appearance of the writer.

Peering unashamedly at the pad in his hand Trudy asked, 'Please, may I look?'

Handing her the pad with a pleased expression and Trudy brought it for Queen also to inspect. The pages contained a series of black-pencilled sketches that portrayed with great dignity the movement of the porpoise under the bow and she looked at him with interest and conjecture. 'You are an accomplished artist, Mr Warr.'

'Just a little hobby.'

'More than a hobby I think, there is life and movement in your work.' Leafing through the drawings again. 'I have seen sketches offered for sale in the galleries of London which could not even begin to compare with these.'

Highly delighted, Francis Warr said, 'Your appreciation is the finest compliment possible.' Retrieving his pad he detached a page and offered it to her. 'This is the one I like best,' he humbly suggested, 'will you do me the honour of acceptance?'

Handing back the sketch, she said with a smile, 'Only if signed by the artist.'

A quick rapport had been established between the two and Queen began to feel like an intruder, a spectator on the sidelines, but after listening to them conversing knowledgeably about sketches and art he forced a significant cough. Understanding, regret showed briefly on her face. A feeling obviously shared as Warr said, 'Wish you could stay a while longer.' Glancing at Queen even as he spoke.

'I have pledged to return Trudy within the hour,' said Queen.

'You are right, of course.' Warr then said to Trudy. 'May I hope for the enchantment of your company again?'

She registered pleasure, then concern. 'My time is fully taken up by my duties, Mr Warr.'

'The ship is too confining to allow of isolation,' said Queen with a smile, 'and we have a long way to go.'

Chapter Ten

Earl of Rothesay smoothed her way over the sea as if enjoying a fair wind and blue water under her keel. Ploughing on ever southerly into the vastness of the Atlantic Ocean. Then suddenly! One dark night! A cockerel crowed three times! A raucous shriek that ghosted over the main deck and immediately revived the superstitious fears of the crew. By morning every chicken had disappeared, necks broken during the night and the carcasses thrown overboard.

'Know of a ship where a cock crowed in the dark hours,' Arnold Waugh's voice, melancholy at the best of times, was positively funereal as he went on, 'within a week the ship foundered and only a handful of men was saved.'

'I heard that story.' Jack Dooley was a sensible type not given to exaggeration but his voice held the dull edge of foreboding as he added, 'She was the old *Southern Cross* out of Plymouth . . . sank within minutes and only eight out of her crew of fifty got ashore.'

The men gathered in the foc'sle were barren faced and subdued as Waugh took up his inflammatory dialogue. 'Gives you the flamin' creeps to hear that Judas cry in the night, and we've just got to face up to it. She's jinxed, and the sooner we get off the better!' Voice hushing with dramatic effect as he concluded. 'I know we all have to go sometime but there's no damn future in just waiting around for it to happen.'

'Must be a few hundred miles from the mainland,' pondered Dooley, 'not much chance of jumping ship out here?'

Jacko Abbot spoke up. 'The smudges of land we saw two days back were probably the Cape Verde Islands. Who's for jumping the duty officer tonight and taking off in the longboat?'

'Not me!' Dooley said emphatically. 'I'm not sailing the Atlantic in a bleedin' longboat! And even if we found the Islands who the hell wants to be stuck in the middle of nowhere like those poor bugger's from the *Southern Cross*. They went out of their minds waiting for a ship to come by.'

Waugh sensed that the men were in full agreement. 'If that's the feeling,' he said, 'we may as well forget it 'til we reach Table Bay. Old Probus won't be able to keep his eye on all of us at the same time: and Cape Town is plenty big enough for us to get lost in. In the meantime we'll let him think all's well below. Lull 'em into a false sense of security then as soon as their back's turned we'll be gone.'

'Suits me,' said Dooley. 'Masters are always on the lookout for experienced men and from a place like Cape Town we could sail out for any port in the world and on a ship that's not jinxed.'

'Keep this away from Vinderman,' instructed Waugh, 'he might just mention it to his friend's back aft.'

'Vindo's alright,' defended another man, 'he's a bloody fine helmsman and I'd rather have him with us than against.'

'Nevertheless,' insisted Waugh, 'keep your eyes open and your mouth shut.'

'The one I'd like to meet ashore is that sarcastic bastard of a second mate.' This from Joe Castellack, ship's carpenter, he also had a small money earner acting as barber to the crew, and went on to threaten. 'If he comes into my workshop with just one more of his private jobs I'll adze him from arsehole to breakfast time.'

Officer Gaywood had established himself as a hard, unfeeling taskmaster and the men were increasingly resentful of the arrogant manner in which he worked the deck watches. Several had suffered punishment for minor offences, and even more significantly, he was now threatening to flog anyone not jumping smartly to his orders. While the other officers were aware of this inflexibility, they could not interfere without undermining authority: and were unanimous in maintaining discipline, for the early sailing men were a hard, uncaring breed ready to seize on and exploit any sign of weakness.

'Aye,' said Abbot, 'Gaywood's beginning to get on my back as well. No telling what floggings he'll be dishing out by the time we reach Table Bay.'

There's always one sour apple,' said Waugh, 'but remember, lads. No violence! Jumping ship is the one thing they can't do anything about, but any sort of your trouble, Jacko, any bloodshed, could have us all strung up on a charge of mutiny. Like I tell you! Do nothing that will spoil our chances. All we want is to finish with the *Earl* before she finishes us.'

Vinderman at the wheel with the ship ghosting through sparkling seas and the sun blazing down, he was stripped to the waist and the matt of hair on his chest was bleached golden brown and his feet straddled the deck planking, braced against the slow, rhythmic roll.

Probus lit a cigar, eyes roving over the ship, every scrap of working canvas set to draw maximum advantage from the zephyr-like breeze, all idyllic, or so it seemed. The rewarding sort of day that made it all worthwhile, what man in his right mind would exchange all this for a stuffy office in Leadenhall St. Glancing at Vinderman. 'What course, helmsman?'.

'Course due south, sir,' alert as he answered, the course had been constant for many days and it was uncharacteristic of the Captain to indulge in idle comment.

Probus looked calculatingly at him. 'Haven't heard you play your lute since we left Tilbury, you did the ship a fine service that night and I never expressed my appreciation?'

'The rum went down well,' replied Vinderman very guardedly, 'but the thanks should go to Mr Queen. The idea was his, not mine.'

'Guessed as much, and made my thanks known to him at the time.' Having succeeded in getting Vinderman talking he then got the dialogue back on course with a casual. 'How did the crew take to that funny business the other night?'

'What funny business?'

'You know damn well what!'

Probus wasn't pleased with Vinderman's evasive attitude and his voice was curt and demanding. No way out for Vinderman and he reluctantly said, 'They soon got rid of the chickens.'

'And cost us a few decent meals in the so doing.' Looking straight at Vinderman and, in a tone that held both enquiry and invitation, he said. 'Damn funny thing that cock crowing.'

Vinderman concentrated on the compass heading.

In similar way to the men of the fo'c'sle, Probus had come to respect the capable Vinderman. 'Come on, Vindo,' he urged, 'man to man talk. Just you and me, nothing you say here will in any way be misinterpreted.'

Looking squarely at his Captain. 'You don't need me to tell you they are scared to death. That the cock crowing is another sign we are in for dire trouble on this passage.'

'And you personally, how do you view all this superstition and talk of impending disaster?'

'If it's honest speaking you're after, Capt'n,' replied Vinderman coldly, 'I think you feel as I do: and all the others who've been years at sea. The ship is unlucky. You've seen the sign's same as the rest of us and find them equally difficult to ignore.'

'Mine is the ultimate responsibility, both for the safety of the ship and the success of the voyage. I cannot indulge in the luxury of these wild imaginings that run rife through the lower deck and you know damn well that seamen love a reason for a good grumble and grouse.'

'Then why didn't you punish them for throwing the chickens overboard: or were you just grateful they'd been got rid of?' Knowing he was close to insubordination but the Captain had invited free comment and Probus stifled instinctive anger to concede:

'You are right, of course, and I can well imagine the state of mind below.' He then queried. 'What do you think they'll do?'

'I'm not in their confidence.'

'Hardly fair to ask, anyway.' Probus couldn't keep still. Stalking a few yards away, he came back to face his helmsman. 'You're an honest man, Vindo, and I thank you for your candour. Tell me,' he pursued, 'what would you do in their place?'

'Can't speak for them. My job is to helm, not anticipate the actions of the crew.'

Knowing he would get nothing more from Vinderman, Probus said in conclusion. 'Then I'll just have to hope for a continuance of these ideal conditions and a fast passage to Table Bay.'

The next morning brought a dead flat calm. Not the slightest whisper of wind. The glassy-looking sea concealed a deceptive swell that rolled the ship down almost to the gunwales. They were caught in the doldrums, an area of complete calm that lies along the equator and in which a sailing ship is trapped without wind and rolling beam on. The yards swung and clashed, never still and in danger of fraying apart with the constant chafe.

'Everything is against us,' cursed Probus, 'certainly gives cause to think the ship is unlucky.'

'We've been stuck in the doldrums before,' comforted First Officer Alan Sethman. 'They are a nuisance and damned uncomfortable but we aren't the first vessel to be delayed this way and we certainly won't be the last.'

'One bloody thing after another,' insisted Probus gloomily, 'and all starting with young Peters in Blackwall dock.' Clad in shirt and breeches and barefoot as his men he still found the heat oppressive and mopped his neck with a spotted cloth. The upper yards creaked as the masts gyrated, while the sails just hung limp. Shaking his head at Sethman's enquiring glance. 'Leave them up,' he growled, 'we'll have to absorb any wear and tear because if there's any sign of a puff we must be ready to take advantage.'

Unconcerned about the lack of activity, Queen, McFie and Verber were taking turns to jump over the side where they would swim around for a few minutes before being hauled back by the other two with the rope prudently looped around their middle. While enjoying the swim they were exercising care lest a sudden breeze might get the ship under way and leave them floundering. Some of the crew gathered to watch the frolics and now several passengers appeared on the quarterdeck, attracted by the unusual sound of gaiety.

Cascading over the rail Queen sprayed seawater over Bonham-Jones. 'Come on, Toby,' he laughingly said, 'you badly need a bath.'

Always ready for a bit of fun, McFie took up the idea and brandished the rope before Bonham-Jones. Mimicking the senior midshipman's accent, he drawled, 'How about it, Toby old boy?'

'Keep away from me, McFie!' Alarm brought harshness to the words but Queen and Verber took close position and with a grin McFie announced:

'Your turn, Toby.'

Bonham-Jones tried to dash for safety but was

trapped against the galley bulkhead. With a shout of triumph the three grabbed him, ducked under his flailing arms and, easily containing his struggles, knotted the rope round his waist and flung him bodily overboard. Amused laughter rippled through the spectators as he came up splashing and clawing frantically at the rope.

'My God,' cried Verber, 'he can't swim!'

'Shark!' High-pitched cry from an observant seaman as a sinister dorsal fin cut the surface about fifty yards away. In the clear water all could see the ominous and fast-moving shape of the giant fish and for one petrified moment everyone froze and the belly of the shark showed sickly white as it turned to dive.

'Pull, Billie!' Queen's wild shout jerked them back to grim awareness and McFie exploded into action. Shoulders bulging with muscle he strained on the rope with Queen and Verber in line behind pulling for all they were worth.

Bonham-Jones was some yards away from the ship's side when he heard the warning cry and his face was suddenly a frightened mask. Jerking a look over his shoulder. Could see nothing! The shark had gone deep, and he sobbed and clung to the rope in panic and desperation. Nearby seamen leant urgent weight into the pull and their tough, experienced hands heaved in rhythmic unison, propelling Bonham-Jones at speed back to the ship. But the shark was swift, master of its element: and hungry! Tumult in the water below and his mouth opened to scream but no sound came and he turned his head in mortal terror as the shark rose to strike. He could see the grinning, gaping mouth open like a dark cavern in the white of its underbelly and jagged teeth closed on his trailing legs as the shark came in at full speed for the kill and he could only stare in hopeless mesmerisation at that awful mouth rising for the first tearing mutilation, but the legs of Bonham-Jones were no longer within reach as he was hauled unceremoniously but safely from the water and the shark's deadly mouth found no target. The great fish thrashed along the ship's side and with a flash of grey disappeared underneath.

Yanked up and over he collapsed in a sodden heap then, shaking off the helping hands with an animal growl he rose to crouch before them in menacing stance.

'Rotten bastards!' The words spat seawater and malice and they fell back before his screaming rage. The three were dumbstruck, appalled by the speed at which their unthinking horseplay had so nearly turned tragic.

'Stand to, you idiots!' Voice of Officer Gaywood cutting across the scene. A blistering glance dispersed the attentive seamen and they moved away to leave him alone with the midshipmen. Stalking around scrutinising each in turn he then looked out to sea where the dorsal fin cruised. 'You're in for it this time,' he snapped, 'Captain's coming and I hope he orders you a dozen lashes each.' Eyes glittering with anticipation as determined footsteps approached, he commanded, 'In line, you four. Attention!'

Standing erect before their Captain. Glaring at the soaking wet Bonham-Jones, he demanded, 'Who's responsible for this outrageous behaviour?'

Bonham-Jones stared straight ahead, a posture that brought contempt from Gaywood. 'All for one,' he scorned.

Probus was in foul mood, in angry, condemning stance. 'Don't you fools realise that we daren't risk further tragedy on board? This lunacy of yours could have given the ship's company even more cause to think she's jinxed. You are supposed,' he said with real threat in his voice, 'to be training as officers and gentlemen but after today I doubt you qualifying as either?' Looking aloft . . . the masts were rolling through a dizzy arc of twenty degrees either side and the yards swung with abandon on their fastenings. 'Put them to dry off on the topmast yard, Mr Gaywood. Two hours up there should help to reduce their appetites.' With this last, scathing comment, he turned away to leave the shamefaced midshipmen at the malice of Second Officer Michael Gaywood.

'Up you go. Two either side: and stay there until ordered down. If I had my way you'd have felt the cat-o-nine tails across your backs.'

Grimacing in evil manner at the thought and as if disappointed at such mild punishment, he ordered. 'Now move, at the run!'

Reaching the topmast yard they inched across to hang over by their waists. The sun scorched down and already their breeches were dry. McFie looked across at Bonham-Jones. 'I just played my last trick, Toby,' he said in penitent voice, 'nearly died when I saw that shark coming for you.'

'You nearly died? I was the one up for shark bait!'

The three were seeing Toby in a new and revealing light and, suddenly, they were closer than at any time on the voyage. Looking at them, he said with a nonchalant grin, 'Must admit it was a bit scary but I knew all the time that you would get me out.'

Verber's dark complexion had tanned to deepest mahogany, giving a rugged and handsome look to his aquiline features. He placed a hand on Toby's shoulder. 'I was proud to know you back there,' he said, 'if it had been me in the water I'd have been screaming my head off.'

Toby thought that his terror stricken loss of voice had earned respect, but didn't enlighten them. Instead he gave Verber a snide glance and a grin and said, 'Let's shake hands all round then.'

Gripping hands in a solemn manner; four young men on the adventure of a lifetime and they were friends: and comrades. McFie gave a whoop of acclaim. 'All for one,' he cried, 'let's give old Gaywood a cheer!'

A great shout rang out from four mouths simultaneously, ringing down from the masthead and scything across the main deck. Probus gave a resigned shrug at his First Officer and a half-smile softened his face. 'At least one section of the ship's company refuses to be downhearted.'

Removing the pipe from his mouth Sethman grudgingly admitted, 'Makes me feel brighter myself and with such exuberance aboard there may yet be hope for all of us.'

Wallowing in the doldrums. This area of ocean where the atmosphere stifles and no trade winds blow. Any slight puff heralded with anticipation only to have hope banished along with the fickle breeze, sails slatting to and fro and the roll of the ship a constant, destructive menace; conditions that were a sailing man's foresight of hell. The sticky, overpowering heat sapped energy and caused increasing bad temper. Fights broke out among the crew, which exhausted the Captain's tolerance. He ordered several men flogged and threatened a dozen strokes of the cat to any further offender.

Probus now attempted to tow his ship out of the calm, using the longboats in relays of two at a time. This served the double purpose of keeping the ship moving, albeit slowly, and also to work off excess energy because no man could row solidly for an hour in this heat without becoming completely exhausted. All to no avail! The glassy sea held them in swelling embrace and not even a catspaw ruffled the surface. By this time Ernest Harper had become increasingly impatient and cornered the elusive Captain on the quarterdeck.

'There is not a damn thing I can do,' reiterated Probus, 'I've known ships to be stationery in the doldrums for weeks on end.' As irritable as Harper, he then snapped. 'I don't presume any influence on the ways of wind and sea and we'll just have to wait this one out.'

'All very well for you, Probus,' replied Harper heatedly, 'but time is money to me: and this is far too much time wasted!'

Fed up with Harper's whining Probus moved away with a final admonition:

'Then direct your plea to a Higher Authority.'

Long days passed, in which the sun blazed down from a sky devoid of cloud. The cloying heat made the crew's quarters unbearable and caused the men to sling their hammocks topside. The forward part of the ship began to resemble a farmyard on washday with hammocks slung in haphazard manner and animals wandering listlessly about. One of the sows produced a litter of twelve piglets, fat and shiny, and these soon took over the affection of the crew and were given freedom on deck except in the stifling hours when both men and animals sought shelter from the steam heat. The sailmaker rigged protective awnings in a vain effort to keep the deck cool but pitch bubbled in the seams and the deck planking began to split open. Not like Probus to allow this kind of untidiness but he was more fed up than anyone and, at the moment, couldn't have cared less.

The passengers, particularly Mr and Mrs Harper, now appeared on deck only in the cooler hours of evening but the squad of marines had been pressed into service and took their turn in the longboats, working through the morning and late afternoon, twenty men to a boat with a midshipman in charge.

Longboat moving in jerks . . . lifting a hawser out of the water with each forward thrust towing the *Earl* sluggishly behind. Clad only in floppy hat and cotton breeches Queen stood hand on the tiller searching for any slight ripple that might be the forerunner of a breeze. Sweat running down his forehead and face and his eyes smarting with his own salt as he urged his crew to maintain effort.

Now a familiar and disliked voice roared command from the mother ship.

'Lay into them, Mr Queen. Put some drive behind them with your whip!'

Taking up the short-handled whip that lay on the thwart he brandished it high. 'You heard him, put some muscle into it!' Cracking the whip over their heads as he jested. 'How about a realistic groan from you, Arnie, you know how Mr Gaywood loves to hear someone suffering?'

'Hanged if I don't like your style, Mr Queen.' Waugh contrived to groan in pain but the smile on his face ruined the effect. Jason Queen was popular with the men and his eagerness to learn all the intricacies of their trade had formed a strong bond between him and the men of his deck watch.

'You put as much effort into that groan as you do in pulling this longboat. How about one from you, Davy?'

Davy Greenwood was about the same age as Queen. Freckled face, untidy head of auburn hair, he said with a grin, 'Don't make me laugh, then,' accompanying the words with a high-pitched moan.

'Squawks like a bleedin' shitehawk,' laughed a seaman and the humour brightened and brought enthusiasm enough to lay into their oars with renewed effort.

Came a call from Verber in the second longboat. Following the line of his pointing arm, Queen saw in the distance a dark patch on the sunlit water and he stood on the gunwhale for a better view. 'Looks like wind, lads,' he said excitedly, 'worth pulling for so put some real effort into your work and see if we can get the *Earl* into that broken water.'

The men layed to with a will and the bow rope sprang taut. Commotion on deck brought a third longboat to join in the attempt to place the ship within that telltale smudge. Wind! Fluky and light: but cool on the sweat of their bodies. Exclamations of relief as the first wavelet slapped alongside.

'Avast there!' came the bold call, 'all boats back inboard!' They didn't need urging and the longboats were quickly alongside and prepared for hoisting. Now the sails began to lift and fill, a few bubbles drifted astern and the helmsman felt the dormant wheel respond.

The breeze died. The sails drooped. The forward motion stilled.

'Away all boats!' the call was weary but not as weary as the men who scrambled back into the longboats.

Three times they pulled the deadweight of the *Earl* into disturbed water but not until evening did a wind finally establish. Light zephyrs, but enough to fill the sails and drive the ship across calm water to resume a painfully slow way southerly. The night was hard and frustrating because the wind changed direction with such contrariness that the sails were continually taken aback and having to be braced round on a new tack. Duty watchmen were exhausted by the time they were relieved and most slept where they dropped. But they were under way and edging out of the doldrums grip and even the vagaries of a fickle wind were welcome after days of soul-destroying boredom. Next morning broke fine and clear, with the atmosphere noticeably fresher.

They were under the influence of the southeast trade wind, light in strength but constant on the larboard allowing a wonderful, broad reach. The wake bubbled and the bow wave deepened into a satisfying growl; music in the ears of Captain Probus who responded by ordering all hands to clean ship. Working with good heart, the crew soon restored her to pristine condition and finished by scrubbing and stoning the deck until it shone. Even the salt beef at suppertime tasted good.

The evening was beautiful. The heavens a blaze of shimmering blue shading to crimson along the skyline and the early moon hung low and incandescent. Off-duty watch lounged on the galley deck and passengers promenaded. Strains of Vinderman's lute drifted aft and his voice took up the melody. Came a drifting of personnel closer to the main deck to listen to the music and enjoy the tranquillity, soothing to the spirits of all aboard.

Taking his turn on the helm and concentrating on the compass, Queen glanced up as watch officer Sethman said, 'Such a night as this stays with a man for a long time and is a glimpse of paradise after the misery of the doldrums.' He was dressed in full uniform, apart from the hat carried in his hand. Just under six feet tall, a robust figure, slightly corpulent, hardly ever seen without a pipe gripped in rather protuberant teeth, Mr Sethman was a competent navigator who, while undergoing tuition classes, had much personal contact with the midshipmen. He was firm, strict, and allowed of no frivolity but they had come to like and respect the kindly First Officer.

Everyone in relaxed mood as the great ship sailed without fuss through the majesty of late evening. Passengers in no hurry to retire, the other two writers, Warrington Smythe and John Symmonds had joined Trudy and Francis Warr at the ship's rail. He imagined the young couple were arm in arm and his smile brought a look of appraisal from the First Officer. 'You don't have a great deal to say, Mr Queen,' he commented, 'and in this respect have much in common with your father.'

This comment brought an eager voiced, 'You knew him?'

'Well enough to know he was a man who indulged in no idle chatter and spoke only when he had something worthwhile to say.'

In agreement with this summary, Queen said, 'Made me look up when he was talking, though.'

'Didn't we all? But he had charm enough when he wished and could command more loyalty from his crew than anyone I ever met . . . before or since.'

Interrogative now, Queen enquired, 'Can you tell me why he so suddenly left the East India Company?'

'You don't know? Thought the story was common knowledge.'

'Like you just said, he wasn't the type to indulge in idle gossip and I had no reason to wonder until I myself came into the service.'

'And met with Mr Passendale,' mused Sethman, 'and his daughter Margaret?'

Queen's face always betrayed him in embarrassing moments and, sensing his discomfort, Sethman smiled in knowing manner. 'Miss Passendale is a most attractive young woman,' he said, 'and how strange it all begins to appear.' Regarding him with shrewd assessment Sethman added in reluctant voice. 'Perhaps I would be doing you a favour by not divulging secrets from the past. Which in some subtle way could exert influence on the present, and even more disturbingly on the future.'

'I don't understand you, sir,' said Queen with furrowed brow.

'You think I speak in riddles?'

'All I know of my father is that he and Mr Passendale were great friends.' Speaking with sincerity as he added, 'Which is why I have been received with such kindness and generosity.'

'I had better take up the story from here.' Probus had approached unseen from the shadows and the light from the compass binnacle cast a ruddy glow on his side-whiskers.

'Wish you would, sir,' replied Sethman and his obvious relief earned a smile from Probus.

'Don't look so worried, Alan, you were evading young Queen very adroitly.' Pausing, he then said, 'James suggested that this would be inevitable.' He gave an instructive nod and Sethman took the wheel, after which Probus took Queen by the arm and brought him to the rail. Bewildered by this exchange he looked to the Captain for enlightenment but Probus seemed in no hurry. He gazed down into the enigmatic waters and all the while music drifted quiet rapture on the night air. 'Once upon a time, long ago,' he said at last, 'there were three midshipmen.' Probus had a flair for melodrama and his voice was resonant with feeling. 'Their names were James Walter Passendale, John Queen and Peter Fitzroy Probus, more commonly known as Fitz, and the friendship of these impetuous youths became almost legendary throughout the maritime section of the Company.' His eyes were far back in the past and Queen had the feeling that the Captain wasn't seeing him at all, then Probus's voice penetrated deep as he went on with. 'Young men make friends easily when thrown together in conditions of hardship and danger and sometimes of unbelievable adventure, forming associations that this way of life moulds into mutual respect.' Speaking as though embarrassed, he then stated. 'Aye, lad, even into love, which can be carried by a man for the rest of his life.' Coming back from memory, he said. 'I see it all again with the friendship that exists between you, Billie McFie and also young Verber. Treasure these friendships, Jason, because such respect and loyalty are not easily earned and become more and more difficult to sustain as the years flow swiftly by and when, sadly, personal ambition and desire intrude upon and obscure the ideals of young and stout-hearted men.' Speaking with the conviction of experience and his eyes warm on Queen. 'You call a man friend,' he declared, 'when he puts his hand in yours and you know inside without any qualification that his life would be forfeit before his word was dishonoured.' The eloquence of Captain Probus was very moving, and he then asked. 'Are you following me, Jason?'

'That I am, sir.'

'I tend to get carried away when I remember those early days.' Smiling, a little sadly, he glanced away to where the last of the daylight suffused the horizon into glorious flame. 'Such a bond existed between us three and the memory consumes even now . . .' hesitant, as if in emotional retrospect, he then resumed his narrative. 'Regrettably,' he said, 'young men grow older and have to go about their separate lives. So, after two wonderful years we finally had to take up our careers as ship's officers and our association ended with advancing responsibility and individual desires.' Glaring straight at Queen as he demanded. 'You wouldn't expect to stay a midshipman for ever and will also advance according to your own drive and ability.' With a sardonic chuckle at Queen's bewilderment, he said, 'I haven't yet explained the reason why your father so abruptly left the Company.' Laughter fading, he became serious as he went on. 'Reasons, Jason, are just words with which we attempt to paint a portrait, but words seldom do justice or bring true life and colour to a canvas such as this.'

Queen's involvement was a tangible thing and Probus looked at him for reaction and as if seeking to justify this obscure statement, then went on to say, 'It all started when John Queen bumped into a young woman one morning in the Company headquarters. She was the only daughter of Sir Roger Farquasan, a very wealthy shareholder, and the beauty of this girl was something to behold. With her looks and inherited wealth you can rightly imagine that most of the aristocratic young bloods in the City of London were pursuing the favours of this incredible young lady.' Shrugging, as he declared. 'The details of their meeting are irrelevant now but sufficient is it to say that the affection that started between this dashing midshipman and the exquisite Elizabeth was somehow inevitable. Theirs was a love story that poets have tried to capture in prose since time began and one so tender and wonderful to witness. Typically, Sir Roger was not exactly enchanted with his daughter's infatuation for a poor midshipman and made it obvious that he saw John as a threat to domestic bliss and to his ambitions for his daughter: but in the end even he had to bow before the encompassing love these two shared.'

Queen heard all this without interruption. He was too engrossed. Probus lit one of his long cigars, taking his time and inhaling deeply of the fragrant tobacco.

'Love,' he then said, 'is a flower that does not flourish in solitary confinement and even people so devoted as Elizabeth and John were desolate at the thought of the lonely years that beckoned. But the greatest threat to their future was the need and driving ambition of John Queen to command his own ship.' Allowing a few moments for this to register, the Captain went on to state. 'Elizabeth had to spend two years at home while we served our apprenticeship on the old *Argo* . . . then for further long months when he served as deck officer . . .' breaking off his narrative to announce, 'this was the record-breaking run we spoke about, for it seemed that John harnessed every fair wind which ever blew to get back to his Elizabeth. But, she was a strong minded young woman and after this voyage told him he had to make his choice, the sea – or herself in a disagreement so upsetting that John finally promised that if she would wait for just one more voyage, in which he would realise his ambition to be Master of a tall ship then he would retire from the sea and settle down to a shore routine.'

'Do you think he would have been able to do this?'

'Not easily, but you are forgetting what I said earlier. When John Queen gave his word, you could stake your life upon it.'

This moving respect for his father brought moisture to Queen's eyes. 'What happened next?' he asked eagerly.

'His ship was caught by a typhoon and to save her they had to chop away her two mainmasts. The records of the Company proudly display how they rode out the typhoon then limped under jury rig across a thousand miles of Pacific Ocean to make a landfall somewhere on the coast of South America and how they cut down two tall trees to replace their masts then sailed the ship home around Cape Horn.'

'Phew!' No wonder his father's name was held in such esteem. He wanted more of this and said excitedly. 'How long did that take?'

'They were more than ten months overdue and in this time the Company had received not a word and posted them missing. In all they were away for twenty-seven months but the really sad part is that everyone had given them up for lost.'

'So the fair Elizabeth didn't wait.'

'Not so hasty with your indictment,' chastised Probus, 'she waited more than two years. A young life, devastated by despair and constant loneliness, even a love such as theirs could not be expected to survive without consummation.'

181

Voice taking on a note of finality, he said, 'She was married just two weeks before John brought his battered ship into the Pool of London.'

It all became clear. All the mystery! All the seemingly inevitable attraction Maggie and he were destined to share. In a voice that held a conflict of loyalties, he exclaimed:

'His sweetheart and his best friend, James Passendale.'

Though frowning at the note of condemnation, Probus just nodded. 'When John heard the terrible news, he packed his sea chest and sailed out on the first ship leaving London.'

'Without seeing them?'

'Such was the way of John Queen. They never set eyes on him again.' Adding wryly, 'Then you walked in like a ghost from the past.'

'Wonder how they felt when they realised he was back?'

'Desperate, I think, and somehow unworthy. But James had always been in love with Elizabeth and they found happiness eventually.'

The Captain had certainly painted a moving portrait, albeit in sad prose 'I'm glad they were happy,' said Queen emotionally, 'for their sake and for mine.' Looking up into the night sky with a prayer of thanks and a thought that soared: exultant.

How else would I have known Maggie?

Chapter Eleven

At The Court of King Neptune

'What are we going to do about crossing the Line?' said Jack Dooley.

'On this miserable ship,' said Arnie Waugh, 'not worth the effort?'

'It's tradition though, and we ought to initiate the newcomers. There's only a few, three midshipmen and young Greenwood.' Then, with a grin. 'Vindo hasn't been this way before, either.'

Smiles broke out. 'Aye,' said Jacko Abbott, 'reckon Billie McFie will be up for it, he likes a bit of fun.'

'We must be close to the Equator, now that we are out of the doldrums at last,' said Dooley, 'what do you think, lads, might liven things up.'

'Can't see Gaywood going for it,' doubted Waugh, 'miserable sod, he'd see us on the punishment rack rather than enjoying ourselves?'

''It ain't down to him,' said Dooley. 'Probus would approve of the idea. I've never yet crossed the line without proper observance, and we owe it to the first timers'.

The men were beginning to show interest. 'Let's get the longboat over the side ready,' said Abbot. Then, with a lewd grin. 'Who's going to play Neptune?'

The twelve o'clock noon observation placed them exactly on the Equator. The officers were congregated on the quarterdeck, attracted by the unusual activity forward. 'What on earth are those idiots doing down there?' said Second Officer Gaywood,

'What do you think,' said Probus, 'we are just about crossing the Line. Even such an unhappy crew like this lot wouldn't let the opportunity slip without due ceremony. Reckon our new midshipmen are in for a dunking.'

Gaywood managed a thin smile. He had to admit that the crew were in need of some amusement and for once he was in approval, and said at last, 'This I have to see.'

'I'll inform the passengers,' said Sethman, moving away, 'they will enjoy a bit of frivolity, for a change.'

Just then a strange figure came up over the rail. Dripping wet, dressed in rags and tatters and with something resembling a mermaid's fin dragging behind. Confronting the amused pair he said, 'I am from the court of King Neptune ... what ship is this me-hearties?'

'*Earl of Rothesay,* of the Honourable East

India Company,' said Probus, making a gallant leg to the arrival.

'Whither bound?'

'Table Bay and places east.'

'Are you ready to receive His Highness King Neptune aboard?'

'Indeed we are,' said Probus repressing a smile. Then with exaggerated courtesy he bowed from the waist. 'Pray take a glass of wine before we welcome his Majesty.'

The forerunner downed the glass in one gulp then said pompously, 'Neptune demands a list of all who have not entered his realm.'

Probus was already prepared and presented the list and, well pleased with his reception, the forerunner disappeared over the side.

'Longboat approaching under sail,' called the masthead lookout importantly, 'looks like King Neptune is calling.'

'Heave-to,' said Probus, 'make ready his carriage.'

The longboat secured alongside, King Neptune was hoisted aboard in a rope sling, followed by his wife and courtiers who quickly took possession of the foredeck. Dressed in rags of multi-coloured bunting, wigs of hemp with seagull feathers sticking out, they were a rowdy, hilarious bunch, obviously enjoying the freedom of the ship. King Neptune's carriage was an upholstered chair on castor wheels and he took his seat with aplomb, brandishing his trident for effect.

Probus had done this several times and greeted his royal visitor with a formal salute. 'We are pleased to welcome you aboard the *Earl of Rothesay,* your Majesty. Will you take a glass of wine with us?'

'Avast there,' roared King Neptune, 'is there no rum aboard this scurvy ship?'

'I beg pardon,' smiled Probus.

Rum was hastily brought and, pacified, Neptune gulped it down in one go. Knowing he would not be revered if his courtiers did not get to share in the libation, he leered and said, 'And a noggin for my faithful followers if you please.'

Probus thought this was getting much too liberal but had no alternative except to join in the frivolity. A cask of rum was placed on the foredeck, greeted with roars of acclaim. Jacko Abbott's Neptune was a fearsome sight – blackened face – flowing beard of hemp, red and white striped shirt, trident in hand, office chain of sea shells around his neck and with a gold-coloured paper crown perched precariously on the top of a bushy wig of hemp. His stomach was huge and rotund, padded out with pillows. Cheered on by the whole assembly he was wheeled to the foredeck where he took seat on his throne – an empty barrel – with a bath of seawater in which to place his bare feet, for Neptune had to be accommodated in his natural element. His wife was positioned alongside on an upturned crate; ship's carpenter Joe Castellack, dressed to kill. Her cheeks were daubed brilliant ochre-red. Flowing skirt of yellow flag bunting, coronet of sea shells, she played to her captive audience with a shameless hand thrust of her voluptuous breasts and her eyes flashing invitation to all. 'Come, me-dear,' she said to Neptune, 'we must get on with the initiation.'

Downing his third noggin of rum, Neptune wiped the remnants off his beard with the back of his hand, then thundered, 'Are we ready to try the offenders?'

'Aye,' came the hearty response.

'Bring forward the first culprit,'

Davy Greenwood was thrust before Neptune. He had been looking forward to this but now, before the awesome assembly, he wasn't quite so sure.

'What is the charge, my Lord Chamberlain?'

The post of Chamberlain was tailor-made for Arnie Waugh. He was dressed in a robe of ghostly white sailcloth that reached to his ankles. His coronet was an upturned chamber pot draped with seaweed. In a very officious voice he announced:

'This ignorant swab doesn't know his sheet-bend from his bowline . . . and did tie a granny instead of a reef knot.'

'What is the sentence of the court?'

'Guilty!' roared the courtiers, 'he must walk the plank, blindfold.'

Davy was hustled on to the plank, below which

was a well, hastily constructed of tarpaulin spread over an open hatch and filled with foul smelling, slime and seaweed covered salt water. A bandana covered his face . . . he couldn't see! Pushed forward he took two fumbling steps, lost his footing and went splashing under, came up gasping festooned with weed. They hauled him out and soothed him with a noggin and the Chamberlain said, 'Sentence completed you are now a courtier to the Realm of King Neptune.'

The midshipmen were stood in anticipatory pose, relishing their turn, as Neptune demanded, 'Bring forward these scurvy three!'

Hurled before Neptune the midshipmen received no dignity. They were stripped down to breeches and their shoes briskly removed. The Chamberlain said with a scowl:

'The charge against these swabs is that they did take liberties with the women passengers when they should have been on watch duties.'

'Ooh!' shouted the courtiers.

Billie McFie wasn't going to allow this opportunity to get away from him. Hamming it up for all he was worth he fell to his knees before Neptune with his hands clasped in supplication. 'Sire,' he implored, 'I beg you . . . it wasn't me! I was only keeping them from having their wicked way with the women.' Bowing his head several times in fervent servility he said in humble, despairing voice. 'Please, don't make me walk the plank when I was trying so hard to do my best.'

'Who is this knave, this buffoon who seeks not to enter my court?' The grin on the face of Neptune showed through his beard and was in dire conflict with his severe tone. Then, rising from his throne. 'What is the verdict on these swabs?'

'Guilty! Guilty!'

The Chamberlain looked at Queen. 'This one has hair on his face. He must be shaved before we allow him into our court.'

'Shave all three,' commanded Neptune.

The midshipmen were thrust unceremoniously to their knees, faces plastered with a foul, creamy substance made up of galley grease and rancid butter and reeking of rotten fish. Jack Dooley came forward brandishing a cutthroat razor that he proceeded to hone on his belt with menacing strokes. He razored off the shaving cream with aplomb, McFie first, then Verber, who protested vehemently, a move immediately regretted as his open mouth was stuffed with the revolting mixture. Dooley hesitated when he came to Queen, he thought he might have cause to regret this, but the courtiers had no respect and shouted in concert. 'Off! Off!' The Chamberlain intervened, saying with an evil leer, 'One side only!'

Secure in the support of the courtiers, Dooley complied. His hand was shaky and the grin on Queen's face didn't help, but he recovered fast and shaved off one side of the droopy moustache, with growing confidence. Then Queen was pulled to his feet and shoved blindfold onto the plank. Trying for balance he missed his footing and went splashing down. They made no attempt to pull him out because Verber was straightaway thrust on behind, immediately fell in and the two floundered about in the foul-smelling water. McFie was held back, they all wanted to see this. Planting the Chamberlain's chamber pot on his head, they festooned him with seaweed and rotten fish before perching him precariously on the plank. Billie played it for all he was worth, tottering, stumbling, recovering, nearly falling, arms and legs weaving in drunken patterns, no way was he going to fall in that stinking water, until Neptune, incensed that McFie was stealing the show from him, tired of his horseplay and came behind and butted him off with a forceful belly. He fell with a shout and a splash so great that the onlookers crowding the edge were deluged in the overfall. He came up with his arms around his two comrades, but Neptune was well gone in rum and lost balance, almost fell in after McFie and only a concerted effort from the courtiers saved him from ignominy as they hauled him to safety and restored him back on his throne. The court was in raptures, McFie was a revelation to all and they enjoyed his clown act almost as much as he. Hauled out, the three held on to each other as though exhausted, but in hilarious stance. 'Is it over?' said Verber with a wide grin.

'Not yet,' said McFie, gulping rum, 'they

haven't done Vindo.' A sentiment shared as the Chamberlain looked craftily around.

'Someone is missing,' he said, 'where is the knave who skulks in hiding?'

'We have him,' shouted the courtiers. No escape for Vinderman, they had found him secreted in a forward chain locker and now rushed him before Neptune, who looked suitably indignant at this affront to his royal throne as he growled:

'Who is this reluctant swab? He must answer to the most serious charge of all, the one of failing to pay homage to the court of King Neptune. How do we find?'

'Guilty! Guilty!' Resounding chorus.

'What sentence, my Chamberlain'

'Shaving!'

Thrust to his knees, Vinderman thought this was ridiculous, child's play, not for a tried and tested seaman like he, but had no time for personal misgiving as Dooley came forward with his rancid shaving cream and proceeded to plaster it on with gusto, making sure that Vindo received a mouthful that effectively silenced his threatening growl. Dooley thought it high time that Vinderman should be shown how real men sailed the great oceans but, even so, he was careful with the razor and Vindo was treated to a very neat trim to his beard, with Dooley laughing all the time because he knew what was coming next.

'Have we yet done with this landlubber?' roared Neptune.

'No! No!' Shouted the courtiers, with anticipation evident. 'Tar and feather him!'

Vinderman didn't like the sound of this but his efforts to get free were smothered with ease. They stripped him to the waist. A bowl of black molasses appeared before Neptune who scooped up handfuls and, with the assistance of his Chamberlain, spread great dollops over back and chest then the courtiers came with a bucket of rice which they threw with enthusiastic abandon on to the black molasses until Vinderman was caked in a sticky mess of "tar and feathers" and looking like a spiky, half-trussed chicken. Then he was rushed on the plank and hurled forcibly into the revolting water below. Justice was done, they had given Vindo a much overdue accounting: they thought he was too clever for his own good.

McFie hauled him out and said with a huge grin, 'Having a good time, Vindo?'

Vinderman wasn't amused, but took it in good part. 'Bloody idiots! How the hell am I going to get this mess cleaned off?'

'I think it very becoming,' said Queen, unable to keep from laughing at Vinderman's downfall.

'The audience enjoyed it,' said Verber. All the passengers had congregated to watch the ceremony and now came forward to express their appreciation.

'A magnificent performance, Mr McFie,' complimented Martha, 'you put on a good show, you ought to be on the stage.' Looking at Queen she couldn't repress a smile at his one-sided moustache. 'Never mind, Mr Queen,' she said, 'half a moustache is better than none.' Linking arms with Trudy she turned to Probus. 'Thank you for a most entertaining morning, Captain, does this happen every time we have to cross the Equator?'

'Only on the first occasion.' Probus was in a happy frame of mind, never had the crossing of the line ceremony been more welcome. Joining his crew on the foredeck he complimented. 'Well done, lads.'

'Rum's all gone,' said Neptune in sly tone.

'Do not pursue good fortune, Jacko,' said Probus icily. Then, relenting, he added, 'A tot for all, but not until suppertime. Now clear the foredeck and prepare to get under way again.'

The crew complied with a will, more than satisfied with the way their performance had been received . . . and appreciated.

The mood of euphoria was destined to be short-lived.

Third Officer David Ashbury had a look of impending disaster on his face as he knocked on the door of the Captain's night cabin and the growling command to enter confirmed a lack of patience at being disturbed so early. Still dressed in night attire his scowl of irritation changed to one of enquiry at the sight of the metal container as Ashbury announced in a voice laden with foreboding, 'Some of our fresh water has turned sour, sir.'

With alarm rampant Probus was up and scrambling for clothing.

'Have you checked all the barrels?'

'The deck scuttlebutt was filled only this morning,' replied Ashbury shaking his head in negation. 'Gimpy the cook straightaway brought my attention to the state of the water.'

Hastily dressing, Probus said, 'Follow me.'

Collecting Mr. Sethman and Castellack the ship's carpenter they went down into No.1 hold. Castellack removed the lid from a huge water barrel, exposing a slime-covered surface and releasing the stench of foul water. Examining every barrel. At least two thirds of the water proved unfit to drink and Probus came wearily up into the sunshine. The news had spread and the crew were grouped in speculative bunches around the deck. Conferring with his officers, Probus informed them, 'We have about four hundred gallons of drinkable water, which is less than three gallons for each person on board.' Stabbing a finger on the chart he stated. 'The nearest land on our larboard beam is roughly one thousand miles. Table Bay is twice the distance or just about ten days sailing time if we can maintain our present rate of two hundred miles per twenty-four hours. This means we can either run for the African coast to find water or keep going for

Table Bay where we can clean and replenish our tanks.'

After a few moments for calculation, Sethman remonstrated, 'Margin's too small, sir. Three gallons for ten days is just two and a half pints apiece, which is acceptable enough as long as the wind doesn't fall light: or head us..' Concluding with the grim thought. 'Could take three weeks or more to reach port?'

'Which is why I intend to reduce the ration to a pint and a half, starting immediately. This will give us some extra time allowance and there is always a chance of adverse weather bringing rain and giving a chance to collect a few gallons. Mr Gaywood,' he instructed, 'have the sailmaker rig catchment canvas, particularly beneath the lower sails.' Eyeing them gloomily Probus said, 'You know how the crew will react to this further bad luck, and this is another reason why I have decided against running for the African mainland. If any of them jump ship on some savage shore they may never be seen again and I don't want such a thing on my conscience. I know the same thing could happen at Table Bay but at least we'll have a chance of taking on a substitute crew, even if we have to sign Lascars to get us to India.'

'Have you considered St. Helena?' asked Sethman.

'My ace in the hole, and if things get too bad we will of course run back to the Island. But you are well aware that we could lose a good number of our crew to the ever-greedy Captains of the resident Naval Squadron, without any chance of replacement. We take our chances with wind and sea and head straight for Table Bay. Have every foul cask emptied overboard and cleaned ready for filling should we be blessed with a rain shower. Bring all remaining water aft under the quarterdeck awning and post a midshipman and marine on watch every minute of the day and night. Anyone caught stealing water will be made to run the gauntlet.' His voice followed after them as they dispersed. 'Pray for a fair wind, gentlemen.'

For two days the wind remained fresh and steady on the beam with the noon-to-noon run estimated at two hundred and forty miles, direction south by east and almost in a straight line for Table Bay. Tension eased as progress was maintained.

But ill-fortune returned to *Earl of Rothesay* on the afternoon of the third day when the wind fell light and began to back round the compass before settling to a gentle blow from the south, the very direction in which they were heading. Neither starboard nor larboard tack proved more favourable and, with the wind so light, little forward way was made. The following noon observation placed them but a hard earned sixty miles nearer to Table Bay. The water ration was reduced to a pint and Probus ordered the animals butchered, all except the milking goats. Fresh pork appeared on the supper table but many a tender hearted seaman pushed his plate away untouched for, as Davy Greenwood sadly phrased:

"Twould be like eating a little pal.'

With the slack wind came the inevitable increase in heat. The only respite was in the late evening when the terrible red ball of fire sank below the skyline and a welcome cool eased the steamy atmosphere. Treasuring every drop, men consumed the meagre offering in individual manner, some hoarding and doling out precise sips to themselves, others downing their twice-daily cup in a single gulp only to spend the hours until the next issue in a state of torment. Discontent was rife as the thirsty days continued.

The water casks were stowed under a canopy on the quarterdeck, sheltered from the sun and kept cool by the wet sailcloth shrouding them. The midshipman and marine on guard were armed with musket and pistol.

The usual crowd of unhappy seamen herded in the forward mess deck. The air was oppressive and putrid with tobacco smoke and the smell of unwashed bodies. Most of the crew were breaking out in salt-water boils on their arms, and even more painfully on their buttocks and lower flesh of their backs. They would have preferred the open air on deck but this was the one place on board where they could discourse freely and without invasion of privacy.

'Many more days of this,' growled Jack Dooley, 'and we'll be past caring.'

'This is without doubt the most unlucky and miserable ship I have ever sailed in.' Birkenshaw the sailmaker was convinced they would never see England and home again as he added, 'These sores of mine make it impossible to rest in comfort.'

'And mine,' agreed Arnold Waugh, 'the only cure for these sort of boils is a long soak in fresh water. I've had salt water disease before but never on the outward voyage.'

'Is there likely to be any homeward passage for this ship,' asked Dooley, 'or will we end our days sailing forever in the bleedin' South Atlantic like a bleedin' ghost ship?'

'Not much we can do about it.' Birkenshaw again. 'Probus is as anxious as we are to make Cape Town but even he can't hope to make against a head wind.'

'You think he realises we'll jump ship?' said Dooley.

'Course he does! But reckon he'd rather lose his crew to another Master than have us all perish on board.'

'Should have made straight for land soon as he found out about the water?' Jacko Abbot joined in the discourse, adding in angry tone. 'At least by now we might have been within reach of some shore or other.'

'Aye! And within reach of some hungry tribe of

bleedin' cannibals as well,' said Birkenshaw forcibly. 'I'd rather stick with old Probus and the ship, unlucky or not.'

The watch changed. The night fell with deathly calm. Abraham Verber came alert, hearing a furtive scuffle from close-to he looked round in alarm but the marine sentry had left him to it and gone off for a smoke and was nowhere in sight. Stepping warily forward with pistol cocked, could see nothing in the impenetrable dark? Turning too late as a rushing figure came from behind, he caught a glimpse of a bearded face and staring eyes before a belaying pin smashed him down. His assailant stooped at the water barrel, set the tap flowing and knelt with his mouth under the precious liquid. Verber had just enough strength of will to fire his pistol into the air. The shot rent the night bringing uproar to the quarterdeck and the intruder scurried away. Coming on the run David Ashbury looked aghast at the water running to waste and shut the tap in one urgent move before kneeling by the inert midshipman.

All hands. Piped on deck at first light. Verber had recognised his attacker as a seaman in his own watch but, reluctant to name the culprit, stood silent before Captain Probus who said sternly, 'If one man is allowed to steal water they'll all expect the same treatment. This is the difference between officers and crew and here, Mr Verber, is where you must assume the mantle of authority.'

Verber's deep-set eyes brooded on his Captain's face and he shot a worried look at his fellow midshipmen. The bruise on his forehead glowed angry red in the sunlight as he squared his shoulders. 'I name you, Jed Ackerman.'

An angry growl ran through the men. Ackerman broke ranks and made a run for the ratlines but was forcibly grabbed by four marines and forced to his knees before them. This is where the subtlety of Probus became apparent; for the seamen were plainly incensed that one of their own should have stolen water, and worse! That he had allowed several gallons to run to waste.

Gauntlet formed. Twenty-four determined men. Twelve either side in line facing each other and each armed with a knotted rope's end that they wound in a loop round their wrists for better purchase.

Unsympathetic seamen stripped off his shirt and hurled him into the space between the two rows. He took off at speed. Moving so fast that the first pairs missed him completely but the third man stuck out a foot and tripped and brought Ackerman to his knees, and immediately a barrage of knotted rope ends lashed down on his unprotected back. Howling in outrage, he started forward. A fiercely wielded rope caught a spreading boil on his shoulder opening a spout of pus and blood and he stumbled blindly between the rows shielding his head and eyes and taking each blow with a howl of blasphemy and pain. Staggering from the gauntlet under a final frenzy of lashes, he fell in a groaning heap. The men dispersed. Justice had been done, cruelly, but by their own hands. Mr Sethman instructed the surgeon to, 'Clean him up, Dr. Quennel, and return him to duty.'

The wind continued light. Frustrating. Lack of water taking its toll on the ship's company: the men beginning to lose appetite and finding food increasingly difficult to digest. Dysentery becoming commonplace and the grim spectre of scurvy a real threat! The officers and passengers had fared better than the crew so far because they had a private stock of wine to help ease their thirst. But now, Probus commandeered every keg of drinkable liquid and had them brought into his cabin, an action that brought vociferous indignation from Ernest Harper. 'I'll make sure this treatment is brought to the notice of the shareholders,' he fumed, 'you have no right to take over our private stock.'

'When will you learn,' said Probus resignedly, 'my wish is my right and I will do whatever is necessary for the safety of the ship?'

'You haven't managed the ship with distinction so far. In fact,' challenged Harper, 'I could run it better myself.'

'Let us hope for all our sakes that you never get the opportunity.'

Two weeks of slow progress brought them to within eight hundred miles of Cape Town. Still, the wind came fitfully from the south. By now many of the crew had become too ill and weakened by dysentery to carry out even the easiest of duties. The surgeon worked continuously in the forward mess and the ceaseless toil had a detrimental effect on his already poor constitution. Stricken down with fever he laid shivering and helpless in his cabin, a situation that brought much needed response from Martha Harper and her companion Trudy.

One of the cooler mess rooms was taken over as a makeshift sick bay and the two volunteer nurses moved through the stinking room dressing hideous sores and giving comfort to the stricken men. No extra ration of water could be made available but a daily, minute tot of claret helped to sustain the poorly. The two women carried out their nursing with patience and consideration and not one grumble or foul word could be heard while they were below.

The Captain and his officers were in consultation when Ernest Harper stormed in, accompanied by Martha and Trudy. Harper seemed beyond restraint as he snapped, 'You've got to do something, Probus!'

'Already told you! I have no control over the elements.'

'You could turn for the African mainland.'

'I could. But the distance is now hardly less than it is to Table Bay and just as hopeless. The time for closing land in such a manner is behind us.'

'You now admit your judgement was in error?'

'Base my decisions on information available at the time and never indulge in futile retrospect.' He was fed up to the teeth with Harper and it showed in the rising tone of his voice and his irritation was shared by Martha. Her dress was stained and dishevelled and she looked ill and weary but had enough spirit to turn forcibly on her husband.

'Wish you'd stop whining,' she said in hard tone, 'if you think you're the only one suffering try looking in the sick bay to see how real men behave.' Looking entreatingly at Probus. 'Is there nothing we can do?'

Taking her hands, he looked deep into her face. 'Martha,' he said with great feeling, 'you and Trudy are a source of strength, to me and to the crew, and I thank God for your presence on board.' With a poor attempt at a smile, he stated. 'The only thing left is to pray for deliverance.'

The next day was Sunday. At Martha's request the morning service was held in the sick bay. Every man not on watch crowded in to take part. Pursuing their way of life along unending seaways and vast ocean wastes seamen were mostly rough and violent men who took their pleasures as and when they could and usually to a point of extreme. Drunken, lecherous louts on shore with a lack of moral restraint that was the distinctive hallmark of the early sailing men . . . but at sea? Constantly at the mercy, and in awe, of the unbelievable power that the elements could unleash, they lived closer to their Maker than other mortals and had neither hesitation nor embarrassment in turning to prayer at times of crisis.

Vinderman's lute accompanying the hymns, Captain opening his Prayer Book, those among the congregation fit enough stood with bowed heads, the voice of Fitzroy Probus reaching every corner. 'O Lord our Heavenly Father. Almighty and everlasting God: who has safely brought us to the beginning of this day. Defend us in the same with Thy mighty power . . .' he had read this prayer many times, but never with such need or feeling and the sick bay was charged with dedication. Raising his head. Eerie quiet falling as a hesitant but distinct tapping came from the deck head. Heads lifting. The tapping became louder. Insistent. Turned into a deluge. Rain! The incredible murmur crescendoed into a shout and all standing rushed topside. The heavens were opening and great sheets of rain splashed over figures that were dancing ecstatic through water streaming across the deck. They knelt as one with faces turned upward and mouths open wide and within seconds everyone was soaked with cold, life restoring rain and the deck up-roared with excitement and thankfulness.

'Duty watch close up!' voice of Alan Sethman bringing order. 'Hands aloft to reef sail!' With the rain had come a shift and also an increase in wind strength, pressing her hard over. Sail was hurriedly taken in and trimmed on the new heading. Though short lived, the downpour had allowed the catchment of many gallons of pure water, enough to quench the long thirst and ease the pain of sick and unwashed bodies. The fierce gale kept the crew constantly aloft but also gave them a swift push toward Cape Town.

They logged three hundred miles in the first twenty-four hours. Then two hundred and fifty as the gale abated, sighting the wonderful, cloud-shrouded Plateau of Table Mountain on the evening of the third day. Smoothing through the night under reduced canvas, they entered Table Bay at first light. Down from the bow the splashing anchor dropped. The last shred of sail was furled and the black and yellow hull of the *Earl of Rothesay* lay at peace in the heavenly calm, sunlit water.

Allowing no respite. All day they toiled. Filled the empty barrels with sweet water. Re-victualled with fresh meat and fruit and green vegetables, enough to tempt the most jaded appetite of crew and passengers alike, a procession of workboats and native bumboats ferrying back and forth. During the early evening the Navy frigate sailed into harbour. The remainder of the convoy still unaccounted for and probably dispersed in the wastes of the Atlantic.

Calling a conference of his officers, Probus looked sternly at them before stating, 'I intend to allow the crew shore leave tonight: as many as practical.'

Mr Sethman nodded approval but Second Officer Gaywood disagreed. 'Begging pardon, Captain,' he said, 'but you must realise that many will not return?'

'I'm well aware of their state of mind, and instruct my officers and midshipmen to also take shore leave and, hopefully, to keep an eye out for deserters. There is a chance that a good roaring drunk will banish some of the despondency that seems to shadow us.' His eyes were sad and so was his voice as he added. 'I will not treat men like slaves regardless of the circumstances and must take a chance on them returning in sufficient number to work the ship.'

'When the rumours about the *Earl* are carried ashore, we won't find it easy to replace deserters. I still feel,' insisted Gaywood, 'that we should keep the crew aboard and under surveillance.'

'Might be here for several days waiting for the other Company ships.' Impatiently brushing aside further protestations Probus snapped. 'When you are Master, Mr Gaywood, you can make the decisions. But until then?' Turning to Sethman, he instructed. 'Make the arrangements, duty watch aboard tonight will be allowed ashore all day tomorrow.' His grimace showed a lack of assurance as he concluded. 'Perhaps our display of confidence will cause them to view the situation more tolerantly.'

Chapter Twelve

In every seaport there is an establishment, tavern or brothel, or more likely a combination of both which is a gathering point for the passage-making men of the ships that sail the trade routes.

Quite often also, such seemingly hospitable havens were places where ship's Masters could recruit replacements for men lost at sea by sickness, or desertion on land. And the tavern keepers were well known to short-handed Captains. These were places where men could be kept in a state of dissipated sloth and then bartered for the price of a man's first month's pay. Countless times, in the dead of night, a back door would open to a discreet knock and inert bodies taken over by a hard-mouthed group, to be bundled on board a ship due to sail at first light. No way back for such press-ganged men. They would awaken from a drunken stupor to find land a dull blur on the horizon and realise they were a member of another ship's company.

Usually, after a couple of days, they accepted their lot with uncaring philosophy; the alternative being a knotted rope across the back and a life of continuing misery.

So it was a cautious Master who brought his ship into port after a long time at sea. He had to tread the dubious line between allowing his crew to carouse ashore and rid themselves of the frustration that builds up in the lonely months, and yet keep his vessel fully manned. Much depended on the Master and the way he ran his ship. One such as Fitzroy Probus would normally find the line easy to define because a fair skipper commanded respect and seamen wouldn't willingly exchange from a good berth. But after a few hours ashore in the hands of the tapsters who served strong liquor and in the warm bodies of the waterfront women who were part of the saloon-keeper's stock in trade, seamen tended to lose control and were easy and willing prey for the traders in human flesh.

It is difficult to understand why men submitted to this slave type of treatment time after time. Perhaps a reason can be found in the sad truth that seamen ashore were welcome only in these taverns of licentiousness, and also in the fact of their tendency to herd together in an atmosphere of their own creating. "Where the liquor flowed and all women were beautiful" and where, for a brief moment of time, they could forget the monotony of sea and ships and submerge themselves in the fleshpot lures of dry land.

One such establishment was the "Bodega" of Rodrigo Svenson: Table Bay.

Probus had to anticipate that he was about to lose a good proportion of his crew. Cape Town was a huge place where men could disappear in spite of constant surveillance. Sad thought, and the first time in his career he had felt such misgivings, berths in the East Indiamen were much sought after and again he cursed the bad luck which shadowed the *Earl*.

Alone on the quarterdeck gazing around the harbour, Table Bay was a meeting place for the shipping of the great seafaring nations. Numerous ships lying in the roads, the Navy frigate was anchored nearby and he took comfort from its uncompromising bulk. He also realised they would have similar problems, although ratings on board a ship of His Majesty's Royal Navy knew only too well that they could be hanged from a yardarm if caught in the act of desertion. A short-handed Navy Captain would not be averse to press-ganging some of the crew of the *Earl* if he had the chance and the thought almost brought a smile. His recalcitrant men may have good cause to regret their reluctance to rejoin.

Anchored at a discreet distance away lay a squat looking ship flying the colours of the

V.O.C. *Verenighe Oostindische Compangnie*. The Dutch East India Company. Named *Zeevalk* she was a heavily armed merchantman with the brightness of her paintwork suggesting she too was outward bound for the Far East.

Rodrigo Svenson ran the biggest, bawdiest bar and brothel on the waterfront. The offspring of a Swedish father and Spanish mother he was a grossly obese man with a constant, overflowing air of good nature that masked an evil and calculating mind. The buttons on his shirt front had long since given up the struggle to contain the revolting mound of his stomach and gaped wide open to expose a pallid expanse of sickly white flesh from the centre of which his navel winked obscenely. His Bodega was long and low ceilinged, with a bare wooden floor sparsely sprinkled with sawdust. The air was stifling and thick with the smoke from innumerable pipes, which over the years had coloured the paint of walls and ceiling to its present dirty yellow. Wooden beams spanned the ceiling, bowed down with the weight of the rooms above. The serving counter had once been a ship's stern and still retained the intricate carvings of some long ago craftsman. The bar was crowded, noisy, women lounging about in open invitation. Women of varying shape and colour with skins varying from a shade of fine parchment to deepest ebony and the stairway leading up from the centre of the tap-room hosted a constant passage of seamen and women on their way up, or down from, the rooms above.

Most of the crew of the *Earl* had been granted shore leave and, to a man, packed into Rodrigo's. Bunched around the base of the centre stairway they were swilling down mugs of liquor as if to make up in one night for months of abstinence. Lurching to his feet, Jacko Abbot threw his arm round the waist of a dusky skinned woman who responded with a suggestive gyration of her hips and straightaway led him up the stairs to an accompaniment of cheers and cat-calls of derision from his shipmates. Just waiting for someone else to go first, several of the others followed Abbot's example, including the master carpenter, leading hand Jack Dooley, and gunner Jancy. Some of the younger men were grouped together around a long table, Vinderman among them who surveyed their animated indecision with no small amusement.

'Are you going up, Vindo?' asked Davy Greenwood in a tone reflecting a mixture of longing and curiosity.

'No.'

'Surely you want a woman after all this time away from home?'

'Not one where so many others have already been.' Taking a deep drink he wiped his moustache with the back of his hand. 'Reckon I'll settle for a pipe of baccy.'

Thumbing tobacco into his pipe he sat back in relaxed manner but Davy perched on the edge of his stool. 'What do you have to do when you get up there?' he asked in a whisper.

'You'd find out soon enough.' Laughing out loud at the innocent way Davy said this, Vinderman then said, 'Fancy you've never made love to a woman that way.' Gripping Davy by the shoulder he looked him in straight in the eye. 'Don't do it, lad,' he implored, 'not here for the first time. Not this way. Save it for some clean living English girl back home.'

'Hasn't the nerve,' goaded one of his mates, 'just look at him . . . wants to right enough, bet he's afraid he won't be up to it?' The remark brought a ripple of humour. The crew were relaxed and beginning to feel the effect of heavy drinking. Vinderman's eyes narrowed when he saw Queen and McFie appear in the bar and he watched in covert appraisal as they ordered wine from a surly tapster while the obese shape of proprietor Rodrigo observed all things from behind his partitioned cubicle.

Dressed in full uniform the midshipmen looked conspicuous and very much out of place but were too engrossed in the atmosphere and in their first experience of a foreign tavern and brothel to care about the resentful glares their appearance aroused. Looking around for their own men, they sauntered over.

'What the hell are you two doing in here?'

growled Vinderman in unwelcome tone.

'Supposed to be keeping an eye on the crew,' grinned McFie, 'but didn't see why you should have all the fun.'

'What's the matter with Davy Greenwood?' asked Queen curiously.

'Fancies getting his cock into one of these coloured gals, but doesn't know how to go about it.'

'Got more nerve than me taking on one of this lot,' said McFie with admiration rife.

'Think it's more in his trousers than in his nerve.'

'Plenty of choice,' suggested Queen as he surveyed the ladies of the establishment but just then Davy lurched to his feet.

'I'm away, Vindo,' he said in challenging voice.

'Suit yourself, boy.'

Davy's legs were precarious and hardly supported him as he made his way to the woman he had been observing. Opening her arms she clamped him to her breast and gave him a gap-toothed smile and immediately led him away up the stairs.

'Could give you ideas, though?' McFie had his eye on a woman who was without doubt the prettiest in the room. Standing in provocative pose with her back to the bar she looked slim and attractive in the lantern light and at that moment a sailor from the Dutch East Indiaman was approaching her. Huge and heavy shouldered he was dressed in wide trousers, and biceps bulged through his cotton shirt as he poised before her but she completely ignored him because she had responded to the obvious invitation of McFie and swayed across to look admiringly at the two clean-cut midshipmen.

'One at a time or both together?'

She spoke with an appealing French accent and she smiled in alluring manner, an effect spoiled by a missing front tooth, and McFie regarded her with a look of pure devilment. 'Just my friend here,' he said, 'but he's too shy to ask.'

Looking with invitation at the tall midshipman she sidled close to put her arms round him, a move that opened his eyes wide in sudden alarm. Her hips moved suggestively against him and she smelled of some exotic eastern perfume, cloying and almost sickening in his nostrils yet so very seductively and he reeled in the touch and the scent of a willing woman. Then, controlling unsuspected wanton thoughts, he looked down into eyes of dark green, disentangled her arms and shook his head. 'You do me great courtesy, miss,' he said, 'yet one I must decline.'

'Move over then, Mr Queen,' one of the crew jumped to his feet and, pulling on her arm, exclaimed. 'Maybe you can't? But I bloody well can!'

She cast a look of regret as the young seaman led her towards the stairs, but the giant Dutchman caught up with them before they reached the first step and pulling the seaman forcibly back, lifted him by the shirtfront and smashed a great fist into his mouth and sent him sprawling against the staircase with his face streaming blood.

'This one's mine,' he growled in guttural accent and, bundling up the terrified girl, he started for the stairs. The speed and ferocity of the attack brought a shout of outrage from the onlookers and the look of desperate appeal on her face brought Queen off in support. .

'You started this, McFie,' he said angrily, 'better back me up!'

The man had been hoping for retaliation and threw her down as Queen came for him. He had a smile of anticipation on his face and Queen knew he was in deep water here and straightaway belted him one in the stomach. Like hitting the side of a barn then a clubbing fist smashed into his chest and he went flying backwards and down in the sawdust. Anger flaming hot and out of control he scrambled to his feet as McFie sprang on the Dutchman's back like a tiger cat but, almost contemptuously, he ripped McFie away and threw him bodily across the room onto the table where the crew of the *Earl* sat enjoying the spectacle. They flared up in instant retort and the place resounded in uproar bringing the crew of *Zeevalk* upright in support of their own man. The stuff of a good run ashore to sailing men and both crews reared for action.

Turning to face the menacing seamen the

brutish Dutch sailor spat on the floor. 'I spit on you cowardly English: I spit on your King.' Clearing his throat in the sudden hush, he spat again. 'And I spit on your miserable, jinxed *Earl of Rothesay*!'

It was one thing to feel bad about your ship but to have this foul mouthed foreigner condemn her so vilely proved something entirely different and bought roaring response and the Dutchman found his neck gripped in hands hard as English oak and he was jerked round face to face with big Jacko Abbot who had come down the stairs in time to hear the man's curse. 'Spit on this then,' said Jacko with a leer, upending a heavy brass spittoon over the head of the surprised sailor. It was half full and the revolting mess slid out over his head and face. The spittoon was then rammed over his head like some old-time knight's helmet and visor and Jacko spun him round and shoved him hard into the advancing Dutch crew, giving him a hefty kick in the backside to help him on his way. The Dutchmen scattered then closed ranks as the English crew piled into them. Fight raging violent and bloody and vicious and the two crews were soon a roaring, fighting mob without thought or care and bruised and battered bodies cursed and battled across the length of the barroom while Rodrigo pounded on the bar top with his high-pitched voice futile against the din and his ladies had already discreetly vanished as if they had seen all this before.

Vinderman fought his way to where Queen and McFie were slogging back to back. A lean Dutchman jumped him. Vinderman's fist met the man's head in mid air and he went down with his nose broken and blood pouring down his face.

'Best fight I've seen in years,' declared Vinderman as he picked McFie off the floor and dusted him down. McFie had a swelling bruise on his cheek and his right eye was rapidly closing. Fighting eased as men reeled apart but Jacko Abbot remained locked in a desperate struggle with the huge Dutchman who pumped a vicious knee into his balls. Abbot sagged back and ducked a scything punch that would have taken his head off his shoulders. His pain-crazed eyes flared with wild, uncontrollable rage and he went for his opponent, stalking and crouching and menacing and ignoring the flurry of blows bombarding his head as the Dutchman fought like a man demented but all the time finding himself driven back. Abbot's lip curled . . . his mouth a vicious wild animal snarl that sent fear stabbing through the Dutchman. What could he do to stop this mad Englishman? Head snapping back as Abbot clubbed a two-handed fist into his face. Knee pumping into his groin and his legs scissored and he started to crumple but Abbot held him with strength born of raging temper then hit him twice with fists like clubs bringing blood spurting from nose and mouth. Fading, but still upright, the Dutchman reeled back, then

Abbot crashed his fist into the throat of the helpless man, a blow terrible in its finality and down went the Dutchman in a gurgling, legs scissoring heap on the sawdust of the floor at the bottom of the stairs.

Abbot kept on blindly after his man but four English seamen jumped him and held him immobile. Crazed, and struggling like a wild man in their grasp, Vinderman slapping his face, once, twice. Stinging blows that brought Abbot back to something approaching sanity. 'Quick now,' called Vinderman urgently, 'let's get out of here! Everyone back on board!' The crew dispersed in haste leaving Vinderman and Arnold Waugh to cope with Abbot and they dragged him outside and along the waterfront to the liberty longboat and the cold night air had a rapid sobering effect that sent a shiver of apprehension through Vinderman. 'Didn't like the way the Dutchman went down,' he said ominously, 'reckon we're in for real trouble if we don't clear out of here . . . and quick. Won't be much of a welcome ashore for any of this crew.'

'Messed up any chance we had of getting off,' agreed Waugh in disgruntled tone before adding warily, 'you know we were set on jumping ship?'

'Thought about it myself,' admitted Vinderman. Reflecting on the semiconscious Abbot for a moment. 'Your loudest advocate for desertion may have given us good reason to stay aboard the *Earl*.'

* * *

Early next morning, main deck ablaze with colour: detachment of Marines from the frigate *Hermes* in two dominating lines between main and quarterdeck. Sir Fauntleroy Cabot, Commodore of the frigate and his Captain of Marines in full dress uniform and wearing tricorn cocked hats with swords buckled at their waists. Entire ship's company of one hundred men assembled in a tight square. The small platoon of East India Marines in formation behind the crew with muskets sloped and bayonets gleaming bright. Slight offshore breeze rippling the clear water of Table Bay, bringing gay movement to the courtesy colours flying at the mizzen mast and crosstrees. Too early for the Harpers but the three writers lurked in the background, wondering what the hell was going on?

Four midshipmen at the head of the formation, the first line of the crew made up of the quartermaster, bosun, and the artisans such as carpenter, cook and sailmaker with the seamen in rank behind as Captain Probus's sergeant of marines stepped forward to command in rasping voice, 'Ship's company, attention!'

Merchant seamen are noted for their lack of respect for drill but they managed to shuffle upright. The marines of both frigate and East Indiaman were ramrod straight as *Hermes* Commodore stepped forward. Formidable in dark blue coat and white silk breeches he stalked up and down before the assembly, silver buckles gleaming on his shoes as he measured his tread as if in significant suspense building. His eyes were keen and penetrating and, as he paused in front of the midshipmen, one sardonic eyebrow raised at the beautiful black eye sported by Billie McFie. Enjoying the tension created by his stalking silence, the Commodore wheeled with dramatic effect to stand square before them.

'A man was killed last night in the fight at Rodrigo's Bodega.' Stabbing voice. Condemning. Not a vestige of emotion showing as he stated. 'A Dutch seaman named Van Dyke, and the shore authorities are demanding that the man, or men, responsible be put ashore immediately to stand trial.' Silent for a long moment to allow this to sink home. 'Further,' he then snapped, 'the proprietor of this Bodega, saloon, whatever he calls it, has presented a bill for damages amounting to two hundred pounds which your Captain will have to settle before the ship can leave Table Bay and which I'm sure will be deducted from the pay of all concerned in this disgraceful shambles.'

Two hundred pounds! At least a month's pay for the entire crew and the murmur of disquiet was instantly stifled by the sergeant's bark for silence. The Commodore hadn't finished and, clasping hands behind his back, allowed himself a brief smile. 'Think we can persuade him to settle for half that amount but this is not the real issue here.' Eyes hardening, he commanded. 'I order the man responsible to declare himself, here and now, before the assembled company and in the sight of Almighty God.'

His Captain of Marines now took charge. A lean and whip-like figure and straight as a flag-pole, he cracked command. 'Man responsible! One step forward!'

One hundred seamen and four midshipmen stepped forward in perfect unison. The Captain of Marines looked at his commanding officer. The Commodore's bushy eyebrows met together in a frown of astonishment. 'Once more,' he said brusquely.

'I repeat.' The Marine Captain seemed to have found new respect for the merchant seamen. 'Man responsible, one step backward!'

One hundred seamen and four midshipmen took a firm pace backward, Probus staring vacantly at them with an expression of amazement as he began to realise that his miserable, discontented crew had somehow been formed into a united and self-loyal group and he stepped hurriedly down from isolation to lend his support but the Commodore showed disbelief as he said, 'Seems we have a dilemma, Captain Probus. Your crew appear to suggest they are to be held equally responsible for the violence of last night?'

'Even though some of their number were on duty watch and still on board,' Probus looked at the Commodore. 'Perhaps you will allow me to deal with the situation, sir?'

'We must resolve this matter, Captain.'.

Probus also could be formidable when determined. 'May I ask you and your officers to retire to my stateroom,' he straightaway said, 'I will join you there in a few minutes?'

He locked eyes with the Commodore, who said, 'As you wish, Captain.'

Stalking the deck Probus surveyed his men. 'All remain on deck' he ordered, 'until I have ascertained the cause of this murderous affair.' Voice carrying conviction as he eyed the midshipmen and they looked at him in alarm as he then commanded. 'You four: follow me!' Stalking away without a backward glance.

The Naval Officers were assembled in the stateroom as Probus and Sethman entered, followed by the very subdued midshipmen. 'Make yourselves comfortable, gentlemen,' said Probus to the officers. They removed their hats with relief and the cabin steward served cigars, and claret from a finely chiselled decanter. Not included in this refreshment the four young men stood stiffly to attention. Lighting a cigar and regarding them through the smoke haze. 'Stand easy, Messrs Bonham-Jones and Verber, I'm concerned only with these two,' eyes boring into Queen and McFie, whose bruised face seemed suddenly conspicuous as the Captain eye-balled him and added, 'because they are going to tell me just what happened last night.' Confronting the apprehensive pair. 'That eye would seem to implicate you, McFie, and if you were involved I know damn well that Queen was in the action.' He looked fiercely at the two midshipmen who stood mute but with their eyes roving warily over the Naval Officers who were also intent on the proceedings and their obvious interest only added to the build up of tension. In a voice ominously quiet, Probus then said. 'You two have to make up your minds just where your future lies. Are you to be officers, or crewmen? Speak up, Mr Queen, does your loyalty lie with me or the men of the fo'c'sle?'

Queen glanced sideways at McFie. 'Our loyalty is to you, sir,' he said, hesitating, before adding, 'and to the ship.'

'There is a qualification in that remark which I find interesting.' Pulling on his cigar Probus blew smoke rings in laconic manner. 'Was there some reason why your loyalty to the ship, and possibly that of the men also, was put to the test?'

Queen was breathing easier now, some of the tension easing from his tingling nerves. 'The crew were magnificent, sir,' he said, 'and should not be blamed for their violent reaction.'

'Don't speak in riddles, man. Reaction to what for God's sake?'

The sharp tone stung Queen to instant retort. 'The man spat three times, sir. Once for Englishmen, once for the *Earl* and once for King and

Country.' Squaring his shoulders he faced his Captain and declared. 'That was when they went berserk'

Probus felt a quick prickling behind his eyes as the proud words flooded him with emotion, and he heard low murmurs of approval from the Naval Officers. The Commodore jerked his hat down over his ears. He wore a look of quiet esteem on his face as he announced, 'Good job the crew of *Hermes* were not granted shore leave last night otherwise friend Rodrigo would have had to rebuild his miserable Bodega. I find no fault here, Captain, but recommend you move your ship at once out of Table Bay.' On his way out, pausing in front of Billie McFie, couldn't repress a grin as he said in humorous tone. 'Wear that eye proudly, lad.' Turning back from the doorway to face the assembly, the Commodore saluted. 'I bid you good day, gentlemen, and thank you for a most uplifting and interesting morning.'

Staying the hasty departure of his midshipmen. 'One thing more,' said Probus in condemning tone, 'may I ask what two of my officers were doing in a house of such ill repute?'

'Obeying your orders, sir,' replied Queen tongue in cheek, 'and keeping an eye on the crew.' The midshipmen scampered out on deck where the ship's company were still assembled and watching with curious eyes the departure of the Royal Navy. They came to life, disbelieving, as the orders roared.

'Crew dismiss! Prepare the ship for sailing, Mr Sethman. All hands! Prepare to get under way!'

Spontaneous cheer, the crew rushing to their stations and running like monkeys up the rigging, relief in this unexpected leniency being plainly shown in the enthusiasm and speed with which they made ready for sea.

'Heave short!' The hands on the windlass hauling round and a rhythmic shanty accompanied the anchor chain as it came inboard.

'I want this done right, Vinderman,' ordered Probus, 'too many Navy eyes on us for mistakes.'

'Aye, aye, sir.'

'Set lower foresails and brace yards.' The sails on the main mast filled, while the topsails of the foremast were braced back. 'Break out!' Freed from her hold on the sea bottom the ship began to move with the backed topsails canting her head round towards open water; topsails hauled round and filling on the same tack as the working sails.

'Steer full and bye!'

'Full and bye, she's sailing, sir,' announced Vinderman confidently.

'Set fore and main courses.'

The sails set like great gulls' wings, white and brilliant and fluttering for a moment before filling with a reverberating thump. She surged forward under the power of the offshore breeze. A solitary cannon fired from the frigate, the percussion salutary and moving as *Earl of Rothesay* sailed smoothly out of Table Bay, breathtakingly beautiful in the midday sunshine.

'Dip our colours to the Royal Navy, Mr. Ashbury.'

The striped ensign of the East India Company crawled down in significant gesture then returned to the masthead. On the quarterdeck stood Probus and Sethman who, as well as First Officer, had been friend and confident for many years. They exchanged speculative glances. 'Stroke of good luck for a change,' murmured Sethman.

Nodding, Probus said, 'Put it down to violence or perhaps danger shared. 'Tis a strange reflection on human nature that loyalties are easier earned when trouble threatens. We must count our blessings. All shipshape and Bristol fashion! So pass the word to the crew, Alan. Well done: and welcome back!'

Chapter Thirteen

During the next two days they had doubled the Cape and were making steady progress along the southern tip of the African mainland. Perfect sailing conditions. Morale of the crew was high and they had found belated pride in the ship and in their work. Fancy rope work began to adorn hitherto untidy falls of rope ends and the men went about their tasks with a willingness that reflected their newly established comradeship. Even Officer Gaywood had difficulty in finding faults and the days were full and pleasant with all aboard taking satisfaction in the engrossing routine of sailing the ship to best advantage. The wind remained constant and the plunging bow furrowed a path through the warm waters . . . eventually turning north by east to keep her fair wind and running parallel with the coast of Mozambique.

The area of Indian Ocean into which they would soon be sailing was notorious for pirates. Madagascar, together with the many off-lying islands and anchorages, were convenient bases for these daring sea rovers but they could also lay in wait off Mauritius or even as far north as the ports bordering the entrance to the Red Sea, waiting for the chance to intercept a merchantman returning heavily laden from India. These waters had earlier been the spoiling ground for two of the most infamous Captains in the history of piracy . . . Captain Avery and Captain Kidd, who at one time in his gory career actually carried a commission from King William "to proceed as a private man-of-war to capture other pirates and freebooters". Ships of any nation were fair game for such ruthless buccaneers, giving Probus due cause to worry about the vulnerability of a lone ship in the Indian Ocean.

The hands were closed up at action stations and drilled constantly in the skills of becoming a fighting unit. Preparing and running out the guns became a contest of speed with a daily competition held between the duty watches, the prize being a tot of rum to the winners. The midshipmen were becoming proficient with weapons and improving all the time. Lieutenant Gascoyne, an accomplished swordsman, was their tutor, and every forenoon they were busy on deck thrusting and cutting.

'Don't try to be too clever,' instructed the Lieutenant, 'no time for fancy swordsmanship when you are facing a half-crazed Frenchman or pirate. Just keep in your mind the certainty that if you don't put him out of action fast: you're dead!'

Not surprisingly, Bonham-Jones and Verber were very competent with a fencing blade while Queen and McFie, though learning fast, were definitely cutlass men with strength and enthusiasm more evident than skill. The marines practised marksmanship every day. Warrington-Smyth and John Symmons entered into these sessions and proved useful with a musket and the former soon became the most accurate on board, with a deadly aim surprising in a man of letters. But all three writers were now vastly different men, when compared to the sea-sick clerks who had joined ship at Portsmouth. Probus kept his crew at practise until satisfied they were more than capable of giving a good account of themselves and he kept the ship sailing at full speed, using the fair wind to best advantage.

Idyllic days, noon-to-noon run averaging one hundred and fifty miles. The Island of Madagascar was sighted on the starboard bow and bringing the pungent fragrance of a tropic land, seductive to nostrils scoured by sea air. The ship's surgeon, Dr. Quennel, had recovered from illness and held morning sick call on the galley deck. He had few complainants.

Francis Warr could always be seen with his sketching pad capturing many a routine moment in the daily life of the ship. No one, from the

Captain down to the cook was exempt from his penetrating crayon and his collection was finally displayed in an exhibition spread on deck like some street artist on the pavements of London.

Many a good face was captured. Some in caricature, some in noble repose. Arnold Waugh holding court. Vinderman playing his lute, Gimpy the cook complete with gash bucket, the wide grin of Billie McFie and the dark good looks of Verber, Toby wearing a coronet. Deck officers on the prowl with disapproval in their stern demeanour. Queen as a buccaneer adorned with a droopy moustache and a single gold earring, he suspected the influence of Martha Harper in this. Martha herself: movingly mirrored in disarray as she tended the sick. Francis Warr could have made a good profit from his amused and intrigued models. Instead he cheerfully gave every interested customer a sketch of their own, stating to all, 'Your approval and interest are more than I have a right to expect.' He had spent much time sketching Trudy Manson and she appeared in several beguiling poses so delicately lined that they brought comment from the ship's company, few of whom had failed to notice the amount of time the two spent together. One of the more interested was Ernest Harper whose portrait was Shylock in its shrewdness.

Regarding the sketches with concern and suspicion, he said to his wife in disgruntled voice, 'Something's going on between those two.'

Martha's outlook on life had changed considerably of late. The unhurried routine and the fulfilment of being so desperately needed in the sick bay had brought new maturity and a sense of confidence in the knowledge that she actually cared for others and she smiled serenely at her husband. 'Surprised you haven't noticed,' she said, 'particularly in the evening when we all have an hour of leisure to share.'

'Thought you would have the foresight to put a stop to this nonsense. Surely the girl's duties keep her fully occupied?'

'We cannot monopolise Trudy every waking moment. She is so very young, Ernest, and there are times on a voyage that seems to go on forever when young people are bound to find pleasure in each other.' Linking her arm inside his as she murmured. 'These tropical evenings are so lovely: and so romantic.'

The romantic notions of Ernest Harper had long dried up in the conducting of his profitable and down to earth merchant's business. 'Trudy must remember her position and the debt she owes us,' he said in dismissive tone. 'I suggest you find her more work to fill these idle moments of which you speak.'

'You are a hard man, Ernest, and seem to forget she is my sister's girl and more to me than just a servant.'

'You know best, but remember how difficult it will be to find a replacement in the wilderness we are bound for.' Patting her arm in patronising manner. 'Now you must excuse me, my dear, I have some accounts to attend.'

She made a face at his retreating back . . . a look of resignation intercepted by a startled midshipman and she looked at him and smiled. 'I beg pardon, Jason, my regretful look was certainly not meant for you.'

He glanced after the scurrying figure of Mr Harper. 'It appeared one of slight disillusion.' His observation was pertinent but delivered with an answering smile that caused no offence, Martha was pleased to have him to herself for once. This young man interested her more than she was prepared to admit.

'The time for disillusion is long past,' she said, 'I just wondered what happened to the impetuous young man I married?' Finding quick humour in the thought, she said wryly. 'Not that Ernest could ever have been described as impetuous, but he had a certain charm.' Looking speculatively at him she then asked. 'What happens to young men to make them dry and sterile before their time, when does the magic begin to fade . . . all the tender romance and the relationship which was once so encompassing?'

He didn't know how to answer her questions and certainly felt most unqualified in such delicate matters but Martha obviously expected an answer and, after thinking about it, he said carefully, 'Perhaps the magic is allowed to fade in the very act of maintaining the relationship, in the way a man has to accept the position of responsibility and the desire to support his family in the style to which they are accustomed.'

The words came out stilted and not in the way he had intended and he quickly wished he had refrained from comment when she clapped her hands in brisk, mock applause. 'Bravo,' she exclaimed, 'Ernest himself could not have said it better, and is a typical man's excuse when his love of life is subordinate to a desire for wealth and recognition.' Disappointed with him, she said scornfully. 'What coward's men are, hiding behind this facade of family. Listen to me, Jason,' she insisted and with an intense, direct look, stated, 'women need to be loved, not surrounded by ambition and barren reason. Life is meant to be grasped firmly and with every hour treasured.' After a brief pause, she added suggestively, 'Such a treasure can be without compare when shared with a kindred spirit.' Moving to the rail, facing him, the hem of her dress lifting in the warm breeze of evening, a strand of ash blonde hair unheeded across her forehead. Martha Harper was a beautiful woman and her eyes were afire with the emotion of her spoken thoughts. The harvest moon shone like a halo on the back of her head and the night sky hosted a myriad stars. Holding out her hand, imperious, and he joined her at the rail and together they looked down into the swishing wave that ran back from the bow and tumbled phosphorescent alongside and after sharing this moment of contemplation she said in a tone that held a note of envy. 'I begin to understand how a man could want a life such as yours. At least you are alive, boldly facing the challenge and the danger: and enjoying this unbelievable splendour.' Pausing her rhetoric in quiet reflection, then she looked up and said as if in query. 'But I have only sympathy for the woman who falls in love with a man such as you, young Jason, for what have we to offer that can compete, year after year, with such compelling grandeur?'

'Why should a woman have to compete? Surely there is room for compromise in this great scheme.'

He was well out of his depth with Martha and his stammered reply earned scant consideration. 'Compromise,' she scoffed, 'I wonder how many lives have been prostrate in that word? What compromise would you make? The only change for you is to give up your career as a ship's officer and seek out some confining job ashore. No, Jason!' Eyes devouring him as she fervently declared. 'You are a pirate! A buccaneer! Taking whatever you wish in demanding hands without fear of consequence and without needing to lay claim to posterity in the shape of impotent layers of wealth and respectability.' Moonlight flashed fire into her eyes as she stormed on. 'Such a man could command a woman's devotion for all time.

She might never marry you but she'd certainly carry the vibrant memory of you for all of her life.' Emotionally moved by her own rhetoric she had to stop for a moment to collect herself . . . then she concluded in a voice that betrayed lack of control. 'But finally, and so very sadly, no woman could bear to forever share the love of her man with so formidable an opponent.'

Looking at her in bewilderment. 'Ma-am, you have me reeling. I somehow feel we have come round in a complete circle.'

'Who can reason with a woman,' she queried, 'perhaps this enigma we pursue here can never reach a satisfactory conclusion. Hesitating, as if searching for the right words, she then questioned. 'Is it love to demand that a beautiful, vibrant man of action should forsake his chosen way of life? Expect him to conform to the accepted pattern and thereby condemn him to be like my own Ernest, long dried up and barren in the need for success and fortune. To see the laughing boy we loved so dearly change over the years into a different person, someone who perhaps is no longer capable of commanding our love.' This train of thought had words rushing and tumbling in eagerness to get out. 'On the other hand, my young pirate,' she went on, 'can it be love that so selfishly expects a girl to wait on her man's pleasure and spend her own life in loneliness?' A perceptive note appeared as she queried. 'Am I correct in my assumption that there is such a girl?' The look on his face was confirmation enough so she shook her head in resigned manner. 'I no longer can presume to know the answer,' she said in quiet voice, 'or how these two extremes can be reconciled and, in the end, perhaps a few moments of blinding passion is enough. To be enjoyed,' opening her hands in emphasis as she added, 'and let go.'

Her observations were too close, and unwittingly had outlined a dilemma that had its beginning with Mr Passendale's own concerned comments. 'True love could find a way,' he said confidently.

'It might, but could also be the snare into which two people are trapped to find frustration and misery.' Looking into his face, as if memorising every detail. 'I begin to agree,' she then said, 'we are moving in circles and in a maze from which there is no obvious and easy escape.' Concluding with a wry smile. 'The subject is most provocative but eventually you will make your own decisions.'

'If they haven't already been made for us.'

'I can't subscribe to that view,' she said firmly. 'We may be presented with the opportunity by our fates or stars, whichever we believe in most, but in the final reckoning the decision has to be our own.' Taking his hand in fond gesture she pressured it for a moment. 'I retire from this profound conversation puzzled and defeated, yet will rest in my berth below secure in the knowledge that you have the ship in your capable hands,' smiling tenderly as she added, 'and perhaps shedding a tear for the beauty of youth: and for its sublime optimism.'

He watched her move with easy grace down the companionway. She looked back, touched fingers to her lips in intimate farewell, and went from view.

Chapter Fourteen

'Deck there! Sail ho! Fine on the larboard bow!' Lookout's cry rang down from the masthead bringing the deck officer on the run. High on the poop deck Michael Gaywood focused his telescope then turned to find the First Officer and a midshipman expectantly by his side.

'Duty watch close up,' ordered Sethman, 'hands to gun stations. Call the Captain, Mr Bonham-Jones.'

Gun ports slamming open. Cannon primed and run out. The regular exercising was evident in the efficient manner the crew prepared for action.

'What is she, Mr Sethman?' asked Probus as he struggled into outer clothing.

'Too far off to distinguish but certainly no square-rigger, from the style of her I think she's an Arab.'

Probus scanned the distant sail. 'Long way off and alone, they'll not tackle us single handed, keep an eye on her and the duty watch closed up at battle stations.'

The morning was fine with a slight wind hardly filling the sails. The sun already high with the distant sighting just a bright sail in the distance and the Captain hurried below to resume his breakfast.

'Your opinion, Mr Gaywood?' asked Sethman.

Taking a long look through his telescope, Gaywood reported, 'Two sails . . . lateen rig and going the same way as ourselves. From what I've seen of Arab dhows we haven't a hope in hell of catching her.'

His summary met with approval. 'There's little to match a well-handled dhow in these waters,' confirmed Sethman, 'but she's too small to cause us trouble and as long as there are no others about we have no problem. Double the lookout and relieve them every hour, don't want anyone falling asleep up there.'

The day continued fine and bright. They were again in the latitudes of extreme heat and the lack of wind kept the atmosphere steamy and oppressive. Action stations were manned all day, but by a minimum crew, the Captain deciding that the more of his men he kept rested the better, if danger threatened. The crew were enjoying the change of routine and an air of comradeship prevailed on the fore deck. Since leaving Table Bay the voyage had been so peaceful and incident free that their superstitious fears had gradually receded. The distant sail remained in sight for most of the day. Becoming more difficult to locate before finally disappearing. Daylight faded with typical splendour to find the *Earl* alone on a calm, darkening sea.

Next morning. Wallowing in a long, slow running swell. Sails hanging limp and the spars groaning in discord as she rolled from side to side, the northern extreme of Madagascar some miles away to starboard, invisible in the damp, clinging mist that surrounded the ship.

Just before dawn, Queen coming on watch. Vinderman by the helmsman who stood hands in his pockets with the wheel untouched, they weren't going anywhere? Vinderman greeted Queen with a growling, 'If it wasn't so bloody hot and sticky I could imagine we were in a Channel pea souper. Known fog like this linger for days.'

'Cheer up, Vindo, nothing lasts for ever.' Nostrils twitching as his smile faded. A strange and nauseous smell hovered on the dank air.

Vinderman's nose also registered disapproval. 'If that's our breakfast cooking,' he said, 'I don't want any.'

'Never smelt anything so revolting,' said Queen with a grimace of distaste. Moving to the side he looked down into clear water, returning to explain. 'Thought we were in a sea of decaying fish?'

'No fish ever made this kind of stink. Only once before have I known anything smell so awful.'

'What do you think it is, Vindo?'

'Dunno.' Stroking drops of condensation from his beard he then said in hard tone. 'Once moored alongside a slave trader . . . there was no cargo aboard but it still reeked with the stink of human filth.'

'If you're right, there must be another ship becalmed, and damn close as well.' Levelling his telescope Queen could see nothing but mist, instinctively taking charge he commanded. 'Have every duty man on the rail both sides and I want absolute silence. We can't see but we may be able to hear.'

Mist clinging, damp and clammy, only sound the creaking of the yards and the eerie atmosphere brought a shiver and a grumble from Vinderman. 'Sailor's nightmare: enough to give you the creeps.'

The sky was lightening but the fog seemed even thicker. They could see no further than the galley deck. Then the steward came out with ship's coffee, a dubious mix of burnt bread and hot water, and Queen instructed him to, 'Call the Captain and ask him to come on deck.'

Probus joined them on the quarterdeck, pulling a loose cape about his shoulders. His scowl of irritation at being aroused so early changed to disgust as he received the full blast of the revolting smell.

'What the hell is it?'

'No idea, sir, but Vindo thinks we are close to a slave ship.'

Glaring, the Captain said, 'You served on a slaver, Vinderman?'

'No sir,' came the hasty reply, 'but I've been close enough to recognise the stink.'

'Close up the gun crews, Mr Queen.' Eyes scouring his ship, 'Got a man at the masthead?'

'And at the rails, sir.'

As the sun made its presence felt the first tendrils of mist began to disperse and a call came from the lookout.

'Deck there! Ship to larboard!'

Telescopes focusing. Probing for a sight. The fog suddenly thinning and bright sunlight clearing a circle round the *Earl*.

'There she is,' pointed Vinderman, 'about three hundred yards on the larboard bow.'

Hazy sunlight reflected on the limp sails of the vessel wallowing ahead. A large Arab dhow with distinctive lateen sails and as she came more into view they could see the hull was painted gold and red and an impressive figurehead of a nubile native girl was carved in ebony with full, naked breasts uplifted as if to keep at bay the surge of bow wave.

'Arab slaver,' confirmed Probus, 'probably shipping Negro slaves from Mozambique to Aden or India. Must be heavily laden or else they would have drifted away from us in the current that runs so strong up this coast?' They all had good reason to know the strongly religious calling of their

Captain and the condemning tone of his voice had them wondering what might come next.

Mr Sethman was on deck by now and joined in to state, 'Looks like the sail we saw yesterday, she must have run into this calm while we still carried our fair wind.'

Now a dirge of sound reached across the water. A moan of misery and anguish that tore into the soul of all aboard and the monotonous, despairing wails brought every man congregating by the rail. The dirge was suddenly punctuated by repeated and staccato whip cracks and so hushed its misery and forced a growling command from Probus, 'Take over, Mr Sethman, I'm going to board her.'

'Not advisable, Captain,' remonstrated Sethman.

'Let me go, sir,' said Queen as he stepped forward.

'And me,' said McFie.'

Looking at them with calculating eyes. 'Our two fighting midshipmen,' said Probus. Perhaps you are right, Mr Sethman, this is work for young and stout hearts.' Focussing his attention on the dhow, he said in authoritative tone. 'These Arabs will not submit without resistance and will only be taken by superior numbers.'

As he said this Mr Harper appeared on deck alarmed by the rumble of cannon being run out and, assessing the situation with a worried eye, he demanded apprehensively, 'Why are we preparing for action?' He was informed in curt tone but Harper showed immediate hostility. 'We have no reason to interfere,' he snapped, 'slave trading is rampant and too profitable to be reduced by any insignificant effort of ours. Why place the ship at risk to free a few miserable savages? To have men wounded or perhaps killed will seriously disable your running of the ship and could place our venture in serious jeopardy.' On the verge almost of stamping his feet in fright and frustration Harper flared up at Probus and cried in dominating tone. 'You have no right to place us at needless risk!'

Rearing to full height and his eyes on fire it seemed the long-suffering Captain was about to give the merchant venturer an overdue statement of his position but Vinderman's voice intruded on the fraught tension. 'I've heard that valuable cargoes of ivory are sometimes carried aboard these Arab slavers,' he casually said

This observation brought an outraged turn from the Captain. He didn't take lightly to insubordination and Vinderman's unsolicited remark was about to bring a severe disciplining but the insinuation penetrated the shop-keeping instincts of Harper who put out a restraining hand. 'Captain,' he grimaced, 'perhaps my assessment of the situation is a little hasty and it would be no credit to our Christian heritage to close our minds to the suffering of fellow human beings: no matter how menial.' Clasping hands over his heart in fervent gesture. 'I agree that we should do all in our power to relieve these unfortunate souls.'

'Your feelings do you credit.' Probus eyed him with distaste and his words were loaded with sarcasm but he was already directing his mind to the Arab dhow. 'Right then, Mr Queen, there is no easy way to do this. We can't use our main armament for obvious reasons and you won't be allowed to board without violence.'

The discourse had given Queen time to consider. 'Can you get the *Earl* closer, sir,' he suggested, 'and our most accurate marines placed high enough to pick their targets? This way we might limit movement on the deck of the Arab. Then if we board her on the far side you could direct your marksmen to give us assistance until we are aboard the dhow.'

Despite the urgency these comments forced a wry smile and a knowing glance from Probus. 'Strategy worthy of John Queen himself,' he conceded, 'yet damn sound for all that. You and McFie get your crews ready. Volunteers only, twenty men to a boat and spread your attack as far apart as possible.' Noticing the appeal on the face of his quartermaster, he snapped. 'No, Vinderman: need you aboard?' The Captain's tone invited no argument and he went on to command. 'Mr Gaywood, organise two boats to tow the *Earl* closer to the Arab . . . ten men and a midshipman in each.' As the Second

Officer moved away with Bonham-Jones and Verber at his heels, Probus rasped. 'Gun crews at the ready, Mr Sethman, every gun on our larboard side brought to bear. Mr Ashbury, run out the bow chaser and place the master gunner in charge. Should there come the slightest puff of wind, have him take out her mainmast.'

The bosun's whistle shrilling, men running to their posts, Warrington-Smythe stood musket in hand before the Captain who said to him sternly, 'You are a passenger, not a fighting man.'

'You know I use it well, sir.'

Probus frowned at the eagerness in his voice but with no time for discussion, said, 'Make your way up to the main top platform . . . you should have a clear view from there.' Staying the hasty departure of Warrington-Smythe with a brusque. 'Pick your targets and don't fire without good reason.'

Commands roaring, Marines scrambling to points of a high vantage . . . four boats already afloat. The men in the towing boats were stripped to the waist and lay to with a will. The ropes came out tight and dripping wet and the *Earl* at first resisted then began to gather ponderous way. High on the fore deck the master gunner prepared the bow cannon while Probus stalked forward noting every detail. The gun crew stood to as he approached and the master gunner knuckled his forehead in salute.

Nobody knew if the gunner had a first name, he

was known only as Jancy. Late thirties, short, barrel chested with a mop of fiery red hair tied behind his neck Jancy was a hard drinking man when ashore and reputed to have a lusty way with the women of the waterfront taverns. He had a temper that matched the flame of his hair, but also a quick smile to his generous mouth. An ex-naval gunner, his one lasting pride was his cannon: and the accuracy of his marksmanship.

'Mr Jancy,' demanded Probus, 'can you take out her mainmast if she begins to move?'

Looking across at the dhow Jancy then sighted along the long, slim cannon and, grinning in suggestive manner, said, 'At this range and in these conditions I could take the tits off yonder lusty figurehead.'

Ignoring the hoots of laughter that greeted this statement, Probus said icily, 'The mast, Jancy, just concentrate on the mast and wait for the order to fire.'

'Aye, aye, sir.' Serious now; intent on the task ahead.

'Declare our intentions, master gunner,' ordered Probus, 'one shot: high and above her bow.' With this he left the foredeck to David Ashbury and the gun crew.

With all preparations complete, Queen and McFie were detailed to go. Scrambling down into the waiting longboats, twenty men and a bosun's mate in each, armed with a mixture of pistol, cutlass and boarding pikes. The deck watches of the midshipmen had volunteered to a man. Jacko Abbot, Arnie Waugh, Davy Greenwood and his mates, bright eyed and eager for action and a relief from monotony.

'Race you, Mr Queen,' cried McFie, 'last aboard the Arab buys rum for all.'

'You'll be buying, McFie.'

The challenge brought a great shout and they pulled away, making a large circle away from the mother ship towards the far side of the stationery dhow. The crews of the attacking boats outnumbered the Arabs but they well knew they would soon be an easy target if the men on the dhow opened fire and they came round in a sweeping arc, for the moment keeping out of range of any musketry. Smoke and flame slamming from the bow of the *Earl*. Splash of water a few yards ahead of the dhow. This, together with the appearance of the longboats brought immediate clamour to the deck of the deceptively peaceful slaver. The *Earl* was closing and as distance lessened the marines in the rigging could clearly see into the waist of the dhow where a row of bearded, hawk faced men clad in long robes with waists girdled and turbans on their heads lined the rail in sinister stance. Brandishing a blunderbuss-type musket one ran to the high pooped stern then sighted his weapon at the oncoming boats. He was joined by several others crouching behind the high-railed transom.

The Lieutenant of Marines looked for instruction but Probus gave a negative headshake. 'Hold your fire,' he instructed, 'there's still a chance they will offer only token resistance. Let them fire first if they've a will to, then make every shot count.' His words heralded a ragged volley from the stern of the dhow, aimed at the boats closing from the far side. The aim was too accurate for complacency and brought splinters flying from the side planking.

'Keep low, men,' shouted Queen. Helming directly at the slaver, bow on and making as small a target as possible. These last hundred yards were fraught with danger. A rattle of musket fire as the marines opened up with an accurate first volley that brought a shout of pain followed by a scattering of figures diving for cover. This brief respite spurred on the longboats and they came at increasing speed. 'Fire at will, Lieutenant!' roared Probus

The second volley blasted a hail of bullets across the dhow and again the motley crew had to grope for cover. The one with the blunderbuss must have cleverly presumed he would have time before the marksmen reloaded and rose to take steady aim at the head of McFie. Shot flamed from the musket of Warrington-Smythe high on the main top and the weapon of the imprudent Arab flew skyward as the heavy ball smashed between his shoulders. His body slumped forward and hung over the rail then flopped into the still waters to be kept afloat by air trapped in his burnouse. A dorsal fin appeared, cutting through the water with two others in frantic chase.

Dhow in pandemonium, the stricken Arabs catching the full force of the Marines musketry but they had an astute leader and a group of tethered, black figures were herded on deck to form a living barrier between the Arabs and marine marksmen. But now the two longboats were alongside and grapple hooks fastened on the side rail, clawing hold and followed by a shouting herd of barefoot seamen. The dhow had little freeboard and it needed but a concerted heave and the boarders were up and over. Word had spread of treasure aboard and they were in greedy and voracious mood but met with a fanatical attack, swarthy, bearded men, curved swords slashing and cutting. Steel ringing on steel and battle was joined! The forty men of the longboats were a powerful force and met the Arabs head on. Queen and McFie forced aft in the melee where a giant, majestic Arab stood alone on his poop deck, aloof from the action as if there was no need for his participation and McFie turned aside to parry an attacker and there was an excited Scottish roll to his voice as he called out, 'You're on your own, laddie!'

The tall Arab stood in formidable, arrogant stance. Loose-sleeved tunic girdled at the waist. Flowing trousers looped at the ankle. White turban wound round his head with a magnificent ruby glowing in the soft folds just above his forehead. His presence dominated the foredeck and Queen approached with every nerve on edge. Would the man fight: or submit? His sabre was drawn and ready. Din of battle all around. No time for conjecture or fear? This one had to be taken!

The Arab had only contempt for Jason Queen, a half-smirk of derision on his face as the midshipman approached then his hand came up wielding a curving, broad bladed sword and he sprang down to face Queen on the wide stern decking. They circled as if oblivious of the screaming confusion but each seeking a chance to strike first. The Arab's eyes were unblinking and diamond sharp on Queen's face then he leaped forward, scimitar scything for the neck. Parrying with instinctive reaction but the force of the blow drove him backwards off balance. The Arab was a silent assassin and swung his blade in a shimmering blur but Queen jerked sideways and the steel chopped into the deck with splintering force and the inertia of the missed strike brought the Arab lunging forward with his blade held tight in the deck planking and Queen went straight in with sabre slashing but his wrist was locked in fingers all steel and sinew and in panic he grabbed the Arab's sword hand, then a robed knee crunched into his groin and drove him back but the writhing agony brought demoniac rage and fire in his brain and he hurled forward and smashed his fist into the bearded face, and again, bringing a snarl from that cruel-lipped mouth. But a fist was no match for naked steel and he was driven back and parrying and defending against a sword that slashed and thrust and he was losing this fight! Had no chance with steel against steel because this Arab was a murderous bastard! To hell with defence! Throwing his sabre at the Arab's head he followed straight in and grabbed him in a bear hug. Heat of battle bringing its own desperation and brute force he head-butted then thrust his head under the bearded chin and forcing him over in a back breaking hold but the Arab was too powerful and resisted with ease and he threw down his sword and with his hands on the back of Queen's head as a lever he kneed him in the balls again, and again, then using Queen's tactics head-butted a stunning blow in the face. Helpless and near unconscious Queen was gripped by the hair and his head forced back and through streaming eyes he saw the dagger poised to slash his throat. Suspended in a red mist of pain and hopeless immobility he could only stare with fading eyes at the hairy brown descending hand, and death seemed so inevitable he was almost composed.

Eyes clearing. Why was the strike delayed? As if in another time, another place the lean body of the Arab seemed to float skyward, lifted with seeming ease up and high in the hands of a giant Negro. Covered only with a loincloth the muscles on his back stood out proud and the leather thong that bound his loins cut deep into straining tissue as he lifted the Arab high in the air. Stamping the deck with rhythmic feet, turning the frantic Arab above his head and beginning a tribal chant, frightening in its primeval savagery. Queen lay in stunned posture, striving to force movement to his battered frame. Battle had ceased. Dead and wounded Arabs prostrate. His own men were stood dumbstruck and as if hypnotised but the dozen or so natives who had been brought up as a living shield had freed their bonds and were standing in a group. Waiting. Expectant!

Giant Negro dancing on: the Arab screaming out loud as he was whirled faster and faster. The dance stopped abruptly. Raising his arms to full stretch the Negro flung the Arab down at the feet of the waiting natives and they took up the macabre dance with feet slapping rhythm. A dozen pairs of hands took the groaning Arab and tearing and ripping the clothing from his body until he was naked. His cries now became hysterical as probing black talons tore at his genitals and ripped open his backside. Streams of blood began to pulse and trickle down the pale skin. The dance stopped, bringing sudden silence: dramatic with savage implication. Held high and stationery, poised, his mouth gurgling insanely. A great chant starting but this time concerted from the depths of the vessel and Queen forced up from inertia and propelled forward but too late . . . a lifetime too late as the giant Negro raised his arm and his hand opened with fingers stabbing seaward and a growling sound started from the group supporting the writhing body then the growl volumed into a roaring death cry as all the slaves joined in ecstatic unison and the bloodstained body went flying, high and wide, and straight into the thrashing path of three dorsal fins. The body seemed to hover in mid air for a terrified moment, then with a shriek of mortal terror he submerged and the concussion of strike was demoniac in the extreme. One hand taloned upward but already a crimson stain clouded and frothed in the water as he was ripped to pieces by the blood crazed sharks. A last, significant swirl as the hungry fish took their prey deep then the water stilled and a deathly silence descended on this scene of terrible retribution and at a sign from the Negro the group fell back as McFie closed up to Queen and looked at him and at his battered face. 'Knew I shouldn't have left you on your own,' he said in awestruck voice, 'you alright, Jase?'

'Do I look as if I am? That bastard was about to take my head off!' Croaking words with blood streaming from his mouth and the untypical foulness in the way he spoke reflected both his humiliation at the hands of the Arab and the awesome revenge of the natives and he shook his head in an effort to regain control of himself and strove to focus streaming eyes on the aftermath of battle aboard the slave ship and the sight and sickly smell of death brought grim and sobering realisation that taking men into action was not a game: and one he would never again take lightly.

Forcing his mind to clear, needing all his will power to focus on the task still ahead, and on the plight of the black cargo. The slaves were stacked in tiers three abreast either side of the centre gangway, bottom row squatting cross-legged on the broad planking of the bilge where it began to level off above the keel. Then a board platform was rigged just above their heads on which were roped another layer of blacks and so on up to deck height. There must have been about fifty males and females, forced to sit and breathe in the droppings and excreta of those above. The stench appalled and in the humid, clammy air the atmosphere was poisonous and many of the natives were in a state of near unconsciousness. Deck crowded, seaman milling around with weapons at the ready. He was in command. The one to whom they looked for instruction. Willing his mind back to reason, to sanity! Dividing his men into two groups, one to search the dhow for anything of value, the other to move the prisoners forward. The Arabs went docilely. They had witnessed the wild-animal ferocity of the slaves and much preferred the sanctity offered by the presence of the English seamen.

'What happens next, Jase?' asked McFie.

'Wish I knew. Ought to release the natives before they all suffocate?'

'Hope they realise we are trying to help. Don't fancy a dose of their deadly medicine.'

Queen looked at the giant Negro who stood aloof with his arms folded in regal stance.

'The big one must be some kind of chief and had already saved me from a slashed throat. No,' he ruminated, 'think he realises we are here to free his people.' Moving slowly towards him one hand held palm forward in what he fervently hoped would be recognised as a sign that he meant no harm. The Negro came to meet him, his hand touching his forehead in a gesture obsequious yet in no way servile and he looked at Queen with eyes that seemed to penetrate yet with no hostility. Like everyone else on board he appeared to recognise authority and was prepared to await decision from this bold and white-skinned man who had just released him from bondage.

Unsure, wondering what to do, Queen met his gaze in equal enquiry then, drawing out his knife he offered it hilt foremost, at the same time gesturing toward the slaves with a rope-cutting movement. Grasping the knife without hesitation the Negro went quickly among the tethered slaves and slashed the main rope and, leaving them to disentangle themselves, came back to where Queen stood. Eyes flashing at the Arab prisoners on the foredeck he gave a fierce gesture that was unmistakably one of throat cutting but Queen shook his head in emphatic denial and held out his hand. Hesitation for a tense second, before the knife was handed back: 'You had me worried, Jase,' muttered McFie. 'Thought the heathen was about to slit your throat: just for the hell of it.'

Queen thought the Negro and he had some form of communication, as if each recognised authority in the other, and the Negro thought these men had just freed his people even though they were now well outnumbered and he thought these men were foolish in doing this but he was prepared to wait and see and anything was better than the Arab's treatment and when Queen made signs for him to be patient he growled command and the nearby natives immediately squatted on deck and Queen asked in relieved tone:

'Casualties, Billie?'

'Cuts, bruises, some bloodstains but nothing serious.'

'Get the injured back on board, also the Arabs while the chief is still in a reasonable frame of mind.'

McFie soon had things organised and with the *Earl* now close abeam the Arabs were transferred out of danger and locked away in the ship's hold where they would stay until a suitable landfall was reached. Then Mr Sethman came aboard with Vinderman eagerly behind. 'My God: but it stinks!' gasped Sethman

'Not so bad when you get used to it,' said Queen with a grin.

Sethman grimaced, and speaking in stilted voice, ordered, 'Captain wants an inventory of all cargo and also wishes to know what you intend to do with your prize?'

'The decision is mine?' Queen gasped in incredulous tone.

'As long as it is made quickly and doesn't saddle us with an unwanted dhow and a cargo of blacks.' Sethman then said in suggestive tone. 'Madagascar is but two days sail.'

'Then with your permission I'll turn the dhow over to the slaves.' Speaking in brisk tone he then said. 'Mr Sethman, sir, please have Francis Warr sent aboard with his sketch pad.'

Wondering at this request and lifting a speculative eyebrow at the manner in which Queen assumed command Sethman took a last look, then, holding his nose, hastened for the longboat. He felt an urgent need to place salt water between him and that dreadful stench.

No cargo aboard except the living one but a row of leather chests was stowed under the shelter of the forepeak. One each for the Arab crew and all stuffed with clothing and curiosities. Investigating the contents he could see nothing of apparent value except one soft leather pouch containing some odd shaped pieces of rough, glass-like crystal.

'Have these chests taken aboard, Vindo, they

might provide Mr Harper with an hour or two of interest.' Then, in gibing tone. 'These Arabs appear to do some trading on their own account but I see no sign of your ivory.'

'Quick thinking though, eh Jase,' countered Vinderman as he moved away to assist the loading party.

The stock of food aboard was pitiful. Some rice and a goodly store of dates. Enough to keep the Arabs going but certainly not the blacks, evidently just enough to keep them alive until they reached the market place. Had they tried to cross the Indian Ocean it was most unlikely that any would have survived and Queen concluded that their destination must have been one of the nearer Arabian ports. Francis Warr seemed in ignorance of the stench as he boarded because his eyes were bright and consumed with interest. 'You asked for me?' he queried.

'Want you to be my interpreter through your sketch pad.'

He brought him before the chief and, with a gasp of admiration, Warr announced, 'What a subject for a canvas!' Gazing with awe at the regal-looking Negro who looked back at him ominously and as if he didn't like what he saw.

'Control yourself, Francis,' said Queen, 'and listen for a moment.'

The first sketch was of a dhow under sail with a smudge of coastline in the background; the second of an all black crew working ship.

Showing instant comprehension, the chief spoke words of command that brought four men from the shambles below. Spreading the sketches with childish delight and, after a short dialogue, the four went straightaway to the base of the mast and pulled on ropes and as the lateen sail began to climb up on its spar Queen relaxed in the knowledge there were experienced sailors among the natives. The third sketch showed a compass rose with the head of the dhow pointing westward. The chief couldn't make this out until McFie gestured at the crude compass, then he shrugged disdainfully and pointed to the sun.

'He knows his way home alright.' McFie was more interested in the horde of natives emerging on deck. Plainly the Arabs only took young and healthy prisoners in their slave trade and there were many women aboard and all naked with round bellies and pointed breasts. Delight in their unexpected deliverance was obvious and they regarded the English sailors with open curiosity, a suggestive appraisal returned with enthusiasm. Vinderman had his eye on a plump Negro woman sitting on the rail close by.

'One or two of these black girls could get closer without me objecting . . .' the words gagged short, 'don't they stink, though?'

'Have you ever done it with a black woman, Vindo?' asked McFie with curiosity rife.

Vinderman shook his head. 'Reckon it all tastes the same in the end,' he said with a lewd grin.

Pointing at one of the women. Slender waist and a finely rounded body and her breasts were firm and enticing. 'Just right for you, Billie,' he suggested, 'reckon she'd soon show you the way.'

Responding to this exchange more of the crew converged and discipline was vanishing fast. 'Leave Billie alone,' snapped Queen, 'he can find trouble easy enough without any prompting from you, and if these blacks' turn nasty we could be very exposed.' The commanding rasp had Vinderman's eyes narrowing and he thought Queen actually relished being in charge. Rather him than me!

'My apologies, Mr Queen,' he replied in compliant tone, 'but with so much naked female flesh about you must admit it's bloody difficult not to get an eyeful.'

Queen could see Probus stalking the quarter-deck with impatient step and, in a tone that had Vinderman moving smartly to the longboat, stated, 'Time we were back aboard.'

The Negro chief had trailed behind them all this time and as Queen and McFie prepared to leave a flutter of wind disturbed the lateen sail and a muscular native took position at the tiller. The chief spoke, and two comely native girls were brought to kneel before them in a servile posture. 'Must have heard Vindo,' said McFie with a grin. 'Looks as if he's giving us these two as a going away present.' Queen shook his head in uncomfortable refusal and the chief regarded him without humour. Again he growled command and a lean-hipped black came forward and unrolled a long fold of cloth that Queen recognised as the silk turban of the mutilated Arab and in the centre of the cloth lay the silver dagger and the dazzling ruby. Rolling the silk into a scroll the chief placed it firmly in Queen's hand, enveloping the whole with his great fist in a gesture clearly indicating that refusal would be offensive.

'All ready here, Mr Queen.' Vinderman had a perfect sense of timing. Exchanging glances the two midshipmen turned to face the chief and their hands came up in salute, an impromptu courtesy that brought a flash of pearly white teeth to the dark face.

'Let's go, Billie.' They left with the Negro still smiling. Francis Warr sat on the rail sketching for all he was worth and they had to forcibly drag him into the longboat.

Victorious crew assembling on deck; flutter of wind bringing movement to the dhow. Tall figure on the after deck standing motionless and looking at them and remaining so until the dhow went from normal vision.

'Hope they don't run into any more Arabs,' said Francis Warr.

'They'll never again be taken as slaves, no matter at what cost,' said Queen confidently. 'The next two days will be hungry for them, but at least they have a useful vessel as reward for hardship.'

Francis Warr made no reply. He was too engrossed in his sketches.

The contents of the trunks were examined and dismissed as worthless except for the pieces of crystal. Mr Harper showed no interest until Verber took hold of the pouch, moved to a closed porthole and scratched a piece across the glass before replacing the pouch in Harper's hand. 'Uncut diamonds,' he said, 'I've seen many in my father's workshop.'

'Quite a satisfactory morning, Probus.' Placing the stones in a large, spotted handkerchief Harper scurried down the companionway like a ferret down a rabbit hole.

Scrutinising the midshipman Probus thought Queen must have been in a hell of a scrap, he looked as if he had been run over by a wagon and team of four. Relieved to have them safely back aboard, he said, 'Well done, you two, only six casualties and all back safe. You even found something for Mr Harper to enthuse about.'

Still smarting from his defeat, Queen thought he hadn't done well at all. Unrolling the length of silk cloth out on deck and Probus gaped open-mouthed at the huge ruby. 'Must be worth a king's ransom?' Unable to keep his eyes of the ruby he picked it up for close examination before stating. 'I'll register this in the ship's prize inventory.' Switching scrutiny to the silver dagger he hefted it in his hand for a moment's contemplation then placed it in Queen's belt. 'Keep the knife,' he said. 'You've earned it.'

Chapter Fifteen

Halcyon days. Glorious sunshine. Blue water. Monsoon steady from the northeast, allowing a satisfying close reach deep into the Sea of Arabia and bringing the north coast of India ever nearer. Apart from a strong blow that kept them hove-to for a few hours nothing marred the forward surge of the *Earl*.

Came the time when the Captain had to turn the ship's head easterly, a move that brought the trade wind more directly from ahead causing them to make diagonal tacks into wind and slowing forward progress. Daily sightings now but mostly of inshore traders between India and the Arabian ports. While Probus was confident in a speedy conclusion to the voyage, he never relaxed vigilance until a safe harbour was under his lee and the crew were summoned to action stations whenever the cry of 'Sail Ho' brought conjecture.

With the prospect of imminent journey's end the mood of the passengers became one of anticipation and qualified regret and they were determined to enjoy the last few days on board. The crew were also looking forward to the next carousel among the fleshpots ashore and went about their work in a light-hearted manner. Vinderman was found on most evenings playing his lute on the galley deck with a regular chorus of seaman joining in. The passengers habitually came down to listen and even to join the singing: when they knew the words. With his music always in demand Vinderman had become the most celebrated member of the ship's company but had courteously declined to play for the passengers on the poop deck with a typical Vinderman summary. 'The officers and passengers are free to come down to the galley deck but the crew can never be allowed aft.' So it was established that quarterdeck personnel were welcome to join the musical evenings as guests of the crew. The arrangement worked well with no resentment caused and an air of comradeship and well being prevailed throughout.

Supper over, officers and passengers assembling as usual on the poop deck, dress was informal and the white shirts of the men showed to advantage the healthy, weathered look of their faces. Attired in gay coloured, off the shoulder gowns, the ladies were surrounded by admiring males. Martha with the officers and surgeon, Trudy with the three writers and with her arm linking with Francis Warr, who regarded her in complete beguilement. No music this evening, for Vinderman had the helm with Queen and McFie idling by his side. This was the informal hour and a time for relaxation, until Mr Harper came on deck with a sour look on his face. Never capable of joining in the pleasantries established on the voyage he concentrated his gaze on the intimate pose of Trudy and Francis Warr. 'When do we arrive at Surat, Captain?' he then said tersely.

'If we have no setbacks, I anticipate entering the river estuary in three days time.'

'So soon?' John Symmons spoke with regret apparent. He had lost his enthusiasm for the coming desk appointment, but the tone of his voice only seemed to irritate Harper.

'Good job too,' he said coldly, 'perhaps then we can resume the duties that some among us seem to have forgotten.' Directed at the three writers, and particularly at Trudy, the pointed reference brought a look of remonstrance from Martha, and the comment carried down to the steering position. Vinderman eyes narrowed and McFie gave a sardonic glance at Queen.

'You'd have thought all these months at sea would have mellowed that ungracious sod,' he said, 'he's nowhere near as likeable as Martha.'

'This is what happens to a man when he spends his life behind an office desk with nothing to do in the evening except count his money.' Vinderman had a lilt of amusement in his voice as he added, 'Seen a few men go that way but never one who had no redeeming feature at all.

Puzzles me how Martha sticks with such a misery guts?'

'Probably finds consolation in all the wealth and power,' said McFie with a grin.

'Don't think so,' said Queen, 'perhaps before she joined ship, but I suspect her personal values have been adjusted very dramatically.'

'You appear to know a great deal about the elegant Martha,' said Vinderman curiously.

McFie dug him in the ribs. 'They've enjoyed one or two cosy chats together, Vindo. Haven't you noticed? Our Mr Queen seems to hold quite an attraction for the ladies.'

Used to McFie's probing wit, Queen only grinned but Vinderman continued the teasing mood. 'Thought he might have been getting close to Trudy,' he suggested, 'but seems to have been elbowed out.'

'Francis Warr and his artistic talents are more to her cultured taste,' replied Queen, 'and I reckon we have a very interesting situation developing, one that old money bags isn't going to appreciate.'

This indeed was dominant in Harper's mind as he glared at the voluble and happy group of young people. 'Trudy,' he snapped, 'it's high time you attended your mistress!'

Silence on the poop deck! Martha's brow furrowed. 'Really, Ernest,' she chastised, 'can't we enjoy the evening and the wonderful company for these last days without unpleasantness?'

'Please be quiet, Martha,' Harper immediately

retaliated, 'I am determined to re-establish our proper relationships.' His tone was bombastic in the extreme and Martha looked about to reply in like voice but, too aware of her husband's position to openly challenge him, she stifled her objection and glanced ruefully at Trudy and the group and they opened out in a show of embarrassed discomfort and Trudy withdrew her arm from Francis. Then, worried by the conflict between her aunt and uncle, she moved toward Martha.

Francis Warr had a decision to make and the time to make it was now! By nature a dreamer he was a mild-mannered man who could never seem to bring himself to anger and, stifling the retort that came to his lips, he squared his shoulders with an effort, went after Trudy and took her by the arm and brought her face to face with Mrs Harper. She looked at him with speculation and Warr said, 'I regret that I have to say this, Mrs Harper, but I cannot allow Miss Trudy to be treated as a servant.'

He appeared to have grown noticeably taller. Trudy gazed at him with adoring eyes but Martha seemed very cool. 'Trudy is my niece, Mr Warr, not a servant, and I must ask what are your intentions towards her?'

The poop deck had a sudden air of expectance and the entire ensemble savoured every moment as Warr calmly said, 'I have asked Trudy if she will be my wife.' Trudy clung to him and Martha smiled in knowing manner, as if the declaration was not unexpected.

'And I refuse! Completely and without qualification!' Dumbfounded at this exchange, Harper straightway addressed Trudy. 'Go below to your cabin,' he ordered in dominant manner. 'I will speak with you later.'

The discourse was plainly audible to the three men on the steering platform and brought suggestive comment from McFie. 'Give him one, Francis. Punch old misery guts on the nose.'

'Shut up, Billie,' said Queen straining to catch every word, 'can't hear a damn thing with you interrupting.'

The officers were beginning to move tactfully away but Warr said, 'Please, Captain, I would like you to hear this.' Confronting Harper as he stated. 'You have given your last order to Trudy and I'll thank you never to speak to her again in such tone.'

Furious at this affront to his authority Harper snapped, 'There is not the slightest chance of my giving permission for you to marry my niece and if you persist in this impertinence I'll insist on your immediate recall to London and also make damn sure you will never again be granted a position inside the Company.'

Shrugging nonchalantly, as if the threat had no impact, Francis Warr said, 'I have already written my letter of resignation, and no longer have any desire to serve in your Company.' Proud and determined as he went on to say. 'In future the only master I serve is myself, and my need to paint: to create life and colour on pad and canvas. As for your other denial,' pursuing the startled Harper he stated boldly, 'Trudy is above the age when your consent is necessary.' Turning abruptly he said to Probus. 'Captain: will you do us the honour of performing the marriage ceremony? Here and now aboard ship before your officers and under this starlit sky.' Glancing round as he concluded. 'No couple could have a more romantic setting.'

'Don't you dare, Probus!'

Fitzroy Probus allowed no man to speak to him in such a way: and this aboard his own command! Pointedly ignoring Harper, he said, 'Give me a minute to get my prayer book.'

'No, Captain!' the forceful voice of Martha Harper stopped Probus in mid-stride and wiped the look of joy from Trudy's face.

'Why, aunt?' Despairing cry from the heart.

'Because, my darling,' whispered Martha, 'I need time to prepare the daughter of my beloved sister.' There were tears in her eyes as she clasped Trudy to her breast and gazed at her 'You are going to be a bride,' she said very emotionally, 'and when you stand before the Captain with your Francis I promise you will look beautiful and have a wedding which remains in your memory for all time and with the whole of this wonderful ship's company for a congregation.'

She took Trudy's arm, facing an astounded young man. 'Your bride will be by your side at eleven o'clock in the morning, Mr Warr, so prepare to wait for a little while longer. I'm sure that she will prove worthy of your patience.'

She swept Trudy away to a spontaneous hand clapping applause and resounding acclaim. Then Francis Warr was deluged under a congratulating crowd of men, until Harper said spitefully, 'You'll never make money as an artist, so what kind of life can you possibly offer my niece?'

Warr had a smile of utter content on his face. 'I offer only happiness' he said in reply, for this is all I have! As for wealth: one moment of surging, creative magic could be infinitely more rewarding than a lifetime of luxury. Tell me, Ernest Harper,' he said in quiet voice, 'what kind of a man has wealth made of you?' Just then the cabin steward appeared as if by magic with a jug of brandy from the private stock of Fitzroy Probus and, offering a glass, Warr said pleadingly to Harper. 'Will you join with us in a toast to the bride?'

Harper shook his head and stumbled away, and down on the steering platform, McFie looked at Queen with his eyes on fire 'That was something, my friend, to make a man feel good inside.' Ears cocked at the sound of merriment from the quarterdeck he crept mischievously up the companionway to return balancing three glasses of brandy. 'Nobody noticed,' he said with a cocky grin, 'they were too busy celebrating.'

Queen and Vinderman raised their glasses in a spontaneous toast to the audacity of Billie McFie. Probus strode down stern faced, hands behind his back. The three froze. 'You surely didn't think you could get away with that sort of trick, McFie,' scorned the Captain. 'Do yourself a favour, boy, and seek not to fool them as have fooled thousands?' His hands came from behind his back with the brandy jug and with a chuckle he filled their glasses to the brim. 'To the morrow,' joining in the toast, he then enquired, 'know anything suitable for a wedding, Vindo?'

Vinderman's grin was pure evil as he replied:

'How about "The Little Coloured Gal from Spanish Town".'

Dong! Dong! Dong! Slow, sonorous roll of the ship's bell tolling across the sunlit deck and bringing every available man to his post all dressed in their number one's. Spit and polish the order of the day, deck holystoned until the planking was creamy white, withevery piece of bunting and signal flag joined together to dress the ship overall and fluttering in gay multicolour. Marines assembled in double line from the passenger's cabins to where the Captain and his Officers stood waiting on the quarterdeck very formal in their blue jackets with lapels of velvet and gold buttons afire in the sunlight, with the surgeon particularly resplendent in a dress coat of royal blue with scarlet epaulettes. Not to be outdone amidst all the splendour, the sun shone from a sky of clearest blue and the breeze sighed a gentle love song through the rigging.

Expectant buzz of anticipation hovering over the main deck, and, as the bell ceased its ringing, Vinderman's lute came loud and clear, he knew no wedding hymn but he had a sense of occasion and his music was a slow, stately march. Came the raucous voice of the sergeant.

'Ship's company! Attention!'

Marines springing erect: swords high and touching in an archway of shining steel. Dead silence reigned then came the Sergeant's command again, rasping. 'Off caps!'

Trudy Manson in the doorway of the passenger's quarters on the arm of First officer Alan Sethman and a gasp went through the assembled men. The bride! Devastatingly lovely in a wedding dress of virgin white that swept in folds about her feet and the filmy veil of her headdress served only to enhance the shining beauty on her face. Martha following behind dressed in a flowing, high-necked gown of embroidered silk, full skirted and touching the deck as she stooped and gathered up the cascading lace of the bride's train. As Vinderman played them forward, a movement came from the shadows behind.

'My responsibility I believe, Mr Sethman.' Ernest Harper . . . clad in top hat and dark coat with a cravat of silk at his neck. The two women looked back in astounded reflex, and Martha's eyes were wet with tears as she gazed in wonderment at her husband.

'Ernest.' Was all she could say. Mr Sethman relinquished his position with alacrity and Trudy's eyes shone through the lace veil as she murmured in ecstatic voice. 'Thank you, uncle.'

Marine guard of honour standing stiffly to attention; with swords high as the bridal procession moved between the two lines of uniformed precision. The music ceased as the bride came before the Captain. Prayer book open, he surveyed first the bride, then the proud figure of Francis Warr. This was the first marriage ceremony Probus had conducted and, determined it should be done right, had been rehearsing since early morning in the privacy of his cabin.

'Dearly beloved.' Calm and penetrating voice that reached every corner of the main deck. Seamen stood with heads bowed in solemn worship. Violent, uncaring men moved to tears by the wonder of the betrothal service, their Captain's voice soaring above all. 'We are gathered here, in the sight of God on this lovely morning, and before this distinguished company, to join together this man and woman in the bonds of Holy Wedlock.'

The service was short and very moving. The great ship ploughed her way ever onward, decks almost level. Sails had been eased so that nothing might spoil the ceremony and the *Earl* behaved like a perfect lady, holding her course with not a single flutter of canvas or an undue lurch to mar the enchantment. Silence fell. Francis Warr raised the veil from the face of his wife then a great cheer rang out as they kissed and clung together in close embrace. The happy couple broke away and threaded their way back through the Marine guard of honour and, as if just waiting the chance, the crew broke ranks and rushed forward and showered the bride and groom, and the grinning Marines, with handfuls of rice and the newly weds ran the last few yards in considerable haste as the roaring crowd of seamen deluged them.

A trill from the bosun's whistle restored some semblance of order. Addressing them from the quarterdeck, the Captain said, 'Thank you, men, you did well.' Holding up his hand for silence as the hubbub started again. 'Just remember we are a ship at sea and that I will tolerate no licentiousness. Off duty watch remain on deck if you wish, but keep yourselves at the ready.' Concluding with a promise. 'With luck we will be in Surat tomorrow and I could be persuaded to look the other way while you have a proper celebration.'

Harper joined him, looking very pleased with himself. 'May I ask the crew to drink a toast to the young couple?' he said, 'anything they wish and at my expense. In fact, Captain, I insist no expense be spared to make this day a happy one.' Hesitating, as if in private thought, he then added, 'For all of us and I repeat: the bill is mine.'

As the steward served drink to the men, cheers of applause rang out and Harper realised it was his own bequest earning acclaim. Overwhelmed, he turned to the Captain in no small embarrassment. 'Thank you for a wonderful service,' he said, 'and for the support of yourself and the entire crew.'

Smiling in warranted self-satisfaction, Probus replied, 'Went well, I think.' Accompanying this with a fond glance at Harper, almost as if seeing him for the first time. 'But it was you, Ernest,' he then said, 'who brought real happiness to our wedding day.'

The Officers and midshipmen queued up to kiss the bride and, as a flushed, quick breathing Trudy emerged from the clutches of Bonham-Jones, Queen, McFie and a not-so-backward Abraham Verber – 'Really, gentlemen,' expostulated Martha, 'you make me wish for youth and beauty again!'

'Midshipmen,' commanded Bonham-Jones, 'do your duty!'

Martha appeared more overcome than Trudy when the last youth released her.

The revelry went on into the night and this time Vinderman gladly accepted the invitation to play and sing on the poop deck. The cook and the officer's stewards had combined to put on a fine buffet supper. Gimpy had even baked a cake, with icing, displaying unsuspected skills. A cask of claret was placed on deck and the passengers proceeded to get good and drunk. The officers were more aware of their responsibilities but the evening was upon them before they realised, so quickly had the day progressed. Mr and Mrs Francis Warr retired early but alas, not too quietly. Hysterical cries of laughter and discomfort reaching the poop deck as their double berth disintegrated under them and Probus's cold eye focused unerringly on Billie McFie.

'You been in that bridal suite?'

Billie said, 'Why do I always get the blame?'

His attempt at sobriety didn't last and laughter bubbled beyond restraint and the four youths collapsed in each other's arms helpless with hilarity. Alan Sethman was fighting a losing battle. A laugh started, grew in volume to become an uncontrollable roar of merriment and he had to lean on his Captain for support but Probus had troubles of his own 'It seems,' he said with his voice beginning to take flight, 'that the madness of McFie is contagious.'

'Deck there! Land ho! Fine on the larboard bow. ' A rush to the side rail as the compelling call scythed down from the masthead. Barely visible, it was a smudge on the far horizon and just a shadow in the crimson glow of sunset. Vinderman was the only one unmoved by the sight of land. His song continued without a break 'Lands and fine dwellings: all shall be thine.' In especially good voice, Vinderman had been soothed with brandy and was in lyrical mood.

'India. Land of mystery and promise.' Harper placed his hand on her shoulder. He had consumed far more wine than normal and his voice was slurred as he murmured. 'You were right, these evenings at sea can be very romantic.' Gazing into her eyes, he said soulfully. 'It has been a very moving day, Martha.'

'More than you know.' Her eyes were tender but wondering and her mouth tremored as she quietly said. 'When you took your place at Trudy's side this morning I shed tears.'

Tracing the line of her lips with gentle fingers, having difficulty framing words he then said with great feeling, 'I'd almost forgotten how lovely you are. But this morning, when I saw Trudy in your wedding dress I began to realise what a fool I am and what a complete waste I have made of your life all these years.'

'I carry the dress with me always,' Martha gave a wan smile as she explained, 'for if we should have a daughter whom one day might wear it.' Remembering the occasion she brushed away sadness. 'But Trudy was lovely,' she said, 'and I'm so glad the dress was needed again.'

'Is it yet too late, Martha?'

'I don't know if it's you speaking: or the claret?'

'Perhaps it's the voice of desperation?'

'And what voice will it be tomorrow, in the cold light of day?'

'Help me,' cried Harper, 'I've been too long in the wilderness to return in a single day. Tell me it is not too late!'

'Not for some things.' Taking his hand . . . holding his eyes with her own. 'The fault is not entirely with you, for I have been engrossed with wealth and position almost as much as you. But these months at sea, away from all the false values that had assumed such importance in my life have made me once more alive to the fact that true happiness is not found in the size of a house or in bored society. It may be too late for children but I won't accept that it is too late for you and me, with understanding . . .' hesitating, as if unsure, before adding, 'and with love,.we can perhaps turn back the clock a little way because I have come to believe there is little we cannot achieve if the desire is strong in our hearts.' Tearful emotion was evident now and the tone of her voice provoked loving tenderness from Harper and he said in vibrant tone:

'Young Warr made comment yesterday that a moment of surging magic might be of infinitely more value than a lifetime of wealth.' Arms creeping about her waist. Gripping tight as she yielded to his embrace and he brought her close with growing fervour. 'Martha!' he said. 'This is such a moment!'

Part Two

Chapter Sixteen

Malacca
Strategically situated it was a convenient stop over and watering hole for merchant traffic sailing between India and the emerging markets of the Orient. Harbour Township an untidy sprawl of wood framed shacks stilted high to keep out the damp and filth of the refuse covered water and the inshore reach bustled with the floating homes of Nomadic natives. Junks. Sampans. Craft of all shape and size and each housing a vast family and hordes of children ran wild among the incredible bustle of the shanty town. Practising beggars all, and grubby little hands pulled incessantly at every shore going seaman.

The East India convoy from Surat arrived in mid-afternoon and soon lay quiet to their anchors. On board the *Earl* was all haste and excitement, shore leave being granted to all who could be spared. The Navy frigate had accompanied them and Probus warned his men to keep out of trouble: this time? And in particular to look out for and avoid Naval press-gangs. Experienced seamen were always needed by the short-crewed Captains of His Majesty's ships, who more than a little envied the way the East India Company creamed off all the best men.

Apart from Ernest Harper only one of the original passengers remained on board. Warrington-Smythe had decided that the post of writer held little excitement and, having bought a commission in the Marines, was now a Sub-Lieutenant and subordinate only to Lieutenant Gascoyne. Martha rebelliously left the ship at Surat, where Harper arranged for her to sail home on a London bound ship. A decision brought about by rumours of war with France and also of further bad news of trouble between Dutch and English settlements, long established rivalries that frequently erupted into bloody violence. They had all been sad to see Martha leave. Bidding goodbye to the officers and, lingering reflectively with the midshipmen. 'You four have helped to make shipboard life most attractive,' glancing at McFie as she added, 'and amusing.' She was especially charming that day and they saluted her departure with regret. 'Look out for yourselves.' Her farewell remark sounded very wistful as she prepared to disembark.

'No point in taking unnecessary risk,' said Probus as the longboat sped shoreward.

'I know we must be realistic,' replied Harper,

'but I worry about her sailing such a vast distance on another ship.'

'She'll be in a strong convoy and soon safely home.' Though speaking in reassuring tone, Probus was relieved to be rid of the problems involved with passenger carrying, a situation that could influence decision should trouble threaten.

'Going to be quiet without her.' Reluctant to give up the re-awakened affection they now shared Harper felt very alone and thought business was a poor substitute for happiness.

Having drawn lots for shore leave and Toby choosing the short straw, Queen, McFie and Verber were on the first liberty boat, agog with anticipation. The *Earl* was anchored a long way out in the harbour and as they left the ship they came under the stern of a bluff vessel they recognised as their old adversary *Zeevalk* At this time a boat pulled away loaded with seamen likewise bound for shore leave and the men of the *Earl* leaned more strongly into their stroke when it became apparent that the Dutch crew were determined to forge ahead. Men hitherto sat as passengers knowingly doubled up the oars.

'Looks like the lads are in a hurry, Mr Queen,' said Vinderman at the tiller, 'take the helm while I lend my weight behind an oar.'

The Dutch boat was about ten yards away virtually broadside on, her oarsmen pulling with impressive power. At the helm sat a wide-shouldered man wearing an officer's hat. His cheeks were pock marked and disfigured below deep-set eyes and heavy black eyebrows. Scowling malevolently across he spat tobacco juice into the sea, deliberately and with contempt. The insult brought immediate response . . . the men were in no way going to move over for the Dutch crew whose truculent manner reflected animosity. The longboat surged forward, a burst of activity matched by the Dutch: and the race was on! Bow waves creaming white with the increase in speed. McFie calling a long, powerful stroke, as if he were Cox of a rowing eight on some quiet Berkshire river and the oar blades bit deep and sure into the calm water of Malacca harbour. They had a start that was used to good effect and, try their best; the Dutchmen could not close the gap. The packed waterway didn't often see boats at this kind of pace and a sampan sculled hurriedly out of the way of the speeding longboats and a frail looking fist brandished with outrage.

'Up oars!' Landing stage coming up fast and Queen had to shout down the excited McFie. Helming alongside. Oars raised high. McFie and Verber jumped ashore on to the platform with bow and stern warps, braced against the surge and the longboat nudged to a standstill. The Dutch boat came in immediately behind to an accompaniment of goading catcalls and both crews spilled out with menacing posture and appeared set for a repeat of the Table Bay hand-to-hand scrap. Facing his men Queen said firmly, 'Move on, lads.'

Wary but triumphant seamen moving off, the Dutch also kept under restraint by a young officer who held his men in check while the English crew cleared the jetty, then led them away while the longboat prepared to return to the ship and Queen breathed a sigh of relief, thinking they could so easily have had another fight on their hands. A spirt of moisture came at his feet, and he glared in outrage at the dirty brown patch of spittle and tobacco juice on his highly polished shoe. Eyes flicking up to the grinning face of the big Dutch officer whose teeth showed black with tobacco stain. From close up he was even more monstrous. Stocky and wide with a flat stomach and legs so thick they bulged through his trousers. His hands were huge, covered with black hair and hung ominous and threatening at his side. A broken nose matted with blue veins dominated his face. A scar ran across his right cheek down to almost to his neck and his offensive posture seemed a deliberate invitation to retaliate.

Uncertain, but not about to back down, Queen angrily wiped his shoe against a coiled rope then moved to confrontation only to find Verber barring his way.

'Captain won't thank you for inviting trouble, Jase. Let it go! He's looking for trouble and the best thing to do is ignore him.' Verber spoke in concerned tone and not without cause, the opposing oarsmen were in a state of anticipation, needing little excuse for another tilt at each other.

'You're right, Abraham.' Turning to walk away, followed by a snort of derision from the Dutch officer and his offensive attempt at ridicule brought a backward glance from McFie.

'Don't think we've seen the last of that ugly brute,' he said.

'Forget him, Billie. We're only out to enjoy ourselves.'

Tension over, the two liberty boats pulled away, and Vinderman relaxed from behind the seclusion of a mound of fishing gear.

Wandering through the teeming waterfront the midshipmen were soon in a crowded, open bazaar. Flies swarmed, the narrow thoroughfare stank of uncleared sewage and the smell forced a grimace from McFie. 'Beginning to wish I'd stayed aboard.'

They had money to spend. An advance on their pay in Spanish Silver Rials, the recognised currency in this multi-national area, and Verber was soon engrossed in the market place. Interested in a lovely, carved figure of ivory he bartered animatedly for a long time before shaking his head and walking away only to be brought back by the nodding trader while Queen and McFie looked on with admiration. Verber couldn't speak Malay but his language of negotiation seemed fluent and he obviously had no intention of being overcharged.

After completing the purchase he looked at them. 'You could buy and sell anything here,' he said excitedly.

'Thought you came to sea to escape from such things as trading in the marketplace?' queried McFie.

'Instinct dies hard,' said Verber with a sheepish grin.

With Maggie on his mind, Queen decided on a figure of jade and again Verber took over. Finally settling for a price almost half the original asking. The native trader was a slant-eyed Chinaman of indeterminate age who appeared to view him with respect and obviously enjoyed the bargaining. Joining in the fun, McFie chose a similar piece of jade and Verber again negotiated on his behalf and as they walked away with their purchases the face of the trader was all smiles as he bade them a bowing farewell.

'He didn't make much profit out of you, Abraham,' commented McFie.

'Don't delude yourself, that wily old Chinaman would never have made the sale otherwise, but whatever his profit, I know these trinkets will be worth a hell of a lot more in London.' Well pleased with his performance Verber added with a smile. 'My father's eyes would pop clean out of his head if he could see the treasures on open display in this market place.'

'Reckon you're just a street trader at heart,' said Queen.

'Comes in handy sometimes,' said McFie.

Engrossed, and enjoying their first real leisure time ashore in a foreign port, especially one that seemed to host all the blends of Asiatic and Oriental mystery. Malacca had formerly been a Portuguese outpost and the association with China and Macao was evident in the Oriental influence of buildings and of market traders and in the dress of the native population. Time sped without realising and they now found themselves in a quieter thoroughfare with Oriental eating houses situated either side from which penetrated an appetising smell. Feeling hungry, and adventurous, they had a brief conversation outside one of these, then they pushed through a curtain of latticed bark into a strange and shaded dining room fitted out with low tables and delicately painted tableware. A bowing Chinaman met them and, displaying no curiosity at their entry, ushered them to a table adjacent to the window, one of the few tables with seats. Ho Chin had seen many seafaring races. He had no allegiance except trade: and money. Placing a tiny cup of rice wine and an earthenware bowl of water before each he then sidled away. Taking a hearty sip, they reached simultaneously for the water. They were formally dressed and though the interior was cool, the steam heat of Malacca lingered on in their heavy clothing and the fiery wine helped to bring beads of perspiration to their foreheads. It was early evening. The few customers in the place were sitting on the floor cross-legged and in strange postures and looking astounded at the entry of foreigners and were more interested in them than what was on their tables.

Three dainty Chinese maids approaching, faces powdered white, at once mysterious and appealing. Small and willowy, long silken gowns tight around the waist and upper body then flowing to ankle length. The maidens wore open-toed wooden shoes and walked with tiny, mincing steps, and they moved in this stilted manner because their feet were bound in strange fashion. Each held a carved board, which they presented before the midshipmen. The one attending Queen bowed low with her lower face covered in her hands. Her eyes were clear and almond shaped and her demeanour portrayed shyness, and subservience. She was delightful and an exotic eastern fragrance hovered around the very impressionable young man. Taking a suspect look at a board lined with rows of lacquered Chinese symbols, McFie asked, 'What do you reckon, Jase?'

'Wish I knew.' Running a finger round the collar of his coat and his discomfort was rewarded with immediate assistance. Her hands dropped away from her face to reveal soft cheeks and a sculptured neck, then he felt them light on his shoulders as the jacket smoothed from him with practised ease and dexterity. Yielding to her gentle touch he smiled appreciatively but her eyes remained inscrutable, as if waiting for instructions.

'She soon got the measure of you,' grinned McFie. Beginning to remove his jacket, and his attendant maid slid it from him and Verber looked shyly at the girl by his side and his jacket joined the others on a wall hanger. More comfortable in their white shirts they sat mute wondering what to do. 'We'd better order something,' said McFie, studying the menu board. 'All Chinese to me.'

Offering his board, Queen pointed hesitantly to a line of figures. Her eyes flashed in alarm. Hurriedly moving his finger down the menu. Shaking her head in negation, but her face was beginning to show definite signs of merriment. He gave up in despair but she pointed to the bottom line and smiled for the first time, showing even, white teeth in the scarlet painted bow of her mouth. The other maids responded likewise to help with the ordering but McFie insisted on choosing his own supper and the maid looked at him, incredulous, and her eyebrows arched in wonder. Then after a few whispered words together the serving maids minced away. 'What the hell did you order, Billie?' asked Verber in admiring tone.

'No idea, and I don't care as long as there's plenty of it.'

* * *

The food arrived with surprising speed, Queen and Verber with identical dishes, consisting of several porcelain bowls. Piping hot rice in differing colours. Curving pink prawns and tiny shrimp with appetising pieces of meat that looked like chicken nestling on a bed of tender bean shoots.

McFie's meal came on a separate trolley. Three tiers hosting bowls of rice, gristly looking fish that resembled octopus, a whole chicken cut into quarters: and glistening with oil. Dish of green beans with huge whole prawns draped over the side. The bottom tier displayed a variety of strange fruits including a whole pineapple and dish of white balls that looked like small onions: and a great hand of bananas. He couldn't believe this? But with impassive face the Chinese maid straightaway commenced to place dishes on the table. Then she laid a slender, cloth wrapped bundle before him and unrolled the spotless lace to expose a pair of chopsticks.

'Now you're in trouble.' Queen couldn't restrain himself and laughter rang infectiously. Verber's dark face was a picture of delighted humour and the maids looked distinctly happy.

Unperturbed, McFie beckoned to her. As she came close, his arm crept around the fragile waist causing merriment to subside in quick alarm. But, looking deep into her eyes, he said, 'O' my lovely China girl,' incredible tenderness in his voice and her alarm vanished as quickly as it had begun and she looked at him with interrogation apparent and doing all in her power to understand this foreign young man with the happy face. The cleft in his chin opened out as he smiled. 'Unless you want to keep me here all night,' he whispered in her ear, 'you had better find me a fork or something,' making a spooning gesture at the pile of dishes. Her face registered comprehension and no small amusement then she moved away to return with a wooden spoon, long and delicately carved with a fine curving end, Billie thought it looked like the back scratcher his father was always wielding up and down his spine. She appeared fascinated with McFie and stood close as if she was enjoying him. He closed one eye in an exaggerated wink. 'Think I'll take this one back on board, just to see the look on Old Gaywood's face.' Attacking his food with vigour, and with conceit as he observed the problems the other two were having with the chopsticks.

'Not too difficult when you get the hang of it,' said Queen. His chopsticks collapsed as he said this and the food fell back in the dish.

Spooning away, McFie said through a mouthful, 'Fancy a chicken leg, either of you?'

Queen's hand was taken and gently fastened around the chopsticks in an instructive manner. Verber was receiving similar treatment. 'Might be unusual and damn difficult to eat,' he said, 'but it tastes good and I'm certainly enjoying the chopstick lesson?'

McFie's maid seemed determined that he

should eat everything on the trolley and as fast as one dish emptied she would replace it with another, and another, until he sat back with a gasp and waved his hands in defeat. She bowed in compliance and with a mixture of awe and respect at the mighty appetite of McFie.

'Reckon you've just eaten a meal that a large family might order,' said Verber. He and Queen had long finished and were again sipping rice wine, albeit with care.

'Wouldn't care to eat this stuff at sea,' replied McFie as he reached for water, 'because it would soon be back over the side.' Embracing his serving maid again. 'What's the next course, darling?' Beginning to understand the antics of this circus clown she coyly offered the menu board but, ignoring the laughter of his friends McFie took her hand, opened the tiny fingers and placed in her palm the figure of jade he had bought for his sister.

Eyes flashing, mouth momentarily gaping in amazement, and pleasure, she clasped the figure to her breast, bowed her head and stooped to kneel before him. He immediately brought her to her feet and her lovely, dark and oval eyes rose to him in wonderment. 'O' my little one,' he said very softly, 'would that we had met at a more leisurely moment?' Completely enchanted with her he was in full emotional flight now and the other two were looking at him incredulously. This was a side to Billie that they had never seen, or even imagined yet they had no choice but to follow his example.

'Here goes a month's pay,' said Verber as he brought out the carved piece of ivory.

'And Maggie's present.' Queen presented his maid with the jade figure.

The composure of the Chinese maids was completely shattered by the gallantry of the midshipmen. They stood confused and appeared close to tears as the three prepared to leave. Queen looked enquiringly at the attentive proprietor who shook his head in a negation that stated clearly he would not be presenting his bill. As the maidens formed in line by the entrance-way, McFie looked deep into her face before moving on but the proprietor stayed their departure with his hand upraised, and they exchanged a glance of speculation.

'He wants us to wait here,' said Verber.

'Perhaps he's going to make us a present of the maids?' said McFie hopefully.

Soon returning, the proprietor led the way out. Dusk had fallen and the air struck cool after the daytime heat. A youth waited outside, skinny thin and dressed in ragged clothing and, after a few words with him, the proprietor hurried back inside to his clientele. After which the youth said, 'I am Ramon Salvador.' Apprehensive. His English near perfect yet with a strong native accent. He had the appearance of a half-caste European and his manner was most courteous as he explained. 'Ho Chin felt you may wish for a respectable guide to initiate you to night time Malacca.' Sensing bewilderment, he hurriedly went on with. 'Ho Chin had a respect for you and feared for your safety in the dark alleyways.'

'Mr Ho Chin seems very hospitable,' mused Verber, 'even to the extent of not accepting payment for the meal.'

'He has not met with your like before: and your generosity to his daughters far exceeded his normal charges.'

'Daughters,' expostulated Verber, 'and McFie was making love to one of them before his very eyes!'

'Consider yourselves fortunate in your choice of eating house, Chinese women are not normally allowed the freedom which Europeans take for granted, but Ho Chin, not being blessed with a son, allows his daughters to be seen in public,' he then added, 'and work for nothing in his establishment.'

'The maid seemed to enjoy Billie's unsubtle romancing all the same,' said Queen. Turning attention to Salvador. 'We have but two hours until we return aboard.'

'I can show you respectable taverns. I also know of many young girls who would be pleased to entertain you.'

Grinning at this, McFie said, 'For my part, a quiet drink in a native hostelry would round off the evening very nicely.'

'How about you, Abraham?' said Queen.

'As long as we keep him away from painted Chinese girls.' Ignoring McFie's derisive look Verber added scornfully. 'How my father would scoff: negotiating a good bargain only to give it away to a girl I'll never see again.' He then threatened. 'Better if we leave you on board next time.'

'Won't have as much fun on your own,' returned McFie, unabashed. 'Let's get on. Time's wasting!'

Salvador in the lead, a pathetic sight, his feet were bare and dirty, his legs like drumsticks below cotton shorts. Intrigued with the dusky skinned Ramon, their rapid interrogation revealed that he was the son of a Portugese seaman and a Malay woman.

'Doesn't explain your knowledge of our language?' said McFie.

Ramon then told how his father had worked for an English shipping company at Penang and how, from an early age, Ramon had mixed mainly with English children. Then after being turned out to fend for himself he had drifted to Malacca and now scraped a living as guide and sometimes interpreter. He modestly admitted a command of three languages. Fluent Malay, workable English, and limited Chinese.

'And it takes McFie all his time to speak English.' Verber dodged a swipe from Billie.

Not wishing to get too far removed from the waterfront Queen halted the procession. 'Can you show us a tavern nearer to the harbour?' he asked Salvador.

'Waterfront bars are not quiet or respectable.' He then said with a shrug. 'I know of one reserved for officers and their – er – ladies.'

'Can always leave if we don't like the place,' said Verber.

Situated in a commanding position overlooking the harbour the bar was a shanty-like establishment with a rambling porch along its front elevation. Dimly lit and furnished with bamboo chairs and tables the place was busy with a fairly even mixture of men and women of varying races. Ordering a measure of rice wine, they sat on stools at one end of the bar. Ramon Salvador had refused their offer of money insisting that he would first guide them back to the landing stage. He seemed genuine and they commented on this as they relaxed and began to enjoy the atmosphere of Asiatic conviviality.

'See who is over there, Jase?' suddenly said McFie.

'Saw him when we first came in. How could you fail to notice such an ugly brute?'

The tobacco chewing Dutchman and the young officer from the longboat sat at a corner table with two coffee-coloured women, brash and big bodied, and noticing the leer of anticipation appearing, McFie said, 'Think we'd better drink up and make our way back.'

'We will, but not in undue haste.'

'Doubt him trying anything in here,' said Verber in hopeful tone.

Joining in conversation, reflecting upon the Chinese maidens and in particular about McFie's performance and the size of his meal and their amusement was watched with increasing malice by the big Dutchman. Suspecting their laughter was directed at him he shook off the restraining hand of his woman companion and lurched across to the bar. But she came with him hanging determinedly on to his arm and he thrust her from him, causing her to stumble.

'Jan,' she implored. Heavy breasted and cumbersome she came to him again only to be pushed roughly away and she fell to a sitting position then, face flaming, she scrambled up and pursued him all the way to the bar.

'He's looking for trouble,' said Verber.

'Think he's found it, with his lady friend.'

Catching up again she tugged on his arm. Annoyed at this, a hard hand cracked forcibly across her cheek knocking her down and she lay sprawled out and sobbing. This unnecessary and brutal strike brought no response from the interested spectators, as if it was normal occurrence, yet Queen left his seat and went to her but she shook him away, uncooperative. Verber came to help and together they managed to bring her upright, while the malevolent eyes of the Dutchman followed every move.

'Look out, Jase!' said McFie urgently.

Swaggering towards them, shoving Verber aside without ceremony, the brute thrust a fist into Queen's shoulder. 'Always you are in my way, Englishman.' Deliberately forcing him back again and anger flared into retaliation and his fists beat an immediate and bloody tattoo across the pock marked face, spreading his nose into a gory mess and sending him reeling against the bar. Queen went straight in after him but found himself suddenly immobile in a vicelike grip, struggling but powerless in the grasp of a huge Chinaman. A second Chinese, heavy as the first, stood in the way as the Dutchman recoiled off the bar to spring at Queen and, growling in frustration, swung a punch at the Chinaman who blocked the swing then moved in with the craft of a professional wrestler and gripped him round the waist, lifted him with ease and wrestled him to the doorway then deftly reversing his hold, one hand gripping his cursing captive by the scruff of his neck and the other on the seat of his trousers, sent him sailing through the swing doors and all heard the shout of obscenity as the Dutchman hit the dirt outside and the wrestler remained on, impassive and huge in the doorway and barring entrance like some gladiator of ancient Rome.

Holding Queen in a bear hug the other seemed to be anticipating violent reaction but Queen gestured compliance and the Chinaman smiled in friendly manner. Releasing his hold and Queen straightened his clothing with some attempt at dignity. A futile effort that brought relaxed comment from McFie. 'Thought for a moment you were about to follow your friend Jan.'

Lingering, looking around the room, the wrestlers appeared to be warning everyone that further trouble would be severely dealt with. Then the young Dutch officer came cautiously across to them. 'I must regret the behaviour of our First Mate,' he said in halting English. Looking at Queen, he then warned. 'Suggest you look over your shoulder and keep away from dark streets on your way back, for Jan Hallmeyer does not forget an affront,' frowning as he added, 'ever!'

'Your Mr Hallmeyer lacks any instinct of decency,' snapped Queen.

The young officer seemed in agreement. 'Hallmeyer is a man of two vastly different faces. At sea he is the finest officer afloat. Hard, even cruel at times, but he never asks his crew to do something he cannot do himself: and better. Then woe betide anyone who does a sloppy job.' Pausing, before continuing in hard tone. 'On shore the other side of Jan Hallmeyer is portrayed as a drunken, licentious beast.' Looking at the two women as he concluded. 'And the strange thing is how he always finds someone who clings to his every word.'

'Even if they have to be knocked about?'

'Was he to come in here tomorrow she would

be all over him just like tonight,' confirmed the officer, 'I have to form the conclusion that there are many women who, in perverse manner, enjoy the sheer physical power of a man like Hallmeyer? I warn you again, beware! He has strong hatred of Englishmen, especially clean looking young officers. Possibly because of his own somewhat repellent appearance.'

'Not exactly a knight in shining armour,' said McFie with a grin. 'Watch out, Jase, he's got a thing about you. Perhaps he fancies the idea of smashing up your face the more to resemble his own.'

'Such is the way his mind works. But please do not think we all feel this way. Many of my countrymen, including myself, regret the hostility that flares between our two countries. We have much in common, your people and mine and it seems a great pity that strong emotions have to be aroused whenever we meet. At sea,' spreading his hands expressively, 'or ashore.'

His courteous manner brought similar response from Queen. 'Will you accompany us back to the harbour,' he suggested, 'perhaps if we are seen in friendly company together our respective crews may realise that such things are possible?'

'That time will surely come.' The Dutch Officer's eyes were deep blue and steady on Queen's face and he appeared to appreciate the sentiment. 'But I cannot allow myself to become involved in a situation that might be misinterpreted. Anyway, I have made plans to stay ashore tonight. We are not sailing for a few days and I intend to make the most of the opportunity.' Offering his hand in farewell gesture. 'Perhaps some other time we will meet as friends, not enemies.'

No sign of Ramon Salvador outside and his non-appearance brought conjecture. He owed them no allegiance but the integrity of his bearing seemed peculiarly at odds with the thought of him deserting his self-proffered job as guide.

'Maybe he couldn't wait,' said McFie.'

'Strange though,' said Queen.

'All we have to do is keep the water on our left hand,' suggested Verber, 'and we must eventually reach the landing stage.'

Setting off at a fast walk. Following the water's edge wasn't easy, for there was a maze of dark passages between the shanty-like shacks that lined the foreshore. Gloomy night, shadow of the dark alleyways making for poor visibility but they made steady progress and the buildings began to open out to form a wider thoroughfare with dirt strewn and smelly byways branching off at varying angles.

Before one of these they came to a sudden halt as out of the shadows appeared the bulky shape of Hallmeyer propelling before him their guide Ramon, while from behind converging the menacing figures of six Dutch seamen. Thrusting

Ramon's arms up behind his back with brute force, Hallmeyer sneered, 'We meet again, Englishmen.'

The intentions of Hallmeyer and his men were obvious and the three midshipmen closed ranks. 'You're a hell of a man with women and boys, Hallmeyer!' The words were hard on Queen's mouth and he took a crouching pace forward, a move greeted with contempt and, after a final jerk at Ramon's arms, Hallmeyer threw him down at their feet. He appeared in great pain and had difficulty in getting up but McFie supported him with a stout arm.

'I am truly sorry,' groaned Ramon, 'he took me from outside the tavern when I said that I was waiting for you.' Casting a frightened look at the menacing bunch of seamen he ran off in panic into the darkness.

'Englishmen and their associates are all fools and cowards,' said Hallmeyer in goading voice. 'Will you also run away?'

'Only seven of you against the three of us.' Deceptively quiet statement from McFie. 'The odds are in our favour, Dutchman.'

Shoulder to shoulder, the narrow roadway so confining it allowed some advantage because the bunching seamen had no room to come at them all together. Then Hallmeyer led them in a sudden rush and the three met them with fists and heads and feet, anything with which they could make contact. One reeled away from the force of

McFie's head in his face, Verber pumping fists at the man attacking him, Queen and Hallmeyer immediately locked in battle.

Aware that the Dutchman could overpower him from close range he was trying to keep his distance, crashing a fist through the crude guard into the already damaged face. Hallmeyer growling in anger as blood began to pour from his broken nose. Reaching for Queen, who kicked him hard on the kneecap. Queen had learned much from Vinderman, but Hallmeyer just spat and came in again. The seamen were crowding them now and driving them back. Verber staggered and nearly fell but recovered fast and flung at his assailant with fists flailing. Abraham was not a fighting man, neither was he afraid but the seaman met him with outstretched arms, folded him in a bear hug and began to squeeze the breath from his body. McFie had two against him and was in real trouble. A clubbing strike drove him down on one knee and brought the two of them eagerly in for the kill and Queen had to turn from Hallmeyer to swing punches at one of McFie's opponents, fierce enough to allow McFie to gain his feet and roar back at the other but, seizing his chance, Hallmeyer grabbed Queen round the neck with hard hands and thumbs digging into the windpipe. Queen belted him in the stomach with little effect, for the pressure on his throat merely increased. He began to sag as Hallmeyer squeezed the life from him. Suddenly McFie was hanging round Hallmeyer's neck with fingers gouging into the eyes and oblivious to the punishment he was taking from a pursuing opponent. Releasing his hold Hallmeyer grabbed for the fingers tearing at his eyes and Queen choked for breath and struck viciously at Hallmeyer, splitting his cheek just below the eye. Hallmeyer's knee pumped, just missing the groin but catching him on the inner thigh. There was no pain, just this consuming mist of raging fire and all he could see was the blood streaked face of Jan Hallmeyer floating before him. Verber was down with a brutal Dutchman kicking into him. McFie fighting mad but being driven back by two more but such was the conflict between Queen and Hallmeyer that they were left to battle alone as if the others realised they had no place in this bitter enmity.

Alley resounding with a rush of feet, Ramon Salvador had returned with English sailors and the accompanying crunch of fists hammering on flesh was sickening, Vinderman's voice cutting coldly through the dark:

'Let's see how you Dutch bastard's shape up against men!'

Bulk of Jacko Abbott looming beside him. Lifting a man from the prostrate Verber, Abbott flung him bodily across the alley into a wooden shack with such brute force that his head smashed through the boarding with his body hanging outside. Then, as Vinderman reached for Hallmeyer,

'Keep out of this!' Growling, authoritative command that stopped Vinderman in his tracks. Casting an astounded glance that quickly assessed the situation he held out his arms to keep the supportive English at bay.

Hallmeyer stood alone, all his men were down and he was surrounded by adversaries, he showed only defiance, and Queen's refusal of support brought renewed confidence. Eyes locked, loathing flared and they hurled themselves once more into brutal conflict. Hallmeyer was solidly built and much heavier but Queen was faster and his shoulders spread wide and his powerful arms gave much longer reach and he met Hallmeyer in mid-surge with a two-handed attack that drove him back on his heels. Hallmeyer kicked out suddenly with a sharp pointed clog but Queen caught the foot with instant reflex and threw him down and wrenched off the clog and dived straight in to take advantage but the tough Dutchmen came up head first into him and they went down together in a heap. Rolling over and first up he belted Hallmeyer with a two-handed blow on the back of his neck as he tried to rise.

'Get up!' Standing over him as the words rasped from his bruised throat.

English seamen in awed silence. This fight had become too personal and desperate for interference or even audible support. Rising to one knee, Hallmeyer lunged powerfully but Queen sidestepped and smashed his fists again into his neck as the forward surge carried his man forward. Hallmeyer hit the dirt and came up fast but Queen belted him a right hand smack on the chin and Hallmeyer's head went back and his eyes rolled but Queen kneed him in the stomach and, as he jack-knifed, grabbed him by the shirt front and drove his fist again and again into the gaping mouth, yet Hallmeyer stayed on his feet though his legs were like rubber under him.

Blood lust pounding in his veins! Eyes like pits of hellfire. Kill the bastard! His opponent could offer no defence but this knowledge only brought only elation and renewed and brutal power and he pumped iron hard fists into his stomach. Hallmeyer began to crumple but Queen still blasted clubbing fists into his enemy and as he slumped to the ground Queen snatched up the discarded clog and flung himself on Hallmeyer and with lethal force hammered the clog across the head of his helpless assailant . . . and again! Hallmeyer's face streamed blood but Queen had lost all control and raised the clog for another pulping strike only to have his hand held by Vinderman who had moved at speed to counter this last deadly onslaught and with the aid of Jacko Abbott he dragged the demented midshipman away from Hallmeyer. The English seamen were beginning to find voice but very subdued and eyeing their young officer with the respect of hard men for violence unleashed: and terrible.

'It's over! You maniac bastard! It's over!' Vinderman had to slap him in an effort to restore sanity but the stinging blows served only to incite Queen further and he wrestled clear and dived again for Hallmeyer but found his way blocked by McFie who screamed into his face:

'Enough, Jase! You've bloody near killed him already!'

The familiar voice penetrated and forced awareness. Clinging to McFie. Exhausted. 'What happened?' The words were a mere croak.

'Ramon went for help and a good job too.' Surveying the inert Hallmeyer as he added, 'That evil sod was hell bent on finishing you and with the help of his crewmen would probably have done for all of us.'

Gingerly massaging his throat. 'Knew it was either him or me.'

'Don't think he ever imagined it would be him. Bloody hell, Jase! You're some kind of bleedin' wild animal when you get steamed up!'

McFie's poor attempt at humour broke through and brought a glimmer of a smile. 'How's Abraham?' asked Queen.

'Somewhat the worse for wear,' replied Vinderman, 'but no lasting damage.' Turning to the crew, he said. 'Come on, lads, liberty boats are waiting and we've an early tide to catch.'

'How about this lot?' Abbott didn't sound the least bit concerned,

'Leave 'em,' said Vinderman.

* * *

Ramon Salvador's disconsolate stance by the landing stage brought concerned comment from McFie. 'Hallmeyer and the whole crew of *Zeevalk* will be looking for him, Jase.'

'He'd better come with us,' far from confident as he added, 'no doubt Captain Probus will have something to say but we'll worry about that tomorrow.'

'Not again, McFie!'

Next morning, crew lined up ready for departure. The Captain glaring at the ravaged faces of his midshipmen and in particular at McFie's black and swollen right eye. Probus was noted for his early morning lack of humour, and irritation brought a biting edge to his words as he thundered. 'Just what is it about you midshipmen that continually attracts trouble and violence? This I promise,' he said determinedly, 'never again will you three be allowed shore leave together.' Turning his wrath on Salvador. 'And tell me who the hell are you,' he growled, 'before I have you thrown overboard?'

'Ramon Salvador, sir,' hastily returned Queen, 'we thought you might approve of having someone aboard who can speak fluent Malay.'

Probus seemed about to explode but Ernest Harper intervened to speak quietly to him, after which Probus conceded, 'Mr Harper approves of your idea.' Glowering at Salvador he commanded.

'In the meantime you serve as assistant cabin steward. We carry no passengers! Understood?'

'Yes. Thank you, sir,' replied Ramon in near perfect English.

'Mr Queen,' said the Captain, 'may we now have your permission to take the ship to sea?'

Chapter Seventeen

Throughout the Great Circle routes there are waterways and channels that are the recognised passages to adjacent seas. Such a gateway is the Strait of Malacca between the peninsular of Malaya and the sprawling landmass of Sumatra, and the East Indiamen used the seaway on their route to Indonesia and the South China Sea. Because of the frequent use of these waterways it was also logical that an unscrupulous ship's master, whether buccaneer or interloper, could lie in wait knowing that a ship laden with treasures of eastern trade would eventually sail within reach of his greedy hands.

The early East Indiamen were aware of this threat and whenever possible contrived to sail in convoy. Unless they had the misfortune to be engaged by a hostile foreign fleet, these convoys were too formidable a force for the average pirate. The Company made urgent pleas to the Royal Navy for such convoys to be shepherded to ensure that valuable cargoes reached homeports safely. But distances were vast and the Navy ships' scattered over a wide area of ocean and they couldn't reasonably expect that every ship trading in the Far East should be given the safe escort of His Majesty's Navy. So it was a very thoughtful Probus who watched the convoy go from sight as the fleet turned easterly through the Straits leaving the *Earl* to plough her solitary way south.

The purpose of Ernest Harper, after leaving Malacca, was to take the ship along the Indonesian Islands to trade for spices and any goods that could be turned into profit. The other ships in the convoy would proceed to China where they were to trade their cargo, mainly of Indian opium, for fine silks and the leaf tea that was fast becoming a popular beverage back home.

The Dutch East India Company was strongly entrenched in Indonesia and regarded its trading rights very jealously. However, some ground had been established by earlier venturers and the Union Jack had flown in quite a few anchorages of this chain of Islands that stretch from Malaya to New Guinea, and which were known by the fragrant name of the "Spice Islands", the very spices so sought after in the cities of Europe for use in cooking and in the preparing of exotic drinks. Their value to the Western world can perhaps be judged better in terms of finance, for an expedition that had left London in the year c1607 brought back as part of their inventory a cargo of cloves that had been purchased for £2,948.15s and yet realised the sum of £36,287 on their return to London.

The immediate destination was the village of Semarund on the Island of Java where a settlement of sorts had been established some time previously for the purpose of assembling cargoes of pepper and other spices in readiness for the merchant ships, and in this way to release Masters and Merchants from the long task of bartering and collecting a profitable cargo. A time-consuming business for an impatient Master and one that could put him in danger of losing some of his crew, both to fever and more worldly pleasures ashore. The Indonesian natives were an easy and fun loving race with the young women particularly attractive to men long devoid of such delightful company.

Anchoring in eight fathoms of crystal clear water. Beautiful, sheltered bay surrounded on three sides by the first wooded slopes of the mountains that dominated the high ground. Some of the peaks were volcanic and hidden almost continually by layers of cloud lying like soft crowns on the heads of the mountain range. The trees were lush and the greenery swept down to a curving beach of silver sand on to which washed and pounded the relentless surf. Getting a long-boat ashore and off again was a wet and exhilarating task.

A swarm of outrigger canoes propelled by lusty, brown oarsmen surrounded the ship, as she lay quiet to her anchor. Natives piling aboard, voluble and welcoming and grasping for the gifts laid out for their benefit. Ramon Salvador proving his worth as interpreter.

The landing party consisted of Mr Harper, First Officer Sethman, Surgeon Marcus Quennel, midshipmen Queen and Verber together with Lieutenant Gascoyne and six of his marines . . . and Ramon Salvador. Sand grated under the keel as the longboat grounded and was pulled up the beach by a horde of near naked, brown skinned and happy natives.

Sethman formed his party into two lines with himself and Mr Harper at the head and two sailors bringing up the rear with the heavy chest of trade goods on their shoulders. They were immediately surrounded by a flower-bedecked crowd of young women who adorned them with fragrant garlands before leading them along a wide, well-trodden path leading from the beach and up the steep side of the lagoon and through dense woodland where wild flowers blossomed in colours of incredible hue and the air was fragrant with exotic scents. Keenly observant throughout, Sethman said to Harper, 'No sign of the men who were supposed to set up shop here.'

The appearance of Mr Harper had transformed dramatically since his reconciliation with Martha.

He was dressed almost casually in a cotton shirt and white drainpipe trousers, his face had lost its pinched, mean look and glowed with healthy colour, and most significantly, he now had a good relationship with Captain Probus and worked comfortably with him in the conducting of the ship's business. The steep pathway took painful toll of legs unused to such exercise and Harper was breathing hard. 'They have been here more than two years without relief,' he said, 'perhaps they've gone native?'

'Not so much that they could resist the sight of an English ship in the lagoon.' The thought disconcerted for a moment, then Sethman added, 'Though the natives seem friendly.'

'Maybe, but I'm thankful that Gascoyne and his marines are with us?'

Natives falling back, a bare earth clearing opening out before them to reveal a circle of bamboo dwellings with palm thatched roofs. A low construction at the far end was substantially larger than the others and leading to which was a curious arrangement of grotesquely carved totem poles forming a lengthy entranceway and at the termination of this stood an authoritative figure. Obviously the Chief he was elderly, with snowy white hair and clad in a colourful knee length sarong. Several others similarly dressed were grouped behind.

Procession coming to a halt, silence falling with the crowd of natives forming a half-circle just behind the shore party. The white-haired Chief advanced a few paces, movements agile and denying the look of age. Raising his hand in peaceful gesture, he said, 'Welcome.'

His manner was courteous and somehow expectant and Harper responded in similar tone. 'I bring gifts and greetings from His Gracious Majesty King George.' At the sound of the Royal title the Chief smiled, displaying even but dark stained teeth. Grasping Harper's outstretched hand he propelled him towards the long dwelling, beckoning to his companions who closed in behind the Lieutenant and the midshipmen and separating them from the wary marines. They were paraded up a short set of steps onto a sweeping porch the floor of which was carpeted in strips of woven bark. It seemed apparent that only the officers were allowed to join the gathering on the porch and the marines were held immobile by a double line of men yet with no hostility in their bearing and Gascoyne ordered his men to stand easy.

Squatting with his elders in an anticipatory semi-circle on the woven bark the Chief beckoned the shore party down. While surprised at the greeting in English, Harper sensed the influence of the Company men who had remained here to trade. As they sat cross-legged on the cool carpet a flurry of women brought to each a half-coconut shell brimming over with a milky liquid and, following the Chief's example they downed it in a single gulp.

Queen heard Verber gasp, the liquid burned in his throat and started a fire in his stomach. Only the surgeon seemed unaffected, glancing into his empty shell with detached interest he fanned his open mouth. 'Make a very good disinfectant,' he said.

The Chief smiled in delight at the response generated by his potent offering. Harper's face was assuming a fiery red and Queen grinned inwardly, wondering what the hard drinking Vinderman would have made of the liquor. There was a soothing taste of coconut left in his mouth and he felt curiously mellow. Now transpired a stilted but interesting conversation. It seemed the Chief and his councillors, as well as members of his family, had learned some English from the group who had come to develop trade and the exchange was understandable with the help of Ramon Salvador who had been brought on the porch along with the chest of gifts. 'Ewin' very good man,' said the Chief, a comment that brought interest, John Ewing was the factor who had been deposited at Semarund..

'Where is Mr Ewing now?' Harper instantly queried.

'Johnewin . . .' pronouncing the two names as one, the Chief said, 'went with the other white men to Batavia.' Apprehensive, voice lowering as he stated. 'Johnewin fight with other white men.'

Sethman looked at Harper. 'His reference to

Batavia and fighting,' he said, 'seems to indicate trouble with the Dutch.'

Harper nodded in pensive agreement. Both East India Companies had many incidents of violence to their discredit.

Ramon came to the fore now, the limited English of the Chief was unable to cope with a lengthy explanation. After a long dialogue he turned to Harper and said, 'Two Dutch ships anchored in the lagoon with the express purpose of eliminating the factory that Mr Ewing had established. They came ashore in force and overwhelmed the English and took them as captives.'

'What happened to the factory building and the goods stored?'

The Chief and Ramon shared a quick exchange. Breaking away, Ramon said, 'The Dutchmen looted everything. Pepper. Spices. All that had been collected. The Chief makes it clear that he has no desire to see his people involved in a trade war and fears that your presence here will only lead to more violence.' He then made an hesitant observation to Harper. 'I think this is just a bargaining counter, he is aware of the rivalry between European traders and I guess he intends to take advantage of this and get the best deal he can: if he allows you to trade at all.'

'Which makes me wonder if our trade gifts are anywhere near impressive enough,' ruminated Harper apprehensively. He had the chest brought forward and immediate expectancy showed on the faces of the Chief and his associates. The contents were lifted out one by one, and presented with due ceremony but, as Harper had feared, they were definitely lacking in imagination and apart from a few pairs of spectacles that were tried on in great amusement the contents of the chest were received with a distinct lack of interest.

Woollen garments. Pewter vessels. Glass toys. Pair of duelling pistols and, by a fortunate piece of foresight by an earlier adventurer, a sack of iron nails. This item at last brought excitement and Harper said to Sethman, 'Perhaps we could find more nails aboard ship . . . maybe a hammer or two? Seems the only thing they have appreciated.'

The goods were spread about the floor and for the most part ignored but Abraham Verber had watched the natives with keen interest during the presentation. 'May I try something, sir?' he said to Mr Harper.

Harper already had reason to appreciate the shrewd instincts of Verber but his eyes remained worried as he gave assent. 'Be careful, Mr Verber.'

Slowly replacing the articles back in the chest, natives shuffling and looking at their Chief, who viewed all things with keen awareness? One by one the gifts were returned until only the spectacles and the nails remained. Verber reached nonchalantly for the bag of nails but the

Chief folded his arms around the sack and gazed without emotion into his face.

'Ramon,' said Verber, 'please explain to the Chief that if he does not care for our gifts we must return them to his Imperial Majesty as being considered unworthy: and that includes the nails.'

After a spirited discourse Ramon said in a very impressed tone, 'If he accepts everything, can he keep the nails?'

'With our deepest pleasure.' No expression on Verber's face, but he turned to the Chief and bowed his head in compliance. The natives broke into lively chatter and following a command from the Chief, carried the chest away into the interior of the dwelling and Harper regarded Verber with a look that held both conjecture and appreciation.

''I'm beginning to realise you are a considerable asset to the Company,' he said, 'and I think it would be advisable if you were to remain ashore here to negotiate on our behalf.'

'The natives are like children when it comes to dealing.' Verber allowed himself a smile and a silent thought . . . if my father could see me now, before advising. 'Shouldn't be too difficult to ascertain what the Dutch offered in payment, and up the price.' Hesitating as Harper frowned at this. 'Only by a little of course, but our business would best be served by not pushing our desire to trade any further at this point. Let the Chief have time to think. He'll be easier to do business with if we allow him to approach us in his own way.' Resisting Harper's eagerness to gain further ground with a pertinent. 'He knows we need to trade but too much urgency on our part will only result in him holding the upper bargaining counter.'

The Chief seemed to have lost all interest in negotiation, and smilingly announced:

'Now we have feast!'

Huge bonfires lit up the beach. Some had been burning all afternoon and in these were placed many smooth stones. As the fire died to glowing embers, an assortment of meats and fish along with bananas and wild roots all wrapped in green leaves were placed between the layers of hot stone. The whole then being covered with earth so that neither smoke nor steam could escape. The feast area spread for some fifty yards with a layer of palm leaves strewn for a carpet.

Longboats ferrying the shore party, foremost were the Captain and his officers, except Mr Gaywood. Beach parties held no attraction for him. He preferred to remain aboard ship where he could reign supreme. The watches had drawn lots, and the disgruntled few sweetened with a tot of rum from the Captain's private stock. So it was most of the ship's company who sat straddle legged along one side with the natives opposite.

Parcels of steaming food . . . unearthed and turned back to reveal perfectly cooked platters of meat, whole fish and prawns and crab and a profusion of roasted bananas. Spiced coconut milk, served in shells was cool and very potent, and the shore party set to with a will. No children were in evidence, and the reason was revealed, as the party got under way.

A group of flower garlanded young girls came in line swaying to a rhythm of resonant drums and hollow bamboo canes. A maiden with flowers in her hair chanted a simple line. The group responded with a chorus and soon they had a background of young women singing and dancing with enchanting grace. They were comely and not a little seductive in their dance and the crew eyed them with lewd appreciation but Probus had given his men a stern lecture before allowing them ashore, knowing well the quickly fired passions of seamen, especially in such surroundings.

The sand was warm under the blanket of leaves. Bonfires smouldering under a velvet sky, crescent moon hanging low and a myriad of stars adding subtle brilliance. Fragrance of a tropical flower garden: music mellow, but with rhythm sensuous enough to set the nerves tingling. Murmur of surf drifting from the reef, and the evening was pure magic!

Across from the officers and midshipmen sat the Chief and his headmen. Then the members of their families, from elderly ladies and proud, muscular men to dark-eyed young women with full, rounded figures.

Nibbling on a huge prawn . . . Queen had already eaten his fill but with the food so appetising it was difficult to resist. The beat of the drums grew more and more lively and the accompanying rhythm of the bamboo increasingly provocative.

'Fancy a whirl, Jase,' said McFie, restraining himself with difficulty.

Looking at the dancing girls swaying about them, Queen was feeling the same way. 'Better hang on, Billie,' he murmured, 'remember what the Captain told us.'

The rhythm changed dramatically, became a vibrant, increasing beat and as if this was a signal the whole crowd of native men rose to form a double line surrounded by the dancing girls. Bamboo sticks beating a frenzied pattern . . . brown legs pumping to the beat. Faster and faster they went, women joining in and the whole native ensemble setting up a musical chant. The dance was sensuous and magnificent and sustained for an incredible length of time. The drums stopped. The native men threw themselves down exhausted but the girls resumed their graceful dance to the rhythm of the bamboo. Four girls approaching the midshipmen, exotic flowers in their hair and legs bare to half way up their thighs. The youths rose in unison, conspicuous in white shirts, ean and eager. Seamen scrambling up as the invitation was extended down the line.

McFie's hips gyrated in a deliberate but vain

attempt to match those of his partner. Teeth flashing in an uncontrollable smile at his clumsy antics she sidled close with soft arms reaching to encircle his neck. His hands found her waist . . . his eyes met Queen's. 'The East India Ball was never like this,' he said with a grin all over his face.

The bamboo kept up its insidious beat and the girls swayed in constant movement and their hips mobile in the extreme. Looking into the dusky face of the maiden who had claimed him, her lips were ruby-red; her eyes shining in the bonfire's glow and Queen caught his breath at her tender beauty. Her eyes moved shyly down and he lifted her head with gentle fingers then took a white flower from the garland round his neck and tucked it into her dark hair. Smiling delightedly she deftly placed a bloom behind his ear and he responded with abandon and whirled her round to the rhythm.

Verber and Bonham-Jones were more than enchanted with their partners who were draped close against them with both hands clasped around the midshipmen's necks in an intimate embrace. Verber was making the most of his opportunity but Toby had difficulty in knowing where to put his hands, finally resting them on the supple and swaying hips of his buxom partner.

Probus, observing all this with growing concern! Harper, conversing with the surgeon discussing the probable ingredients of the coconut liquor that was being served in copious draughts . . . Harper appeared in no discomfort. Alan Sethman, look of longing on his face as he watched the progress of the midshipmen, coming back to earth as Probus nudged him. 'Some of the men will be disappearing into the bush if we're not careful.' Eyeballing Sethman for a moment. 'What the hell are you looking so soulful about?'

'Just watching . . . and wishing the years hadn't slipped away so unnoticed.'

'Control yourself, Alan.' Then, with rare indulgence appearing in his voice. 'Unlike you to be so easily seduced into nostalgia.'

'Must have something to do with the beauty of the night or the rhythm of the drums,' swirling the drink in his coconut shell, Sethman took an appreciative sip, 'or maybe it's this subtle concoction of the Chief's? Either way,' he concluded, 'the mixture surely makes the blood run warm!'

Chapter Eighteen

The ship had sailed, leaving behind a garrison of twelve to rebuild the warehouse and establish a settlement. There were four able seamen and a security force of five marines with a corporal in charge. Reluctant to lose one of his officers Probus ordered Queen and Verber ashore; he wasn't leaving McFie and Queen together? With an abundance of willing labour a long structure was soon erected, with sturdy branches and roof thatch, laid in double layers to keep the interior cool . . . a receiving house, stacked with woven banana leaf sacks full of pungent spices and nostril stinging peppercorns. Life was pleasant and carefree, the natives soon known by name and a happy relationship developing between Javan and English.

The seamen and marines slept and ate in the factory dwelling with a pair of women natives acting as servants and preparing the daily meal, taken in the evening for the heat of the day was not conducive to early appetite. Queen and

Verber were invited into the home of the Chief, whom they soon realised must be addressed as King Wanu. He had two wives and a brood of seven children the eldest of whom, Tuamoto, was about the same age as them and, as heir apparent, was treated with a deference equalled only by that shown to the King. The ages of the children progressed in stages of about eighteen months down to the youngest, a tiny, sloe-eyed girl, four years old and completely captivating. The second oldest was the maiden who had claimed Queen on the night of the feast. Cheeks soft with the bloom of youth, her hair black as night and hanging in luxurious length down her back. She dressed in a gay coloured linen sarong reaching to just above her knees. A shapeless piece of material in itself but which, stretched tight across the hips and upper body, showed to advantage the body shape that was such a becoming feature of the native women. Tuamoto constantly teased her because of her incessant chattering, not that Queen had seen any evidence of this loquaciousness, whenever he or Verber was about the maiden remained mute and shy looking, with her eyes ever hidden under long, dark eyelashes.

King Wanu's two wives appeared to get on well together and ran the household with casual efficiency. The children were much in evidence, laughing and mischievous, and with their hair neatly combed and faces shining with vitality. The King seemed bewildered by it all and was more comfortable when sat with his statesmen sharing a jug of his potent brew.

A strong friendship soon established between the two midshipmen and the King's number one son, who took much pleasure in leading them on frequent expeditions into the mountains, through lush vegetation and up into the high peaks. Sometimes they would halt on a craggy ledge to gaze appreciatively over the Island where waving coconut palms and banana trees spread down to the encircling sea, its turquoise fading to mist in the distance and the rollers creaming onto the silver beaches. These were the moments, though endowed with pleasure, when Queen would think of the *Earl* and wishing he were out there.

'Makes you wonder what the ship is doing at this moment,' said Verber. A comment made often to each other, particularly when they could sit on a point of high vantage and look down on a seascape that seemed to stretch away into eternity.

'Do not be sad, my friends.' Tuamoto's was a simple philosophy. 'Be happy today, the future is too uncertain.' A magnificent figure, clad only in strip of batik cloth around his loins his arms were powerful, and rippling muscle was the only flesh seen on the column of his stomach. Of medium height he was about half a head shorter than Queen yet this seemed insignificant when compared with his vitality and athletic ability. His hair was the colour of ebony and his eyes were darkest brown under equally dark eyebrows that lifted expressively when he was speaking. He had a smile that was completely infectious and could banish any sign of gloom, and his compelling good looks together with his prominence as heir apparent, caused him to be much pursued by the young women of the village, a situation he accepted as one to which he was entitled: and that he exploited to personal advantage.

They never brought food on these trips, he could always provide. On every side were forests of banana trees some of which were twenty feet high and laden with fruit. The native Prince would usually follow the track of a mountain stream, leading through a steep-sided ravine where the silence was broken only by the urgent splash of water over countless waterfalls. This is when they would sleep out at night and where they became pupils of Tuamoto. He showed them how to cut strips of vine to splice into a rope. Bamboo stems for rafters and the leaf of the banana tree for a thatch and within a short time they could construct a shelter for the night with sun-dried leaves to make the softest of beds. He would locate a piece of peculiarly white wood and by briskly rubbing a blunt-pointed stick into a groove made in a similar piece until the friction ignited dust caused by the chafing, would then carefully blow this into flame and fire. The stream yielded eels and crayfish. Young leaves abounded, green and tender like spinach, and there was wild yam and a soft brown root that had a sweet taste and was eaten for dessert. All washed down with sweet water from the stream, sometimes with coconut milk . . . every meal a feast.

Queen learned enthusiastically and was soon confident of being able to sustain himself in these idyllic surroundings. His shirt had gone from his back. His hips were covered with a pair of cut down trousers and as the tropic sun burned his skin to a dark mahogany it would be difficult to recognise Queen as an English seaman, and he took a savage, almost primitive delight in the awareness of his ability to survive in the forest and on the mountain.

On one occasion, when Verber had gashed his foot on a jagged stone, Tuamaoto showed them how to make up a sticky paste from earth and the ground up bark of the cinchona tree.

'Good medicine,' said Tuamoto as he explained how to make a bitter liquid from the cinchona bark to drink sparingly in relief of fever. His knowledge was endless and engrossing.

The favourite spot for the midshipmen unquestionably became the lagoon, and in particular one recess that had been scoured into the rock and sand of the hillside allowing fresh and salt water to mingle in a sheltered basin, deep and crystal clear and where the white sandy bed was clearly visible. The mountain stream cascaded, splashing tiny rainbows and here, on a high bank of tender green, they could lie in the shade and munch on coconut or dive in and join the young islanders swimming in the shallows. Verber looked up as Queen came back on to the grassy verge. Regarding him for a speculative moment. 'I'm beginning to find you indistinguishable from the natives.'

Shaking water from shoulder length hair he sprinkled it over Verber and sat down cross-legged. 'Wait 'till I get my ears pierced,' he said with a grin.

'You're never!' shuddered Verber.

'Tuamoto is getting his mother to do me . . . just one,' he added hastily at the horrified expression on Verber's face.

'You really are taken with this native existence.'

'Might as well enjoy it while we can, for it's unlikely that we'll get the chance again?' Gazing around as he asked. 'Have you ever known anything so beautiful or people who are so sublimely happy and content?' Laughter from the pool confirmed the statement. Birds of incredible colour flew overhead and the distant reef thundered a crescendo and he said with conviction. 'What more could a man ask?'

'Is it enough though? With every day spent in idleness and self indulgence life could lose its purpose.'

'What purpose,' scowled Queen in mock severity. 'Think you miss the challenge of wheeling and dealing and wonder sometimes whether trading for a load of spice is enough stimulation for your hereditary instincts?' Spreading down beside him. 'This is a whole world away from Hatton Garden and your father's workshop.'

'You're right, and I seem to have lost all former desire for business of such nature. But just think, Jase,' he said with excitement suddenly rife in his tone, 'of the trading empire that could be built out here . . . with stout ships and determined men there is no limit to what we could achieve?' This vision changed his mood to one of impatience. 'Wish the *Earl* would return so we could get on with it.'

'We already have the warehouse full and done all that could be expected of us.' Queen then drowsily said. 'I know what Vinderman would do in our place.'

'Sit with his back against a coconut tree, smoke his pipe and strum his lute and find some plump native woman to keep him happy at night.'

'Aye, and not question his good fortune.'

Days drifted lazily into weeks, bringing concern about the non-appearance of the *Earl*. The long delay left them with little more to accomplish and it became increasingly difficult to keep the men occupied, a condition that appeared to give no cause for complaint, including Queen, who decided to make a solo trip into the interior.

Telling only Verber and Tuamoto of his scheme, to spend the night and return. This, he thought, would give him the chance to try out the survival training taught by Tuamoto. Early morning, again following the course of the cascading stream. His only weapon the silver dagger of the Arab slaver. All day he trekked. High into the mountains until the vegetation grew more and more sparse. The stream at times was just falling vertically over rocks worn smooth and polished by the rushing water. Banana trees flourished, much smaller now but still prolific with fruit. Climbing until he had the most fantastic view, the sea looking quiet and peaceful with the pounding surf betrayed only by a faint line of white on the off-lying reef. Poising on the rocky knife-edge with the breeze rippling through his hair and bringing the exotic fragrance of the tropical rain forest below.

Making up a house of bamboo. Gathering his supper, succulent leaves, yams, prawns by the handful from a pool formed among the rocks. It took a long time to light his bits of wood but eventually a fire burned brightly with bananas roasting between the hot stones. Sitting back in the fading sunlight satisfied with his performance with his eyes closing drowsily. Tuamoto came from behind a copse, a sudden appearance that jolted him and he said, somewhat resentfully, 'You followed me . . .' words trailing off as he realised Tuamoto was not alone, for Riana was just behind with eyes downcast and her face buried in her hands as always. She had an endearing way of greeting him with her face graciously shadowed by the linking fingers of her hands, palms outward across the lower part of her face. There was a white flower in her hair and two tiny blossoms nestling in the lobes of her ears. Her eyes were deep but shy and almost afraid yet they burned right through him. He brought her forward to the fire then she knelt down and opened her hand to offer an exquisitely carved ring of pure white. Looking at her in startled anticipation as she beckoned him down and with deft fingers removed the slender sleeve of silver wire from his newly pierced ear, fitted the shark tooth and threaded the whole easily back in place.

After a close scrutiny, Tuamoto explained, 'She's been carving this ring for days.'

Deeply moved by the gift and the manner of the lovely Javanese girl he cupped her face in his hands and gently kissed her forehead. Her eyes shone with reflected fire and her lips were red and full and without hesitation he kissed her on the mouth then placed his cheek against her's. 'Thank you, Riana,' he whispered in her ear, 'for your lovely gift.'

Eyes wide and wondrous at the compelling tenderness of the tall white youth she bent her head to shadow her face: and to conceal ecstatic confusion. Grinning all over his face at this revealing performance, Tuamoto examined the campsite with an expert eye then helped himself to a roasted banana. 'Knew you would be just like a Javanese.'

'So why did you follow after me?'

'Riana worried, so we came.'

Using a warm leaf as a platter Queen served her with food. 'Thank you, Riana,' he said, 'your concern is a great compliment.'

Looking up, as if puzzled at his words, and Tuamoto spoke quickly to her in native tongue. 'She speaks English good,' he said to Queen, 'but not when you make the big words.'

Smiling happily, she sat down by the fire. The sky was beginning to darken with the cooler air of the mountain already chill on bare skin. Tuamoto's eyes were on the silver dagger being used to portion out the food and on an impulse Queen handed to him. Delighted, he polished the blade on a handful of dry grass until the silver gleamed. The sailmaker aboard ship had made up a soft leather sheaf for the dagger and also stitched in a fine decorative pattern. Unbuckling his belt and moving behind Tuamoto he fastened belt and sheaf around the hard-muscled waist. Tuamoto stood very still throughout this manoeuvre, the two face to face. Then Queen slid the knife into its sheaf and said, 'For you!'

Springing into the air doing an energetic war dance, dagger in hand. Replacing it in the pouch he pulled it out and pushed it back several times and his delight in the gift was obvious and very rewarding. Then, joy subsiding he came to stand before Queen. 'Now I have knife fit for a King,' he said, somehow sadly, 'but I have nothing to give in return, my friend Jason.'

He started to unbuckle the belt but Queen stayed the move. 'Please, Tuamoto,' he said. 'You have already given a gift beyond value.'

'I have given nothing,' puzzled voice and manner.

'You have given me of yourself and of your knowledge and your instincts. You have taught the wonders of nature and how to exist in such natural surroundings.' The bewildered expression brought laughter from Queen. 'I make the big words again.' Taking his arm and standing by his side, he pointed out to Tuamoto the little night shelter, the glowing fire and the food steaming among the hot stones and, finally understanding, Tuamoto spoke excitedly to his sister. But his initial reluctance to accept the gift had made Queen very much aware that he had nothing with which to return Riana's offering. He moved away leaving the two at the fire uneasy at his departure then he re-emerged from the undergrowth with an armful of wild, exotic flowers and kneeling before her to spread them in her lap, chose a fragrant blossom to thread in her hair, then stood back with a formal bow. She looked at him in wonderment, and her eyes were deep and moist and shining bright, and she clutched the flowers to her breast as if she would never let go of them.

'My sister is happy,' said Tuamoto from behind. 'I am happy as well.'

'And I am happy!' Shouted Queen in a burst of exuberance and they laughed together like children and all the while her gaze riveted on him.

Night fell and brought intense cold and they burrowed deep into their bed of leaves. Waking to a rustling sound, Riana nestling by his side with her body close and seeking warmth. Enfolding her in his arms and her eyes looked into his, content, then they closed in sleep with her head resting against his shoulder. Her warm, and softly rounded body aroused disturbing emotions inside. Looking down into her face, her lips were slightly open and very inviting and all the while the moon shed wondrous light into the little shelter. Spreading a mound of leaves about her he laid awake for a long time, before finally easing out his arm. She muttered a sleepy protest and then was quiet.

The growing attachment between the midshipmen and Tuamoto was the final link in bonding together the English and Javanese. After hearing the story of the flowers and the gift of the silver knife, King Wanu decided to adopt the two young officers.

So another feast was held on the beach, and bonfires again lit the night sky. The ceremony of adoption was a simple one. A small incision made in the wrists of all three brought blood mingling as their wrists were lashed together. The drums began a frantic beat and the natives danced in wild abandon.

'Now we are brothers,' said Tuamoto, adding with a teasing smile, 'but Riana is not sister.'

Dancing girls approaching, selecting partners. A swaying maiden beckoned to a very eager Abraham Verber. Shrugging at Queen. 'What the hell, Jase, enjoy today and let the future bring whatever.' Joining the dancers with his hand held tight by his attractive companion. Then Tuamoto disappeared into the throng propelled forcibly by a laughing, plump-bodied young woman, leaving Queen alone to sense a preconceived plan. He knew she would come for him and got up with anticipation as she approached with arms beckoning. She wore a grass skirt that barely covered her hips and her thighs were plump and shapely and so very inviting. Looping a garland round his neck, her hips swaying, and he took up the rhythm, bare feet stamping on the warm sand.

She took his hand. 'Come, Jason.' The first time she had spoken his name and he yielded willingly to the touch of her possessive fingers.

The feast went on until the late hours and then the dancers began to steal away in pairs. Walking her home hand in hand to the house of King Wanu. The elders were waiting on the porch and he formally returned Riana to her father and bade them goodnight. Abraham had not returned and he lay on his rug with sleep elusive as his thoughts raced disturbingly over the events of the evening. He lay very still as a quiet movement interrupted his reverie and a shadowy figure came to kneel over him and he knew without opening his eyes that she had come to him and he could smell the seductive fragrance of her and wanton thoughts were suppressed only with great reluctance. Forcing his eyes to remain closed, feigning sleep. She knelt for a long minute as if waiting, then her lips brushed his and they were soft and trembling, then she was gone as stealthily as she had come. He couldn't get to sleep. With thoughts in turmoil he was still awake when the grey of dawn brought Abraham creeping into his bed across the room. He slept finally, but to a disturbing return of his dream: the girl who pursued him was once again without a face!

Idle days. The warehouse filled to bursting point with little work remaining for the shore party. So the natives were asked to build a second warehouse to accommodate the accumulating stack of spices. Already two seamen and three of the marines had taken up residence with the willing native women. Verber appeared to have lost much of his nervous energy and was openly enjoying the attentions of the willowy girl who had enticed him into the dance. The King's daughter, Riana, was by now a constant shadow to Queen. Wherever he was she would appear, except during the brief hours when he worked with the seamen. Discipline had almost vanished, and after the morning roll call he seldom saw the men of the shore party.

'May I have a word with you, Mr Queen, sir?' The Corporal of marines had a concerned note in his voice.

'What is it, Ruben?' Surnames had been discarded by now.

'The thing is, sir, the men are more and more going native and if we don't see the return of the ship soon there is a good chance they won't be eager to rejoin.' Hesitating, he went on to say. 'Always supposing they do come back for us.'

'Can hardly blame the men,' said Queen with a grin. Then, sobering at the appeal on the corporal's face. 'I know the ship is overdue but they must have good reason, there is nothing we can do about it and will just have to be patient.'

'It has been six weeks now,' persisted the corporal, 'Lieutenant Gascoyne anticipated his return within a month.'

'Captain Probus is in charge, and Mr Harper still has the final decision in trading policy.' Thinking the corporal deserved some recognition for his concern Queen said briskly. 'You are right, Ruben, perhaps we had better tighten up our routine. Call the roll in the evening also, and keep the men busy on the new factory building during the cooler hours. But for now . . . let's get this lot tallied then I'm off for a swim.'

* * *

Stretched full length on the lush greenery above the lagoon with drops of water trickling from his skin and in his hair. Splash of waterfall soothing, warmth of the sun caressing him into drowsiness and his eyes closed. A tickling sensation came around his mouth and he brushed it away with a lazy hand. The tickle returned, accompanied by a low murmur of amusement and his eyes opened to see her kneeling by his side with a whisper of grass poised over his mouth. Her hand was held in its descent and her laughter stilled to leave her mouth curving in a half-smile. The pressure of her fingers was firm and persuasive and she gave him a look of complete devotion and his stomach muscle tightened in a breathless knot. The look of a young girl in love was on her face and wracking him with its fragile appeal, she was irresistible and he fastened his hands behind her head with uncontrollable yearning and murmured her name, 'Riana.'

All merriment had gone from her face and her eyes were deep and held the luminosity of a tropic sea exploding its power then her head came down and their mouths searched with a hunger beyond any hope of denial. Her body sagged against his, so soft and compliant and he rolled her over and down in urgent movement and she lay passive and her eyes were wide open with invitation and acceptance and her hand stroked his side in a caress intimate and provocative and he couldn't do anything about it but kiss her and her lips trembled against his then opened to the pressure of his mouth and her arms were round his neck. 'Again, Jason,' she murmured. So he kissed her and then his hand came from her waist to ease away the sarong and caress the luscious curve of her breast and her skin was satin smooth and the exquisiteness of her devastated with a rush of emotion that had him gasping. A low murmur of desire came from her mouth and there was invitation in the sudden arch of her body and in her hips moving with a rhythm so sensuous it sent a tidal wave of breathless passion surging and his loins rose . . . erect with a heat demanding satisfaction.

The moment he had tried so hard to resist but every passing day found his resolve growing weaker and affection more dominant and now all inhibition was swept away on a flood tide of passion. Hands soothing through the luxury of cascading, black as a raven's wing hair, then down over her shoulders and stripping away her garment as they moved onto the voluptuous curve of her hips and they clung to each other with animal intensity that flooded and fired with the frantic need they had for each other and his mouth fastened on her's as he eased across her, and body and mind surged with the scent of her desire and he spread her legs wide. Tenderly: but decisive.

Boom! Reverberating percussion of the ship's

cannon! Blasting tranquillity and a thousand birds took to wing. Again the shock of explosion thundered. Bringing awareness. Then resentment: and reluctance. He was a churn of contrasting emotion, staring with dismay into the eyes opening wide below. 'The ship!' Unbelieving.

'No. Jason!' Words choking from a despairing mouth. Sense of panic lending urgency to her cry of, 'Not yet!'

Pressing her down again. His weight on her was sweet. Then he began to rise, bringing her up but she clung to him with her arms tight around his waist and there was deep yearning in her eyes, and with the mist of tears as she grasped him unashamedly and brought her naked body to him again. Holding her. In torment! Wanting her! The cannon insistent that he had no right! He caressed the wondrous curve of her hips with desire rampant but again the thunder of cannon belted into his seething mind, forcing sanity, and the first retreat from wanton passion.

'Oh, Riana! Riana my love!' Kissing her. Mouthing the words against trembling lips. 'That cannon was fired from heaven to shield innocence.'

She felt his withdrawal and her face raised. He cupped her cheeks with hands shaking with the emotion that was in him, and again he said her name, 'Riana.'

Her eyes closed. A tear crept out of one corner.

'You do not love me enough.' Simple words,

but a cry from the heart causing him to clutch her in possessive grip. What could he do? He had always known that her standards were more basic than his own and he needed to find some delicate balance to restore the dignity of his enchanting Princess.

'Riana, my darling, I love you so very much.' Yearning to hold her. Capture her. Never let her go! Queen's wish for the return of his ship had been replaced with an overwhelming confusion at her intervention. But, mature beyond her years, with understanding that was native, she sensed indecision and took it upon herself to bring easement to the youth she worshipped.

'I know you well, my Jason. And in my heart I have also known that you will soon be leaving us. I ask nothing of you except for you to love me for a little while.' Her voice tremored the words as she cried. 'And perhaps share yourself with me.' Taking his hands and gazing up at him. 'But I am sure now,' she said, 'from the strength of the love we just shared, that had your ship not returned you and I would have been as one: and this knowledge will warm my heart for always.' Her assurance was natural. She needed no words to understand. She sought to make it easier for him, pulling on his arm, started to lead him away but he stayed the move and brought her to him and she came willingly and murmured. 'Kiss me again, as if it was the last time.'

Clinging hopelessly to her. Leaning on the

strength she now imparted, he crushed her mouth with a hunger that would never have the chance to be fulfilled, and then she smiled, so sadly. 'I am happy now,' she said, 'to know at last that my love is returned.'

Holding her in close embrace with his face buried in the perfume of her hair, he said in with deep longing in his voice, 'If only this moment could last for ever.'

'But it will, my Jason, and the memory of you will light the darkest hours for as long as I live.' The cannon boomed command and she frowned, then wriggled into her discarded sarong. 'I think it is time to find your uniform and return you to the Captain.'

Bonham-Jones and McFie came ashore in the first longboat to an enthusiastic greeting. They swam in the lagoon and were feasted in the home of King Wanu. Glancing appreciatively at the figure of Riana as she hovered over him to serve at the banquet then went on to linger at Queen's shoulder. 'What have you been up to, Mr Queen?' said McFie with mock politeness.

'Nothing much.' Deliberately misconstruing the question. 'Swimming. Exploring the interior. Learning the way of the Islanders. It's been sheer hell really.'

His bland look fastened on the scornful face of Billie McFie and Verber choked on a smoking hot morsel of crayfish. 'If hell is like this,' said

Bonham Jones in sardonic tone, 'you can reserve a place for me.'

'Fortunate that we came back in time to put an end to this misery,' said McFie. 'I can see it must be real hardship having to put up with this marvellous food and a cosy berth, to say nothing of such alluring female company.'

'Don't read more into the situation than there has been.' Teased into response by the probing wit of McFie he said sharply. 'Riana is but a slip of a girl, and has been shown the courtesy to which she is entitled as the daughter of King Wanu.'

'Who said anything about Riana,' countered McFie, 'slip of a girl she may be but when she looks at you she has the eyes of a woman? I begin to realise, Jase,' he added knowingly, 'how this native life can do more harm than good and I can only repeat . . . it's a good job we have come back for you.'

'Must admit it will be great to be back aboard the *Earl*,' said Verber, but his anticipation was stifled by Bonham-Jones.

'From what I hear,' he said, 'Old Harper is coming ashore for a stay, to get another shipment together.' Grinning as he explained. 'Mr Merchant Harper is a little distressed by his inability to obtain a profitable cargo from the other islands and is to remain here where he is sure of some kind of shipment, while Captain Probus takes the ship into the waters of the Molucca's.'

'How does that affect me?'

'Because, Abraham, our Mr Harper seems to have great respect for your acumen in matters of business and wants you by his side. But not you, Jase, Captain orders you back aboard. He was reluctant to leave either of you ashore any longer in case you go native on him.'

McFie cocked a quizzical eye at the two oddly attired midshipmen and Verber said in disgruntled tone, 'Won't be much fun with merchant Harper ashore.'

Chapter Nineteen

Work began in earnest the following morning to transfer the spices from shore to ship, emptying the store sheds in readiness for further collections. King Wanu was paid in silver coin for this trading. Spanish Rials: the most acceptable currency throughout the Far East.

The shore party had managed to dress more traditionally that morning but Probus looked with disdain at his returned crewmen. 'Sloppy looking bunch,' he said contemptuously to Queen, 'hardly a credit to you.' Glaring into the drooping-moustached face and at the shark tooth ring in his ear lobe. 'For God's sake get rid of that fearsome earring, you look more like a bloody pirate than one of my officers!'

Stiffly erect and resentful with problems of his own to reconcile he was in no mood for chastisement and made no reply but his eyes were flaring and hostile and Probus regarded him dourly in the sudden realisation that his midshipman had become a damned formidable young man. An almost sinister replica of his father, John Queen, and one he would rather have on his side than against. A cold shiver ran inadvertently up the small of his back then, reasserting personal authority, he said, 'At least McFie will be relieved to see you back. Haven't had a single prank in weeks from that clown?'

Unaccustomed to the chill of a sea breeze he hunched into his coat. Evening fast advancing. The last dog watch, with the harbour already opening out on the larboard beam. The Sunda Strait stretching before them, darkening green. Levelling his telescope shoreward, tiny figure standing in isolation on the beach... too far away now to recognise but he knew she was still watching the ship depart, while a score of outrigger canoes and their chanting crews accompanied the ship out into deep water beyond the lagoon. Bound southerly, through the Straits into the Indian Ocean and then on to the Islands of Indonesia. The intention was to cruise off the southern coast of Java, down through the Islands then northerly up by Timor into the Flores and Banda Seas and the area of the Moluccas. This quieter route chosen because of the number of Dutch vessels, both Naval and merchantmen, that were sailing off Sumatra and northern Java.

The *Earl* had already run from such a convoy shepherded by a couple of frigates and a ship of the line of seventy-four guns. A formidable force! Not one to encounter

Queen lowered his telescope with an expression of melancholy plain to see. 'Trouble with the fair maidens again, Jase?' said Vinderman in sardonic tone.

He didn't want to talk about it then with a disconsolate shrug, replied, 'The King's daughter. A Princess in every way... seeking only to please and keep me happy.' Speaking in low voice as if thinking out loud, assembling reluctant thoughts. 'I learnt a great deal from Riana and her brother Tuamoto. The people of the Island have natural grace and a dignity wonderful to be amongst. A sense of enjoying whatever they have at any particular moment with the future unheeded.' Vinderman made no response but a half-smile of appreciation curved his mouth as Queen went on in sombre voice. 'The young women are so different in outlook from anything to which we are accustomed. They take pleasure in some strange reversed manner by waiting upon their man's comfort and to his every desire.' Eyes focussing on the distant figure on the beach. Trying to keep her in sight as long as he could but the distance just merged her into an indistinguishable blur and he murmured sadly. 'I know truly that Riana was happiest when she was serving me in every way, yet her very servility made me feel humble and good inside. Vindo,' he exclaimed, 'she would have denied me nothing!'

'You mean you didn't?' Vinderman shook his head in disbelief. 'What a waste!'

The scornful tone brought only renewed anguish. 'There were times,' said Queen defensively, 'when I wanted to submerge myself in the complete wonder of this lovely girl. Wrong it may have been but I always had this sensation of knowing she was wishing me to in open invitation. What was I to do, Vindo, realising I was soon to sail away, perhaps for ever?' Voice taking on a pleading note as he cried. 'I could offer her nothing!'

'Perhaps this philosophy of their's to take what is offered in enjoyment at the time and let the rest go is the answer. What's more natural than two young people pleasuring and loving each other?' Vinderman then outlined his own philosophy on such matters. 'You loves 'em for a while then you leaves 'em: and everyone's happy.' After a short pause for personal reflection, he said in jibing tone. 'Perhaps the first time might be a soul-searcher for someone so noble minded? But once you've been there, Jase, you won't ever again look for reasons against.'

'For an uncontrollable and wanton minute there I came so very close. Oh, God! I wanted to!' Thoughts ravaging again. Then he took a deep breath in an effort to regain control. 'It just isn't fair! She was so very young and soon I would be gone from her, but I still feel as though I turned away when she needed me most.' Try as he may the searing ache just wouldn't go away and in a vain attempt to justify, he suggested. 'Perhaps there is a difference between love and the ultimate desire, and in this way I may have been shown the difference.'

The forlorn way he said this brought an in-depth study from Vinderman. 'Wonder just what influence Miss Passendale had on this unsought gallantry and control,' he said, 'or how you would have reacted to your native Princess had you not the thought of a probable accounting with your sweetheart back home?'

Brow furrowing, thoughts of Maggie had receded of late but this perceptive comment brought her back clearly in his mind and provoked new and disturbing mental patterns and, he needed a moment to allow these to be absorbed. 'You are saying my actions were more selfish than gallant,' he said in snappish tone, 'and that the fear of alienating the affections of Maggie Passendale was the over-riding influence.'

'Something like that,' grinned Vinderman, 'but let me ask another question. Would she ever know?'

'Make no mistake, Vindo. She would know!'

Next two weeks were spent winging down the chain of Islands that span the Flores Sea from Java to Timor, into the unceasing trade winds that blow from the south and east. Neither tack more favourable and averaging only about a hundred miles over the ground each day. Conditions were ideal and the *Earl* responded bravely to the challenge of the adverse trade wind. Heeling to the gusts with all working canvas set taut she was a picture of grace and beauty and a delight to the men who sailed her.

Came the day when they could turn on a northerly bearing and head up for the Moluccas. Picking up speed as the wind came more abeam and the sheets were eased off to free the sails. Sea miles flowing by . . . steady trade wind blowing without restraint across the fetch of the Pacific, allowing a speedy and exhilarating reach deep into the Banda Sea and the inviting sprawl of the Moluccas. Running fast up the Molucca passage, again crossing the Equator where the heat was stifling and made bearable only by the strong breeze. Ropes of the standing rigging bleaching white, pitch bubbling in the deck seams, crew kept busy with deluges of salt water. They had seen no other sail for weeks and it began to seem they were alone in the blue waters of Indonesia.

Trading first at the northernmost island, Morotai. Freed from the restrictive influence of Merchant Harper, who's instinct to squeeze the last penny caused resentment ashore, Probus traded well among the little native kingdoms. Dutch power was not so widespread in these more distant lands and the ship began to settle deeper in the water as her holds filled with fragrant spice. Working their way down the tiny ports and harbours. Trading was keen but carried out in amiable fashion and it was soon apparent that they would be returning home with a rich cargo. The local Kings and Chiefs of the native tribes were more than willing to barter their lush produce for the variety of trade goods carried aboard: and for gold and silver coin.

So it was a satisfied if somewhat thoughtful Probus who stood on the poop deck observing the Island of Obie open up behind them. Lighting up one of his long cigars, he said, 'A week of this should see us in the Sunda Straits, Alan.'

'With the south east trades behind us all the way.' Puffing his pipe and sharing his Captain's mood of well-being. 'We've done well, Fitz, much better then when Mr Harper was doing the trading. Might just about find room for his sacks of pepper?' Embers from his pipe snatching away on the wind even as he spoke.

Probus nodded in agreement. 'This load will show a tidy profit on the London market.' No personal connotation in the statement, the Company had a clause that stated "*due inquisition shall be made into all and every ship. By search of all chests, boxes, packettes, and other means whereby discovery may be made of this breach of ordinance.*" This simple clause was one of the basic principles of the Company's East India Policy and strictly enforced. Drawing contentedly on his cigar Probus was in a contemplative frame of mind. 'Just one more stop at Semarund to load the last cargo. Take on food and water. Then we can bid farewell to the Islands and set course for Cape Town and home.'

'London will seem a little shabby after all this.' Sethman emphasised the remark by pointing his pipe at the appealing sprawl of Obie. Pale light of evening, crusty mountain peaks smoothed green and reaching high into the velvet sky, crescent moon of silver hanging low in the heavens and the seductive, spicy fragrance of the land still with them.

'London is home and nothing can compare.' Speaking with calculation in his voice, Probus added, 'You will be back before you know it, Alan, but for me? . . . I begin to lose my appetite for these interminable ocean voyages and suspect that I'll soon be content to tend the roses in my little cottage garden and sit quietly in the sunshine with a jug of ale to hand.'

Sethman grimaced at the thought. 'Hard to imagine Fitzroy Probus pruning roses when there are fine ships to sail.'

'Probus will be just another retired old sailor and swiftly erased from the minds of young men.' Drawing fiercely on his cigar he then stated. 'Think you know how I used to dread the idea of retirement. Of leaving this compelling life of ours and with the optimism of youth and good health I saw no reason why it shouldn't go on for ever.' A strain of melancholy crept unsummoned into his voice as he explained. 'It is no longer a question of me giving up the sea, more like the sea giving me up and insisting I move over for the young and eager men who press their claim for recognition and, in the end perhaps, the decision might not be too painful. At least, I have had the supreme pleasure of a vessel like the *Earl* and you more than most, Alan, can imagine how rewarding it is to command a fine ship and bring peace and content aboard,' hesitating, before committing himself to admit, 'after such a disastrous inception.' His cigar had gone out in the pursuance of his thoughts and he threw the stub overboard, before going on. 'As it is we are in the happy position of having secured a fine cargo and virtually on our way home.'

'Long way to go yet, Fitz.'

Chapter Twenty

Sweeping a diagonal line across the Flores Sea 'heading for the passage between Bali and Lombok at the eastern end of Java. Wind fair and abaft the beam in most kindly manner. Heavily loaded, but making an impressive average day's run of two hundred and twenty miles.

Twelve noon on the fourth day of their passage from Obie, the Channel for which they were heading in clear view, Mr Sethman, David Ashbury and the four midshipmen occupied in taking celestial observations from the poop deck with First Officer Sethman instructing in the finer points...a finishing off process because they were very proficient by this time and he was more than satisfied with their navigational ability.

Second Officer Gaywood by the steering position under the quarterdeck awning, very correctly dressed and seemingly oblivious to the heat, he sprang to life as the lookout called from the masthead. 'Deck there! Sail Ho! On the starboard bow!' Racing up the ladder on to the elevation of the poop deck he focused his telescope. 'Two of them,' he announced with foreboding. 'The rear ship looks like the seventy-four we saw earlier.'

'Call the Captain, Mr Ashbury,' snapped Sethman. Turning to Gaywood he ordered. 'Pipe all hands to action stations.'

The ship was immediately transformed into readiness as all hands were called on deck and hatchways spewed hordes of men rushing to their gun stations. Battle exercise had never been relaxed and they closed up with efficiency born of practice. Marines at the double buckled on belt and powder horn as they formed up.

Appearing on deck calm, but anxious-eyed, Probus asked, 'What ship, Mr Sethman?'

'Two Dutch men-of-war on a converging course.'

Calculating look along the main deck, assessing the efficiency with which the guns were being prepared, Probus then viewed the distant sails through his telescope. 'They're hard on the wind,' he said confidently, 'and not as manoeuvrable as us.' The warships were many miles off and bows on into the steady breeze, while the *Earl* was running free. Lombok was close on their larboard beam with the wide channel between it and Bali in plain view. 'Be hours before they can get a fair slant.' said Probus, taking in every detail. Alter course, Mr Sethman, we'll take the southerly option, enough to give us a long reach down yonder channel and into open water under cover of darkness.' Snapping his telescope shut. 'Set all sail, Mr Gaywood, I want her flying.'

'Aye, aye, sir.'

'Larboard two points,' said Mr Sethman..

'Larboard two points, sir.' Vinderman and Dooley at the wheel. Davy Greenwood standing by as replacement. Straining her round. Grunting at the effort needed to increase the angle of rudder against the water rushing along the hull. As the head came round, Vinderman acknowledged. 'Larboard two points on, sir.'

She settled on a course that would take her between the Islands. Ploughing into the swell, sending rainbow coloured spray high into the forepeak. Mountainous ground of the two Islands high and dominating, coastline a dazzling contrast of vivid green and sunlit sand so bright the eye could not focus without discomfort. But the officers gathered on the poop deck had no time for scenic beauty. Their thoughts were only for the menace of the Dutch battle fleet and Gaywood asked the question dominant in their minds. 'Do they know we are in these waters, or is it just a recurrence of bad luck?'

Probus didn't care for the insinuation. 'I don't believe in coincidence,' he said tersely. 'It's the same squadron we turned away from and I'm sure they know of our presence and are on the prowl looking for us.' Thinking about this he said in thoughtful tone. 'On our previous sighting there were three of them and I'm more concerned about the whereabouts of the other frigate. Double up on the main top, Mr Sethman, and choose only sharp-eyed men. Report every two minutes until they are out of vision.'

As he had forecast it were several hours before the Dutch men-of-war could turn away from the restrictive headwind and point up in pursuit . . . hours during which the *Earl* sped onward until she was long out of sight. Watches were kept up, but only at half strength now and the air of tension eased as evening fell and the horizon disappeared into the dark void betwixt sea and sky. Probus gave up the deck to David Ashbury and turned in.

'Call me at first light.' Brusque order, leaving no margin for complacency. Ashbury pacing about unable to relax: thought it was going to be a long night.

The watch changed at midnight, then again at four a.m. The square-rigger swept with purpose out of the channel into the Indian Ocean off the southern shore of Bali. Arriving on deck without summons and squinting into the early brightness. 'Be damned glad when Harper and his cargo are aboard,' said Probus, 'so we can set course for Cape Town. Little chance of being intercepted once we clear the Islands.'

Trade wind dead astern, all sails full and drawing and set square before the wind with the ship fairly flying over the water. No sign of the Dutchmen, men relaxing on deck after breakfast. As the day wore on Bali went from sight and the coast of Java rolled by in rewarding progression.

'Deck there! Dutch frigate. On the bow!' The cry held a note of panic. The bosun's whistle summoned action stations. Telescopes weren't needed. The Dutch frigate had been lurking in the lee of an off-lying island and now came out from cover under full sail and clearly visible to the naked eye.

'Caught like a rat in a trap! To turn and run would bring us under the guns of their seventy-four.' There was a note of inevitability in the comment and the look on Probus's face bore bleak testimony to his words. 'This is the reason for their lack of haste yesterday. They had no need. Just to make sure we came south within reach of their frigate.' Officers gathered aft. The ship was standing into danger and though outwardly calm they knew the Captain was in a dilemma, knowledge confirmed when he asked. 'What do you think, gentlemen, do we strike our colours: or do we fight?' Most uncharacteristic of him to invite a share in decision making. Probus was in command and the responsibility was his alone and carried squarely on his shoulders. But, with a certainty that chilled him to the bone, he knew that if they engaged the frigate they would suffer terrible casualties before the action was over. So he asked the question. Inviting their opinions and Sethman immediately responded:

'We have the initial advantage of speed, sir, and I doubt the frigate matching us for manoeuvring ability.'

Second Officer Gaywood spoke up. 'I'm with you, sir,' he said firmly, 'any way you decide. But I would hate like hell to strike our colours without making them fight for it.'

'So would I,' snapped Probus. Looking closely at them. 'Are we in agreement, gentlemen?' Nodded response, so he ordered. 'Break out the battle ensign, Mr Ashbury: we'll see what the Dutchmen are made of?' Determined of voice, indecision over with the support showed by his officers, he commanded. 'Right then, Mr Sethman, prepare for immediate action. Close up the gun crews. Position the Marines aloft and call Vinderman and Dooley to the wheel.'

About two miles away and closing, the frigate was hard on the wind and heeling well over to larboard. On the gun deck of the *Earl* all was bustle and ordered efficiency. Gun ports crashing open. Cannons loaded and run out. Every free man occupied in stacking hammocks against the bulwarks and when they ran out of hammocks sacks of spices were brought up to reinforce against the fiery cannon ball that would soon be blasting the ship's side.

It was done. Time for nothing more! The great battle ensign broke free at the masthead and flared proud, stiff as a board in the fresh breeze. 'Run straight for them, Mr Sethman,' ordered the Captain, 'make ready to wear ship and pass them on their lee bow.' This strategy would give their own guns elevation and bring the heeled over side of the frigate on the weatherboard of the *Earl*, with more than a fair chance to strike first and run on.

Two ships closing: fast! Cannon firing from the frigate's bow and the warning shot splashed ahead: the signal to heave-to. 'Bloody impudence,' growled Probus, 'they won't get us so easy.'

The Dutch Captain had fought the English before, hoped they would submit but didn't expect them to. He brought the frigate's bow up in an attempt to prevent the merchantman crossing ahead but he was already hard on the wind and couldn't point up any higher without putting his ship into stays, a position where the wind was dead ahead and effectively stopping the vessel.

'Wear ship!'

The *Earl* came smoothly round. Changing course swiftly and crossing ahead of the frigate, which was heeled to larboard, depressing the elevation of her leeward battery. But the frigate mounted eighteen guns either side as well as high-mounted bow and stern cannon: and her Captain was a competent seaman. Shot flamed from the forepeak. The ball fell fifty yards short.

Jack Dooley had seen action before. 'Just a range finder,' he said to Vinderman, 'the next one will be closer.'

Wha-am! The two crouched with reflex action as two cannons fired from the frigate's bow and the shot screamed overhead with a banshee whistle.

'Fire as you bear, Mr Gunner.' Sethman on the main deck among the gun crew. Master gunner Jancy crouched at the foremost gun training his sights with deliberate care. Touching flintlock to powder hole, he stood back in controlled haste as the cannon erupted into smoke and flame, then covered the fire hole with a horny thumb to quench the spark back. The cannon recoiled into its breeching rope and the gun crew straightaway prepared another charge. Jancy watched with disgust as the ball flew high, tearing a jagged hole in the forward main course and the taut sail split from head to foot but already the frigate's men were hauling it down and bending on a replacement.

Converging . . . four hundred yards apart. Jancy sped down the gun deck depressing the guns one wrench of his lever and firing as he went and the rippling volley thundered into the frigate's topside, a fearsome din that deafened the ears and distorted the senses. The frigate rolled violently as the broadside crashed home carving holes in her topsides but her upper battery of twenty-four pounders roared in devastating reply and the *Earl* shuddered to the hell of a Dutch broadside from close range. Cannon balls ripping into the hull, a section of bulwarks disintegrating in a mess of flame and flying wood . . . jagged and lethal splinters wreaking bloodstained carnage among the forward gun crew. Two forward guns out of action; blown spread-eagled across the deck and crushing two men to agonising death. Officers Gaywood and Ashbury among the larboard gun crew urging the men on as they reloaded and again ran out the cannon. Sick bay stretcher party hurrying wounded men into the hands of the surgeon working below. Wet sand hurriedly spread across the deck against the risk of fire: and effectively covering ominous stains where men had fallen.

'Come up under her stern, helmsman.' Probus calm amidst the battle din. Vinderman and Dooley spun the wheel. No time for formal acknowledgement. Bonham-Jones crew of seamen pulled on the running rigging, swaging the yards round on the new course. The wily Dutch Captain had anticipated this and he countered by wearing ship to free his wind. The larboard battery of gunner Jancy bore on the swinging stern for a brief minute, but enough to burst a gaping hole in the ornate woodwork and ignite a sudden flame that flared brightly through the shattered windows of the stern cabin. Guns recoiling. Smoking hot. The din was devastating on shattered eardrums. Still the frigate came round and Probus was forced to run from the menace of her monstrous starboard battery of twenty-four pounders. Jancy's broadside had not impaired the frigate's mobility. She swept back to attack with the wind now behind and the advantage of the *Earl* was lost. She ran off down wind with the frigate in pursuit but the merchant ship was heavy-laden, slower through the water and now paying the penalty for long weeks of successful trading.

'They're gaining, sir.' McFie was the captain's runner. Probus knew without being told. Volley thundering from the man-of-war. Too soon for accuracy and the shot fell short. Gunner Jancy on the high poop with the two long carronades, this might have been a routine exercise for all the apparent lack of urgency in his preparation. Jancy about his business, doing what he knew best. The two guns roared in concert. A section of the frigate's beak head disintegrated and the raking bowsprit snapped off at its heel.

'Wanted the forward mast,' cursed Jancy, 'not the bleedin' bowsprit!'

'You're doing well, Jancy,' encouraged Sethman, 'the Dutchman knows he has a fight on his hands.' The frigate came on unchecked and a thundering broadside flamed from her double gun deck. This time the aim was good and cannon balls smashed along the entire deck of the *Earl* and she seemed to sag in flight with the impact. Men were hurled back and maimed and broken bodies lay sprawling across the main deck and

Vinderman wrestled with the wheel as she slewed. Dooley straining alongside with his face a mask of anguish and, with the ship again steady, Vinderman had time for a brief glimpse at the harrowing scene and relief showed when he located Queen working side by side with Bonham-Jones striving to drag men clear of the debris. David Ashbury was prostrate, blood from his shoulder pouring down his shirt. The prophecy of early doom had caught up with Arnold Waugh; his lean body lay in a blackened and grotesque heap under an overturned gun carriage. Difficult to pick out individuals among the carnage, battle was still joined and a rattle of musket fire came from high in the frigate's rigging, instantly returned by Gascoyne's marines. Lieutenant in full uniform: immaculate as ever and directing his men with calm precision.

'Marines. Fire at will.' His last command. A marksman in the frigate's maintop bore on the bright tunic and Lieutenant Gascoyne staggered and went down as the musket ball smashed the life from him. Warrington-Smythe had not seen his commanding officer fall because he was concentrating on the upper works of the frigate, his musket flamed reply and the Dutch sniper rose in slow grace, held against the press of ropes then plunged headlong into the sea. Warrington-Smythe reloaded his musket.

Another broadside, a rhythmic, rippling and murderous volley. The starboard guns of the *Earl* flamed defiance and both ship's heeled violently, with the recoil of their own cannon and with the impact of a heavy shot in their topsides. Vinderman felt the wheel limp in his hands. With a despairing look at Dooley, he said, 'Rudder's gone, Jack.'

Dooley's face was grim and his voice hopeless. 'I'll tell the Captain we're out of control.'

The ship was on fire. One of the smoking hot cannon balls had blasted clean through the topsides and burst open a cask of brandy in the hold and the fiery liquor spread a carpet of flame that ignited bales of linen and raced up the dry timber of the bulkheads. The deck was a sickening sprawl. Bodies of dead seamen and marines draped over wreckage and broken gun carriage and the groans of wounded men were subdued and unheeded in the soul-destroying din of battle. Flame and thunder again from the relentlessly closing frigate. The mizzen mast lurched and began to topple, held only by its standing rigging. Then the ropes parted under the strain and the mast fell with a splintering crack along the side deck, scattering seamen and falling across the after guns, putting them out of action. Officer Gaywood hastily reorganised the gun crews while Jancy calmly sighted the six cannon, which was all that remained of his starboard battery. Moving fast behind them with a long, flaming torch match, touching powder holes as he passed.

The cannon thundered. The *Earl* reeled under the recoil and the shot screamed into the frigate at almost point blank range smashing into gun ports and punching great holes in her side. Cannon ball and scything spears of wood ploughed among the Dutch gun crews and their frantic shrieks were plainly heard in the momentary hush. But a return broadside ripped across the upper deck and brought the greedy roar of flame as the fire was fed with debris. Sighting his remaining cannon with great deliberation, Jancy stayed with one, aiming and elevating the barrel. At his command the diminished volley flamed into the frigate but six guns were no match for the man-of-war's remaining starboard battery and the return broadside was accurate and deadly and the *Earl* rolled like a drunken sailor under the impact. The ship came up. Steadied. Jancy waiting. His crew working like maniacs to swab and recharge. Jancy poised; match ready. The frigate rolled towards them as she recovered from the recoil of her own broadside. Jancy's cannon fired and the mainmast of their attacker jumped as the base was taken out by the cannon ball. Shout of triumph from the English crew as the giant mast plunged down into the forward mast and taking both in a mess of rope and ripped sails over the side. The frigate stayed its forward surge, the gap between them narrowing as the two immobile vessels drifted helplessly together and the rudderless *Earl* slewed into the path of the frigate.

'Fire's spreading to the lower deck, sir,' rushing back with his report Bonham-Jones said in desperate voice, 'and has almost reached the forward magazines.'

'Prepare the boats for launching, Mr Bonham-Jones.' Looking at the desolation in horror and self-accusation but his voice was composed and without feeling as he ordered. 'Get the wounded topside and into the boats and ask Dr. Quennel to attend them, his work below is finished.' Then to Vinderman, still by the unresponsive wheel. 'Spread the word to abandon ship. She's going to blow in a few minutes and I want all hands in the boats or in the water.'

Aye, aye, Capt'n.' Relieved of his post Vinderman ran off the quarterdeck. Wreckage everywhere, and the sand on the deck was wet not only with saltwater but with the blood of dead men. Destruction beyond belief and he gagged without control as he jumped aside from the legless corpse of Michael Gaywood. Grabbing at McFie who was using all his strength in a solitary effort to bring one of the few upright guns to bear.

'Leave it, Billie!' Having to shout to make himself heard above the noise. 'We're abandoning ship!'

Still crazed with the din of battle, McFie looked wildly around. 'Where's Jase?'

'Helping with the wounded somewhere. Hope so anyway. Too late, lad! Save yourself while you can.'

As he spoke a spurt of flame shot skywards from the centre hold. She was burning fiercely now and the few scraps of canvas still aloft were on fire. McFie gasped with relief when he saw Queen supporting a bandaged seaman, and as he ran to help, Queen instructed, 'Take this one! There's only one man left below, apart from the dead.' Relinquishing the wounded man he was gone before McFie could speak, so he placed his arm round the seaman's waist and struggled him along the deck where willing hands took the burden.

Down in the waist of the ship Sethman was directing as the men wrestled with the boats. Getting these overboard from the wreckage was extremely difficult. One of the longboats was lying askew, its back broken, and Sethman flung oars into the water along with any piece of timber that would float and support men. Unheeding the call of Mr Sethman, McFie dashed back as he saw Queen's head poke through the forward companionway with a seaman unconscious over his shoulder . . . McFie's grip was sure and gentle as he took the man in his arms. Queen scrambled on deck, clothing covered in blood, black and scorched with fire. Shaking his head at McFie's gasp. 'I'm all right,' he explained, 'this blood isn't mine,' gesturing below, 'no one left alive down there.' Looking around as he asked. 'Have you seen Ramon?'

'Reckon he's safe, been hiding away back aft.'

Two boats afloat, already loaded to the gunwales. Sethman had the situation well under control by now. Probus appearing from the wreck of the quarterdeck with the ship's papers and log wrapped in a waterproof bundle, gash under his eye, a long furrow oozing blood down his cheek and neck. 'All ready here, sir,' announced Sethman.

'Over you go, Alan.'

Handing over the ship's papers and the way he spoke brought Sethman's eyebrows angling in outrage and in a voice which expostulated both foreboding and intuition, he queried, 'Fitz?'

Queen and McFie were just behind the Captain when this exchange took place and their eyes met in a look of realisation and resolve and they poised with studied patience close to him while the fire crackled and raged all around but their deliberate posture served only to enrage Probus and, with his eyes wild upon them he growled in furious tone, 'You two! In the longboat! Now!'

'Fitz,' implored Sethman, 'don't sacrifice yourself for some bloody-fool tradition!'

'You're wasting time. Cut the boats free.' Sudden illumination, spark and flame climbing the wreckage of the foremast. Fire roaring. Heat and smoke enveloping. Probus held as if in a trance, gazing at the ruin that had been his greatest pride, and Sethman climbed wearily into the last longboat where the sardine-packed seamen were becoming frantic at the incomprehensible delay.

'Now you two,' again commanded Probus.

'Age before beauty.' No humour in the jest of Billie McFie.

'We won't leave until you do, Captain,' said Queen.

Came a menacing rumble from the bowels of the ship as the bulkheads collapsed and all the while the Dutch frigate drifted nearer with her crew panicking in a vain attempt to keep the two ships apart. Glaring into the faces of his midshipmen, Probus dare delay no longer, or he would be condemning them with himself to inglorious demise. Sensing a weakening of resolve they moved forward in unison. 'Would you like us to help you down, sir?' cheekily suggested McFie.

Pride was one thing, but ignominy? 'Heaven preserve me from fool midshipmen,' said Probus in resigned tone almost relieved to have decision taken from him. Damn fool idea, anyway! He had no choice. Without further comment he clambered down and Queen and McFie splashed into the water and were quickly hoisted aboard the crowded boat. The oarsmen bent their backs with an urgency that had no need of command. The longboat pulled away from the *Earl*: for the last time. Came a sickening crash of wood, the frigate had finally drifted into the East Indiaman! Shouts of alarm and panic as the men aboard realised the extent of the fire.

'Pull away, men.' Sethman helming, and his command jerked the oarsmen from their fascinated stare at the two locked-together ships. A gentle but fatal wind fanned flame from the rigging of the *Earl*. It was an invitation to her warm embrace and immediately the scraps of sail still up on the frigate were on fire. Sudden, blazing explosion shattered the forepeak of the *Earl*. All diving for cover as a searing sheet of flame surged along the black and yellow hull then the entire bow flew skyward in a blistering roar of fire and exploding gunpowder, enveloping the frigate in smoke and burning debris. Series of muffled explosions starting from way down in the frigate, culminating in a final blast of such ferocity that the frigate was torn into two separate parts, freeing the *Earl* to drift away.

Taking off his hat Probus stood bare headed while the noise echoed away into the distance. The night was bright as day with the fire from the two drifting hulks. The whole upper decks of both were ablaze and the men in the longboat were as if mesmerised by the end of two fine ships. The *Earl* was settling and hundreds of tons of salt water flooded through the gaping hole that was once the proud bow. A mushrooming cloud of steam and smoke enshrouded her and her last moments were unseen as she plunged the depths of the Indian Ocean.

The two sections of the frigate were burning fiercely. An ear-deafening explosion blew her stern apart. Powder store erupting: showering blazing debris all over the enigmatic water. Darkness descending, sudden and obliterating as the last fragments disappeared below the surface and Probus broke the awesome silence. 'To your oars, men! We have a long pull ahead.'

Rowing throughout the night towards the coast of Java. By the cold light of dawn they could make out the high ground of land on the bow and, now confirmed of their direction, Probus had them set up the small mast and lugsail to aid progress towards land. Away to larboard sunshine reflected on a white sail and a buzz of approval ran through the crew with the realisation that the other longboat had got safely away. All the wounded had been taken off in the first boat and Probus was concerned for them. There was only a limited amount of water in the boats along with a little hard biscuit and barely enough to sustain a normal crew much less the numbers now carried. 'Double up on the oars,' he ordered, 'they'll need some extra muscle aboard.'

Every man who was able took his turn and the distance between the two sails became steadily less and with the assistance of a light onshore breeze so did the coastline begin to take on shape and colour. Soon they could distinguish the bulk of an off-lying island behind which the mainland curved into a sweeping bay many miles wide from headland to headland.

Closing to within hailing range, Probus called across for information. Bonham-Jones was the only fit officer apart from the surgeon, who was fully occupied with his patients. They had also rescued four injured Dutch seamen, and Bonham-Jones called back in weary voice, 'Could use another ten fit men on the oars.'

The two boats came together and the sorry state of the wounded was soon evident. Short of water and roasted by the midday sun, no shelter in the longboats, several had died during the night and Probus ordered them put over the side. Silencing the low murmurs of dissent with a ruthless, 'Our concern is only for the living.'

Mr Sethman and ten men clambering across, relieving the exhausted few on the oars . . . Bonham-Jones dropping prostrate against the steering thwart. Now equally manned and drawing support from each other they kept together and slowly closed the coast of Java. By late afternoon they had passed inland of the island and were in the calm waters of the bay where they could see waves rolling on to an inviting stretch of sand, shining like burnished copper in the afternoon sunshine.

Vinderman took the tiller from McFie. Queen stood in the bow watching for any change of colour in the translucent green water, a shade that might indicate shallowing water or a dangerous ledge of coral reef. Ahead the land rose abruptly from the beach; a thin strip of sand bordered by sparse greenery then nothing but barren mountainside. Volcanic crater of the highest peak was clearly visible and betrayed by a pillar of steam rising vertically into a cloudless sky. Away on the starboard hand an unbroken stretch of lush green followed the curve of the coastline. Picking his way aft, Queen looked at the Captain in speculative manner.

'Something on your mind, Mr Queen?' His eye was closed and matted with puss and the other squinted against the dazzle of sun on sea.

'May I suggest, sir,' said Queen pointing ahead, 'that we take our boats further down the coast. We'll more likely find food and water amongst the forest than on the mountain.'

Nodding in confirmation, as if he couldn't care less, as if decision-making was no longer his prerogative. 'Do whatever you think is best.'

Resigned, leaning again into the oars, running parallel to the beach for three weary hours before Queen called enough. A final flurry brought the boats through the rollers in a rush up the sand. Barefoot, pulling the boats high and dry out of reach of the clutching surf. Reactions mixed, some running about excitedly to explore while others just dropped wearily in silent relief. Probus gave them a few minutes then, assembling all fit men, he instructed that the wounded be brought ashore and carried into the shade of the undergrowth. The need to find water was imperative so Queen and McFie were detailed to take a small party and explore the immediate area and report on the availability of water and vegetable growth. They soon were back with great armfuls of bananas and yams and the sweet root that Queen knew was so sustaining. They had also located a cool running stream, which he suggested would be an ideal site to make camp.

Several of the wounded were recovering quickly enough to sit up and take interest in their delivery from the eternal rocking motion of the boats but there were others whose condition was deteriorating fast for want of fresh water and food. Stretchers were hastily made from bamboo and strips of bark and the stretcher party made its slow way inland. The proposed campsite was but a quarter of a mile, but more than far enough for weary men. Darkness had descended. It was all they could do for now. Lighting a fire. Chewing on bananas, but there was plenty of drinkable water and the wounded were made as comfortable as possible on a bed of dry leaves.

Cold light of dawn, stretching, stirring to life, stamping feet and pummelling muscles stiff with incessant hours of rowing . . . another two of the seriously injured had died during the night and all of the rescued Dutchmen. A grim faced burial party scraped shallow graves in the sand. Probus said a sad prayer as the holes were filled over.

Numbered among the dead was Gimpy the cook. 'We'll miss that old bugger,' said Jack Dooley in sad tone, 'he was a miserable sod but one hell of a good cook.'

'There'll be a few more alongside him before

this is over.' Davy Greenwood wiped away sweat as he straightened from the task of scooping sand over the bodies. His face was dirty, with an unkempt growth of beard, and Probus strode briskly among them.

'Less of that kind of talk,' he snapped. 'English seamen do not give in so easily.' Lining them up on the beach. 'Men! Our first concern must be for the wounded, so I intend to make camp here for a few days. The fittest will make organised search into the immediate inland area. There may be a native village nearby where we can find help and local medicine. I want a fishing party formed right now, and we are fortunate to have our boats intact for such a purpose.' Looking them over. Smoke grimed and in tatters and their despondent manner brought a scowl that made his scarred face even more menacing. 'You look dreadful! Get yourselves cleaned up.' Snapping them into action with the brisk command. 'All hands to bathe!'

McFie's shirt was off in a flash and lying on the sand with his smoke stained breeches and his bottom showed white against the suntan of his back as he ran naked into the sea. His whoop of delight was contagious and he was quickly joined by a noisy, though somewhat less enthusiastic crowd of shipmates.

Now the skills taught by Tuamoto became of real value as Queen instructed how first of all to build native huts using bamboo uprights and rafters and bind them tight with strips of bark skinned from trees. How to weave leaf from the banana tree into thatch for the roof and the clearing was soon ringed with tidy looking huts. They constructed a larger dwelling for use as a sick bay where the surgeon could work in a cool and quiet atmosphere. Here the wounded lay on stretcher beds of woven bark suspended between bamboo struts. Seamen are adaptable, used to taking care of themselves in any situation and they soon learned how to live and eat well in such a hospitable environment. Making up nets to catch fish. Searching the pools and shallows for crab, prawns by the canvas bucketful and always the produce from the land, green, spinach-like leaf, coconuts and bananas in plenty. Even wild sugar cane was found. Probus looking on with thoughtful conjecture as Queen assumed control and organising the men with an ease to which they responded as if recognising and welcoming authority.

The lad's a natural, thought Probus. Beginning to feel like an onlooker he confronted Queen and, after a speculative glance, said, 'Whatever became of the shy young man I first met by the old *Pandora*?' His face was starting to mend but the scar ran from just below his right eye across to his ear, giving his face a lopsided, almost fearsome appearance. 'I'm beginning to wonder just who is in charge here,' he then said, 'you . . . or me?'

His manner seemed almost benevolent and Queen wondered what the Captain had on his mind. 'I have been fortunate in my tutors, sir,' he replied respectfully, 'both aboard ship and ashore at Semurund.'

'All of which confirms my belief that you are the man to lead a party across the island.' Drawing a sketch in the sand. 'This is roughly the shape of Java, and we are here somewhere on the south-eastern end.' Outlining this with a pointed stick just as Mr Sethman approached with Bonham-Jones, and Probus sought confirmation from his First Officer. 'Correct me if I'm wrong, but from my memory of the chart I calculate the island to be about fifty miles wide and that the nearest port of convenience is Surubaya on the north shore?'

Sethman nodded assent but Bonham-Jones queried, 'Thought the Dutch were strongly garrisoned in the east of Java, sir?'

'That's right, but there is a possibility that their Naval squadron is still at sea looking for their missing frigate and ourselves. If so, they'll be undermanned and it may be possible to acquire a vessel large enough to transport us to somewhere within reach of an English settlement.'

'Acquire?' Queen questioned, with emphasis.

'Desperate situations call for desperate remedies.' Allowing a moment for this to register, Probus calmly stated. 'Anything seaworthy will do. Perhaps an Arab dhow or even a large trading-junk as long as it sails and stays afloat. The alternative is to turn ourselves over to the Dutch and hope for repatriation in the distant future.'

'When they find out we have sunk one of their proud frigates it might be ages before any of us see England,' interrupted Sethman. Taking a quick look at the formidable mountain range, he grimly added, 'But it will take any shore party a long time to travel fifty miles, especially when trying to find a way across that flaming volcano. In fact, they would do well just to average ten miles a day. Say about a week or so to reach Surubaya, then heaven knows how long we would have to wait for their return: and us not knowing whether they would even be coming back.'

His serious mode of speech reflected misgiving but Probus was unperturbed by this show of reluctance. 'I've given much thought to the matter,' he instantly replied, 'we are suffering no hardship here and still have many wounded who require rest and medical care. Thanks mainly to Mr Queen we have learned to sustain ourselves and there is no doubt we could be very much worse off.' After this sombre admission he then said with determination hardening his voice. 'This may be a virtual paradise but safe harbours rot good ships and good men and we must make every effort to get back to civilisation while the will to do so remains strong.' Strident tone, dismissing any objection, and he now proceeded with the desperate idea that had been formulating in his mind for some time. 'This is a volunteers only task, Mr Queen, apart from yourself and Ramon Salvador who I'm sure will be needed. You will be acting under my orders at all time and your command will be subordinate only to my own. There is no possibility of giving written orders but I promise to accept full responsibility for any unlawful act on your part and Mr Sethman will bear witness to this pledge.'

'Here's one volunteer,' said Bonham-Jones, 'and I will be proud to serve under Mr Queen.'

This statement pleased Probus. Toby was the senior of the two and could have resented not being placed in charge. 'Which makes three midshipmen,' he said, 'for I can't imagine McFie letting you go off on your own.' Smiling wryly at this, Probus then added, 'I estimate a force of thirty, which will leave about the same number here, including the wounded. Muster the hands, Mr Sethman, and have all weapons assembled.'

The curious crew gathered in the clearing; every man a volunteer. They were all fed up with the monotony and Probus detailed off the required number. Choosing with obvious intent the roughest, most violent men for the trek inland. Jacko Abbott. Dooley. Ackerman. Gunner Jancy, and of course, Vinderman. All the physically robust, he was certain this would be no easy task.

This left behind the two senior officers. The wounded David Ashbury. Ten fit seamen and a few convalescents. Also retained, for defence of the camp, were the four surviving marines under sub-lieutenant Warrington-Smythe. Only half of the original ship's company were left after the battle, and the weapons also were very depleted, being reduced to just a few muskets, soon to be useless for shortage of powder. Similarly with pistols, and the defence of both marauding party and shore garrison was very obviously dependant on naked steel.

Spending the rest of the day in preparation. Making up sacks of leaves to carry food. Water was a problem. They had no containers for this precious liquid but Queen planned to follow the stream into the hillside and this should be adequate . . . at least for the first few days.

Assembling at dawn, a fearsome looking bunch. Bearded. Sun-blackened. Bandanas round their heads, knives in their belts and cutlasses glinting in the morning light. The midshipmen had a brace of pistols in their belts, with just one charge to each. The dress of the assembled men was an unbelievable assortment. Baggy matelot trousers, tattered shirts or jerkins, some even had coloured cloth over their upper bodies in native fashion and Probus had difficulty in recognising any of them.

'See you have that damned earring in again,' he said with a snort of derision.

Queen's beard was stubbly and unkempt; bushy moustache hiding his upper lip. His belt was a broad sash of native cloth and an unbuttoned jerkin strained across his shoulders. With a strip of cloth round his head and the shark tooth earring he bore no resemblance to a ship's officer as he replied in unrepentant tone, 'I was told good fortune would always be with me when I wore the shark's tooth.'

Bonham-Jones and McFie were equally colourful. Toby had long since lost his fleshy and indulgent look and his waist was a lean, hard column bound with a leather belt from which the handles of two pistols showed their menace, and a rapier in its scabbard across his shoulder was ready for instant withdrawal. McFie had managed to retain his blue striped shirt but his breeches were ripped off below the knee showing a shapely calf and large feet in incongruous, black, silver buckled shoes. Shaking his head in disbelief as he stepped back from inspection. 'What am I breeding here,' said Probus, 'such a pack of cut-throats I never before clapped eyes on?' As he opened his prayer book quiet descended, bringing an atmosphere of reverence to the morning air. After a short service the Captain closed his prayer book and his head lifted proudly. 'May God go with you.' Deep feeling in the words, eyes piercing at them as he ordered. 'And at all times remember you are Englishmen.' Facing the midshipmen. 'They are in your hands, gentlemen. Make your decisions wisely.'

'Mr McFie,' said Queen, 'bring up the rear with Vindo. I want no stragglers.'

The column moved away two abreast. Glad to be on the move. Doing something positive. Probus and Sethman were joined by the surgeon who said in mournful voice, 'Going to be a long wait.'

'Rather be with them than waiting for their return,' said Probus, glancing at the surgeon, he enquired. 'What's the state of the injured this morning?'

'Improving, but slowly, and I'm in dire need of medicine,' adding thoughtfully, 'this diet of fruit and fresh vegetables is doing good work and a few more days should see some of the less severely injured on their feet again.' Smiling as he suggested. 'Think Mr Ashbury might be on deck today, he's beginning to look very restless.'

Chapter Twenty-one

Dense greenery and clinging vine, hacking with cutlass to force through. Progress slow and uncomfortable as the midday sun made itself felt. Insects buzzing and swarming and a constant irritation on sweat-streaked flesh and combining with the difficult terrain to erode enthusiasm . . . forcing a change of plan.. 'We'll have to lie up during the hottest time of day,' said Queen to his fellow officers, 'and hope to make progress in the cooler hours of morning and evening. No sense in sapping energy in this kind of heat.'

They made camp on the fringe of woodland and mountain where the lush green of the forest began to open out into scrubby, sparse and a barren hillside. One of the men had chafed ugly blisters on the heel of his right foot and, as Bonham-Jones scrutinised his foot, he insisted, 'I can carry on, sir, just let me get my shoe back on.'

'It's no good, Mullen, you'll only slow us down.' Beckoning Queen over. 'This man will have to return to base camp, he'll never make it up the mountain.'

'You must have been in agony with that foot,' said Queen kneeling down. 'Can you make it back on your own or shall I detail one of the men to accompany you?'

'No trouble in back tracking, sir, and you'll need every man when you reach Surubaya. Thanks for the offer but I can make it on my own.' Adding forlornly, 'It's downhill all the way from here.'

On the move at first light, snaking a slow path up the steeply ascending mountainside. Out in the open exposed to the full blast of the tropic sun, hot on their backs and shimmering up from the hard ground; mountain towering above, its peaks in stark outline. Little vegetation now . . . just a few dwarf trees laden with bananas and with piles of rotting fruit at their base bearing testimony to the unending harvest. Food no problem, and still the water trickled in the narrowing stream. Calling a halt just before midday when they reached the sheltering recess of an overhanging bluff. This gave some shade and they crawled thankfully into the deepest corners of the cleft.

Coming up with the last of the climbers Vinderman's face streamed and he took off his bandana to wipe his beard then sank onto a clump of rock. 'Thought Dartmoor was rugged,' words rasping from his throat, 'but this bloody mountain is beyond belief!'

'Can't see the volcano,' said McFie, peering up the mountain, 'must be miles to climb yet. Suppose there is a way round?'

'Wish I knew,' replied Queen, adding with a distinct lack of confidence, 'but if there is we must find it.'

Delaying the start until late afternoon. Making steady progress they were soon climbing over volcanic lava with the mountainside becoming steeper and with gaunt, overhanging rocks confronting them and barring the way. The column had to make several looping diversions around impenetrable areas and it was all uphill and hard going. Two midshipmen ahead at all times scouting for an easier route up or around but, as night fell, they were again held up before a sheer rock face. After the energy sapping heat of the day the night air in that high altitude penetrated scant clothing and the men huddled together for warmth with voices subdued, until sleep stilled the last murmur. Examining the rock face by dawn's early light with Bonham-Jones and McFie at his side. 'Are you certain there is no way round, Billie?' asked Queen.

'Not without going right back on our tracks and starting all over.'

'See that the men breakfast while I try to climb this flaming peak.'

'Let me do it,' drawled Bonham-Jones. 'I have done some rock climbing at our summer home in Cumberland.'

'Up to you then, Toby, but no unnecessary risks.'

Looping the stout rope they had brought from the longboat around his shoulders, he started the slow ascent up the almost vertical rock face.

'Not so bad! There's a narrow chimney here that we can use.' A clattering of small stones accompanied both the remark and the rope that came snaking down. 'Send them up one at a time,' Toby instructed, 'it's difficult, but only for the first few yards.'

The men had finished breakfast. Jed Ackerman threw down a banana skin. 'Used to like these bleedin' things, but I'll never be able to look one in the bleedin' face without feeling sick.'

The mournful tone brought a grin from McFie. 'Think you must enjoy grumbling, Jed. Here we are eating ripe bananas for free and lying under a tropic sun. Thousands back home would love to have such a grumble.'

'And bleedin' welcome, I'm supposed to be a seaman: not a bleedin' mountain goat.'

'Come on, lads,' urged McFie, 'can't be much farther to the top.' Stirring them into life, saying insistently. 'How about showing us how it's done, Jancy?'

The ginger-haired gunner looked up, spat on his hands, and said in dour tone, 'Last time I volunteer for a trek inland.'

By this time Queen had joined Bonham-Jones on the rise above. The chimney ascent was hard work, but now on the top, he looked around with interest. This last steep climb brought them almost to the summit where an area of raw looking lava carpeted the plateau, from out of which towered a mass of broken rock culminating in a huge crater. Fearsome. Pillared by an ominous column of smoke that polluted the atmosphere with the heavy odour of steam and sulphur. Away on the right hand the land began to drop away and descend into a distant area of sparse green, with the far horizon obscured with an early morning mist, a scene of desolation from which he turned with a sense of foreboding. Jancy poked his head over the ridge, coming on all fours over the edge, breathless and with perspiration showing wet on his shirt.

'Blimey,' he gasped as he staggered past and flopped down.

The rest came up in steady progression and showing varying degrees of exhaustion but the rope kept everyone safe and the party re-assembled on the plateau. Under way again, travelling due north, with the sun climbing in the eastern sky on their right hand. An occasional rumble from the bowels of the ground followed by a spurt of smoke from the crater kept the ranks closed up tight. Bringing up the rear, Davy Greenwood cast a wary eye at the crater. 'Wouldn't want to be up here when that thing blows off.'

'You'd surely get your toes warm.' Placing an

empty pipe in his mouth, Vinderman sighed. 'Wish I had some baccy.' Eyes narrowing in anticipation as he forecast. 'Some clumsy Dutchman is going to find my hand in his pouch before long.'

No shelter on the plateau. Sun blazing down with a heat that devastated. Trying to shield heads and eyes from the torment they stumbled in a congested line with Vinderman at the rear allowing no one to fall behind. Lack of water would soon become a desperate plight so Queen sent McFie ahead with two seamen. The ground fell steeply away from the summit and at times they were sliding down on their backsides to brake their speedy descent. The scouting party were waiting by a sheer rock face falling vertically some sixty feet to a green sward, and McFie greeted them with the optimistic comment. 'Seems like the last of the volcano.' The land below the ledge appeared gentle in slope and a few clumps of bush sprouted from fissures in the rock. Again the rope was brought into use and Bonham-Jones demonstrated how to descend a vertical rock face with a turn of rope around the waist and feet thrusting off in great descending jumps.

'Didn't realise the extent of our Toby's talents,' said McFie

Gazing around at the mountain scenery, Queen said, 'Let's hope it's all downhill from here.'

Descending one by one, most risking burned

hands by sliding down the rope with their feet against the rock in ungraceful, running steps. These were not mountain men but ropes were their business and all bottomed out safely. Ramon Salvador alone had difficulty and his awkward handling of the rope brought smiles and calls of benevolent encouragement. Little had been noticed of Ramon on the trip, the men were themselves burned to a dark hue and the half-caste was no longer conspicuous, but his acceptance of hardship had been impassive and in many unobtrusive ways he had earned the high regard of the seamen. Ramon hid his rope-burned hands from sight.

Resting awhile, but lack of shelter, the unbearable heat and the consuming need for water drove them on. Reaching the first fringe of the wooded area. They had spent four days working over the mountain and all were hopeful that the worst part lay behind them.

Slashing at the undergrowth, cutlass in either hand. Chopping their determined way inland. The sun disappeared above the foliage of the treetops and suddenly it was cooler: and also much darker. Birds in the trees above squawked a warning at the intruders and the wooded area reached out before them as the shrill cry heralded the approach of humans into solitude. The going became easier and as Queen hacked alongside McFie he saw the undergrowth open onto a broad leafy track. Came a blessed sound of running water and McFie took off at a run and with a shout of triumph on his mouth then the shout turned into a cry of shock as a section of ground opened beneath his pounding feet and he fell headlong into a gaping hole and the expectant cries of thirst-parched men changed to awesome silence at the plunge of Billie McFie.

'Wait here, men,' commanded Queen urgently. 'There may be more of these holes about.' Moving forward with care followed by Bonham-Jones. Crouching horror struck at the edge of the excavation, revealed now as a primitive trap for wild boar or other game and being a pit about five feet deep and as wide across with a wicked bed of stakes sticking up from the base and across which was impaled the body of McFie. As men converged in awed silence, Queen eased down into the pit, placing his feet carefully between the sharp-pointed stakes.

McFie lay still and ominously quiet with blood oozing from several places on his body and a spike of wood protruding from his left leg above the knee and clean through the lower thigh.

'Is he dead?' asked Bonham-Jones in hushed voice.

One eye opened. 'I'm bleeding aren't I. How can I be dead if I'm bleeding?'

A laugh of relief rippled through the entire company. Joining Queen in the vile trap, Big Jacko Abbott eased his arms under the inert body. 'This is going to hurt, Billie-boy.'

Queen moved to lend support, McFie arched in agony and a groan escaped his tight mouth as Abbot lifted him clear, the weight of his fall had been taken mainly by the stake that had pierced his leg and the other wounds were hardly more than deep scratches, but blood poured from the holes in his leg as Abbot carried the helpless man to the side of a running stream, the very stream that had enticed him into disaster. Bathing his face and body. Trying to staunch the flow from the two ugly holes in his leg. Then Vinderman took over. 'Have to use a tourniquet,' he stated with foreboding' and you know what that means?' Using his headband, Vinderman bound it just above the wounds then inserted a stick and twisted the cloth tight and the blood immediately slowed its life destroying rush. McFie's eyes were closed and his breathing laboured. He seemed unconscious, and the chance was seized to wash all his wounds with clean water. Queen searched with haste born of panic for a cinchona tree. Knifing off great strips of bark. Grinding them with water into a soggy paste which he then plastered over the awful holes and on every other visible cut and all the while silently thanking God for the native knowledge of Tuamoto.

Draped in bunches by the stream grateful for shade and the relief from thirst. Scrambling to their feet as Queen approached but he waved them down. 'Easy men, rest while you are able. We have done well so far but there is a long way still to go and Billie will not be able to walk.' The men nodded in general accord, so he added, 'I'm going to make up a stretcher big enough for six men to handle. I know this must delay us but given willing hands on the stretcher we can still make reasonable time.' Scrutinising for reaction but none was forthcoming. 'There's no chance of sending him back,' he then said, 'so we'll take him with us.'

'Think he'll last the distance without medical attention?' asked Davy Greenwood.

'I don't know but we'll do our best for him.'

Long bamboo canes, thick creepers entwined to bind them together. Carry points fixed three either side. 'Don't waste time and energy, Jase,' said McFie as they placed him on the stretcher. 'I'm quite comfortable and would rather wait here until you return for me.'

'Ants and spiders would have you for breakfast and you know damn well that I won't leave you behind.' With a poor attempt at humour he suggested. 'The lengths some people will go to for a free ride.'

Making a determined effort, McFie insisted, 'I can manage to walk.' Falling back with pain creasing his face. 'Maybe not.'

Under way again, two men ahead carving a path and viewing every leafy track with suspicion and a very tired and frustrated ship's company made camp that night. The stretcher parties were changed frequently because the weight of the injured man soon brought weariness. The tourniquet had to be loosened every half hour and there seemed no likelihood of the blood stopping its crimson flow each time the artery was freed. He was running a high temperature and by evening had started rambling. Queen forced a little of the bitter cinchona liquid down McFie's throat but could not coerce him to take any nourishment. As the night grew cold, he started shivering so they covered his body with mounds of dry leaves and sponged his face as the sweat streamed. It was a long night for the sick man but by morning he seemed conscious and sensible again and his eyes roved and conjectured as he viewed the preparation for departure. Fortunately, his leg had stopped bleeding, allowing the tourniquet to be removed. The twin holes had just a faint seepage of pus through the drying crust and as Queen knelt in scrutiny, McFie said emphatically, 'You've got to leave me sooner or later; I'm only wasting valuable time. You know it: and so do the men.'

'Stop whining! You're a long way from being finished and the decision is mine, not yours.'

'Quite the little Captain, aren't we?'

Something of the old note of banter had crept into his voice and brought a smile from Queen. 'Never forget it!' With this he rose to supervise the stretcher party. Not a single complainant among the men. It seemed they were prepared to carry the midshipman until they dropped.

Making progress while the air remained cool. The ground over which they were making was hilly and undulating. Often they would have to labour up a slow incline with the going leg wearying. Food and water were again plentiful and as evening came, the campfire glowed through the dusk and roasted bananas were the main course at supper.

McFie's condition appeared much the same. The superficial cuts on his body had begun to heal and gave no concern. But the wounds on his leg were angry red and causing intense pain and there were beads of perspiration constantly on his face and his headband was soaked through.

Evening meal over, Bonham-Jones and Queen sitting by the stretcher, McFie's eyes were bright with fever but still watchful. Then Vinderman lounged across with smoke curling from his pipe.

'What the hell are you smoking?' asked Bonham-Jones.

'Dried leaves, not much on strength but better than nowt.' Vinderman puffed smoke rings with relish. 'How's our Billie making out?'

'Don't ask them, ask me,' growled McFie, 'nothing wrong with me that a few weeks running before the south east trades wouldn't put right.' Talking seemed to exhaust his strength and he lay back again.

'When do you think we'll strike the south coast,' said Bonham-Jones.'

'Estimate about another three or four days,'

said Queen looking at Vinderman for confirmation, 'depending on the depth of undergrowth we have to hack through.'

Drawing on his pipe, Vinderman nodded. 'Give us all a lift to see the coast no matter how far off it might be.'

With this thought always uppermost in his mind, Queen got to his feet. 'Think I'll take a stroll to the next rise before it gets too dark, just to se what the ground ahead has in store. Keep your eye on Billie while I'm gone.' He walked away with Bonham-Jones in company. Peeling a banana, Vinderman offered it but McFie shook a morose head and Vinderman eyeballed him sternly.

'You're not helping much by refusing to eat,' he said, 'just making yourself weaker.'

'Less weight to carry,' said McFie in a tone that brought a look of concern from Vinderman. Now they had reached lower altitudes the flies were again troublesome so he covered McFie with the woven-leaf blanket made up by the crew. Puffing smoke over his head, the mild and aromatic leaf burned well in his pipe and was a deterrent to the hordes of winged insects.

'Never knew Billie McFie so gloomy,' said Vinderman.

'It's bloody gloomy lying here and a drag on you all and with a leg on fire and slowly rotting.' Fatal tone of voice, reflecting acceptance, then he grumbled. 'Suppose I'll get that damned mud slapped on it in the morning.'

'Mr Queen seems to have a lot of faith in it,' consoled Vinderman.

'Talk to him, Vindo! He's got to leave me and press on as fast as he can.'

'And what will I tell your parents when they ask,' Queen had silently returned in time to hear this plea and, after a pause, said in derisive tone, 'how I left you, wounded and helpless to die alone in a dark forest? And this after promising your Jeannie that I would keep an eye on you.' Kneeling by the stretcher and pulling back the cover. 'Now let's have a look at that miserable leg.' The wound was blue and nasty with an inflamed area of red spreading below the knee. Holding his nose to the strip of cloth that served as a bandage. 'Think it looks worse: but at least it doesn't smell rotten.'

'Pleasures to come,' said McFie as a dollop of cooling mud was spread and the bandage replaced. Then, with eyes that were deep caverns in the ashen colour of his face, he said. 'Answer me one question, Jase, with honesty. What would you want to do if you were in my place?'

'The same as you would in mine.'

Next day, going progressively rougher. The forest wasn't too dense for the trees were high and wider spread but the sun brought steam heat and the brash and undergrowth seemed to have been undisturbed since time began and every yard had to be hacked and slashed clear, men chopping ever more listlessly at the unending barrier, stretcher party stumbling over strewn branches and debris. An unsighted rear bearer fell to his knees and the stretcher fell sideways almost throwing McFie off. No sound escaped his tight lips but his face was a pale mask of pain. Flies swarmed in droves over his head feeding on salt sweat and his hand hung limp, offering no resistance to the winged pests.

'Careful now!' Anxiety bringing the first sharp words. Queen changed the stretcher-bearers. 'Another half hour then we'll break until late afternoon.' Driving them without restraint, the men wondering if this backbreaking toil would never cease, tempers beginning to fray.

'Think we're going round in circles,' grumbled Jed Ackerman.

They were sprawled out by a tiny stream and, from a prone position, Vinderman said in terse voice. 'Don't you believe it. Our heading is due north and as long as the ground keeps its downward slope we're in the right direction.'

'Slashing through this bleedin' forest is hard enough without having to carry a dying man with us. He won't last out until we reach the coast anyway and every step must be sheer agony for the lad.' Glancing round for support, Ackerman suggested. 'Mr Queen should show mercy and let him die, with dignity!' The first time anyone had ventured such a sentiment but the silence that greeted this comment intimated that several were of the same mind but a seaman from McFie's old starboard watch spoke up.

'You forget it could just as easily be one of us lying on that stretcher . . . wonder if you'd be so eager to be left behind?'

'Mean the lad no harm, Les Bate,' replied Ackerman, 'but where's the sense in prolonging his agony, and holding us back at the same time?'

'Billie's a bloody good sport,' insisted Bate, 'never had so many laughs on watch, and I wouldn't wish it on my conscience to leave him to die alone.'

'Many more days like this and we won't have to worry about him,' interrupted Davy Greenwood, 'without rest and medical care that leg will surely poison him.'

'Talk's cheap,' said Vinderman coldly, 'it's them that assume responsibilities who alone have the right to make decisions. Aye! And have to live with 'em after, and I suggest you keep your miserable gossip out of earshot of Mr Queen, because there's a man who grows older and more desperate with each slow mile we cover.'

At that moment Queen was climbing a tall tree, hoping that in the last light of evening he might possibly catch a glimpse of the sea. Of coast, or anything that might bring encouragement to the men. He well knew their morale was being eroded by the endless battle with the forest and by the exhausting trek. For these were sailing men used to life aboard ship with their personal items of comfort always with them and with an ordered routine. They were not cut out for this primitive, soul-destroying existence. His thoughts were morose in the extreme as he reached a point of high vantage. Nothing! View of endless green, sloping downwards all the time but always with another hump of hill in the distance. Scrambling down, with the plight of McFie urgent in his mind, insistent that he reached the coast before it was too late.

Bonham-Jones sitting by the stretcher, glancing up with the question unspoken but Queen shook his head. 'Seems to go on for ever.'

'You'll never make it with me along,' said McFie forlornly.

'Shut up, Billie,' adding quietly, 'bad day wasn't it?'

'Known better.' Wishing he could make them understand. He felt drained. Of strength: of desire to go on. And the self-effacing knowledge that he was placing the whole expedition in jeopardy was the worst of his pain. 'Let go, Jase,' he cried urgently, 'you can't hang on to me at the expense of all.' Then, appealingly at Bonham-Jones. 'Make him face up to it, Toby.' Anguish showing in the pain rimmed eyes but Toby shook his head and said firmly:

'All for one, remember.'

A grasping hand reached out and Queen took it in both his own as McFie said directly into his face. 'You have to let go, Jase! I no longer have the strength to hold on for you.'

These desperate words were knife thrusts to Jason Queen. Letting go of possessions that were dear to him was something he had always found great difficulty in facing up to. Farm animals had lived on to old age and long after their useful life. Boyhood bits of treasure had been retained and carefully stored. Acquired skills diligently practised lest their hard won secrets should escape from his fingers and so make waste of the time given to their learning. Nothing he once had loved was ever relinquished without enduring pain. With the practise of long years he closed his mind to the plaintive appeal and he looked deep into the eyes of his friend. 'No, Billie, there is no easy way out of this.' His voice held the rasp of desperation. 'I won't let go! Not while there is life in you: or me. I swear that we will reach the coast. I will lift your head and let you look once more upon the ocean and bathe your wounds in clean salt water.' Choking on the words, emotion bringing tears to his eyes. 'Then if you insist on dying, you will at least die with salt air in your lungs . . .'

His voice faltering, he stumbled away like a wounded animal leaving a very sombre quiet, eventually broken by McFie. 'He's wrong, Toby,' he said, 'I love him . . . but he is so wrong!' His eyes were gaunt and somehow hopeless and Toby looked at him with an expression of puzzlement which turned aghast as McFie pleaded. 'Leave your pistol, Toby. Let me end it clean. With dignity! And set him free!'

Smoothing hair back from the clammy forehead, Toby said in a voice consumed with tenderness. 'Oh, Billie, please don't ask more of me than I have to give, and, one thing above all,' he added with a glance at the departing figure, 'were we to take this decision it would surely be the destruction of Jason Queen. Hang on, Billie, just a little while longer: if only for his sake.'

On the move at dawn, the time of day when they were refreshed and the air was cool and they could settle into an easy rhythm and make good progress while conditions were less inclement.

Perseverance and determination finally prevailed. Slashing out of the clinging brash into more open countryside. Cutlasses were sheathed with relief and the party halted for a rest on the fringe of forest and sloping plain. Optimism returning in full measure, the men declined to take a midday halt and eager to make ground over easier terrain and ignoring the penetrating heat of a sun blazing from a sky devoid of cloud.

Now Queen felt confident enough to send Bonham-Jones and six of the fastest men to scout ahead. Seeking for any sign of a hostile Dutch settlement or perhaps the longed for sight of the northern shore of Java. The rest of the group moved along in double line formation with the stretcher party at the rear. McFie was asleep most of the day, merciful oblivion easing the agony of the jolting ride and allowing the bearers to make faster time.

Making camp early well pleased with the distance covered. Laying McFie under a shady tree with his face washed and the bandage adjusted round his thigh, Queen ground up the last of the cinchona bark to make up a clear liquid which he eased drop by drop down his throat. Then he strode off to meet the scouting party, eager for news of the route ahead. McFie opened his eyes to find a bearded face peering upside down over him.

'Bloody hell, Vindo! Thought it was the devil himself come to claim me.'

'Sounds a bit more like our Billie McFie,' said Vinderman with a grin of extreme pleasure.

'Any sign of the coast?'

'No, but we made good time today and tomorrow should see us within spitting distance.'

'Anything to eat?'

'House plate special.'

'Not roasted bananas?'

'None finer.' Producing a large leaf full of steaming bananas. He also brought a flat piece of wood to use as a spoon and looked on with satisfaction as the food was wolfed down.

The scouting party returned with information that the way ahead eased all the time and there was still no sign of habitation. Sprawling down as if exhausted, Bonham-Jones said, 'How's Billie?'

Gesturing, Vinderman said, 'Woke up, stuffed his face with bananas then went back to sleep. Perhaps that poisonous muck of Mr Queen's is doing some good after all.'

Bonham-Jones chewed on a handful of sweet root. 'Might see the coast tomorrow,' he said, 'looks as if we might make it after all and without losing Billie on the way?'

Queen had joined them by this time and the comment brought a very relieved smile. 'Something to be thankful for, even a one-legged McFie is worth many a man on two good legs.'

Bonham-Jones and his scouts were seated in anticipatory posture on the brow of the hill as the main group came up the crest and a spontaneous buzz of excitement ran through the men. The view was overwhelming, a carpet of green opening out below and spreading almost into the silver sea with a long sweep of pale sand showing like a water mark on fine notepaper. Air fragrant with the scent of blossom brought on the gentle breeze fanning over the placid water and up through the glades to the peak on which they stood.

'What do you think now, McFie?'

'Knew all the time we could do it.' Excited, he struggled to a sitting position. 'If I could just get on my feet I'd do you a one-legged hornpipe.

How about making me up a crutch so I can get rid of this flamin' stretcher?'

'You'd only slow us down and, as I recall, would be the last person to suggest such a thing.'

'Mr Queen! You've made your point: just don't sound so damn smug! You may have need of me before this trip's over.'

Chapter Twenty-two

Low upon the water, her hull an overall, sinister black, two tall masts with not a suggestion of rake, either fore or aft. Her stern was wide and a slim bowsprit angled sharply up from her beak head. All sails furled, somewhat sloppily to the critical eyes of the English sailors and the ship lay quiet to her anchor. Press of men like ants ashore, busy with rope and tackle. The bay was peaceful, the water calmed by a finger of land creeping seawards to make a sheltering breakwater. 'What do you make of her, Vindo?' asked Queen, surveying the scene with interest.

Sprawled in covert posture on a cliff some two hundred feet up, they had come across this remote lagoon while making along the coast to their destination of Surabaya. Vinderman viewed the men below with a knowing eye before taking a closer look at the ship through the telescope. 'Twenty-four guns,' he stated, 'and she really is a beauty. She looks very French but wears no distinguishing flag.' Telescope snapping shut, he declared. 'My guess is a privateer . . . why else would they be skulking in this out of the way anchorage, and I reckon they are about to careen her and give the bottom a scrape and clean.'

'How long will that take?'

'Two or three days, depends on how much they like work.'

'Pity,' mused Queen, 'but we can't wait around for them to finish.' Surveying the work below. 'Must be about thirty of them, and probably as many aboard.' Shaking his head in dismissive manner. 'She looks fast and efficient but too much of a handful for us and we must try for easier prey at Surabaya.'

Another long day's trek before the port of Surabaya was in sight. With the approach of habitation they had to leave the well-trodden dirt road that skirted the curve of the coast. The going had been easy and they had travelled more than fifteen miles that day, diverting around several small settlements and taking evasive care. They made camp in the cover of thick undergrowth. No fire being made for fear of their presence being detected.

Queen and Bonham-Jones looked down on the harbour from a point of vantage. River estuary shining in the morning sunlight and the waterfront was an untidy mess of shacks and warehouses, deserted and somehow forlorn. Too early for movement on shore but out in the estuary they could see the battened sails of a large junk, almost stationery as it stood into the harbour. Little merchant shipping on view, only two ships of any size lay at anchor and after a minute for speculation, Queen said, 'Inter-Island traders, probably falling to pieces for lack of maintenance. I'll take Ramon and explore the waterfront. Find out the strength of the Dutch, and pick out a likely vessel.' Ruminating on this, he added with a boyish grin. 'Martha Harper must be smiling right now, she always thought of me as a pirate.'

Main party resting under waving coconut palms but in no way careless, men were posted on all four flanks to keep vigilance. Queen had shed all items that might betray nationality and was clad only in a skirt of cloth tight round his hips. With skin colour brown as any Malayan he looked as native as Ramon himself. Waiting until the settlement came to life, hoping to remain inconspicuous among the bustle before making their way down the hill and along the waterfront. Harbour surging with colour and movement. Sampans working between the pools and rock fissures for shellfish; offshore fishing fleet of small junks already out in the river and heading for the Straits separating the island of Madura from the mainland. One of the trading brigs was hauling in its anchor cable and preparing to hoist sail. Topsails dopping from the yardarms, sheeted home. Sails that were dirty and patched,

'That canvas would never stand up to a prolonged blow,' said Queen, dismissing this and the other trader as a potential prize. Sauntering without haste along the waterfront. It was a township on stilts with a congregating mass of wooden shacks spreading untidily down into the wet filth of the river where the water was the colour of mud and strewn with floating debris. Stench of sun-baked refuse: with bloated flies and other insects buzzing about their heads in constant irritation. The Port bustled with teeming humanity all milling and jostling in the market place. Numerous carts and rickshaws sped along the dirt road propelled by barelegged coolies in wide brimmed hats of straw, adding their own mixture of dust to the stale odour of waterfront garbage. The population seemed a blend of Malay and Chinese and the two mingled unobtrusively into the motley throng.

Dutch flag flying above a parapet walled, two-storey fort, two armed guards patrolling in front dressed in the uniform of the Dutch militia. The fort was in a position overlooking the harbour entrance and a row of cannon poked their suggestive noses through slits in the parapet wall. A curving jetty had been built out in front of the port and along this on both sides lay a disorientated jumble of native craft roped and rafted together and swaying and undulating with the disturbance set up by the swell. Small junks . . . covered over sampans and dhow-like vessels all jostling together. A virtual shantytown of houseboats and it appeared that much of the population lived afloat. To free one of the inside craft must have needed a manoeuvre of some intricacy.

'What exactly are we looking for, Captain?' asked Salvadore.

'You promote me too soon, Ramon,' said Queen in surprised reflex, 'my rank is midshipman.'

'For this trip everyone knows you are Captain.'

Brow furrowing at this, he said, 'You make me realise my responsibilities.' Glancing across the harbour, eyes serious and scrutinising. 'I'm looking for a craft big enough to transport what remains of our original crew to a place of safety.' Just then a squad of Dutch marines came marching at a brisk pace towards where they were idling and Ramon broke into a torrent of abuse in Malay, directed at the bowed head of Queen. The officer in charge looked neither to left nor right as the marines marched through the gateway into the fort.

'Didn't understand what you were shouting, Ramon, but it sounded damned fierce.'

'You would be most offended, my Captain, was I to interpret.'

Queen had more urgent things on his mind, for just then a glimpse of a topsail appeared over the low cliff that formed the western arm of the hillside. Must be a tall ship to show above the cliff that way, and soon three masts under plain sail were in view then a great ship swept with imposing grace around the point. A cannon roared from directly above them, belting their eardrums and causing them to jump in shock. Another cannon fired, them another. Crashing about them and echoing back from the hillside in a salute to the oncoming vessel.

'Dutch battle cruiser,' said Queen as the guns of the ship returned a rhythmic greeting. Watching the seventy-four ghosting in, her sails furling one by one, leaving up just a backed mizzen. She poised, her anchor dropping with a rattle of windlass and the vast three-decker drifted astern on her anchor cable. All very professional! Her bulk monopolised the harbour. From under her stern crept the junk they had seen earlier, the gestures of the crew making it obvious that they didn't appreciate the man-of-war taking their wind. Calls of abuse came clearly across the water and Queen viewed the junk with conjecture growing. Much bigger than he had supposed. From so close he estimated she must be about sixty feet long, with two bamboo slatted sails set square across the main and mizzen masts. She came easily over the water and a thrust on the helm brought her head up into wind. Sails furling down like roller blinds and a tiny anchor splashing from the bow as a fleet of six sampans disengaged from the tangle of boats and each with a solitary figure sculling at the stern sweep came alongside the junk where the crew immediately began throwing silvery fish into the waiting sampans. Queen commented on the curious structure at the stern of the junk.

'Stern lanterns they use to attract fish at night,' said Ramon.

'You mean they go out every night then return in the early morning?'

Ramon nodded in confirmation.

'So they remain at anchor all day, and probably sleep,' said Queen calculatingly. 'Come, Ramon, we have work to do.'

They came into Surabaya during the dark of late evening in two's and three's, like pilgrims on a quest considered worthy, with McFie between the supporting shoulders of Jack Dooley and Davy Greenwood, his leg rigid in a restraining splint of bamboo.

Taking the junk was child's play to determined men. Two swam out and cut loose a vacant, outlying sampan. The little craft drifted alongside the junk with just Ramon hunched over the single sculling oar and with ten men supported along its far waterline, heads down and well out of sight. The crew of the junk were on deck preparing for their night's work and they looked with contempt at Ramon, pouring abuse on his plea for a single fish for his poor supper. Ten seamen came dripping up behind them, barefoot, making no sound. The fishermen turned in alarm but too late. Manhandled, they were stripped naked and locked at knifepoint in the forward cabin.

The sampan brought the remainder of the English aboard in relays, the whole operation being carried out in silent haste. McFie was hoisted up and propped against the after bulwark and sail was hoisted while she laid head to wind. The anchor hove up short, then broke out as her head paid off to seaward. Gathering way she moved off without fuss then left harbour as she did every night about her normal business and with no apparent unease at the strange hand on the tiller.

Chapter Twenty-three

Dawn flared the morning into light with the junk standing out into the gulf formed between the eastward coast of Java and the Island of Madura. Water calm . . . just a restless swell deceptive in strength until it pounded and broke onto the outlying coral reef with the explosive power of seas driven across thousands of miles of exposed ocean by the monsoon wind. Sun warm and the air sharp with the tang of salt, junk rolling from side to side as they reached deep into the gulf. Coastline lush, crowned by undulating palm trees. Sea of translucent emerald paling in colour as it surged into the shallows only to stay its rush on the strips of beach fringing the calming water, with the reef ominously marked by a line of white capped breakers.

Distinct lack of variety in the food aboard: they didn't care. They were at sea again! In their own environment; doing what they knew best. Breakfasting on fish and boiled rice, swilling down bowls of steaming, smoke-scented tea . . .

taking turns with the limited domestic utensils. But it was a veritable feast after existing on a diet of fruit and vegetables.

The junk wasn't built for speed but she was a sturdy sea boat riding well through the water, the bow wave swishing back alongside the low waist and the coast changing shape and colour as lagoon and craggy cliff slid by. Two green-slant eyes were painted on the bow, one either side.

'Ship no have eyes, how see way?' Instructed Ramon Salvador in an exaggerated Chinese accent but also with a serious expression that indicated belief.

'Hope they work for us,' said Vinderman from the helm, 'there's bugger-all else to steer by?'

Their course planned to run along the coast deep into the southern corner keeping land in sight but well out in deep water, then to come about on a long tack into wind which would take them on a close reach for eighty miles and clearing the tip of Java before they could turn southerly through the Straits of Bali. Only then could they free their wind and make course directly to the southern point of Java and along the final westerly route to where Captain Probus must be counting the days with either impatience: or acceptance of failure.

Little to do as the junk ploughed on with seamen relaxing on deck enjoying the wind and sunshine and just happy to be at sea. The watch changed. First dog watch taking over. Off-duty men preparing rice and fish for the evening meal as Vinderman handed the telescope to Queen with a question in his eyes. They had just passed a finger of rock that curved out of a deep lying bay and as the shoreline opened out they could see clearly into the entrance. Queen closed the telescope with a decisive snap.

'She's afloat again and lying to her anchor.'

He was prowling like a caged animal about the narrow bridge deck and Vinderman looked at him. 'They outnumber us two to one.'

'Not when they're asleep.'

'We'd never be allowed near enough to board,' said Vinderman with conviction.

Bonham-Jones joined them, he too had seen the anchored privateer and as the coastline slid by closing off the entrance into the bay, said, 'What a lovely thing she is, and there is no doubt that such a ship would be the answer to our problems.' Looking at their own crowded deck. 'This junk is nowhere near large enough to carry all the crew of the *Earl* any great distance.' Sensing conjecture, he added with a grin. 'Wouldn't it be rude justice to pirate a privateer?'

'Won't stay there much longer now she has a clean bottom,' said Vinderman.

'Keep under way until we are out of sight, then heave-to around the next headland.'

They hove to by dropping all sail and lying ahull. The junk rode easily on the swell but Queen stared in dismay at the line of pounding breakers between ship and shore. There appeared no way over the encircling reef but, with an idea formulating, he ordered, 'Toby, have the skipper of the junk brought up, and bring Ramon also.'

The skipper was a wizened old man with a goatee beard of silver. They had allowed him to dress in a Chinese smock that reeked of fish and opium. He seemed docile but his eyes were penetrating and hostile as leading hand Jack Dooley poked him forward with a pistol and the old man shuffled towards Queen with his hands buried in the wide sleeves of his smock. 'Watch him,' warned Vinderman, 'might have a knife up his sleeve?'

Showing a toothless grimace, the old skipper opened his empty hands. 'Perhaps he understands English,' said Bonham-Jones.

'No matter.' Queen instructed Ramon to explain that he wanted to get the junk inside the reef but the old man broke into a torrent of abuse.

'Says there is no way in at this point,' announced Ramon, 'and fears you will destroy his ship.'

'He should worry; he's lost it anyway. Explain our intentions and also the fact that if we are successful he can have his ship back, but only if he can put us ashore close to where we are now.'

A spirited conversation followed. It was plain that the skipper's interest had been aroused. 'He calls this ship the scourge,' explained Ramon, 'and says that if you challenge the notorious Captain Swally you will soon be joining your dishonourable ancestors.'

The slant eyes glittered through calculating slits and Bonham-Jones wryly suggested:

'He seems quite enchanted with the thought.'

Ramon engaged in a long dialogue with the skipper, then interpreted, 'The only gap is about four miles further up the coast but once behind the reef you could sail inside almost to where we are now.'

'Will he pilot us in?'

'Only if you give him back his ship.'

'If we take the pirates, otherwise it won't matter much to us anyway.' He had no intention of giving back the junk should they fail because he intended to leave a prize crew aboard capable of sailing the junk to the aid of Captain Probus. Thinking about this for a moment, before ordering. 'Up sail, Vindo, run parallel to the reef.'

As the junk got under way the old Malay spoke urgently to Ramon. 'He wants two of his men on deck to help pilot us in,' said Ramon.

'Bring up two, Toby, under close guard.'

Racing along the edge of the reef still in deep water, the motion much more violent because now the onshore wind came directly abeam so the slatted sails bellied deep and bar taut with the driving wind. She responded quickly to the pull of the rudder and she heeled and the lee rail dipped into the rushing bow wave. A half hour passed without any apparent way in and still the surf pounded against the barrier of coral.

'How about there?' Vinderman had seen a smoother slick in the line of broken water.

'Run her off a point. Let's take a closer look.'

The change of direction brought alarmed response as the old Malay pointed a skinny arm at the fast approaching slick and, shaking his head, gestured frantically to a point further down the coast.

'Forget it, Vindo! Bring her back on course.'

The Malay cackled urgently with Ramon, who said, 'Needs his crewmen on the bow.'

The two took up position on the forepeak and the old Malay allowed himself a little smile as a dark swirl of water at the place they had been making for brought a scared comment from Bonham-Jones. 'This reef gives me the flamin' creeps, think we ought to pull back into safer water.'

Queen took a quick glance at the diminutive old skipper who seemed quite composed and with his eyes fixed on the men at the bow. Still racing on, the land beginning to curve away and soon could be seen the indentation of a small lagoon and the recess of what appeared to be a river estuary. Corner cleared, their searching eyes could now make out the broader sweep of a semicircular bay flanked by an expanse of white sand. Man on the bow raising his arm in a signal. The skipper made a swerving gesture and

Vinderman turned the junk towards the reef. The waves were certainly less menacing although a line of white caps foamed between ship and shore and all the while the junk rolled gunwhales under. Both natives now had one hand above their heads in a signal to go ahead and Vinderman looked at Queen in alarm.

'What the hell, Vindo, do we have a choice? Get on with it!'

The junk heeled sharply as a creaming wave lifted her then she surfed along on the crest. The roar of sea surging against that coral reef was the most forceful and fearsome sound and the English seamen stared at the onrushing breakers with fright clearly showing on their faces. Broken water all around, tip of coral showing three yards away on the starboard beam, instantly covered by a swell of foam. The junk rolled beyond control and Vinderman cursed as he wrestled with the jerking tiller. A giant wave reared astern, seemed to hang over them, then the top broke and tons of water roared down and lifted the junk like a piece of driftwood and slewed her round in a broach-to. Queen jumped to the helm where Vinderman was fighting a losing battle to keep stern on to those fearsome seas. They were being carried bodily sideways and another such wave would surely bury them.

Struggling . . . wresting her head round heedless of the derisive cackle of the old skipper, they managed to get her pointing shoreward again just as the next following sea caught up with them. Bursting under the transom. Deluging high and over them. Men on the foredeck were waist deep in green water, the whole length of the deck awash with foaming seas. But they were over the reef and in quiet water with the junk speeding shoreward, the surf outside growling a sullen disappointment at their safe passage. The wind died away in the shelter of the lagoon and the change from onslaught to peace and tranquillity was so sudden they could only feel relief and thankfulness.

'We'd better get some sail off.' Vinderman's laconic voice snapped Queen from appreciative reverie.

'Not yet! Bring her round. I want to run as far inside the reef as we can.' Turning to Dooley, he commanded. 'Return the skipper and his crew to confinement.' He had the distinct impression that the old man had a smile in his eyes as he moved with shuffling gait down to the fore cabin.

'Don't trust that old man, he looks a cunning little bastard!' Bonham-Jones said with feeling.

'He's hoping this Swally character will remove us from his sight, permanently,' replied Queen. 'Check that they are properly secured, Toby, don't want them breaking out with only a prize crew left on board.'

Ghosting up the channel formed between reef and shore. Spray flying from the reef and they could hear the incessant booming of the breakers but inside all was calm, the water like crystal with the sea bed a pure white sand beneath them. A quarter mile wide the lagoon narrowing sharply with the beach to larboard fringed with waving palms. The men had been as though hypnotised as they blasted over the reef. Expecting any second that they would be catapulted into the raging torrent, their relief was obvious and voluble, while ahead the steep hill crept seaward making a dead end and forming a beautiful lagoon.

Waking up, McFie looked around with his mouth open. 'What happened?'

'Missed all the fun, McFie, and the ride of a lifetime.'

'Where the hell are we?'

'Just over the hill from the privateer, I hope.'

The sails rolled down like a window blind and the anchor plunged into the seabed to bury its point in the sand with the cantenary of the anchor warp threading down and clearly visible in the shallows. The junk snubbed against the anchor and lay still and the early evening sun cast a long shadow from the palm trees with the only sound the thunder of sea against coral reef.

'Have the men to a cold supper, Toby. No galley smoke to betray our presence and absolute silence must be observed while Vindo and I take a look ashore.'

'How about me?' McFie struggled up as he spoke.

'Can do without you falling down holes again.' Easing him down on a hatch cover. 'Sorry, but you remain aboard, need you to organise a prize crew.'

'We got in safe,' said Vinderman, 'getting back out over the reef against that onshore wind could be another matter.'

'The skipper will pilot his boat out safely,' said Queen, 'particularly if he thinks he's getting it back.'

The only link they had with the shore was a tiny shell of a ship's boat . . . a flimsy thing with a shell of animal hide. With Vinderman at the stern sweep the little craft sped buoyantly over the few yards to shore where the sand was soft and dry underfoot. Moving without sound to the first slope of the hillside. Climbing stealthily . . . reaching the crest and looking down on the other side to find the pirate ship had been warped close to the lee of the hillside and lay anchored a bare hundred yards offshore.

'They've come under the lee to keep out of the onshore breeze,' whispered Vinderman, 'so they're not planning to leave before daybreak.' The ship lay below them, they had a perfect view of her sheerline sweeping a gracious curve aft. Her name was painted on the bow, the lettering in commanding gold against the black. She was named *Restitution* but showed no register of a native port, and Vinderman said emphatically, 'Something about this sinister beauty brings out the worst in a man.'

Sounds of revelry aboard, press of men gathered on the main deck. The crew seemed to be of many races with brown skins predominant and all drinking freely from bowls that looked like half coconut shells and their untidy dress and lack of restraint caused Queen to say, 'Not much in the way of discipline.'

'None the less dangerous when it comes to a fight. We could never take them by force.'

'What do you reckon, then?'

Looking at them with the eyes of experience, Vinderman said, 'Let's hope they carry on drinking. Once they get the feel for strong liquor, they might drink themselves into a stupor.' These words heralded the arrival on deck of a colourful figure. A big man, and round like a barrel. Flowing, wide-sleeved shirt of brilliant red tucked into a broad belt that ballooned over the great mound of his stomach. His head was completely devoid of hair and his scalp glowed in the late sunshine and a black beard covered his face from the eyes downward. Wide trousers pouched below the knee. Bare feet. Sword over his shoulder and, staring wide-eyed at this formidable apparition, Queen gasped:

'Swally!'

'What a bleedin' monster,' said Vinderman, 'no wonder the junk skipper's shit scared.'

Swally dominated the main deck with his colour and restless energy. Though grossly obese he moved with the grace often found in fat men and ran easily down the short companionway to join his crew. Seizing a drinking bowl from the hands of one he swaggered over to a keg of liquor that stood on the top of a similar keg and not bothering to run the tap just stove in the top with a single blow from his clenched fist and scooped up a bowlful and downed it in one swallow and threw the bowl back at the man from whom he had taken it. His exuberant guffaw carried loudly across the water. The pirate crew roared approval and Swally's teeth showed in the dark of his beard. Swaggering among them he clapped his hands in a summons and a stoop-shouldered seaman hastily placed a fiddle under his chin and began to scrape a lively tune. Grabbing a man by the scruff of his neck, Swally thrust him headlong into a space cleared by the expectant pirates. The man was small in stature and had only one leg, the other being just a wooden peg. Gyrating to the tune of the fiddle, stamping his peg leg in staccato rhythm, round and round in an endless dance then, clapping again, Swally shouted, 'Faster!'

The tempo of the fiddle quickened and the dance became a frightened scramble to keep up the rhythm and the two onlookers watched in mesmerised silence as the scene took on a desperation that had little to do with the music. The dancer began to tire and a pistol appeared in Swally's hand. He fired deliberately at the wooden peg and the bullet ploughed splinters in the deck and the man jumped away with his peg leg pumping with desperate energy. Cheers of encouragement rang out from the circle of men and Swally replaced his smoking pistol with another significantly aimed weapon. The fiddler's bow scraped a wrong note and the one-legged man staggered and nearly fell as the heavy ball splintered at his feet. Laughing all the time at the plight of the dancer Swally levelled another pistol and the little man collapsed in a heap, huddling himself against the next shot but Swally had tired of his fun. Striding to the keg of liquor and picking it up with ease in his hairy hands he splashed the fiery spirit over peg leg's head.

'What a waste!' Vinderman groaned.

Another cask was stoved in and serious drinking resumed with the recent fun adding to the air of abandon but Swally barked command and two men moved reluctantly away to take up position in the bow of the vessel.

'Seems confident that he's unassailable here,' said Vinderman, 'but still sets an anchor watch.'

Looking at the scene on deck with increasing conjecture Queen said, 'Swally rules by fear and by virtue of his own brute strength and this might be to our advantage. From what we've just seen I doubt them being eager to die in defence of him.'

The words sounded confident but didn't do much to inspire Vinderman, who answered with a cautious, 'Let's hope for a dark night.'

* * *

Queen stood on the steering platform of the junk looking down on them. Most stripped to the waist with a knife in their belt and cutlass slung over their shoulder. Any resemblance to law-abiding seamen had long since disappeared and they looked as fierce as the cutthroats whose ship he was determined to take. Allowing a moment for quiet before addressing his men.

'You are all aware of our situation. We need this ship if we are ever to get off the Island and return to England. We are outnumbered at least two to one but have the advantage of surprise . . . and if we can board her while they are asleep should take them without too much bloodshed. If our plan fails and we have to fight, there is no doubt that it will be bloody and violent with no quarter given.' Grim, but confident tone as he concluded. 'Twenty-four English seamen are worth a hundred miserable pirates, and I know you will give your best.' A low, affirmative growl confirmed the validity of this compliment, so he now outlined the details of the take-over plan. 'Mr Bonham-Jones and Mr McFie will remain on board with a prize crew. If we fail . . . their task will be to sail this junk to the position of Captain Probus.' Pausing for effect, Queen then said. 'And don't forget that the *Restitution* will be a valuable acquisition and I promise you all a fair share of the prize money.'

Big Jacko Abbot spat in his hands. 'Sounds good enough to me, Capt'n.' Came a murmur of accord and the crew rushed for the side. Anchored in a few feet of water, they were soon ashore.

Prize crew of four . . . Bonham Jones in charge. He had raised passionate objection to being left behind but finally bowed to reason and to the fact that he couldn't swim: and how else would they be able to board the privateer? Cursing the ill luck that kept him immobile McFie grumbled in frustrated tone, 'Don't know what you'll do without me at your back?'

'If we succeed, I'll send you a signal. Free the old skipper and leave him to pilot himself over the reef.' Looking at Bonham-Jones he said with a semblance of a smile. 'It's all yours from here on, Toby. I'll leave one man on the ridge as observer. If it goes wrong put all the prisoners ashore except the skipper and get out as fast as you can back to base camp.'

Reaching out his hand Toby said, 'Good luck, Jase.'

McFie looked decidedly miserable so Queen ruffled his hair in consoling gesture.

'Cheer up, Billie, I need you aboard this old junk.'

'Give 'em hell,' was all McFie managed to say.

Sprawling under cover on the hilltop. Darkness falling fast, incandescent moon hanging low in a velvet sky and shining silver light across the water so brightly they could see the reflected shape of the privateer in the water below and the two masts rippling down into the depths. Noise of revelry going on unabated and the waiting brought tension to the silent observers, then a light flared from the bow and tobacco glowed red in a pipe bowl.

'Two still on anchor watch,' observed Vinderman. Whispering the words because the slightest sound carries far across the water on so still a night. 'Must take those two first or lose our advantage.'

'What the hell is that?' The murmur escaped the open mouth of Jacko Abbot and the seamen stared in apprehension as the immense figure of Swally emerged on deck. In the half-light he looked more gigantic than ever and his moon-shadow spread grotesque and darkly satanic across the deck. He moved with speed among the carousing crew and the onlookers could clearly hear the crack of a whip as he lashed through them, scattering them from the barrel of liquor. Picking it up, Swally threw it over the side where it bobbed for a minute then sank in a flurry of bubbles.

'The monster has no regard for good liquor,' growled Vinderman, 'if he had to buy it he mightn't be so quick to throw it overboard.'

'Suspect he wants an early start,' mused Queen.

'Drunken men sleep heavy,' said Jancy with a knowing wink, 'give 'em half an hour and they'll be dead to the world.'

Pirate crew stretched out on deck, some had slung a hammock but most slept where they dropped in a stupor and the deck was littered with recumbent bodies.

The two best swimmers among the crew were Jack Dooley and able seaman Les Bate. Together with Queen and Vinderman they crept down to the water's edge. The foreshore was strewn with driftwood and they picked out a half submerged and rotting tree stump, quite long and three feet across it floated easily when slid into deep water. The four waded in either side and swimming with silent care began to cross the lagoon, pushing the log with their hands gripped tight in the pulpy wood they drifted slowly across the exposed stretch of water and along the shaded side of the anchored ship. Dooley and Bate held the log off and, treading water, Queen poised by the midships where the freeboard was at its lowest but even so, deck level was still several feet above their heads. No handhold or hanging rope, the only sound a muted discord of snoring from sleeping men above. Movement from the bow caused them to squeeze further under cover of the ship's side as one of the men on anchor watch urinated over the bow. Holding their breath until his silhouette disappeared.

Queen made ready to take a look. The others grasped firm hold on knobbly branch stumps to steady the log and he straddled across and carefully rose to his feet, balancing himself against the black hull. Head clearing the rail, eyes alert for any movement. Paunchy figure asleep directly below him: prostrate men in various states of abandon. Air reeking with the smell of stale rum and unwashed bodies and he cursed the moon that was bathing the deck in revealing light. Pulling himself up and over he dropped in a crouch behind the bulwarks, Vinderman coming up with a knife in his teeth, bare feet making no sound as he took up position alongside, then knotting a convenient length of rope, he lowered it for Dooley and Bate who pushed away the log then scrambled silently up. Moving clear, the log resumed drifting progress back to shore. Queen inclined his head at the bow then with Vinderman picked a careful way to the other side and began to move forward: with exaggerated caution. Taking a belaying pin from a rack by the mainmast shrouds, Vinderman beckoned Queen to do likewise. Now two either side, the four men moved with ghostly menace through the sleeping crew. One stirred and grunted in his sleep causing them to freeze in their tracks but there was no further sign of waking and they crept forward and came with stealth up the companionway that connected to the foredeck.

The two men on anchor watch sat on a windlass. Facing forward over the bow they appeared half-asleep but there was a naked expanse of foredeck to cross before they could be reached. Hefting his knife Vinderman beckoned to Dooley then raised his belaying pin and threw it over the bow. It fell with a dull but audible splash. The two watch keepers looked questioningly at each other then moved to lean over the rail and look down. The last movement they were ever to make because Vinderman and Dooley were on them like wild animals with a hand over the mouth and cold steel in a death dealing thrust between the ribs. Vinderman twisted his knife clear and wiped it clean on the shirt of the pirate who was draped over the bow gazing sightlessly at the ripples caused by the thrown belaying pin.

Queen had seen men die in battle but this was his first encounter with cold-blooded murder! The sheer speed and savagery left him aghast and reeling, then he remembered the chilling words of Captain Probus. "Do whatever you have to do". Movement on shore caught his eye and his arms moved up and down in signal, following which men slid into the water and a line of moving heads began to close *Restitution*. Creeping back down the starboard side, the four found a boarding net furled on the rail and this they lowered over the freeboard.

Dripping seamen came silently on deck. A pirate stirred, as if sensing the presence of intruders. Les Bate smashed him unconscious with a belaying pin, a sickening crunch, loud on the night air. 'Wake 'em up,' said Queen. 'One by one!'

Drink sodden pirates were brought to sudden life when a calloused hand was clapped over their mouth and a sharp knifepoint pricked their throats. It was a situation that called for no explanation and all weapons were taken from the bemused sleepers before they were sufficiently aware to resist. A pistol fired suddenly as a hidden pirate realised the danger. Blasting the quiet, and answered immediately by the pistol Vinderman had taken from the dead watch keeper. Deck in uproar as the remaining pirates woke into bewildered life. Stealth over the English crew flung themselves upon the pirates. The battle was short and bloody but the pirates were a drunken, disorganised rabble against cold determination.

'Where the hell's Swally?' The terrible din should have brought the Captain out by now but Swally had woken to the knowledge that his ship was under attack and he was working his way through the lower deck gathering every man below.

The English were in control of the main and quarterdeck and they had all captives bunched together on the foredeck where gunner Jancy had loaded one of the bow cannons with grape shot and, with a flintlock to hand, the muzzle of the twelve pounder swung to cover the prisoners. Queen had felt almost a bystander during the action, always surrounded by Vinderman, Abbot, Bate and Dooley, who appeared to be playing the role of Good Shepherd while the rest of his men overcame any resisting pirate. Then a forward hatchway burst open and splintering under the impact of Swally and his motley few. Armed with cutlass and pistol they came out in a foul-mouthed rush. Two men fell under the fusillade and an answering fire prostrated several of the rushing pirates. Swally was a fearsome sight. Stripped to the waist and whirling a sword above his head he charged without hesitation into the fray and men reeled before his scything blade but his own crew had no heart for a fight where the odds were not favourable and offered only token resistance. Swally and another man, a villainous looking dwarf with shoulders wide as a barn door were surrounded by a horde of English seamen, but resisting all attempts to take them. The language of the Captain was foul, yet English, and Queen stepped forward with a loaded pistol. 'Submit, Captain. Or I blow you apart.'

'Shoot and be damned!' Swally parried a blow that would have severed his head. The dwarf officer staggered from a sabre slash and went down on his knees but Swally fought his way clear to the ship's side as Queen crouched with pistol aimed. Swally's eyes flared wild. His rage was audible and obscene and he glared without fear at Queen and, sensing he was hesitant, shouted in a loud, contemptuous voice. 'You ain't got the belly for it!' Realising suddenly that he was alone in the struggle, his men either down or without resistance he leaped on the rail and reversed his double-handed sword and raised it to throw like a spear and Vinderman screamed frantically. 'Shoot the bastard!'

Finger tightening on the trigger but he just couldn't force himself to fire. Swally laughing at him! Loud. Demoniac. Arm drawing back for the killing throw and bright moonlight glittered on the naked blade as Vinderman shouldered Queen aside and made to grab the pistol but his move was too late: and unnecessary. Swally's body lurched . . . eyes flaring in desperate agony. The sword fell and his hands clutched his belly, gripping the handle of a knife that had come from nowhere and was buried to the hilt in the gross flesh and streaming blood over his grasping fingers.

'Die, Swally! Die! You black hearted bastard!' The words spat from the mouth of the little man with the peg leg who had appeared unnoticed. Stumping forward with another knife, which he threw with deadly precision into the obese belly and just above the first knife. Jerking in agony, Swally grabbed for the rigging and held on, refusing to let go, but his eyes were glazing yet focussed in fading surprise on the man with one leg.

Peg leg did a dainty pirouette.

'Watch me, Captain,' he gloated, 'while I dance for you.' Stumping gleefully around. A macabre dance of death for Swally! Hands grasping the rigging but sliding down all the time. Hanging on for a last moment. Rigging holding him, but his weight finally brought him down and he fell spraddling across the rail then overbalanced and dropped with a great splash into the dark water and Peg leg shouted in a voice high pitched with elation. 'I've been owing you that one, Swally: for a long, long time.' Turning to Queen he said scornfully. 'You've a lot to learn, lad! Fight like a gentleman with the likes of Swally: and you're dead!' Coming briskly to attention he knuckled his forehead. 'Able seaman Joe Laval, late of the trading brig *Serenada,* out of Lisbon.' Laval spoke with a distinct but excited cockney accent as he explained. 'We were taken by Swally and his cutthroat six months ago in the South China Sea and those of us left alive had the choice of serving under Swally or being fed to the sharks. That butcher carried no passengers, any man who wasn't able went over the side.'

'Any other English aboard?'

'Six of us left . . . take us with you, Capt'n, never thought we'd live to serve under an English flag again.'

Queen had more urgent matters on his mind. Shrugging this request aside, he asked, 'Casualties, Vindo?'

'Ten wounded, but only one seriously.'

He could have shouted in ecstasy. The surprise attack had succeeded beyond his most optimistic assessment. Thrusting away euphoria. 'Send a man to inform Mr Bonham-Jones then load a longboat with the wounded pirates and put them ashore.'

'How about the rest?'

Glancing at the prisoners on the foredeck. These were guarded by a ring of seamen and the menace of Jancy with his loaded cannon and, reassured, he said, 'They won't give us trouble without Swally. We'll make swimmers of them as soon as Toby and his men join ship.'

Several pirates were lying dead on deck, and these were thrown overboard without ceremony. The injured had their wounds dressed from the limited sick bay stores then lowered into the ship's longboat and taken ashore. A performance viewed with disdain by peg leg Laval. 'You wouldn't have received such tender treatment from Swally.' Stumping alongside, acting as guide while Queen explored the ship. The state cabin was luxurious with teak furniture and Oriental carpet and screwed to the floor close against a bulkhead was a huge four-poster bed with sheets and covers of finest silk and lace. The cabin was situated aft and faced seaward through a curving line of windows that enhanced the great sweep of the stern. Casks of liquor were stowed in an annexe off the main cabin and Queen was wide eyed in appreciation at the grand style of pirate Swally.

'He certainly lived well off his plunder,' he said out loud. This thought, together with the realisation that these could be his own quarters for the journey back to Captain Probus, brought a thrill of provocative anticipation. His own command! Savouring the thought, before turning his mind to immediate matters. Laval was eager to serve and the full extent of the ship's stores revealed plenty of food aboard and the water casks had been filled from shore the previous day. Magazines crammed full with powder and shot. The ship hosting a vast armoury of weapons . . . muskets, pistols, and a long row of boarding pikes in a rack by the mainmast.

Satisfied that the ship was in all respects ready for sea he regained the upper deck. Their own wounded had been taken below where Vinderman was dressing wounds with his usual competence. Young Davy Greenwood was seriously injured and lying prostrate on a canvas cot. Queen moved through the makeshift sick bay, having a quiet word with each of the stricken men. Pausing by Greenwood. 'How is it, Davy lad?'

The youth had suffered a cutlass thrust high on his shoulder and Vinderman had swathed him so tight he was almost immobile. Pain showed in the pallor of his face as he hoarsely replied, 'Tot of rum would help, sir.'

'Already on its way, don't worry, Davy, we'll soon have you in the hands of Dr. Quennel.'

Jacko Abbot appeared with a jug of rum so Queen left them in Vinderman's care.

'Shore party boarding, sir,' reported Dooley by the boarding net as Bonham-Jones and four men clambered up, with McFie struggling in a rope sling. Dropping awkwardly he got to his feet with a frustrated curse. With dawn breaking and a cool wind blowing across the deck there was no reason to delay and after greeting Bonham-Jones, he ordered:

'Prepare ship, Toby, we get under way immediately. Hands to breakfast when we are at sea and on course.'

The prisoners were bunched in a sullen heap on the foredeck. They stirred into movement as he approached and said to peg leg Laval, 'Pick out every Englishman.' Five men detaching and forming in line. 'You men wish to serve as East Indiamen?'

Nodding in unison. 'Aye, aye, sir,' said one, 'and damn glad of the chance.'

Thirty pirates left. No time for niceties and, gesturing with his pistol, Queen snapped, 'Over the side!' They looked with alarm at the cold water, making no move. 'Jancy,' he said with a nonchalant shrug, 'give them a taste of their own grape.'

Jancy gave an evil grin, fished a lighted match out of the tub at his feet and brought it close to the touchhole. The pirates hesitated no longer. Scrambling away from Jancy's twelve-pounder, they dived in desperate haste over the side.

'Watch them every moment,' said Queen, 'put a shot into the head of anyone who turns back.'

'That grape shot would have spread them over the foredeck like fruit preserve,' said Jancy in uncaring tone.

'Was banking on them not waiting around to give you the chance, form yourself a gun crew, Mr Gunner, I want us ready for action at all times.'

'Aye, aye, sir.'

Jancy scampered away as McFie approached. 'Vindo has been telling me how you nearly got yourself killed,' he said with a despairing head shake. 'You're too bloody soft, Jase . . . knew you'd be in trouble without me.'

'Trying to pull that trigger was the most difficult thing I've ever had to force myself to do but I'm learning fast.' Pausing, with reflection plain to see as he went on to say. 'Killing a man in the heat of battle I can accept, but deliberate, cold-blooded execution is something else entirely.'

'Even if it costs your own life?' McFie retorted sarcastically.

'We're ready, Mr Queen,' announced Bonham-Jones, 'what ensigns have we aboard?'

'Dutch. French. Spanish. Pirate skull and crossbones. Plenty of choice.' Producing a white flag with a red cross. 'We sail under the colours of St. George and England.' Scrutinising aloft, men strung out on the yards ready to untie. 'Don't just stand there, McFie, take over the foredeck.' Grinning as McFie hopped his way forward with a growl of indignance.

'Make ready all plain sail, and heave short!'

In came the anchor cable until straight up and down.

'Set topsails aback.' The bow came round under the thrust to point deep into the bay.

'Break out!' The anchor came free. The topsails were sheeted round. The ship's head paid off, steadied under the pull of the rudder then began to move away from the beach in a long tack into the centre of the bay, entrance opening out to starboard.

'Stand by to tack.'

'Helm's a lee, sir.'

'Ease headsails! Ready about! Main course haul! Lee ho! Let go and haul!'

Restitution came round without fuss and pointed her bow straight through the entrance and out into the waiting ocean. With all plain sail set she heeled to a gust as they cleared the headland, then surged forward as if relishing freedom after the confines of land and settled into a fast reach towards the north eastern tip of Java. Handling the oiled teak steering wheel with loving precision Vinderman said, 'Nicely done, Mr Queen, but don't be over conceited. This lovely lady sailed herself out of harbour.'

Chapter Twenty-four

The captured ship proved as fast and efficient as her clean lines had forecast. Wind steady and fine on the starboard beam . . . allowing them to lay a course parallel to the coast and by late afternoon they rounded the tip of Java and came about to bring the wind broad on the larboard beam. Sheets were eased. Night fell to find the speedy vessel romping through the narrow waterway that separates the Islands of Java and Bali. It was normal practice at night to take off the upper sails and so ease the ship through the dark hours, but Queen was determined that all haste should be made to reach base camp so he doubled up the helm and kept all plain sail up and working.

Justly pleased with themselves. They had rummaged throughout the ship hoping to find treasure but Swally was too canny a captain to keep his loot aboard, and they had to be content with the personal possessions left by the pirates. Dressing in a colourful, motley assortment. Shirts of vivid reds and yellows, baggy trousers, bandanas . . . anything was better than scraps of native cloth. Happy to be at sea in a real ship! Sense of cocky impudence prevailing, reinforced by a double measure of Swally's strong rum served just before supper. Salvador volunteering to act as cook

'Mr Queen knows how to keep a crew happy,' stated Jack Dooley. Wiping his tongue around his moustache, savouring every last taste. 'Now there's my idea of a fine skipper.'

'Aye! Something to be said for a pirate's way of life,' Les Bate's dark face lit up in a rare smile as he spoke, then raising his mug, 'couple of jugs of this and I'd be ready to take the Royal Navy on.'

'Deck there! Sail Ho!'

Call from the main top in the early light of dawn. McFie was watch officer and showed keen anticipation as he lowered his telescope. 'Looks like our Old Dutch enemy *Zeevalk* and we could intercept if we came up a point'

Scanning the ship ahead. 'They're setting more canvas,' said Queen, 'perhaps they recognise *Restitution* and don't fancy a dose of Swally's deadly medicine.' Temptation adding a decisive rasp to his voice. 'Up helm a point. Set royals and studding sails.'

'Helm a point on, sir.' No reaction from Vinderman. Just doing his job.

One of the features of the privateer was the amount of fair weather sails she carried. Designed and built for speed she flew through the water under the thrust of additional canvas. The bluff bowed Dutch East Indiaman was no match for the privateer and the distance between them narrowed at rewarding speed. Then *Zeevalk* showed her stern as her Captain wore round in an attempt to run away.

'Makes you realise just what could be achieved with so fast a ship.' McFie wasn't alone in this idea because all the crew were on deck, conversing eagerly and staring with growing excitement at the ship they were overtaking with such ease. Bloodied in battle, they were confident and eager for engagement. Bonham-Jones stood tall and relaxed. He had assumed great maturity since leaving behind the restraining influence of Captain Probus.

'Are we going to take her?'

The question brought a frown to Queen's forehead. The crew had closed up to action stations without command. Jancy was moving along the larboard battery calmly opening gun ports. McFie couldn't keep still, hopping about on one leg.

'The way the Dutchman's heeled we could come up under her lee,' he said with anticipation rife, 'give 'em a broadside before they know what's hit 'em.'

'Permission to speak, sir?' Jack Dooley said from the helm.

'Speak up, Jack.'

'Just want to say, sir,' said Dooley with a shifty glance, 'that the men are with you all the way.'

'Even in piracy?'

'Aye . . . not that they'd think taking a Dutchman could be considered piracy.'

Vinderman looked on without humour. The southeast corner of Java was now abaft the starboard beam and already they should have turned westward to bring the wind astern on their passage to Captain Probus. What had started as a capricious chase had fast developed into a provocative and intriguing situation? How tempting the thought? Taking *Restitution* into action! Insidious, tormenting Queen, with tension mounting all the time, then clearing his mind of wanton thought he shook his head in dismissive gesture. 'Think she's trying to work a spell on us,' he said, somewhat reluctantly, 'she's been a privateer too long to resist such easy pickings.'

It seemed the speeding ship was indeed set on such deadly business. Surging in the wake of the Dutchman with an exhilaration felt and shared by every man aboard, yet Queen commanded, 'Run her off, helmsman. We are law-abiding seamen and can't allow ourselves to be deviated from our task, and also,' he added, 'we must get our wounded into safe hands. Stand the men down, Mr McFie, and have Jancy close up the gun ports.'

The crew were muttering together in open disappointment as she came round and away from the chase. Yards braced round again, she settled on her new course and running free with the wind astern.

'We had her by the bleedin' short and curly's,' snorted Jacko Abbot. Peering over the side at the bow wave rushing past. 'Never knew a ship could be so fast?'

'Must be a very puzzled lady,' said peg leg Laval, 'first time in her career she's turned away empty from a merchantman?'

'Buccaneering sods!' Breathing hard after his struggle from the quarterdeck McFie gave a fierce look as if passing responsibility onto them for his own sense of disappointment. 'Mr Queen was just giving the Dutch a fright. So next time wait for orders before preparing for action.'

Stalking along the sand with Mr Sethman in step. 'What do you think. Alan?' said Probus.

He had posed this thought many times and Sethman shrugged it off. 'Same as before,' he said, 'they have a long way to go and an even longer way back to us.' Turning to retrace their steps as he added, 'We're comfortable enough, the wounded are all on their feet and life here is peaceful. In fact, Fitz, we have much to be thankful for.'

'I know all that!' Probus didn't slow his frantic pace. Breeze plucking at his tattered shirt, scar livid on his face, eye half-closed in a permanent, leering wink. Squinting into the sunlight with one hand protecting his eye he said in unhappy voice. 'But I'm beginning to wonder if I made a wise decision in asking them to cross the Island with an inexperienced midshipman in command.'

'We'd never have got back, Fitz, and well you know it. Those midshipmen of ours are as capable as any men to whom I have had the privilege of teaching the principles of navigation and never forget they have the mighty Vinderman along to say nothing of men such as Dooley and gunner Jancy, and together with brutes like Jacko Abbot they are a considerable force.' Squaring his shoulders, breathing in the clean, tangy salt air, he declared. 'And who amongst us could be a pessimist on a morning such as this?'

The sun bathed them in warmth from a cloudless sky, breeze moving lazily through the palm trees and the silver sea stretching before them. Cramming dry, aromatic leaves into his pipe, Sethman puffed away with obvious enjoyment.

'You have a damned annoying philosophical turn of mind this morning.' Relaxing his impatient tread Probus regarded him with fond approval before going on with. 'You are aware of course, Alan, that I have recommended you for a command of your own, and this on quite a few occasions, yet you persist in sailing as my First Officer.' Sethman made no answer and Probus hesitated, as if embarrassed, then said quietly. 'Your loyalty is one of the most treasured things in my life.' The tenderness in his voice would have surprised any of his men who might have been within hearing, and he added in similar tone. 'We have sailed together for a long time and I have to admit that I would miss the comfort of your presence. But I have been selfish too long and when – if – we get back to London I will insist that you take a ship of your own.'

'Have you never thought I may not wish the responsibility of command, and am more content to sail as First Officer to the formidable Fitzroy Probus?'

'The time is fast approaching when Probus must step down, I am the last of my generation and time is running against me.' A disturbing thought occurred and he faced Sethman. 'In fact, Alan, I begin to realise you have been nursing me along of late. Have I been thinking you were leaning on me when the support is the other way around?'

'Probus leans on no man.' Sethman knew his Captain felt very badly about the loss of the *Earl* and suspected this was the real cause of his untypical self-deprecation. 'If you have recommendations to make,' he then said, 'put forward the young men like David Ashbury. New ships need new men with the optimism of youth to pave the way to fame and fortune.'

'What price experience then?' Probus challenged, 'experience such as yours and mine . . . earned on the oceans of this world and paid for with the years of our lives. Such knowledge is beyond valuation and should not be discarded lightly.' The dialogue had reversed his melancholy train of mind and he said firmly. 'The energy and drive of youth are not without its advantage, this point I concede without hesitation, but show me the hand of experience at the helm and I'll show you a tight ship.' Eyes coming back from the depths of nostalgia, focusing on the running figure of gunner's mate, Cassidy, moving awkwardly because his arm was in a sling. Skidding to a breathless halt, he announced:

'Lookout has sighted a sail, sir, standing in towards us and Mr Ashbury asks permission to light the bonfire and make smoke.'

'Not yet,' snapped Probus, instantly alert, 'wait until we find who she is and what her intentions are.' Cassidy ran off with the two officers hurrying behind to gain a point of vantage above the camp site. Everyone gathered in a bunch and staring excitedly out to sea as Probus took the telescope. 'What do you make of her, Mr Ashbury?'

'Haven't seen her like before but she doesn't look much like a merchantman?'

The Captain handed over the telescope with an ominous expression on his face and, focussing for a long time, Sethman said in pensive tone, 'Certainly not an East Indiaman: more like a privateer.'

'This is just what she is. Low in the water, black and very sinister, I've heard of this one. She's the

Restitution, skippered by the blackest-hearted man ever to pirate and loot a law-abiding vessel.'

'Swally!' Sethman exclaimed with foreboding.

'Aye. Swally and his *Restitution*. A ship feared and envied by every Captain who sails the South China Sea.'

Ashbury was glued to the telescope. 'Pirate she may be,' he stated, 'but she is flying the red cross of St. George at her masthead.'

'Ensigns don't mean a damn thing,' retorted Probus, 'and is a typical pirate ruse to get in close.' But he was both intrigued and puzzled and, taking another look, mused. 'Strange sort of coincidence though.'

Voicing the thought uppermost in all their minds. 'Could it be Mr Queen,' said Dr. Quennel. 'I mean, sir, why would pirates be coming ashore here?'

'Water. Food. Either way we'll soon find out.' Surging into action. Snapping orders. 'Break camp! I want every man assembled within two minutes with all available weapons. If it is Swally we'll take to the forest but keep your eye on her, Mr Ashbury.' Probus smote his hands together and cried. 'By God, men: if Jason Queen has taken *Restitution* from the murderous Swally he ought to be recommended for a knighthood!'

Forming up. Ragged. Four marines and their sub-lieutenant Warrington-Smythe, with his head swaged in a cloth bandage...a handful of sailors, the surgeon, David Ashbury and the two senior officers. A few muskets and pistols but hardly any powder or shot. The rest was going to be down to cutlass and knife.

Looking at his crew with sadness and pride mixed in his eyes. There was no chance of them putting up much of a fight against a marauding, well-armed crew, but at least they were all mobile and could flee inland should need arise.

'They're signalling!' Ashbury again: rampant.

She was coming in at full speed. With naked eyes they saw the red and white ensign flutter down then rise to the masthead again. Several stirring their feet in anticipation but Probus warned, 'I'll shoot the first man who moves into view.'

Ashbury closed his telescope. 'I can see men waving from the foredeck.' There were tears in his eyes as he added joyously, 'It's our own crew aboard!'

'Not yet, men,' insisted Probus, 'wait until we make sure it is them?'

Consternation at the lack of activity ashore, Bonham-Jones questioning, 'Strange, not a soul in sight?'

'Capt'n probably recognised the ship,' said Vinderman with a lilt of humour in his voice. 'He'll know her for a privateer and has taken the men into the forest under cover.'

'Position a leadsman in the bow, Toby, and drop the hook when he calls six fathoms.' Queen then said in hopeful tone. 'Wish we could see somebody.'

Upper royals and topgallants furled, the ship slowed her headlong rush and glided in to the bay.

'By the mark! Six fathoms and sand.'

'Bring her head up, helmsman.'

'Head to wind, sir.' Down splashed the anchor. Bringing up against the cable, she snugged short, then drifted back to lie still.

'There they are!' Straggle of figures emerging hesitantly from the undergrowth and a great shout of greeting ripped across the water from the men aboard. This roar shattered all inhibitions and the shore party broke ranks in a frantic, cheering rush towards the beach.

'Away ship's boat! You and I, Toby, will report to the Captain and request Dr. Quennel to attend our wounded.'

Probus entered the sick bay breaking Dr. Quennel's concentration and causing him to look up from the patient stretched out on a table where his leg was under scrutiny. The twin holes were closed and darkly puckered but the tissue around them seemed normal. The leg had a permanent bend and try as he may, McFie could not straighten it.

In full possession of the details of their adventure Probus had a word with each wounded man. Davy Greenwood was still very weak but in no danger, while the others were in various stages of recovery. 'Don't like the look of that leg,' said Probus to McFie.

The attempts to straighten it out now the splint had been removed brought beads of perspiration on McFie's forehead. 'It's a wonder he has a leg to worry about,' said Dr. Quennel. 'With so serious a wound, needing a tourniquet to stop the bleeding there is no doubt gangrene should have set in and being so far removed from medical care he shouldn't even be alive.' Puzzled and intrigued as he resumed examination, he then announced. 'Had Mr McFie been in my hands a week earlier I would definitely have amputated.' Billie was already suffering and this remark caused him to move hastily off the table.

'Think I prefer Mr Queen's treatment, sir, if you will pardon my saying so.' Looking wistfully at his crooked leg. 'Might not be much to look at: but better than none at all.'

Smiling at this, Dr. Quennel said, 'I'll have the carpenter make up a crutch to keep the weight off your knee.' Addressing the Captain he suggested. 'McFie is in considerable discomfort, and I ask that he may be excused duties for as long as possible.'

'I'm short of capable officers, Mr McFie,' said Probus with a knowing glance, 'and am reluctant to lose you.'

'I can stand my trick, sir,' came the quick reply from McFie, 'just let me loose on that crutch.'

Movement made him lose balance and, clutching hold of the table, he queried. 'Are we at sea, sir?'

'We are, heading for the Sunda Straights and Semarund to pick up Mr Harper and his party. But before you assume watch duties I want a written report on your venture across the Island, particularly the return journey.' Probus paused, before adding, 'Mr Queen's own report seems very brief so I'm instructing Bonham-Jones and you to fill in more detail.'

Standing on the poop deck watching the bay slowly blend into the background with the camp site already gone from view, Sethman's thoughts very confused as he reflected on the fact that soon all traces of their occupation would be obliterated as the site reverted back to its natural habitat. Sensing the same reluctance he too had recently known, Queen enquired, 'Regrets, sir?'

'Yes.' Filling his pipe he seemed eager to talk about it but spent a long time lighting up. 'There is great satisfaction in wresting survival from the wilderness: and even to appreciate a more basic and primitive way of live. Things assume a proper place in the scheme of life. The false values that society conditions us to accept and work towards are exposed by the stark need just to stay alive.' Drawing deeply on his pipe. 'Nature provides everything for peace and enjoyment, yet we always seem to want?' Searching for words, he concluded with . . . 'More!'

'Philosophy again, Mr Sethman?' Probus approached unobtrusive as ever and, after pausing for personal thought, stated. 'I've said this before. Safe harbours rot ships and men and to stagnate is to abdicate from life and from our responsibilities.' Frowning now at Sethman as he added, 'I believe you really enjoyed being shipwrecked on a tropic island, but I question if you would be quite so lyrical if you had to face up to the fact that we could have been marooned there for countless years, think perhaps your enthusiasm for the primitive life may have become a little sour as the months dragged by.' Gazing shoreward his voice softened as he murmured. 'For all that, paradise wasn't so very far away.' His tone of voice brought contemplative silence, after which he turned abruptly. 'Now then, Mr Midshipman,' he demanded, 'what have you been doing to my crew?'

The sharpness of the question startled and brought confusion and a hesitant, 'I don't understand your meaning, sir?'

'I mean they look and act like a crowd of buccaneers. They swagger about as if they own the ship, and further,' said Probus with emphasis, 'I form the distinct impression they look to you for command: not me! Even McFie, who said he prefers your treatment to that suggested by Dr. Quennel, not that I blame him for that!' Allowing himself a smile, before resuming his attack. 'Am I to believe that a few short weeks under your influence has turned first rate seamen into an undisciplined mob of rum-swilling pirates?'

Expecting applause, not this kind of censure, Queen was taken aback and, angered by the unfair description, he stood his ground and retorted, 'I know you have read my report, sir, in which I explain that the men are looking to me for a fair share of any prize money realised for the capture of *Restitution*.' Looking fiercely at the Captain he added proudly. 'And they had an extra ration of rum because they earned it.'

'Hear they wanted to take a Dutchman for good measure?'

'*Zeevalk*,' confirmed Queen. 'Very tempting but we had more urgent matters to attend.'

These words brought a murmur of appreciation from Sethman and caused Probus to look deep into Queen's face, noting the gaunt-high cheekbones and the lines of tension etched deep around his mouth, and severity changed to approval 'You did damn well,' he complimented, 'far in excess of anything we had a right to expect or impose upon you, and have no worry about the men because I will be pleased to honour your promise.' Probus had something else on his mind, and now including Mr Sethman in the discussion, said to Queen. 'We're short of officers with Gaywood gone and Ashbury unfit for duty so I'm promoting you to acting Second Officer and Bonham-Jones as Third. Both temporary and unpaid,' he added quickly and with a smile that faded at the expression on Queen's face.

'With respect, sir,' he said, 'I would rather you reverse the order of promotion. Bonham-Jones is senior midshipman and entitled to the higher rank.'

Sethman nodded approval but Probus frowned in defence of his own position. 'He seemed happy enough to serve under you before.'

'Circumstances were different then and I know that a severe strain would be imposed on our relationship if the seniority is not restored.'

'I stand corrected,' said Probus very formally, 'and your judgement does you credit.'

'Can you also promote McFie, sir?'

'To what?'

'How about senior midshipman?' interrupted Sethman with a smile.

Sharing in the laughter Probus said, 'He will no doubt see the humour of the appointment, being the only midshipman. You will share the same quarters aft, and I'll expect you all at my dinner table when weather and duty permit?' Fixing Queen with his good eye he slyly enquired. 'How did you like residing in the great cabin of pirate Swally?'

Not about to reveal that he relished command best of all, Queen replied tongue in cheek, 'Unused to such style and extravagance, sir, I must admit to feeling very alone.'

Chapter Twenty-five

Semarund. Beach deserted, just a few canoes on the waterline. 'The sight of *Restitution* in harbour seems to have everyone running for cover,' said Probus.

'Something we'll have to get used to,' confirmed Sethman. 'Swally has become a legend over the years and his ship is well known and notorious even in these little used waters.'

'Prepare a shore party, Mr Bonham-Jones.' Scanning the shore, not liking it, Probus instructed. 'Arm yourselves but be careful not to invite attack from King Wanu and his warriors.'

Longboat grounding. Shore party forming up. No sign of movement. So unlike their previous visit and the lack of activity brought a concerned query from Queen. 'Thought we'd have been shown a welcome by now?'

'Too damn quiet,' said Bonham-Jones, 'but you must admit we don't look much like lawful seamen.'

The men's clothing was a mixture of patched,

sailor's ware, supplemented by items from the ship's slop chest. Hair and beards long and unkempt, and the untidy appearance together with pistol and cutlass in their belts made them a piratical bunch to which any normal person would give a wide berth.

'Better take a look inland.' Bonham-Jones formed them into a column, leaving behind two men to guard the longboat. With a man ahead as scout they worked a careful way up the well-trodden path to the village.

'We're being watched, Toby,' said Queen urgently.

'This is nothing like their usual welcome,' said Toby, fingering his pistol.

As he spoke, the scout came back at a run. 'Village is in ruins! Burnt to a cinder!'

'At the double, men,' ordered Bonham-Jones. Leading the way at full speed and as they burst into the clearing, they came to sudden halt to stare with horror and apprehension at the heaps of charred rubble that had once been dwellings and warehouse buildings. Every structure razed to the ground and the smell of damp charcoal hovered acrid over the stricken village. As they looked on with dismay, a stealthy, encircling movement had the men reaching for weapon.

'Steady now,' cautioned Bonham-Jones, 'keep your hands empty and in open view.'

By now a ring of warriors had emerged from the bush to encircle them, armed with spears which they rattled menacingly as they stalked nearer. A gap appeared in their ranks and the King accompanied by his elders came to face the two officers. There was no welcome in their approach and a sense of deep foreboding brought lines to Queen's forehead. Stepping forward with hands raised in greeting, a move that brought an immediate and frightening rattle of spears but he felt more concerned at the non-appearance of Tuamoto, and the fact that not a solitary woman could be seen. Stilling the challenge of his warriors, King Wanu spoke in his native tongue, causing a disquieted Queen to bring Salvador forward.

'He recognises you,' explained Ramon, 'but no longer wishes to speak your language. He also makes it plain that you are not welcome and insists you leave the harbour immediately.'

Pushing aside two husky warriors with spears at the ready, looking directly at the King, whose eyes were hostile and evasive, Queen said in hard tone. 'Who has done this, and why do you blame us?' The question brought an angry torrent of words directed at Ramon, who heard him out before interpreting in more economic length.

'The Dutchmen came and because the King had befriended and allowed you to build your trading post they took all the stored spices, and then looted the village, robbing and pillaging and helping themselves to everything including the women then fired the entire village as a warning, and all this after they had been made welcome in traditional Java manner.'

'Ask him what happened to Mr Harper and the others.'

Salvador seemed uneasy at the King's reply. 'The marines tried to hold the Dutch forces,' he then explained, 'but were annihilated and the rest taken as prisoners.'

'Does he know the name of the Dutch ship?' He didn't really need to ask.

'*Zeevalk*.' The name spat from the King's mouth like poison on a viper's tongue.

Down on one knee before him, Queen asked humbly, 'What can we do to help?'

The King said, now in halting English, 'Can you bring back our dead or honour to our women?'

Shaking his head in sad response. 'No, but we can help to rebuild your village.'

'So the Dutch can return and burn us down again?' Harshness softening before the acute distress of the man on his knees before him, gripping Queen by the arm he brought him to his feet and said, 'I ask only for you to leave because we are not strong enough to resist the men from the ships and from Batavia: and we can never allow you to trade here again. As for those evil men with skins like your own?' Voice fired with threat as he exclaimed. 'They will be made to pay! Over the years our vengeance will claim their youngest and finest. Not in open conflict for we would be the losers. But secretly, from the shadows we will kill every Dutchman within reach until they regret forever that they abused our hospitality.'

The King spoke in hard terms but the underlying sadness and despair in his manner brought rampant concern, and, looking around, Queen asked very hesitantly, 'Where is Tuamoto, and Riana?' King Wanu's face was like stone. He made no answer. 'Where is Tuamoto,' asked Queen again, holding his arm up to expose the significant scar on his wrist, 'where is my brother?'

Deeply moved by the appeal and the passion in this cry, the King nodded in slow acquiescence. 'Come,' he said simply. With this he elbowed through his warriors, who closed behind them but without hostility and the squad relaxed a little. Bonham-Jones watched them go from sight before turning back.

'At ease, men, this might be a long wait.'

King Wanu led through down a pathway arched over with lofty palm trees. Queen straightaway knew where they were heading and they came out onto the grass verge overlooking the lagoon where he and Riana had enjoyed so many times together. But the scene was vastly different, deserted, no children laughing in the shallows, even the birds had left this place. The sun was shining and the waterfall splashed its tiny rainbows yet the lagoon was desolate, the atmosphere tomb-like, and Queen felt the chill of foreboding, like ice across his shoulders, even more so when King Wanu came to a halt, turned to face him and say in condemning tone. 'When the Dutchmen came and we finally realised they would abuse our welcome I ordered all our young women to flee into the forest.'

Hearing the words with apprehension and with a strange reluctance to hear more yet he had no choice as King Wanu said in a voice deep with grief and revulsion. 'One of them caught up with Riana on the very patch of green on which we are standing, and he took her: with violence and brutal lust.' Unprepared! Queen was motionless and open-mouthed as the King continued his distraught narrative. 'She was still lying here, torn and bleeding, when we found her and carried her back home.' The memory brought renewed anguish and tears formed in his eyes as he said in tones of gaunt, wracking emotion. 'We watched over her and nursed her for three weeks and then one day she disappeared from her bed.' As he said this he glanced up and Queen mutely followed his gaze to where a noose of vine hung suspended above their heads. The sight brought a sick, dreadful reaction. He wanted to look away! To hide! But couldn't tear his eyes from that awful neck loop. Then the King said. 'We found her hanging by the neck.'

These terrible words shattered all control, face buried in his hands . . . mind and body reeling in mortal despair. His exquisite Princess:

ravaged by a marauding Dutchman! Flame of anger kindling deep inside, and a fast rising desire for blood retribution brought depth to his voice as he cried, 'Why? In God's name! Surely she would have forgotten, given time?' The cry screamed from his very soul. 'She had no right to take her own life!' He couldn't accept! No words would bring her back but the plea shuddered from his mouth and so desperate and just as futile because King Wanu droned on as if sharing might ease his own pain. Remorseless. Trying to explain. To justify!

'Riana was so very young,' he said. 'With all the dreams and growing up pains to which a maiden is privileged to cling and you of all people should not judge her too harshly, for she had a strong feeling for you, my son, and I know she could never face you with such dishonour.'

The words were a cutlass thrust through his heart. 'The fault was not Riana's,' he sobbed, 'surely you could have made her accept this truth?'

'The dishonour was not only in her violation, this unclean beast who fouled her body left her with the pox of the white man . . . the cursed disease that rots the tissue of the face into premature ugliness and weeps its unending misery from the loins.'

He couldn't take any more! Reeling away to huddle against a tree for support. Pounding his fists without feeling into the rough bark and his sobs retching and uncontrollable.

'Can you still blame her for choosing death rather than the slow destruction of shame and dishonour?' The words reached him but as if from a great distance, then the King growled in menacing tone. 'My son waited on the beach for him to come ashore, armed only with the dagger you gave him. It took three of them to hold him while the man killed him with a sword thrust.' Spitting in distaste, the King contemptuously stated. 'They couldn't even fight like men.'

Queen felt the surge of hatred and his hands taloned with an insatiable urge to close on the throat of a Dutchman. A feeling that took permanent root inside. No pain. Just cold: and lethal! 'How will I know this man when I catch up with him?' he rasped with terrible intent.

'You will know . . . Tuamoto cut off his left ear.' Words cold as the sea. 'And he has the silver knife.'

Queen's fingers were following the mark of a cross cut deep into the tree against which he had sagged. 'Riana?' he asked vacantly and looked down for a burial mound but the King shook his head.

'Tuamoto also, but the cross is only for remembrance.' Pointing over the lagoon and far out to sea. 'We placed them in a war canoe among soft leaves and dry wood. Then we lit the fire and took them out into deep water beyond the reef.

The funeral pyre burned for a long time before the sea claimed them for its own.' His face taking on a more normal, inscrutable expression, he concluded:

'We cleansed her body with eternal fire so that her spirit could be at peace.'

Chapter Twenty-six

'Jason's been very withdrawn since we left Semarund and I think we both know the reason.'

Bonham-Jones's comment brought a nod of agreement from McFie. Hopping about on his good leg, practising mobility without the aid of a crutch he was achieving a lopsided, but speedy type of gait. Second only to Vinderman in knowing Queen's mind, he said, 'He can't come to terms with the way his native Princess died and has developed a thirst for Dutch blood.'

'Never knew a man change so quickly,' agreed Bonham-Jones, 'so different from the easy-going Jase of old. Just imagine how he couldn't bring himself to fire his pistol at Swally ... don't reckon there would be any hesitation now?'

'He feels worse knowing we had *Zeevalk* at our mercy and just when she was leaving the Island with Abraham and the others in chains. Pity we didn't give more thought to just what they were doing in Java waters and if it wasn't for Old Probus being in charge I think we might now be on our way up the South China Sea chasing the Dutchman.'

'Under what flag, I wonder?'

'Bet it wouldn't be the Honourable East India Company's.'

Off duty watch gathered in the forepeak, Dooley and Abbot in conversation.

'What a bleedin' let down,' said Abbot, 'sailing for home with our holds empty and sod-all bonus for anybody.' Looking at his mates, slyly. 'For a while there I thought we might have a chance to take us a prize or two, you never know what kind of treasure ship we may have come across?'

'That's daft talk, Jacko, Probus has lost one ship and he ain't about to risk another,' replied Dooley scornfully. 'Anyway, the Capt'n is too strait-laced for privateering. The best we can hope for is a cargo of tea when we dock at Trinco.'

'Lot of good that'll be,' interrupted Les Bate, 'by time the tax is paid we'll be left with just our pay, no clothes to our backs and flat broke: again.'

'Don't forget we have a share of prize money when *Restitution* is sold off.' Dooley again. 'Should be worth a bob or two?'

'If we ever see it,' sneered Bate. 'I've heard promises before.'

'Mr Queen gave his word . . . and there's a man we can trust.'

The men were in agreement. 'I'll go along with that,' said Bate, 'wish he was still in command.'

Tongue snaking round his lips as he added, 'Rum sure tasted good, and plenty of it.'

'Aye,' agreed Abbot. 'Mr Queen's a skipper I would follow any day of the week.'

'You can count me in,' said Davy Greenwood. His arm was in a sling but he had resumed light duties.

'Why don't we mention it, casual like?' Les Bate said.

'Aye,' said Abbot again, 'but Vinderman is the one to speak to him, them being such good chums an' all.' No malice in his voice for the ship's company had been joined together by their misfortunes and successes and a strong bond of comradeship had become established among all the crew.

'If you think Mr Queen will talk mutiny you're off your heads,' scorned Dooley, 'or any of the others for that matter? Not a chance, Jacko, they're too fond of Probus ever to go against him and if I were you I'd be very careful what was said. Mutiny is a hanging offence and I ain't going to dangle by the neck from a yardarm for you or anybody.'

'No one's talking mutiny,' said Abbot impatiently, 'but what harm would it do to let Mr. Queen know we'd be with him if he fancies taking *Restitution* after the Dutchman. I wouldn't object to a share of her cargo?'

* * *

He paced the quarterdeck with stalking tread and Vinderman's gaze alternated between the binnacle and the newly promoted Third Officer, comparing him with the gentle mannered youth he had met on the northern slopes of Dartmoor. He understood some of the anguish tearing into Queen with each sea mile that sped by. Courteous as ever, perhaps, but he had retreated into an inner shell of brittleness since they had left Semarund. A veneer hard to penetrate and Vinderman grimly reflected that he wouldn't wish to be a Dutchman aboard *Zeevalk* if they ever came within reach of a *Restitution* broadside.

'Watch your course, helmsman!' Probus had noticed the uncharacteristic swerve in the ship's wake and snapped. 'You feeling alright?'

'Aye, sir.'

Probus also felt troubled and closely observing the animal prowl of his Third Officer, said with concern evident in his tone, 'Mr Queen seems to have something on his mind.' The gash on his cheek had healed into a jagged scar but his eye remained half-closed and gave considerable unease. Good eye piercing at Vinderman. 'Do you know what's troubling him?' Vinderman made no reply and Probus cast a jaundiced look at him. 'Then let me hazard a guess, Daniel, and I won't mind you correcting me if I'm wrong.' The familiarity had Vinderman's eyebrow's meeting but Probus paid no heed and, continuing his train of thought, stated. 'I would be pleased as any of you if we could meet up with *Zeevalk* and take back Mr Harper and the other members of our crew, and I deliberately sailed into the Malacca Strait in the hope of an encounter with the Dutchman instead of taking advantage of the more direct and quieter water south of Sumatra.' Pausing, in the hope that the announcement would get back to his disgruntled crew. 'But I will no longer delay the safe return of our wounded. They need care and medical attention and I have no desire to waste valuable time hanging about the South China Sea in the hope of a chance interception.' Voice taking on a biting edge. 'We are law-abiding seamen and will at all times act as such.'

'The Dutch don't seem to share your ideals, sir.'

'Their actions will be called to account one day and this to a higher court than either you or I could commission. Vengeance, Daniel, can never be ours. At least,' he qualified, 'not to deliberately go in search of.' Finishing with a perceptive. 'I think we agree on the reason for Mr Queen's foul temper?'

Vinderman shrugged in the realisation that his own contribution to this conversation was non-existent while the Captain aired his own thoughts. Silent for a moment, he then said, 'He has been prematurely brought face to face with the savagery of the human animal and his ideals have been torn to shreds. He'll get over it. Has to? For we all have to realise that men are not equal in their standards.' Concluding his narrative with. ''Tis a condition known as growing up.'

'For someone who claims a lack of education,' said Probus, 'you show a damned remarkable insight into human nature.'

Just then the surgeon came looking for him. 'I've repeatedly asked you to keep this eye away from strong light,' he said curtly, then brought Probus under the shade of the quarterdeck awning. The Captain's eye was angry red and weeping yellow puss and the surgeon stated in determined tone. 'You refuse to wear a bandage even though I have told you over and over that such stubborn foolishness could lose you its sight.'

'You want the men to know their Captain is blind in one eye?'

'You're not blind yet, but certainly will be if you refuse treatment. There is infection in that eye of which I have scant knowledge and I warn you that it could spread to the other.' The surgeon had found authority of late and now added scathingly. 'Mr Sethman is more than capable of running the ship and I must insist you either keep off deck during daylight hours: or else wear a bandage.'

'Don't fuss, Quennel, I'm not going to spend all day skulking below. Bring out your damned bandage if you must? But allow me to decide who'll run the ship.'

* * *

Marcus Quennel enjoyed the position of surgeon and his prominence, as a much needed member of the ship's company. Holding sick rounds every morning, accompanied by his assistant, Robert Gilpin, a tall balding man, who had volunteered his services after their battle casualties and who had displayed a natural ability in the sick bay, which still housed several patients. The surgeon's main concern being the lack of equipment and medicine aboard, he formed the conclusion that Swally was a Captain without care or scruple. During his rounds he confronted McFie. 'How is the leg progressing, and why haven't I seen you in the sick bay lately?'

'Didn't like the way you kept eyeing it,' McFie found difficulty in being serious but now looked intently at the surgeon to suggest. 'You might take a look at Mr Queen though?'

'His injuries are not as obvious as your own, and my experience of mental strain is very limited.' Probing at McFie's leg as if still bewildered, he said with a reassuring smile. 'I'll have a chat with Mr Queen, if he'll allow me: and explain how concerned you are.'

Her face intruded, dusky, and appealing . . . the lower part hidden behind slender fingers. He took her hands away as he had done so many times and held them tight with fierce possessiveness, fragrance of the flowers in her hair hovering. She was soft and tender and so very fragile. She haunted him. Sometimes in daylight and unceasingly at night, with her eyes dark and her lips opening for him. He reeled with the remembered enchantment of her and, clasping his hands tight around his shoulders in sudden chill, 'Riana,' he murmured despairingly, 'why do you torment me so?'

Vinderman observed all things with a shrewd eye. His own position had become so elevated that he was treated virtually as a ship's officer and because of the limited space aboard had moved his gear from the fo'c'sle and taken accommodation in a tiny retreat just aft of the quarterdeck in a cabin made up of wood struts and canvas. One that would be dismantled hurriedly at action stations because of the twelve-pounder housed there. Vinderman sorely missed his lute, which had gone down with the *Earl*.

The evening tot of rum had just been served by Ramon Salvador, the cabin steward, savouring the fiery liquor he rolled it round his tongue before swallowing it down in one gulp. 'If you don't want your rum, Mr Queen,' he suggested, 'I wouldn't object to sharing a drop?'

Shrugging, Queen slopped half his measure into the proffered mug, drank the rest in one gulp. 'For God's sake stop calling me Mr, we've been friends too long for such formality.'

'Does this friendship entitle me to comment on the meanness of your disposition?'

'Is it so obvious?'

'Not just to me either! Capt'n has criticised, Billie's worried . . . and the crew complain because they don't know what the hell's going on.'

'Just can't help it, Vindo. We should be after *Zeevalk*. Take back our men, Abraham and Mr Harper. Then blow her miserable hull to eternity: and her bastard crew with her!'

'Foul language doesn't become you, Mr Queen.' Probus had been waiting his chance and now added sternly. 'How easy it is to comment on matters over which we have no jurisdiction.'

Standing erect with his hands clenched at his side, the uncompromising demeanour brought hard words as Probus snapped, 'Forget *Zeevalk*! We have injured men to put ashore and I will not place lives at risk to satisfy a thirst for vengeance. We are a merchant ship, not a Naval man-of-war, and fight only in our own defence and there is no possible justification for wasting time on a selfish vendetta.' Having got this tirade off his chest he simmered down a little and with a keen, one-eyed glare, queried. 'Mr Queen, I put the question to you . . . what would you suggest we do?'

This untypical request came as a shock to Vinderman but, with this situation always uppermost in the fury that consumed him, Queen instantly replied, 'Place our wounded ashore then take *Restitution* back up the South China Sea.'

'You seem to have great faith in the ability of this ship,' returned Probus dryly, 'do you have the same confidence in your ability to command her?'

A pertinent query, probing into Queen and he thought he had commanded her damn well already. Repressing an affirmative reply he said instead, 'The situation does not arise, sir.'

'Unless you are so obsessed that you would take matters into your own hands?'

'You misconstrue my anger, sir.' Astounded and also bewildered at the allegation he then asserted in sure voice. 'It is directed towards the Dutchmen and I would die before I turned against you.'

'Nevertheless,' murmured Probus, 'your attitude is perilously close to rebellion.' Turning abruptly on his helmsman. 'What is the feeling of the crew, and yourself?' Vinderman didn't like this conversation at all and his reluctance to speak brought impatience as Probus snapped. 'I asked you a question, Vinderman.'

'Since you ask, sir,' he replied in reluctant voice, 'reckon most if us would be with him.'

'Disloyal to a man!' His own suspicions confirmed, Probus showed no surprise as he said firmly. 'But like you just said, Mr Queen, the situation does not arise.' The Captain's forehead and left eye were swathed in a wide loop of bandage and he had to turn his head to focus along the main deck. Concentrating attention on the seamen lounging between the cannon that lined the ship's side. 'Must admit she doesn't look much like an innocent trader.' Addressing Queen again, he queried. 'Have you considered the difficulties involved in the running of a pirate ship?'

'Sir?' He couldn't follow this reasoning and his obvious bewilderment brought further, caustic comment as Probus scorned:

'Just imagine you are sailing in pursuit of the Dutchman. You wouldn't find a single friend among the Islands. Neither merchantman nor Naval ship would look kindly on you. Expecting Swally and his cutthroats they'd fire on you without warning. All the pirate strongholds would be closed because they would see you as a threat.' Glaring at him, Probus exclaimed scathingly. 'Don't you realise, man? You'd be outcasts! Isolated from every form of shipping and with no haven to supply the basics of food and water.'

'Wouldn't have to seek far.'

Queen's confidence penetrated and caused Probus to think hard for a few moments before confirming, 'Semarund? King Wanu and his warriors were not exactly cooperative on our last visit. Why should they now be any different?'

'Because their hatred of the Dutch is greater than ours could ever be and I have no doubts about their assistance.'

'You appear to have given the matter much thought,' insinuated Probus in a voice acid with disapproval and, receiving no further response, turned away in dismissal. 'I'm ending this conversation before one of us says something too provocative to ignore. I may admire your resolve, Mr Queen, but do not share in your motivation.'

Ploughing a lone furrow through the Malacca Straights, speeding up the coast of Sumatra and gradually the northernmost tip of the Island dipped below the horizon. Changing course, skirting the Nicobar group and making their westing towards a friendly port. Five days out from Semarund a hail from the masthead brought the officers to the poop deck. The sighting was well ahead and steering in the same direction.

'Set more sail, Mr Sethman,' commanded Probus, 'let's see if we can catch her.'

The pursued ship was overtaken with ease. She was slow through the water and as they drew within sight Probus and Sethman exchanged amused glances.

'East Indiaman, ' said Probus, 'and running from us fast as she can. Do you recognise her?'

'Looks like the *Lord Ellesmere* and from her appearance has seen action.'

In plain view now, topsides badly disfigured and with new patches of wood planking conspicuous down her freeboard and her beak head was in a sorry state. Her sails were patched, and overall she looked very much the worse for wear.

'John Attenbury is Master,' confirmed Probus, 'his first command. Make signal, Mr Bonham-Jones, show her we're friendly before she gives us a broadside.'

Restitution flew English colours but ensigns alone are not trusted in dangerous waters so the early East Indiamen had other ways of identification, with varying sail patterns that were secret to the Company and to ships of the Royal Navy.

The signal was for the ship to windward to hoist an English flag at the fore topgallant masthead, and for the leeward vessel to answer by furling the mizzen and hoisting a French jack at the masthead. To further identify them Probus had the main topsail lowered and also hauled up his foresail . . . this display being peculiar to a homeward bounder. These signals were in no way permanent and for obvious reasons were altered in their nature at frequent intervals.

The other ship replied immediately but kept her gun crews closed up. With the breeze steady and the sea calm they closed on the East Indiaman and the two ships drew parallel. 'Heave-to, Mr Bonham-Jones, and lower the longboat,' ordered Probus. 'I'll board her.'

Lord Ellesmere reduced sail and backed her topsails, crews lining the rail with some speculative waving from both sides. Piped aboard with normal courtesy, Probus soon returned and, waving away eager enquiry, instructed Mr Sethman to, 'Muster all hands.' Bosun's call brought the men running, assembling on deck, Probus addressing them in brisk tone. 'I intend to place all the wounded aboard the East Indiaman immediately. They also have been in action against the Dutch and have lost many men, two officers, and the Captain is badly wounded. Their cargo is still intact and they are on their way home but require assistance and capable officers.' Allowing a few moments for this to register, he then delivered his bombshell. 'So I am transferring Mr Sethman and I to take command for the long haul back to London.' Raising his hand to quell the sudden buzz of interest, he then stated. 'Any man wishing to join me has five minutes to pack his gear and get in the longboat. The rest will be under the command of Mr Queen, who himself will be under orders to return to Indonesia to search out for the Dutchman *Zeevalk* and take back our men held prisoners.'

Excitement surged through the crew at this rasping statement. The midshipmen gaped incredulously at each other as Probus, making every word count, said in commanding tone, 'If you have not made contact within three months you must return home forthwith. Is that very clear, Mr Queen?'

'Yes, sir.'

Dumbfounded, his stammering reply brought a scornful response from Probus. 'Then I suggest you pull yourself together and call for volunteers. But let me make quite clear that if you do not have sufficient support I will order you to take the ship home,' With this final demand Probus moved away leaving the main deck to the bemused officers and crew.

'You heard him,' said Queen. 'The ship is ours, if we want it.'

'Let's get started then,' said Bonham-Jones.

'Look out *Zeevalk*,' said McFie.

He had needed their support, his shoulders squared and as he faced the crew, fifty pair of eyes focussed on his face. Their expectant posture brought a sense of justification and he stalked before them unable to maintain composure for a brief second then, with pride and authority rampant, he announced, 'Crew of *Restitution*, my orders are to take the ship back to the South China Sea. Be under no illusion! We will be acting as a privateer . . . on our own and recognised by neither the Navy nor the East India Company but by the same yardstick any rewards will be our own. I give you no guarantees, except a fair share of any profit,' confidence growing all the time, he added with a smile, 'and perhaps a celebration jug or two as before.' This remark brought return laughter and he paused, before continuing. 'Captain Probus had insisted this be a volunteers only mission and those not wishing to sail with us are free to go with the Captain.' The ranks remained unbroken but an air of expectancy hovered and brought excited chatter. Moving among them he confronted peg leg Joe Laval. 'This is not your concern, you and your original crew mates should take the offer and sail for home.'

'Been away so long the South China Sea is

more home than anywhere else,' came the instant reply. 'I'll sail with you, Capt'n.'

Nodding approval, he moved on. 'You're not fit, Davy. Go aboard the East Indiaman.'

'I'm as fit as Mr McFie,' retorted Davy, 'Sir,' he added hastily.

'I'll vouch for Greenwood,' said Dr. Quennel, 'but there are a few others who should be retired from active duty for their own sake. As for me, I have a taste for more adventure. They have a surgeon aboard already, and suspect you will have need of my services.'

Reaching for his hand, Queen said, 'Thank you, sir.'

Dr. Quennel's handshake was equally warm. 'Leave me to weed out the unfit. They seem reluctant to go without persuasion.'

Probus came up with his sea bag to find Sethman ready along with David Ashbury and the other wounded. The marines and their sub-Lieutenant were also ready, having decided there could be no benefit to them in what they unanimously considered just a waste of time.

'This few?' Probus showed no surprise and, addressing Queen directly, said in chilling voice. 'You have the ability to inspire devotion, but beware, lest you reward such loyalty with decisions based purely on personal motive. Command does not rest easily on young shoulders and you will soon come to realise there is more to Captaincy than giving orders.' He hadn't yet relinquished authority and now insisted. 'My last act of command is to appoint Vinderman as your sailing master. Take heed of sound advice and be in no hurry to question his judgement. The final decision must be yours but at all times respect the voice of experience.' Transferring his attention to the crew, he lectured them as if they were children. 'Know well what you are getting into. You are all volunteers and must be prepared to stand by your decision. I say again! If any of you wish to return home decide now while you have the opportunity.'

Eyes flicking across the water to the poised East Indiaman as he delivered this last warning, but no one moving, so he swung away saying emotionally, 'Then God go with you.' Eyes stinging, he descended the boarding net with bustling haste followed by Sethman and the wounded, several of whom had to be lowered in rope slings. The longboat soon returned and was hoisted inboard. The *Lord Ellesmere* swaged her yards round and her ensign dipped in farewell.

'Give our Captain a salute of eleven guns, Mr Jancy.' Queen's thoughts were very mixed as the cannon fired. Feeling suddenly alone, yet with a sense of satisfaction because the crew had stood by him and were even now awaiting his orders, an embracing thought that stirred him from reverie and, rejoining his officers, he announced. 'Toby, you are First Officer and navigator. Billie is Second Officer and Vindo our sailing master.'

'Unpaid again?' McFie said with a grin.

'Something which is very much up to us,' said Vinderman.'

Glancing at the homeward-bound ship, hull down and running free, Queen said, 'Good sailing, Captain Probus.'

'Aye,' said McFie.

'Orders, Captain?' Bonham-Jones queried.

Grinning boyishly at the title. 'Bring her round, Toby. Set all plain sail and plot our course for Semarund and as soon as we are snugged down for the night issue a double tot of rum all round.'

'What colours?'

'St. George and England,' said the Captain.

Chapter Twenty-seven

Several days had passed since Captain Probus relinquished command and sailed for home. The coast of Sumatra was again visible but this time to starboard as they tacked into the southeast trades . . . days of activity with the crew working the ship to maximum efficiency and also exercising at battle stations. If the crew expected leniency from their new officers they were disappointed, so responded with a will and settled enthusiastically into the routine of maintaining their ship in a state of readiness.

One of the most rewarding aspects of this hard work was the ability of the ship to claw to windward. The old square riggers were built to run before the trade winds and when the contrary wind blew from ahead forward progress was slow and hard-earned but the designer of *Retribution* had endowed his creation with more then just beauty of line, and the crew found great satisfaction in keeping her moving fast into wind, doing a long and short leg down the Malacca

Straits . . . the long leg being a rewarding surge southerly.

'Deck there! Sail ho! On the bow!'

'Call the Captain,' ordered Bonham-Jones.

'What ship?' Queen asked as he came on deck.

'Too far off to recognise and going the same way as ourselves.'

Glancing aloft, the night canvas had been replaced with working sail. Heeling rail down, they were on a speedy tack towards the coast of Sumatra. He could see no urgency.

'Keep her on course, Toby, whoever she is we'll close her before long. Have the crew stand by. No point in closing up just yet, be several hours before we see her colours.'

Just after dawn with the the sun not strong enough to warm away the chill of a stiff breeze. Hunched into his sea coat, Queen felt the tingle of nerves and his fingers fumbled with a stubborn button. Fear, he wondered, or just apprehension of how he would conduct the ship, and himself, in the event of action. Remembering Probus, and his prophecy of command not resting easy, then he shrugged aside the doubts and concentrated on the ship ahead.

Smoothing to windward, catching up fast, he focused on the distant sail. The style of the vessel provoked interest. 'Get Jancy up here.' The gunner came cap in hand. Handing over the telescope. 'Your opinion, Mr Jancy?'

Steadying against the mast rigging, taking his time, after a good scrutiny Jancy stated, 'English man-o-war. Too far away to say for sure but she looks like a two-decker frigate and I think she is one of the old forty-fours.' Pausing to reflect on his naval experience, before suggesting. 'If I'm right, she carries twenty-two eighteen pounders on her gun deck and twenty-two twelve's on the upper. One hell of a broadside, sir.'

'Don't intend to come within range.'

'She's coming about,' said Bonham-Jones.

'Gaining sea room,' said Vinderman. 'They don't want to be caught on a lee shore but perhaps we can squeeze through before she closes.'

'Doubt it,' said Queen, 'their Captain would have allowed us free passage if he had kept his course. Think he plans to take a look at us.'

Let's hope he believes our ensign,' said Vinderman, 'otherwise it could be very interesting.'

'Close up your gun crews, Mr Jancy, but run out no cannon or even open a gun port. We'll show no hostility.'

'Aye, aye, sir.' Jancy moved smartly away and his commanding voice resounded along the main deck.

With the sun now warming, they peeled off their topcoats. The plunging bow sent spray flying over the foredeck, forming brilliant rainbows. Foresails bar taut and showing damp as the bowsprit rose up from the white caps. Bow wave foaming along the lee rail and rushing by in a cascade of foaming water, but spectacle ignored, the officers had eyes only on the frigate's progress.

'Keep her moving as she is, helmsman.'

'Aye, sir.' Jack Dooley was now chief helmsman. His hands were sure on the wheel. Then the frigate's sails momentarily flapped free and she seemed to hover then her head came through the wind and the sails filled again, a significant alteration that brought her on a course to intercept.

'Bring her about' said Queen, 'we'll meet the curious Navy Captain head on but stand by to make our signals of recognition.'

On came the frigate and closing fast. The appropriate signals were made but received no acknowledgement.'

'What do you reckon, Vindo?'

Pointing with his pipe, Vinderman said in ominous tone, 'Yon' frigate's Captain seems hell bent on engaging. Be worth a good promotion if he could sink Swally and his pirates.'

As *Restitution* came around and settled on the opposite tack the ships angled towards each other about three miles apart. All telescopes training on the frigate. Starboard gun ports dropping open . . . cannons of the two-tiered gun deck poking their noses through in silent menace.

'Christ!' Ejaculated Vinderman.

'Repeat signal, ' ordered Queen. A hopeless gesture, the frigate standing on in full battle array.

'You could turn and run from them,' suggested

Vinderman in a voice laden with urgency, 'they'd soon see a vanishing stern.'

'And lose all the ground gained these last hard days. Not only that, because we'd be scared to come down the Straits ever again for fear of meeting the Royal Navy.' Adding in determined voice. 'They'll only get one chance at us then we'll be clear.'

'One broadside could be plenty enough,' said Vinderman.

Two miles only separating them . . . a matter of about five minutes at the speed they were coming together. Telescopes were no longer needed. Contemplating the frigate for brief moment. 'The way she's heeling must limit the scope of her starboard battery,' said Queen, 'and I doubt whether her guns will be effective at long range.' Making up his mind, he ordered. 'Bring Jancy up here.'

As sailing master, Vinderman was virtually in charge of sailing the ship, and with no remaining doubt of Queen's intention, he moved closer to Dooley at the helm to assume responsibility for ship handling. Assessing with a keen eye, he ordered, 'Larboard one point.'

'Helm larboard on, one point.' The wind freed. Sheets were eased. The sails bellied deep and she fairly flew towards the frigate. Jancy reporting aft, breathing hard with all this running up and down, but explaining in terse voice, Queen said, 'If the frigate's Captain is determined to engage we must slow her down.' Observing for reaction. 'How close do you need to be to bring your bow cannon to bear?'

'Fire on the Navy!'

Jancy couldn't believe this and the expression on his face bore testimony to shock and abhorrence but Queen said again, insistently, 'How close, Jancy?'

'Less than half a mile.'

'If I position you within seven hundred yards?'

Jancy nodded in mute acquiescence.

'We'll try to get through without engaging,' said Queen in understanding tone. ' Train your guns on masts and rigging only and, if it proves necessary, take them out.' Grasping the gunner by the shoulder, he consoled. 'Know how you feel, but they seem intent on taking us.'

'Aye, aye, sir,' said Jancy.

'Wait for the word, Mr Gunner.'

The two guns on the foredeck were masterpieces of the gunsmith's craft. While the shot they fired was comparatively small, they had the virtue of long range and accuracy. Jancy assembling his best crew; Vinderman discussing tactics.

'We'll run straight at them and come up under her stern to keep her main battery from bearing.'

'Her Captain may have some ideas of his own,' said Queen.

They could make out the cluster of officers on the frigate's quarterdeck. Distance less than a mile now and there seemed vast numbers of men closed up at the gun positions. Even as they watched her head came round, yards swaging to free the wind and she came up to a more even angle of heel.

'He's giving no advantage,' said Queen.

'Would we?' Vinderman asked brusquely. Keeping an eye on Dooley, he growled. 'Hold your course, helmsman.'

'Aye, aye, Mr Vinderman,' Dooley looked at him askance. 'This could be bloody interesting, don't much fancy taking on the Royal Navy.'

Two puffs of smoke belching from the frigate's bow, a double detonation that belted against unprepared eardrums. Shot falling short; waterspouts disturbing the green water.

'Larboard one point,' instructed Vinderman. She rolled sharply then raced to round the man-of-war's stern. Pointing with his pipe. 'She's coming round,' he said.

The frigate's Captain responded instantly to the change of course and his ship came round to counter this move. After an initial pause her sails filled and she picked up speed again.

'Ready about.' With all inhibition cast aside Vinderman was enjoying sailing the ship to full potential and followed this with an ecstatic. 'Mainsail haul! Let go and haul!'

The forward battery again spat fire from the frigate's bow. But sailing flat out and about her deadly business *Restitution* made a very fleeting target and the telltale splashes were well astern. So the frigate's Captain again wore ship to cover his opponent.

'She's slow to pick up speed when she wears.' Viewing the frigate . . . concentrating on this hesitation in gathering way when turning, Queen incisively commanded. 'Bring her about, Vindo. Now!' Hand raised in signal to his master gunner. The frigate had her larboard battery trained and a fearsome, rippling broadside, thundered death and destruction but *Restitution* was already about and the bewildered Navy gunners saw the shot plunge harmlessly into the wake of this elusive target. Five hundred yards between them and, as the frigate's Captain wore ship to cover this new tack, his ship poised for a brief minute.

Wha-am! Jancy fired one. It recoiled into its slinging as a tear appeared in the frigate's main course. Depressing his second cannon while his crew swabbed, loaded, run out, he touched flintlock to powder hole. Wha-am! The din was unbearable . . . returned by a volley that screamed overhead with a banshee whistle, but a great shout came from the crew as Jancy's second shot smashed into the frigate's foremast. The topgallant yard lurched and sagged, suspended by one rope and swinging wildly overhead before crashing down, causing pandemonium on the gun deck. Then, Jancy back with the first cannon took careful aim, waiting for an even keel, suspense nerve wracking. Wha-am! The frigate's foremast jerked under the impact then cracked off at a point ten feet above deck level. Hanging suspended from its own rigging for a dramatic second then its vast weight snapped the ropes and the whole plunged over the side, wrenching sail and yardarm from the main mast as it fell, scattering debris and tattered sailcloth all over the deck. Forward drive instantly slowing . . . frigate's upper decks in chaos with seamen chopping and heaving frantically to restore vision and mobility.

Restitution swept across the frigate's bow and was soon showing only her stern. A vain, last broadside slammed from the man-of-war, but no more than a defiant gesture as they surged out of range. Matter of minutes and a full mile separated the ships.

'Heave to, Vindo.' Queen needed to check that the damage to the frigate wasn't serious. They lay almost stationery under backed headsails while the officers surveyed the confusion aboard their would-be attacker.

'That little encounter won't exactly endear us to the powers that are.'

Bonham-Jones drawl seemed more exaggerated than normal but McFie said unrepentantly and in cocky tone. 'Their own damn fault! Old Probus was right when he said we'd be fair game for all.'

Queen turned from appraisal. 'It's fortunate the Navy is overstretched in these waters, or they'd soon be after us in strength.' Adding thoughtfully. 'Swally left a legacy we could well do without.'

'If we can take on the Royal Navy,' said McFie, 'we haven't much to fear from the average merchantman.'

The encounter had put all on board in a mood of exuberance and confirmed the lethal manoeuvrability of the pirate ship and Queen went down among the men with words of congratulation for the unflinching way they had engaged the powerful man-of-war.

'Beggin' your pardon, sir,' said Jancy, 'but I wouldn't care to fire on a ship of His Majesty's Navy very often.'

'Nor I, Mr Gunner, you did well and I couldn't ask for better and if there had been any alternative apart from running I would have taken it.' Looking Jancy straight in the eye. 'Somehow doubt the frigate's Captain showing us the same charity.'

'Damn right, sir, taking us would have brought a tidy sum in prize money,' adding with a self-satisfied grin, 'got a little more than he bargained for this time.'

Leaving the crew to resume normal work, Queen returned to the quarterdeck where his officers were in rapt contemplation of the day's happenings. Allowing a minute for mutual congratulation, he then instructed, 'Make all plain sail, Toby, and bring us back on course for Semarund.' Casting a last look at the frigate still making stubbornly towards them. 'Dip our ensign to the frigate's Captain, Billie, and pray that we meet no more ships of the Royal Navy.'

Alone in the privacy of his aft stateroom, stalking about unable to keep still, pouring a large brandy he held the glass at eye level. The liquor was rock steady and he couldn't help but be surprised at his calm demeanour. Much more than this . . . he was jubilant! He had taken on the might of the Royal Navy and his crew had backed him all the way. He'd sailed *Restitution* into action and had proved himself a worthy Captain. He saw his face mirrored in the clear liquid and knew the ecstasy was more than mere triumph. His mouth had a sardonic, almost cruel and untypical half-smile and now he came face to face with the fact that desire for revenge was not the sole reason for his recent moroseness of manner. Just as assertive had been the resentment against other hands being in charge of this witch of a ship. She had ensnared Swally, and now sought his own subservience to her lethal beauty. Downing the brandy with one gulp he threw the glass down with a flourish that could have been Swally's own, but he no longer needed to hide behind protestations of outrage. The reason was out in the open and he could face it without flinching . . . wanted to shout it out loud. 'The ship is mine!' He was Master! And the real lust was for command: for power!

Lust for power has dominated man over the ages. Power for Jason Queen at this moment came in the form of a deadly fighting ship named *Restitution*. The brandy also was untypical, yet filled a need and allowed time for reflection. Was all this perhaps a legacy from his father, John Queen, whose own early career had been dominated by this same need for command? Now he remembered other things . . . what would Maggie think of him now? Her face came, lovely of mouth but with eyes questioning. How he remembered? Then he looked around revelling in the opulence. The eighteen pounders, one either side facing outboard was in grim contrast to this luxury and he pictured the carnage of such a shot crashing into his quarters. The thought instantly sobered and brought him back from conceit to the stark realisation that responsibility for the ship's safety and the lives of all on board was in his hands.

Though relishing command, Queen had yet to come to terms with the isolation. Without any preparation he had to stand aloof, a situation to which his fellow officers appeared to contribute. He couldn't quite make out whether they or he had erected the barrier, or if they had unwittingly conspired to build the restraint that must always be the dividing line between Captain and his officers. If anything, he found more friendship from among the men of the fo'c'sle who seemed to regard him with a mixture of affection and deference and who had no difficulty with what to them was a traditional relationship. Vinderman as always ... just himself, ready to listen and offer his experience and bridging the gap with ease but Queen missed the association of midshipmen days, especially with McFie. He was learning the isolation of command and in all his solitary style of life had never felt so alone. He could almost hear the humour in the voice of Captain Probus, who was no doubt saying. 'You have the chance you yearned for, get on with it man!'

Squaring his shoulders. Mouth hard again. Time enough for normal relations when he had taken back Abraham, Mr Harper and the others, and also, had his hands on the neck of the beast that had fouled his enchanting Riana.

He unrolled the chart of the South China Sea.

Chapter Twenty-eight

Semarund. Where the anticipation of King Wanu's support soon proved justified. After a stop over of two days, they sailed fully provisioned and with the men festooned with exotic garlands. Queen declined the King's offer of his finest warriors but gladly accepted his insistence of a return to Semarund when they had found *Zeevalk*. All in the village seemed to accept without question the success of their venture.

On their way through the Sunda Strait they plundered a French merchant ship, relieving them of some silver coin and a goodly store of cognac. The French vessel showed little resistance and a couple of rounds from Jancy brought her to a hove-to position. Her Captain couldn't believe his luck when his sword, and his ship, were handed back.

Patrolling the waters north of Java and Sumatra for a further three weeks, they took every sail within reach, mostly small vessels who had no hesitation in striking their colours when

Restitution came at them with bow cannon roaring yet Queen resisted any inclination to take such ships as prizes, for this could only serve to reduce the size of crew aboard his own command, and after one such encounter Vinderman scrutinised him with an expression of disquiet in his eyes. Captain or not . . . he had no fear of plain speaking to the man in whose company he had been for so long and whom he had accompanied into adventure beyond imagination. Pulling hard on his pipe, he said, 'Reckon you're deliberately engaging every ship we meet yet take possession of none. In fact, apart from keeping ourselves well supplied with strong liquor and provisions, we're not finding the kind of reward that would make our efforts worthwhile.'

'The men aren't complaining.'

'Have you asked the wounded?'

'What the hell are you talking about, we have no wounded?'

'Not yet.'

'They knew the risk when they volunteered, and at least, the surgeon is well stocked with medicines as a result of our actions, and you do not go short of tobacco!'

'Long as we don't get into the habit of pirating for its own sake.'

Unmoved by the irritation that hardened his Captain's tone Vinderman blew smoke rings and observed for reaction through the smoke haze but Queen seemed unconcerned as he said, 'You know as well as I that an efficient ship keeps in fighting trim only by constant engagement.' With these words Queen stood tall to confront him and Vinderman's eyes narrowed at the dominant manner of his bearing as he stated. 'This is our insurance because the Dutch ships are heavily armed and won't be taken easily.' Speaking with conviction and a surety which had Vinderman nodding in reluctant agreement. 'When we meet up with *Zeevalk*,' Queen then said, 'I'm determined that we'll be successful, and efficiency alone will be the deciding factor in an engagement where we will be the smaller, both in size and firepower.' Slowing his dialogue and a glimmer of a smile broke through. 'You're right though, for every sail sighted is viewed as prospective plunder but we haven't yet sailed under the black flag of Swally nor have I completely succumbed to the spell of *Restitution*, although I admit that she becomes harder to resist. But as Captain Probus insisted many times, we are English seamen and will conduct ourselves accordingly.'

Under reduced sail . . . cruising among one of the many groups of islands north of Sumatra seeking a possible haven where they could top up their water supply. They were not short of water but every opportunity was taken to replenish and keep the ship in readiness to stay at sea for long periods. They had been cruising back and forth across this area in the hope of intercepting the return of the Dutch ship. The early charts had no details of such diminutive islands and Queen scrutinised ahead. 'See any way in?' he asked.

Vinderman shook his head then drew attention to a boat scudding from under the sheltering spur of a high cliff. Rigged with a lateen sail like an Arab dhow she seemed small and harmless but they were in strange waters. 'Could be the local pilot boat,' he said cautiously.

'Close up the hands, Toby, but show no hostility. We'll give them a chance to close us.'

The dhow was well handled by a crew few in number who skilfully manoeuvred alongside some yards away and keeping good way on. Ramon Salvador again proved his value as interpreter and after a short, shouting discussion, explained, 'They claim many ships come here for water and offer to guide us over the reef.'

'Ask the price first.'

After a quick exchange the price was agreed.

'What's your opinion, Vindo?'

'We're in deep water. Seems no danger; and the crew would welcome a run ashore.'

'Ramon, tell them we'll follow.'

Dhow moving ahead at reduced speed with *Restitution* sailing slowly behind. Little way on now, sail up just a scrap of topsail. Noticing a change in the colour of the water Vinderman snapped, 'Leadsman forward!'

'By the mark, ten,' came the call from the man

sounding the depth. Ten fathoms were adequate. The call repeated. 'By the mark, ten.'

Beginning to round the spur of high ground, Vinderman straining for a glimpse of the entrance.

'By the deep, seven.'

The ship drew about twelve feet. Seven fathoms was plenty of margin, but Vinderman suddenly said, 'I don't like it! I'm coming about.'

'Gun crews close up,' commanded Queen.

'Look at this lot!' The shout came from McFie on the foredeck as a fleet of dhows swept from under the lee of the headland and speeding towards the slow-moving ship. Then the supposed pilot dhow reversed direction and came winging back and a horde of men appeared on deck armed with swords and peculiar, flare-barrelled muskets.

'By the deep, five, and coral!' Alarm now evident in the call.

'The bastard's trying to run us ashore,' growled helmsman Dooley.

'Get her moving, Vindo!' Leaving the quarter-deck in haste and running to the gun positions, Queen shouted in urgent voice. 'Prepare broadside.'

Gun ports slamming open. Cannon running out either side. The Pilot dhow was well ahead of the others and closing at speed.

'Orders, Capt'n?'

'Sink them, Mr Jancy.'

The ship was turning, but slowly . . . almost in

stays . . . head reluctant to come through the wind. Canvas dropping from the buntlines, swaging round, setting: all urgent but orderly under the control of Bonham-Jones. Jancy crouching over the larboard cannon, impatiently waiting for the ship to come round and settle. Small shot flaming from the nearest dhow, a ball thudded through the rail and across the deck, sending splinters flying.

Wha-am! Jancy fired one. High! Depressing the second and third. Wha-am! Wha-am! Recoiling . . . the twelve-pounders blew the front of the dhow away. The bow gaped wide and the dhow pitch poled. Its stern reared and men flew high with the force of the explosion and with the forward momentum. *Restitution* was slow in gathering way. Wind on the beam and too light for acceleration. The dhows were shallow draught and easily driven and coming at full speed with men lining the rails, half naked and fearsome. The larboard guns flamed a broadside into the dhows. A mast dropped from one and sails tore asunder from others but still they came on and closing fast.

'Load grapeshot, Jancy!' Intent only on survival: no time for niceties.

Guns reloaded, depressed to minimum elevation and aimed at point blank range but the pirate fleet had split up and came approaching from bow and stern away from the ship's broadside, bringing a foul curse from Jancy. 'The crafty bleeder's have done this before.'

McFie in charge of the seamen, Bonham-Jones busy issuing cutlass, boarding pike and pistol. 'For God's sake, Jancy,' roared Queen, 'pour it into them!'

Din of battle raging, and the roar of the broadside only added to hysteria as the Dhows cleared the shelter of stern and bow and took the blast from close range. Men were cut down into bloody heaps. Screams strangling from mutilated mouths but the remaining pirates took no heed and the last Dhows came crashing down the freeboard... grappling iron and boarding nets hurtling inboard.

'Prepare to repel boarders.' Frantic command. Unnecessary as the crew rushed the pirates crowding the rail and scrambling up to engage in hand to hand fighting and the boarders were met with pistol and slashing cutlass.

'Bleedin' cheek!' Big Jacko chopped down a bearded Malay then swung at another nearly severing his head. The pirates were hacked down off the rail. A yardarm swung out holding a net of cannon shot which then dropped onto the foremost Dhow to crash through the deck and stoving a gaping hole in the bilge planking with pirates swimming in panic away from pistol and musket fire.

Under way and gathering speed as her press of canvas harnessed the breeze to full advantage. Grapple ropes chopped free; last of the Dhows falling astern. Jancy's stern guns were primed ready and he glanced expectantly but Queen shook his head. 'Let them go. They'll remember this day and think twice the next time a ship approaches.'

The action had been short-lived but they had come out practically unscathed. The men were jubilant as the full potential of their ship and gunner Jancy was tried and tested but the officers were not so self-congratulatory. 'A lesson in complacency,' said Vinderman in hard tone, 'and the first time we've fired in anger.'

'Gave 'em rice, though,' said McFie, whose sober countenance seemed in strange contrast to the elation in his voice.

'We're equally at fault,' said Queen, 'thought we were unassailable and it took a bunch of Malay boatmen to prove how dangerous it is to assume?'

'Aye,' said Vinderman, 'if they had managed to put us aground they could have done with us as they pleased.' Just then Ramon Salvador came with rum, he had already anticipated his next order.

'Measure all round, Ramon: and a double tot to our master gunner.'

On constant patrol between the Islands of Sumatra and Java, acting on the advice of Captain Probus, who had explained that the logical route for most Dutch ships returning from the ports of China and Indonesia would be to call at Batavia for victualling and then on down the Sunda Straits and out into the Indian Ocean for the long haul around the Cape of Good Hope.

Long weeks of sailing, in good weather and foul and the monotony brought the first sign of discontent. The crew were becoming expert at the trade of piracy but not a single ship worth the looting came within reach and it began to seem that all the rich merchantmen were sailing other waters. Pickings were lean and they could foresee the frustration of a return home with empty pockets.

Queen was a hard Captain, driving his ship ever onwards without sympathy for any murmur of complaint, but even he began to wonder if *Zeevalk* had slid by under cover of darkness and was already on her way homeward. Short tempered and despondent, the three-month commission granted by Captain Probus had almost run out and he would soon be on borrowed time. He didn't much care, for he was Captain now and would make his own decisions. But he fully realised how this long stay at sea with its accompanying lack of reward was sapping morale and, more potently, time had begun to erase the bitter memories, and the fire that burned in his soul was slowly being extinguished. Pacing the poop deck. Aloof . . . not allowing of any frivolous approach. Causing his fellow officers to keep their distance, with the association they once enjoyed no longer apparent.

He requested their company to dinner in his stateroom. Dr. Quennel in attendance.

The meal was eaten quickly and with only formal and very stilted conversation. The dinner guests sat back with brandy and patient conjecture. The first time in weeks they had dined in such style . . . knew there must be a reason. Uncomfortable with their presence and obvious curiosity Queen opened the dialogue. 'The way I see it we have three courses of action.' Interest was immediate so he outlined his options. 'Continue as we are in the hope of intercepting *Zeevalk*. Give it all up as hopeless and obey orders to return home or try for more remunerative pickings in other waters.' He had given much thought to this last alternative. Frustration had brought a decimating lack of purpose both to the ship's company: and himself.

'Are you asking our opinion?' McFie said sarcastically.

'It's time we gave up on *Zeevalk*,' said Vinderman, 'and began to look out for ourselves, because you know as well as I do that everyone is fed up with cruising up and down with nowhere to go and the only time we set foot on dry land is to top up our victuals and the way things are going we won't be able to pay our way much longer.' Concluding with a laconic. 'Reckon we're wasting our time.'

'She could have slipped through, we can't expect to cover every square mile, but I would still like the chance to find Abraham and the others. They might still be alive?'

'We must be damned unlucky privateers,' said McFie, 'maybe we've boarded a good few but never a sign of profit.'

'We are here for a specific purpose,' said Dr. Quennel, 'seems premature to give up at this stage.'

'The way we're placed we meet only inter-island traders.' Vinderman again. 'Such ships have no value to the likes of us.'

'Perhaps we are in the wrong position,' said Bonham-Jones.

'If I was Master of a homeward bounder,' suggested Vinderman, 'I'd take the shortest route down the South China Sea and up the Malacca Strait into the Indian Ocean, so it must follow that this is where the returning Indiamen are likely to be and where the rich cargoes are also to be found.'

Having posed this provocative thought he left them to think about it while he thumbed tobacco into his pipe but if he expected a chance to light up he was forestalled as Queen demanded, 'Suppose you were Dutch with a base at Batavia?'

'I don't have all the answers, but if you don't soon provide the crew with either profit or a lengthy run ashore among the flesh pots you'll lose their support.'

'We still have a week or so before time is up.'

'If we decide to turn for home,' said McFie, 'we

could look out for any potential prize. Anything is better than returning home in humiliation and with our holds empty.'

'So where do you all stand?' Queen asked curtly.

Dr. Quennel. 'Not my decision.'

Vinderman. 'Look for easy prey on the way home.'

McFie. 'I agree with Vindo.'

Bonham-Jones. 'See out our three months as ordered by Captain Probus.'

'Thanks, Toby,' said Queen. 'We wait one more week then try our luck in the Malacca Straits or the Indian Ocean.'

The next week was but a repetition of its predecessors and he reluctantly gave orders that turned the ship northerly. Indecision over, officers and crew alike were in a much happier frame of mind. There was enthusiasm in the routine handling of the ship as anticipation replaced boredom. He knew the ache of resentment. Of futility! How could he have expected to intercept the Dutch ship in this boundless seaway? Needle in a haystack would have been easier. It was finished. All over! He had a duty to his men and also to *Restitution* who seemed to enjoy her release from the confines of narrow waters, and it was just a day's speedy romp before the Island of Bangka on the eastern end of Sumatra came into view. There were several off lying islands in this area and careful attention to navigation was needed. Darkness fell before the hazards were cleared and they could reduce sail for the night. Retiring to his cabin, relieved to have the confidence eroding weeks of uncertainty behind him, but also with an overpowering feeling of self-recrimination. He had failed his ship, his crew, and worst of all: he had failed Riana!

Chapter Twenty-nine

On the way home with all hope abandoned. Despondency and sullen acceptance! On a northerly tack to clear Bangka ... dawn breaking with typical splendour.

'Deck there! Sail ho!' The lookouts call held a note of unusual query that brought speculation to the deck watch. Snapping his telescope shut and, with satisfaction rampant on his face, Queen announced:

'Dutch merchantman on course for Batavia.'

Posing the question dominant in their minds, McFie said excitedly, '*Zeevalk*?'

'Certainly looks like her.'

'Do you think they've seen us?' Bonham-Jones queried.

'They're seamen are they not,' said Vinderman, 'be sure they've seen us.'

'She's standing on regardless.'

'So they should,' replied Vinderman, 'she must be at least twice our size and her Captain is probably confident of his ability to scare off any single attacker.'

A formidable vessel, *Zeevalk* mounted fifty guns, mainly thirty-two pounders. She was also heavily built with high topsides that presented a conspicuous target to a skilled gunner. Standing on . . . sails becoming larger and very distinctive. Stowing his telescope, Queen's face had the contour of Dartmoor granite. 'It's she right enough. Pipe all hands to battle stations and hoist the death-head flag of pirate Swally. Let them know they can expect no quarter.'

The bosun's pipe brought everyone running. Gun ports slamming open. Cannon run out. The decks spread with wet sand to reduce the risk of powder burns causing fire. *Restitution* mounted twelve guns either side on her single gun deck. These were eighteen-pounders, with two lighter cannon on both fore and poop deck, mounted high for maximum elevation. It was customary to issue a double tot of run when action seemed imminent and this was duly served. The fiery spirit! The expectation of looting a valuable cargo, they could return home rich! This was why they were here! Long months of frustration about to earn just reward and the crew closed up with anticipation and with excitement in their animated buzz of conversation.

'She's altering,' snapped Vinderman, 'giving her guns more range. Bring her up two points, helmsman, we'll force her further over.'

'Up to points on.' Dooley might have been

helming up the English Channel so matter of fact was his voice.

Gunner Jancy moved without haste along the gun deck supervising the loading. Coming up on the poop deck he bent over the twelve-pounders. Apparently satisfied he gave a quick salute. 'All ready larboard side, sir.' Looking over the lee rail to state. 'If we heel any further the gun ports will have to be closed.'

Bonham-Jones and McFie at their deck action stations, Queen and Vinderman at the steering platform, Dooley and Bate doubled up at the helm. *Zeevalk* had run off to starboard but closing fast because *Restitution* was speeding directly at her.

'Back on course, Vindo,' ordered Queen, 'keep just out of range then come up under her stern for a broadside.' Thoughtful for a moment, he then said to Jancy. 'Aim high, Mr Gunner, I want her crippled not sunk. Remember that our crewmen might still be aboard.'

'Aye, sir,' hurrying back to his guns.

Main deck in a state of readiness, rows of cutlass and boarding pikes in well positioned racks. Marksmen climbing the rigging as the ship surged back on her original course to race along the side of *Zeevalk*. The menace in her approach instantly invited a thundering broadside from the two-tiered gun deck of the towering merchantman. Water spouting fifty yards away as the shot fell short.

'Wear ship,' cried Vinderman.

Dooley spun the wheel. Yards braced, the stern came round. Wind directly from behind and as she raced towards the bulky East Indiaman the low hull of the privateer was almost level in the water. Double shot flamed at them from the high transom and heads ducked involuntarily as the fiery ball screamed a banshee whistle through the upper rigging.

'Fire as you bear!' Twelve cannons fired one by one as they bore across the stern of *Zeevalk*, crashing death and destruction into the high poop. Jancy aimed his stern chasers. They fired close together and the lateen mizzen mast lurched sideways throwing sailcloth and broken wood across the after deck, with the damaged mast swinging dangerously overhead. Recoil brought the guns back into their breeching ropes and men worked with feverish haste to sponge out. Cartridge and wad rammed home and a man ready with shot as the rammer came clear. At close range aiming was hardly necessary, the vital need being to fire as rapidly as they could. An efficient gun crew could achieve a rate of about a round every two minutes and the guns were soon prepared and run out again.

'Good shooting, Jancy.' Queen had time for encouragement as his ship came round in the wake of *Zeevalk* whose pace had hardly been slowed by the loss of her mizzen, but with commotion on the after deck as debris was cleared.

As they closed her fast to leeward twin chasers blasted from her stern and a section of rail shattered inboard. Splinters flying ... jagged and lethal and men were cut down, not with cannon ball, but by scything spears of teak that sent the foredeck men scattering. Two men appearing through the melee supporting the limp body of a shipmate, a sliver of wood protruded from his mangled shoulder and they hurried him below to Dr. Quennel.

The ship was moving fast and flew down the leeward side of the Dutchman raking her upper deck with a full broadside. Her main mast jerked but remained upright as a cannon ball gouged a great chunk from its base. The wind-taut main course disintegrated in shreds and her guns blasted a defiant and hasty reply but the angle of heel was acute and sent the shot just short of the waterline. Jancy's broadside had succeeded in slowing the heavy Dutch ship and the fleet-footed *Restitution* swept on ahead.

'Ready about,' roared Vinderman.

'Prepare starboard battery,' shouted Queen.

The speed and deadly power of their ship fired every man to exhilaration and the whole ship's company were battle crazed and intent only on returning for another devastating attack. The sail handlers were under the control of Bonham-Jones and McFie with not a single movement or moment of time wasted. Pulling smoothly on the sheet ropes, sails filling on the opposite tack and back she swept. The men aboard *Zeevalk* could only watch and wait with increasing fear as the black-hulled ship once again ran alongside.

Gun crews moving smartly across to the starboard battery, already loaded and run out. Jancy poising with flintlock in his hand . . . intermittent cannon fire flaming at them, din of battle raging and creating its own demoniac style of madness. Jancy wouldn't be hurried. Firing the first cannon, covering the vent as it recoiled. The shot was short; he elevated the next one quick wrench and fired. The ships were virtually beam on and focussing on the shattered main course of his target Jancy moved easily along the gun deck. Elevating. Firing. Crouching by the next. An easy mark for the master gunner, his rippling volley smashed death and chaos across the main deck of the Dutch ship. Her damaged mast cracked like a carrot and fell, spreading a net of rigging and sailcloth across the guns and trapping seamen and gun crew alike. Cannons on the Dutch poop fired at close range and *Restitution* shuddered and swung off course as the shot smashed a swage of shattered wood and broken glass through the stern cabin walls. Then they were past and beyond accurate range before the cannon could be reloaded for another shot at them.

'Once again, ' roared Queen, 'then we board her!'

Wearing ship, closing up on the crippled

merchantman. Dutch stern chasers belted fire and smoke and the privateer replied with flaming cannon. *Zeevalk* rolled sharply, topsides and gun positions blown apart as the smoking shot blasted through men and gun carriage. A loaded thirty-two pounder exploded throwing bodies around like rag dolls. Great splinters of oak ripped the crew into a screaming, running horde trying in vain to get free of the slaughtering carnage. The ships came together with a shriek of tortured wood and immediately the English crew secured with grapple hooks. Muskets crackling from high in the rigging as they poured up and over and were met with a volley of small arms fire from a squad of Dutch Marines, felling several boarders but also many of their own men who had rushed to repel the attack. Marksmen aloft poured musket shot into the Dutch Marines who broke and huddled for shelter.

Queen and Bonham-Jones in the forefront, chopping, shouting at top voice and cutting a murderous swathe inboard surrounded by a screaming, hysterical mob and deafened by the din as sword and cutlass clashed above the cries of stricken men. The boarders were engaged by Dutch sailors; who came rushing at them from the foredeck but a second boarding party hurtled over the side, swinging on ropes to get further inboard. The English were outnumbered but more than made up for this in sheer determined and murderous fighting ability. Chop! Slash!

Thrust home! Kill the bastard! Fire in the blood and brute power in the strike. The deck was in shambles as battle surged across tangled rope, broken yardarms and the bodies lying prostrate between wet sand and pools of blood.

McFie was doing great work with his crutch. A bearded man reeled away, head broken by a swinging blow, and every crunch of wood on exposed heads was accompanied by the foulest of oaths from McFie.

The Dutch seamen seemed to have no heart for this death-dealing encounter and, laying down their arms fell back in submission, leaving just one group holding the quarterdeck led by a heavy shouldered brute. Hallmeyer! The sighting brought remembered, raging antagonism and Queen ran forward with a group of seamen to engage this last defiance. The Dutch were well organised at this point and seemed to be holding firm but the support of Queen and his men soon had them under pressure and they were forced back. Men went down with a terrible toll among the defenders but Hallmeyer fought with the strength of a madman. Then shock! Disbelief! The sudden appearance of Queen stopping him in his tracks but only for a split second then, with an obscene snarl of recognition, he sprang to engage. Cutlass hilts locked together . . . neither giving way. He spat deliberately into Queen's face; who pulled clear and slashed a cutlass strike that took away shirtsleeve and flesh. Blood spurted, bringing foul blasphemy and he came back with a knife appearing in his left hand. Queen reared at the sight of the silver blade and his strength was maniacal as he straightaway chopped his cutlass down on Hallmeyer's wrist and feeling only elation as it crunched deep into bone and sinew. Hallmeyer screamed in agony and the cutlass fell from nerveless fingers as Queen moved in close to seize the hand wielding the dagger. Holding it by the wrist in demoniac grip, glaring into pain crazed eyes he deliberately ripped away the bandana covering his head and his eyes narrowed into slits of hell fire at the hideously disfigured face exposed from under the coloured cloth. A face made even more grotesque by the puckered, twisted flesh that had once been his left ear.

'Hallmeyer!' Voice unrecognisable as his own, harsh and consumed with a lethal intent born by the side of a tropic lagoon: and nurtured under a hanging tree. Then he growled in condemning tone. 'It had to be you!'

Fighting around them had ceased. Dutch giving up the struggle as the last pockets of resistance were overwhelmed but Queen had heed of nothing but the man before him. His eyes were evil and Hallmeyer almost cowered before the uncontrolled venom on his face, then Queen snatched the dagger from the unresisting hand. Helpless now with blood gushing from his shattered arm, Hallmeyer shuddered, with pain and in bewilderment at the viciousness of the man savaging him. 'In the name of mercy,' he gasped, 'what have I ever done to you?'

'That ear condemns you to death, Hallmeyer.' No mercy in this barren voice. 'Never again will you murder a native Prince on the beach at Semarund or despoil a maiden with your vileness.'

Eyes flaring in sudden realisation, 'For God's sake!' cried Hallmeyer. 'She was only an ignorant savage!'

'She was young and completely innocent: and she hung herself rather than live with the shame you inflicted on her.' Dagger reversing in the hand of Jason Queen: voice taking on the rasp of executioner as he snarled. 'Take your foul disease to hell with you!'

Stroke of the assassin: upward through the ribs and deep into flesh and vital organs. Hallmeyer screamed once in mortal agony then his eyes rolled and blood gushed unchecked from between his lips. Queen lunged and buried the knife deeper, twisting and gouging on the blade with wild-animal ferocity, then let him fall with the knife still embedded. A sickening crunch came from behind and he turned fast to find a Dutch seaman lying unconscious with McFie standing over him brandishing his crutch.

'He tried to sneak up and run you through while you weren't looking,' said McFie. 'Good job I was watching your back: again!'

Queen had just killed a man. Deliberately and with hate in his very soul and, now feeling the reaction couldn't stop from shaking, but he wasn't allowed time for personal feelings as Bonham-Jones reported, 'Prisoners all forward.'

'Keep them well covered, Toby.' Forcing his mind to function, to shake off the dull ache of vengeance accomplished he turned to McFie and said in an out of control voice. 'Take our wounded aboard and get back here as fast as you can.'

The Dutch Captain, waiting on the poop deck, offered his sword hilt foremost but Queen shook his head in negation. 'I want neither your sword nor your ship, Captain, both will be returned when we have stripped everything of value to us.'

Registering surprise and looking astounded at Queen. 'You are not the usual type of China Sea pirate,' said the Captain, 'I expected Swally and his murderous crew.'

'We are late of the East India Company's ship *Earl of Rothesay*, sunk by your Navy off Java,' said Queen very formally, before adding, 'why didn't you run from us, Captain, like you ran once before?'

'Run to where! Your ship is much too fast for us to have reached safety. Anyway, we are more powerfully armed and should have done better.' Shaking his head as if in disbelief 'I never saw such gunnery.' His manner was composed and he seemed to have bowed to the inevitable. 'Privateers normally seek easier prey than such as us but it was almost as if you were lying in wait for us.'

'Your downfall started when you repaid the hospitality of Semarund by burning the village and allowing your men to rape and pillage. The outrage of your crew! The killings! And the imprisonment of our crew were reason enough to seek you out.'

'War makes animals of us all. Are you any exception?' Deliberately emphasising the words, surveying the carnage on deck and looking directly into Queen's face as he asked. 'What justification can you possibly offer in defence of your brutal and totally unnecessary murder of Jan Hallmeyer?'

'Such a monster must expect retribution,' said Queen in hard tone.

'You presume to elect yourself judge and executioner. Remember that one day you will also be judged.'

'So will we all.' Impatient now, he asked. 'You have English prisoners aboard?'

'Six only: in chains below.'

'After you, Captain.'

Escorted down into the after hold. To a dungeon, a tiny black hole some eight feet square with neither light nor ventilation. Stink of urine, human excreta and the rank odour of unclean bodies. Six men roped to iron brackets and sprawled in their own filth. Difficult to penetrate the gloom but a gasp of wonder and surging hope came from a man on the floor. 'Is that really you, Jase . . . wondered who was causing all the commotion topsides?' The croak came from Abraham Verber, almost unrecognisable under all the hair and dirt.

Dropping to his knees to cut him free. Cradling him in his arms like a baby, supreme fulfilment as he said tenderly, 'Aye, lad, we've been searching for a long, long time.'

The men lifted Verber and carried him topsides. All the prisoners were incapable of movement without support and were taken from the cell with extreme care. Queen had his arms round a frail body that seemed without life until the eyes opened to peer in bewilderment.

'Thought we'd never live to see a familiar face,' words high-pitched with delirium but unmistakeably those of Ernest Harper.

'You can't imagine how pleased we are to find you, sir,' said Queen in a voice full of ecstasy and self-justification.'

As they gained fresh air Harper seemed incapable of clear speech but his eyes registered astonishment at the scene on deck and half-formed questions came rushing from his mouth.

'Later, sir.' Transferring his charge to the men on sick bay detail, he turned his attention to where McFie and Bonham-Jones were supervising the looting of the cargo.

'Struck lucky this time,' announced McFie.

The cargo was mainly of tea, stored in earthenware jars with intricate Chinese style paintings, but one hold contained a quantity of silks and other exotic goods. Exquisite porcelain: figures of jade and small but weighty sacks of gold pieces. Vinderman came on deck with a small box, which he threw open with a flourish. 'Something to be said for being a successful pirate.' The box overflowed with pearls, shining and lustrous.

It took all night and most of the following morning to loot the huge merchantmen of the cargo she had acquired during months of trading. The two ships drifted together during the dark hours with just a scrap of sail set to give steerage way on. The holds were stocked full of the items they considered valuable, except the chests of gold pieces and the pearls that were stowed in the aft cabin, hastily being repaired by the carpenter. They could absorb nothing more. Reluctantly calling enough, the bosun's call brought the last man scrambling.

'I give you back your ship, Captain.' Last to leave, Queen bowed arrogantly then threw the Captain's sword into the deck planking where it stuck, vibrating between them.

'Thank you for your courtesy,' looking up at the black flag flying at the masthead, a chilling sight to any merchant seaman, the Dutch Captain said in ominous and threatening tone. 'You realise that I will report you as a murderer and a pirate to my owners: and to my government.'

Queen couldn't have cared less. Too proud: too full of his own importance. 'Will you also report your bloody work at Semarund,' he said with scorn rampant. 'Count yourself lucky, Captain, for if this really had been Swally and his cut throats you and your ship would have been resting on the seabed by now.' He sprang on the rail where stood a row of seamen headed by Bonham-Jones, poised and alert for any hostile move.

'The next time you look upon this flag,' stated Queen in arrogant and cocksure tone, 'I suggest you run for cover because it appears the Dutch can only wage war against simple natives.' With this he slashed the remaining ropes. *Restitution* smoothed away from the crippled ship. Raising his cutlass in mocking salute, then he jumped down among his crew.

'Well done, men! Ramon, break open a cask of brandy! Double measure for everyone!' A cry of agony from below sobered his triumph. 'Better start with the wounded,' with this he went below to the sick bay where Dr. Quennel and his assistant were hard at work . . . five men lying in shrouds.

Wiping his forehead with a bloodstained hand. 'There'll be one or two more before this day is done,' Dr. Quennel said wearily. 'Can you have the corpses moved, I have no room for dead men?'

Casualty count revealed seven dead and several

more wounded, of these only three were hopeless. Continuing his rounds he came to Abraham Verber propped up in a corner. Alongside him lay Ernest Harper, cleaned up and sleeping. Coughing over a sip of brandy, Verber's face had the colour of faded parchment and Queen kneeled down by him.

'Having you safe makes it all worthwhile.'

'How about getting me up on deck, Jase, fresh air is the only medicine I need.' His voice came out as a hoarse croak but he had so many questions bubbling on his mouth. 'What devil ship is this? Where are Captain Probus and Mr Sethman? How the hell – ?'

'All in good time, Abraham, rest for now and I'll come for you soon as we resume normal sea-going routine.' Surveying Ernest Harper for a moment. 'How did our merchant venturer accept captivity?'

'Philosophically at first, but the close confinement drove him further and further into himself no matter how we tried to cheer him up, think he was beginning to lose his reason. Good job you came, he wouldn't have lasted much longer . . . they put us into that black hole when we refused to work ship.' Pausing for breath, he then asked. 'Where are we bound, Jase?'

'Semarund for provisions, then we set sail for England to return you and Mr Harper to the bosom of your families.'

* * *

They buried their dead at sundown. Sewn tight in shrouds of sailcloth they slid one by one over the side. The last was peg leg Joe Laval. He had finally come home to his South China Sea.

Part Three

Chapter Thirty

The cab came to a halt outside the wrought iron gates. Stepping down he shouldered his sea bag and paid off the driver with a silver coin that had the man starry-eyed.

'I'll walk from here.'

The cabby didn't question his good fortune and flicked the reins to move the big chestnut mare forward. Closing the double gate behind him, Queen hesitated for a brief moment then, giving way to impulse, walked off the driveway and through the close-cropped grass sloping towards the river.

It was late afternoon . . . the sun still high and warm so he shed his jacket. His shirt was white silk, a ruche up the front with the neckline open to reveal the strong column of throat and the colour burned deep into his skin. Eyes alert. Tiny sun wrinkles dancing from the corners. He hoped? Knew she would be there, and he dropped his bag to watch her moving slowly among the trees with her head bowed. She was wearing an ankle length dress of emerald green with a hooped skirt that revealed those tiny red boots he remembered so well. She looked so petite . . . so alone.

Waiting. Enjoying this, willing her to look up. She turned to retrace her steps then her head lifted and bewilderment flashed in her face as she beheld the tall stranger looking down on her.

'Jason?' She couldn't believe her eyes.

Feet taking wing he flew down the grassy slope then stayed his headlong rush a yard away . . . all the wild anticipation and the plans he had made for this meeting evaporating in a surge of shyness and uncertainty.

'Maggie!' His hand tentatively reached out and her fingers gripped with a pressure that tingled.

'Are you ever going to kiss me: you great lumbering oaf!' Deep yearning in her voice and he drew her close with renewed confidence then, cupping both hands round her face, he held it just a few inches from his own in tender but urgent embrace. Her lips trembled and parted, a nervous reaction immediately stifled by the demand of his mouth. Breaking away with a gasp she buried her face into his shirtfront, breathing deeply of the pungent aroma of hemp and Stockholm tar pervading from the white silk. Holding her tight, almost crushing in his need for her and she sagged into him, elation and surging emotion racked through her and left her almost delirious.

'Maggie! Maggie! How I have longed for this meeting.'

Her head came up. Her eyes were soft and very moist. Her finger traced the line of his brow, across his eyes and down his nose, then lingered on his bushy moustache. 'There is something different about you,' she murmured, 'and it isn't just the hair on your face?'

Whirling her round in delirious abandon, his arms were strong around her then he closed off any further question with a searching mouth but she broke away breathing hard. 'Unhand me, sir, you seem much too sure of yourself: and of me.' The words were delivered in a coy and far from indignant tone and she hung onto his arm with a fiercely possessive grip. 'What a fright you gave me? Hardly recognised you, and that droopy moustache didn't help. I had the strangest feeling: as if some long dead ghost had come back to haunt me.'

'As I have been haunted, all these long months.'

The words sent icicles shivering cold down her back and she drew away to say in a tone that held a note almost of accusation, 'Papa told me that Captain Probus came home months ago. There are awful rumours about you and some pirate ship and it seems you were in no hurry to return to England: or to me.'

'Something I had to finish.'

His voice was cold and the way he said this

caused Maggie to look at him with sombre, indecisive eyes and, not caring for the change in his manner, said, 'I find you frightening, and prefer the shy, idealistic young man I used to know.'

'So much has happened since then and no one can expect to remain forever the same.' His voice penetrated as he added, 'But believe me when I say that one thing above all remains inviolate.'

Their eyes met in understanding, his arm went about her shoulders and they walked slowly along the bank of the peaceful river. Some of Maggie's ecstasy had been replaced with the warm glow of happiness and she rested her head against his shoulder. 'What does it matter, my love, as long as we can again share this magic of ours?' Her fingers crept around his waist, he could feel the softness of her against him as she cuddled close. 'How I have dreamed of this moment,' she said, 'every single day when I walk here wearing the same boots that I knew would one day bring you back to me.'

'And I surely knew when I came through the gateway that this is where I would find you.' His two years of absence were almost forgotten and once again strolling this familiar green sward it seemed as if he had never been away, but Maggie couldn't stop talking. Excitement and surging happiness in reunion brought chatter beyond any hope of control.

'Did you dream of me?' she then asked.

'Only once.' He couldn't lie to her, even to please.

'Once! In more than two years?'

He laughed out loud at the tone of disappointment, then her obvious petulance brought quick recovery. 'It's your fault more than mine, because you no longer had the need to chase me through the night, knowing I was yours beyond any hope of escape.'

'How clever you have become, Jason Queen, and much quicker than I remember,' flattered and pleased by his complimentary phrasing she added, 'begin to realise there is much to learn about the time you have been away.' Then, with a sideways, hooded glance. 'Papa also said you had women passengers on the outward voyage?'

There was childish question in her voice and, unable to resist the temptation to tease, he said in deliberately reflective tone, 'There we were, thousands of miles from home under the dark velvet of a tropic sky with the harvest moon hanging low and all the stars in the heavens shining bright and the night so warm and romantic and the surf thundering wonderful music from a distant reef.' Pausing, as if reliving the scene, he said with a sly grin. 'Then out came husband Ernest to spoil it all.'

The scornful, indignant look on her face brought laughter flooding but Maggie was well acquainted with the Harpers and her mouth curved into a reluctant smile as she realised he was only teasing. Then, considering his words and the manner in which he said them, her brow furrowed. 'Mrs Harper is quite beautiful, I suppose,' she said questioningly, 'but I had the distinct impression that you were talking about someone completely different.'

Queen thought he was in dangerous waters, had no inclination to pursue this line of thought and, regretting his capriciousness, said quickly, 'Maggie, there is so much I have to tell. Of all the new and wonderful places and the long weeks of crossing oceans that seemed to have no end, when all I had to do was think of you and of being with you.'

'You were sure I would still be here?'

'Not really! In the beginning perhaps, but as the months passed I had to wonder if the memory of me would fade and whether some dashing society blade would sweep you off your feet and out of my life for ever.' Clasping his arm around her possessively, before admitting. 'There were times, on deck in the depths of night when such thoughts would torment, but when daylight swept over the horizon and the sun shone again I would remember and be confident once more.'

His arm slid down to her waist and he pulled her to him, hungry for the touch of her. She came easily into his embrace with happiness shining in her eyes and allowing no mood of melancholy to spoil the wonder of this first meeting. Her body moulded against him, her fragrance invaded his senses and his mouth crushed her's, insatiable and with a growing fervour returned in equal measure. All the old magic revived, but two years of separation and also of growing more adult no longer allowed of former innocence, and body demand brought passion and intensity and increasing abandon to his embrace and she forced away. 'Think it is time we went in to meet Papa,' she said with a gasp, 'lest you become too ardent a lover for a maiden to resist.'

Dinner that evening was a celebration feast with conversation brisk and stimulating as the endless questioning about the voyage unfolded some very colourful episodes. Sir James was reliving his early days and was very reluctant to have it all come to an end.

'Truly amazing,' he said with a wry shake of his head, 'and difficult to believe that one so young should accomplish all of this.'

'You credit me too highly, sir, and underestimate the support of Bonham-Jones and McFie. You also forget that I had the magnificent Vinderman for my tutor and sailing master and there were many times when he controlled the ship, not I.'

Regarding him with a look that held both admiration and speculation, Sir James swilled brandy round his glass. 'Your modesty is becoming but the praise or blame will be yours alone. As Captain of *Restitution* you will be the one to be either uplifted: or cast down.'

'Cast down, Papa,' exclaimed Maggie heatedly, 'why should this be even considered?'

'Perhaps because I look too much on the reverse side of the coin, yet I also know of the envy and intrigue that obscures fair-mindedness among many of my associates who, though small in their own stature, imagine themselves giants in the world of commerce and who do not take kindly to being overshadowed, especially by one so young and, if I may be so bold,' adding with a smile, 'so diminutive in rank.'

'You make it sound as if it is some kind of contest.'

'Make no mistake, Jason. Life is a contest. A continuous struggle to haul oneself ever upwards: and to hell with the rest.'

'This is a cynicism to which I cannot subscribe,' countered Queen, 'for many times have I seen men place their own lives at risk for a comrade and for a cause of which they were sure.'

'There speaks the sublime voice of youth. Hold on to your ideals, Jason Queen, for as long as you are allowed: ideals that we have all held though in less measure perhaps. Men in action and at times of danger are vastly different animals than those who exist only for profit in either cash or personal advancement. Unfortunately,' he concluded, 'these are the men with power and the position to use it with malice.'

'Surely you exaggerate, Papa?'

'Wish it were so.' Came the quiet reply, and Queen had the feeling that Sir James was warning him in some way, a feeling reinforced as he stated. 'My advice to you is to ship out as soon as possible before some petty official decides to enquire into the many questions that have been bandied about since Captain Probus returned home.'

'He's only just arrived!' Maggie sounded distraught and Sir James saw the look that passed between them.

'Nevertheless.' Filling his brandy glass he raised it high. 'A toast to you, Jason Queen, to your return and to all the fascinating stories you share with us. Adventures which bring life and colour into my house.' Sensing her impatient eye on him and suddenly feeling like an intruder at his own dinner table he pushed back his chair. 'I have some very dull papers to write and regretfully will have to leave you. Shall I ask Mrs Bronson to keep the proprieties?' Smile starting. 'Perhaps not.' His amusement was audible as he left the dining room.

Talk of shipping out had brought a mood of melancholy and her downcast eyes bore mute testimony to her retreat from euphoria. In a vain attempt to console, Queen said quietly, 'Don't look so troubled, Sir James surely overstates the urgency.'

'Papa seldom overstates.' Anger and despair

brought a sharp response and an equally tart. 'Is this the way it will always be? A few hours to spare then you are gone, and I am left to face an empty future.'

Her distress, and her pertinent statement, was like a knife thrust in the back and his chair screeched as he thrust up and stood over her to forlornly declare. 'I love you, Maggie, more than life: more than anything.'

'But not more than commanding a tall ship! Tell me,' she cried, 'does this love of yours devour so much that you cannot bear the thought of ever leaving me or do the words just mean you will spare me a few fleeting hours every two years. Do you think love can survive without contact, without a sharing, of touching, and of knowing the wonder of life dedicated to just one other human being? Jason,' she said sadly, 'I don't think I could bear to see you sail away for more lonely years. I need to take life firmly by the hand, to establish a rightful place in your life. I must establish roots, my own roots, not just extrusions of your own needs and ambitions.'

He took her hands, feeling the trembling fingers reaching out to him. His mind blazed with a picture of pursuing red boots as he strove to assure, to make her understand. 'Oh. Maggie,' he said, 'I'll be taking my Master's ticket next time and assuming my own command. Then it will be possible for you to accompany me to all the wonderful places. I'll show you green mountains rising sheer from a tropic sea, all the unending glory of sun and wind across blue water.' Slowing his enthusiasm to say pleadingly. 'It won't be forever! There will be plenty of time left to put down roots. Our own roots! You and me together.'

Fired by his rhetoric . . . his vivid declaration lodging pictures that the wanton parts of her mind sought to hold on to, then with a negative headshake. 'Such impossible dreams, my darling.'

'Dreams we can make come true if only we can hold on to our love for a short while longer.'

His voice held a confidence that she couldn't share and taking his arm she led him to an armchair. 'Sit here,' she ordered, 'so I don't have to look up at you all the time.' Pushing him forcibly down with her hands on his shoulders she looked him straight in the eye. 'Ask yourself what would happen when we had children: and I know from the way you look at me? From the strength of emotion that flares every time we touch that there would surely be children. Wouldn't the position then be exactly the same as now with our lives being lived in separate worlds where the only words exchanged would be hello, and just as fleetingly . . . goodbye?'

'The time would come,' he feebly insisted, 'when I could no longer bear to be parted from you.'

'But what of the lonely years, while we are young and should be happy together exploring this wonderful relationship that binds us so close?' A note of exasperation had crept into her voice. 'Jason, I need you now! I want to be your wife and live with you always, but you are asking me to share with some ocean-bound sailing ship?' Eyes narrowing as a further thought intruded and her voice tremored, then recovered as she exclaimed. 'Not even share! Just accept what few hours your other life can grant me.' The thought devastated, then her shoulders squared and there was determination in the set of her chin. 'Look at me, Jason,' she said firmly. 'I know a wife has to subordinate her desires to those of her husband. This I would happily accept, but a way of life such as yours would mean living in a constant state of suspension. A wife, yet still a maiden. To be subordinate to you,' she repeated, 'is something I would welcome but I'm not about to prostrate myself before your selfish pursuance of a career in which I can have no place. No, Jason. There is a compromise somewhere, this I know, but compromise is a double-edged sword that must cut both ways: or it will surely sever us.'

His eyes flared as he remembered Martha Harper's scorn of the word and her scathing, "how many lives have been prostrated in compromise", so he returned heatedly, 'We have our whole lives ahead . . . are a further two years too much to ask?'

'Women mature quicker than men,' she instantly replied, 'and tend to wither away when so much time is spent alone. I can no longer spend my days in idleness or in writing foolish letters which in the end have nothing to communicate and for what purpose when you will probably never receive them anyway.' Shaking her head resignedly and hesitating, before adding, 'And the saddest part of all is the fact that you and I both know our lives are not just our own but a strange and wonderful extension of a love from the past. A love that has waited so patiently to be realised and which implores us not to repeat the misery and utter waste.'

'What would you have me do? Stand behind a dusty drapery counter selling needles and cotton!'

It was a heart's cry of torment from the mouth of Jason Queen that was devastating in its anguish, and she clung to him, to comfort, love and sadness bringing tears to her eyes. 'Oh, no, not you, my darling' she sobbed, 'for this would surely destroy you. Then you would be the one who was prostrate. That is something I could never live with and would just as equally be the destruction of our hopes and dreams together.'

Her distress shattered him and he pulled her down on his knee. She was light as thistledown and so very soft, and passion flamed as she flung her arms round him and he said in anguished tone, 'I'll never let you go, Maggie.'

The way he said this brought a frown to her brow and she regarded him in a perceptive manner, as if reading his mind. 'Isn't this the crux

of our situation,' she then said, 'you can't let go
. . . either of me or of your need to command a
tall ship. I wonder how many other times have
there been when you couldn't let go?' Struggling
in his fierce clutch, protesting, 'You are hurting,
my impetuous darling.' Her eyes were deep and
enigmatic as a dark sea and her mouth an inviting
curve. 'Are you going to take me by force?'

'If I have to, and if this is the only way for you
to submit.' Arms gripping tight as he murmured
in a voice husky with desire. 'The very nearness
of you is more than I can stand without wanting
to touch you, to kiss your lips and plunge myself
into the exquisite fragrance of you.' Kissing her
on the forehead, then his lips moved down
her cheek to hover over her mouth and she
trembled in his embrace, overwhelmed by seething emotion. Her body fired into a wakening,
responsive passion, and she reached for his head
with both hands pulling his mouth to hers and a
moan of longing wracked her as they clung to
each other with desire rampant. His demanding
pressure eased. Sensing withdrawal, her eyelids
flickered open. His face was flushed but troubled
as he released her. 'Forgive me, Maggie,' he said,
'for being selfish again and as always, insensitive
to your own needs and desires.'

Bewildered and also frustrated by his change of
mood she reared away and said with great indignation, 'Desires you arouse only to discard so
arrogantly.'

'Would you have me take you in a moment of wild passion?' Breathless but tormented words, and she hastily rose, straightening her dress with faltering hands. His arms reached to pull her back on his knee; a futile move and her resistance brought a despairing. 'Oh, Maggie, Maggie! There is no need for me to say how much I want you, for it must be obvious every time I hold you or look into your eyes. These are the signs that tell more than words how I love and need you.' His face reflected deep turmoil and sagging as if exhausted, he said despondently. 'I fight a constant and losing battle to keep my hands from your body.'

She suddenly knew, and with a sureness of which she became aware for the very first time: of her blooming womanhood. A revelation that brought confidence and maturity and she drew away. 'Then you should restrain yourself, sir,' she said with studied aloofness, 'lest your emotions lead you into a situation beyond control.'

He knew well that she also was emotionally unstable whenever they embraced. How else could this fire be so mutually overwhelming? 'Maggie' he said despairingly, 'I am tormented with a need that will not be reconciled until you are my wife.'

Shaking her head in firm negation. 'I'll not be your wife in this present circumstance and your indecision,' pausing significantly, before finishing, 'in all things, does little credit either to you or me.' With this she swept haughtily from the room leaving him in abject misery and dejection. Looking dolefully after her, knowing he had failed: again! Then his eyes narrowed into slits of blue fire. The eyes only his men would recognise.

The night was dark, the balcony in shadow, she pulled the glass doors shut and prepared herself for bed. She had not seen him since their impassioned encounter and felt very much concerned that he had made no attempt at reconciliation. Wishing now that she hadn't left the room so decisively she began to undress by the light of a solitary candle, then reached for her nightgown. Sound of movement coming from the veranda, her hand went to her mouth in fear as through the glass doorway she saw a dark and strangely garbed figure leap over the parapet wall. Her throat was dry as dust, half-scream just a gasp. She stood motionless with her nightgown held before her as a shield. The casement doors crashed open and her eyes flared wide as in swept a commanding figure. He wore polished thigh boots and white silk breeches and a sleeveless jerkin coloured jet black and open at the front. The hair on his chest was bleached fair by long exposure to sun and wind; the skin burned deep mahogany, as were his powerful arms. A naked sword hung from his belt and a broad band of red silk girdled his waist. His hair was tied behind his neck with a leather thong and a single; shark's tooth earring hung stark white against lush sideburns. An incredibly colourful yet frightening figure, he stood tall with eyes arrogant and piercing. 'I've come to pick you up in my strong arms, Maggie Passendale,' he boldly declared, 'and carry you off into the depths of the night.'

Remembering the words, spoken in jest to a highly embarrassed young man on this same balcony so long ago, she whispered, 'Have mercy on me, sir.'

'There is no mercy. A pirate takes whatever his heart desires . . . ruthlessly and without fear of consequence.' Reaching her in one stride he plucked the nightgown from her nerveless fingers and let if fall at her feet. She was naked. His eyes roved insolently over her exposed beauty. 'You are truly magnificent, Maggie.' Lifting her effortlessly in his arms, a clean tang of salt air hovering about him. All her apprehension vanished to be replaced by an exhilarating sense of unreality. She yielded to strength and domination. To Jason Queen . . . the pirate who had come to claim her for his own. This was a man she had yet to know, strong willed and sure of purpose. Looking without fear into the bold, arrogant eyes, she softly said:

'What will your heart desire on the morrow.'

'Think not of tomorrow if tonight be sweet.' Moving with easy tread he laid her on the four-poster bed. His sword fell to the floor and there came a whisper of lace as the drapes around the bed were closed. They reached for each other in the soft glow of candlelight. Her lips were open for him and trembling and murmuring and, unheeded in their impassioned embrace, the name she murmured was not his name but a ghost whisper from the past, hovering and vapouring and repeated over and over.

'John! John! I have waited so long!'

A Navy platoon marched in on them during breakfast. The officer in charge held papers in his hand and announced without any introduction. 'I have a warrant for the arrest of Midshipman Jason Queen.'

Sir James's chair crashed back as he flared up in startled outrage. 'What nonsense is this, Lieutenant! How dare you intrude into my home?'

The Naval officer was courteous and almost apologetic, but very determined. 'I offer my personal regret, sir, but I have orders to detain Mr Queen until a court can be convened.'

Livid of face Sir James demanded, 'On what charge?'

'Murder! And piracy on the high seas!'

Chapter Thirty-one

He remained held in custody for several weeks during which period the only persons allowed to visit him were his solicitor and law advocate. These two learned gentlemen made clear that the cause of his arrest was without doubt the fact that he had paid off his crew with the proceeds of the plundered *Zeevalk*. They also intimated how certain shareholders of the Company felt very strongly that any cargo profit acquired by their employees would be more advantageous if placed in their own coffers and were determined to make a scapegoat of Queen as a deterrent to other officers who might be likewise inclined. Doubly unfortunate was that fact that the recent hostilities with the Dutch were short-lived and all over by the time he docked his ship in the Thames, thus lending extra weight to the Dutch Government's formal complaint of piracy.

With typical resource, Vinderman managed to smuggle a note of encouragement into the prison but Queen's return message instructed him to keep the crew well out of sight.

Because the company shareholders didn't wish any accusation of prejudice laid at their door the Court was convened in the Admiralty building, presiding judge Rear Admiral Lord Nathaniel Temple. Grey haired and stern of countenance, he was flanked in court martial fashion by four high-ranking Naval Officers.

In front of the bench sat the law clerks and notaries who were to assist and record the proceedings and a further row of Navy personnel sat sentinel-like behind the two long tables separating the officials from the public auditorium, on which both defence and prosecuting advocates had laid out their papers.

Great double doors closing on the assembly, attendance strictly limited and allowed only after intense pressure. Margaret Passendale took a seat alongside her father and just in front of Martha Harper and the Verber family. Queen's spirits lifted as he saw them arrive in court; perhaps he wasn't so alone after all. Sir James had made strong protest about the charges but even his power and position had no influence on the course of justice.

He had not been allowed a change of clothing or a chance to clean up before being brought to trial. Unshaven and dishevelled, he stood tall in the dock with eyes alert on the proceedings.

Prosecuting counsel for the East India Company was a plump, smooth-faced man with a shiny pink complexion that appeared positively damp under his silver wig. He was powdered and perfumed like a court dandy but Queen's solicitor had shown great concern when he learned of the appointment of Mr Maurice Chapman as prosecutor, warning Queen not to be taken in by an appearance that deliberately served to conceal the razor sharp mind of an experienced advocate.

The prosecuting council addressed the court in a practised accent.

'We will prove, your Lordship, that midshipman Queen unlawfully attacked a Dutch merchant ship. Did plunder her cargo and brutally murder her First Officer! Also, deliberately fired on a ship of His Majesty's Navy on station in the Far East, inflicting crippling damage and wounding a Lieutenant and seven ratings.'

Queen flinched . . . this was the first he knew of casualties sustained aboard the frigate.

'Call William McFie!'

As he stumped in with his leg swinging McFie looked enquiringly around and his face showed dismay at the prisoner's unsavoury appearance. Queen felt pleasantly surprised when he heard Billie being called as first witness for the prosecution and became suddenly reassured.

McFie taking the oath . . . Maurice Chapman approaching.

'You are William McFie, a midshipman in the service of the Honourable East India Company?' it seemed more statement than question and McFie inclined his head, waiting for the next.

'Please answer yes or no!' Advocate's biting tone brought the witness's eyebrows together. .

'Yes,' blurted McFie.

'You also served aboard the vessel *Restitution* as Second Officer?'

'Yes.'

Surveying him for a long moment, Chapman suavely asked, 'There were three midshipmen aboard at the time including Mr Queen?'

'Yes.'

The other being Mr Bonham-Jones?'

'Yes.'

'Tell me, Mr McFie, which of you is the senior?'

Sensing danger, McFie's delay in answering caused the Rear Admiral to instruct, 'Speak up, McFie: just the name of the senior ranking officer.'

'In strict order of seniority Bonham-Jones held the higher rank.'

'And yet,' said Chapman nonchalantly, 'Mr Queen assumed command: in spite of the fact that he was outranked.'

'Only because – '

'Just answer yes or no!'

'Yes!' jerking the word, incensed at not being allowed to explain.

Chapman was amused at this reaction but defence counsel gained his feet. He seemed bored to tears as he said, 'Wish my learned friend would get to the point.'

Addressing the bench, Chapman said in conciliatory tone, 'My lord, I am seeking to establish that Mr Queen was subordinate in rank and hadn't the seniority to captain *Restitution*.'

His Lordship looked impatient but allowed the question. 'Proceed, Mr Chapman.'

'Let us now look back to the events prior to your departure from Semarund.' Smoothly into his stride as if there had been no distraction he queried. 'At this time Captain Probus was still in command with Mr Alan Sethman as First Officer?'

'Yes.'

'You had lost the services of the Second and Third Officer?'

'Yes.'

'And your Captain, who I believe was handicapped with a serious eye injury promoted the three midshipmen to take over the vacant positions?'

'Yes.' Billie could see the direction of this questioning and answered in worried tone.

'Will you now outline the order of promotion?'

'Mr Bonham-Jones as Second, Mr Queen as Third, and myself as senior midshipman.' Adding with a snappy. 'All unpaid!'

A smile warmed the faces of the Naval Officers.

'Just answer the questions, McFie,' said Lord Temple

'So we must accept that Captain Probus recognised Bonham-Jones as senior.'

'Yes!'

'Mr McFie.' The prosecutor walked slowly up and down as if trying to collect thoughts and information in condemning order. 'The village of Semarund had been the victim of a violent attack by the crew of *Zeevalk*. Can you provide us with more detail of this outrage?'

Seizing his chance, Billie straightaway replied, 'The Dutch had learned of our trading settlement and came ashore in force attacking and killing several of our garrison and taking the rest on board in chains. Then burned the village to ashes.'

Chapman nodded sympathetically. 'We would all agree that this is not civilised behaviour but were there not further incidents while the Dutch were ashore?'

All in court intent on every word but defence counsel again interrupted. 'Objection, my Lord! Surely we have heard enough of the atrocities committed by the Dutch and I fail to see how these can have any further connection with the case before us.

His Lordship seemed to agree and looked at Chapman, who said, 'Just one more question on this subject, your Lordship. I intend to show that the defendant had very personal reason for this act of piracy.'

Queen was granite faced as the question was allowed.

'Mr McFie, is it true that the Dutch seamen did – er – amuse themselves with the native women?'

'Against their will and by force.' Billie was fed up with answering these loaded questions of Mr Flaming Chapman in monosyllables and this outburst brought sharp reprimand from the Judge:

'Will the witness please restrain himself!'

Ignoring the interruption, Chapman went smoothly on. 'In particular with a certain native girl whose company Mr Queen enjoyed during his stay on the Island.'

'Yes!' Temper beginning to take over he fairly spat the word.

Chapman smiled, taking pleasure in provoking this fiery young man and devoted friend of the defendant who, more than any other, could unwittingly cause great doubt to be cast on Queen's motivations. Resuming attack to ask. 'What was the end result of this native girl's ordeal?'

Noticing the bleak expression on Queen's face and knowing the exposure would only reopen old wounds, Billie jerked out in compelling fury. 'She hung herself rather than live with the shame of his disease!'

A murmur of indignation rippled through the courtroom, Lord Temple hammering for quiet with his gavel, Margaret Passendale's face had turned pale and she looked across at the haggard figure in the dock with distraught eyes, wanting to run to him and throw her arms round him for support, but froze in her seat as Chapman went for Billie again.

'It is reasonable to assume that Mr Queen was very upset by the tragedy of this native girl, whose charms he probably considered as his own private pleasure.'

McFie's eyes flared on the bland face of advocate Chapman. 'Jason Queen never took advantage of anyone in his life,' he said angrily, 'and what right has someone like you to make foul accusation on circumstances you know nothing about!'

Hammering on the bench Lord Temple snapped in hard voice, 'One more outburst from you, McFie, and you'll be held in contempt and dealt with accordingly.'

Chapman allowed the court to settle down, then continued his probing.

'Tell us now of the mood of midshipman Queen when you sailed from Semarund?'

'As acting Third Officer he carried out his duties as required.'

'Would you say he was his normal self during this period?'

'Objection!' Defence counsel couldn't allow Chapman to get away with such liberties and said forcibly. 'Surely the witness holds no qualification for such a professional conclusion.'

Nodding in agreement, Lord Temple instructed, 'Rephrase or withdraw, Mr. Chapman.'

'Was Mr Queen depressed and moody about these duties?' Chapman suavely asked.

'Suppose so.'

The judge looked down angrily but, sensing his chance, Chapman asked, 'Did he express the desire to go after the Dutch ship *Zeevalk*?'

'Yes,' admitted Billie. He was trapped. Had no choice? But his reply assumed Judas-like overtones.

'Contrary to the expressed opinions of Captain Probus?'

Billie couldn't bring himself to reply and the delay caused the Judge to lose patience as he growled, 'Will you answer the question.'

Queen felt for Billie, knowing how painful this must be. His eyes met the distressed stare from the witness box then Billie turned shamefacedly away.

'Contrary to the opinions of Captain Probus,' insisted Chapman.'

'Yes.' Defeated tone, and Chapman almost smiled

'No further questions for this witness,' he announced. 'I feel that I have proved to the court that the defendant had personal and vengeful reasons for his pirating of the merchant ship.'

Billie remained in the witness box in considerable dismay. Wanted a chance to shout out! To make them appreciate all the happenings not just the damning facts as presented by the wily counsel, but he wasn't given the chance because defence counsel, from a sitting position, merely said, 'I have no questions of this witness.'

Giving the impression that McFie had done enough damage he told him to step down. Swinging his leg with frustrated anger he paused to face the dock and Queen's rueful smile. 'Sorry, Jase,' he said forlornly.

'You did well, Billie,' said Queen, and the warmth between the two could be felt throughout the entire courtroom. Lord Temple's gavel stayed its demanding swing. Maggie felt her eyes smarting and reached for her father's supporting arm, but Billie said in determined voice:

'They haven't got us yet!' With this he stumped hurriedly through the doorway.

The cross-examination had taken a long time and the court adjourned for the midday break. The afternoon session began with the Captain of *Zeevalk*. It appeared that the shareholders had spared no expense to prove the case against their recalcitrant midshipman. Duly sworn in the Captain established his identity.

The prosecutor looked sleek and plump after his expensive meal and approached the witness with anticipation. Speaking slowly because of the Captain's inadequate English, he enquired, 'Captain Van de Stadt, when did you first see the defendant?'

'When he came over the side with a knife between his teeth.'

All eyes flicking involuntarily towards the dock as Chapman continued.

'Did you know his nationality at this time?'

'Privateers are international. They have no homeland.'

'You had fought a running battle before they boarded?'

'For two hours.'

'Isn't it customary for a ship intent on action to first fire a shot across the bows to allow the defending ship a chance to submit without bloodshed?'

'Not always,' replied the Captain, then with an expressive wave of his hands, 'there are few rules along the great seaways.'

'Was it so in this case'?'

'No.'

'The Captain of Restitution seemed hell bent on engaging?'

'It appeared so.'

Realising he had rapt attention from the courtroom, Chapman pondered for a few moments, prolonging suspense before continuing. 'We know that your ship was crippled and how the pirates finally forced your men to submit. Did you suffer any unusual atrocities during the action?'

'Only in the hand to hand fighting.'

'Will you please tell the court how your First Officer died?'

Looking away from the prosecuting counsel

and around the courtroom as though he wanted everyone to hear. 'The battle was almost over,' said Van de Stadt, 'apart from the terrible struggle between Jan Hallmeyer and the pirate Captain.'

'This went on after all fighting on deck had ceased and after you had surrendered your weapons,' prompted Chapman, 'you felt it was personal matter between the two?'

Rising in protest the defence counsel was waved down by Lord Temple and sank back in his seat realising the court's attention was riveted to the witness, who said, 'I had to wonder about the reason for such extreme savagery.'

'In the end your officer had to submit?'

'What else could he do? Sword arm almost severed at the wrist. Bleeding from neck and shoulder. He was completely without defence.'

'So tell us, Captain,' moving away so the court would not miss a single word, 'of the ultimate fate of your First Officer?'

Pointing with dramatic effect at the prisoner in the dock, Van de Stadt said in condemning tone, 'He grasped Hallmeyer's dagger and stabbed him to death.'

Gasp from the crowded court but Chapman pressed home his advantage. 'Not in the heat of battle but deliberately and in cold blood after Hallmeyer had submitted?'

'Yes.'

'No more questions.' Chapman was satisfied,

knew he had done a good job of damning Queen in the eyes and ears of the court.

Mr Joseph Helford, the defence counsel, came to cross examine but in a resigned manner and giving the impression that he felt no purpose could be served but had to do something to justify his fee. Walking up and down in thoughtful pose, he then asked, 'Captain Van de Stadt, will you enlighten us on the size and armaments of Zeevalk?'

'One thousand tons burthen. Mounting fifty thirty-two pounders on the two gun decks and with stern chasers aft.'

'Formidable. Would you expect to be engaged by a ship so much smaller in size and mounting fewer guns?'

'Do not be confused by figures,' countered the Captain, '*Restitution* is a ship feared by all Masters sailing lawfully in eastern waters. We had no reason to suspect she was in other hands and fully expected pirate Swally would be in command.' Hesitating . . . resigned expression on his face as he added, 'I have to concede that we were no-match for such a ship. She easily out-manoeuvred us through the water and her gunnery was unbelievable.'

'How were you personally treated, and your crew also?'

'Courteously and with reasonable consideration.'

'Your ship was returned intact?'

'After she had been looted of her most valuable cargo.'

'I must insist on a straight answer. Were you given back your ship?'

'Yes.'

'Is this normal among pirates?'

'No.'

Helford walked back to his desk, consulted his notes and returned with a question that had Van de Stadt squirming in his seat.

'The violence of your crew at Semarund . . . is this typical behaviour for Dutch East Indiamen about their business of trading?'

'We had orders to destroy the settlement,' said Van de Stadt before adding carefully. 'Violence is unavoidable in times of conflict between nations.'

'Even attacks on native women?'

'I do not condone such behaviour, but are your own men any different after such a long time at sea?'

'Allow me to cross examine,' insisted defence counsel with a cold glare at the witness. Then he asked a very peculiar and unwise question. 'You defend your men because you claim they were acting under orders and because our two Countries were in conflict. Why do you not extend the same consideration to Mr Queen in his command of *Restitution*?'

Astounded at the question Van de Stadt boldly said, 'Because he was sailing under the black flag of piracy!'

Queen forlornly watched the defence counsel retreating. No hope now. The last exchange had condemned him in the eyes of the court.

Now the frigate's Captain took the stand, impressive in full Naval uniform he had the grand sounding name of Walter, Beuregard Hamilton. The prosecuting counsel's questions were brief and to the point. After giving details of time and position, the Captain then told how on approaching *Restitution* his mast had been broken by cannon fire, wounding a Lieutenant and seven ratings when it crashed to the deck.

Moving in wearily, defence counsel surveyed the Captain in sympathetic manner then casually asked, 'Can you remember what colours she was flying?'

'Red cross on white of St. George.'

'Yet you still moved to engage?'

'It is common practice to show the wrong colours to confuse an opponent.'

'Did she not also fly the recognition signals you would expect when meeting an East India Company ship at sea?'

'This is so, but I had no knowledge of such a ship sailing under English colours and had to assume she was an enemy.'

'Dare I suggest that you recognised her as the infamous *Restitution* and refused to accept her signals?'

Long silence.

'I'm waiting, Captain.'

'Possibly this influenced my decision,' admitted Beuregard Hamilton, 'but let me make quite clear that I do not gamble with the lives of hundreds of men under my command. She was an enemy: and I acted accordingly.'

'And had your mast shot from over your heads.' Probing on with scorn apparent. 'Couldn't your – er – enemy just as easily given you a broadside amidships?'

'We would have blown her to kingdom come if I could have brought my guns to bear,' blustered Hamilton, 'it was a damned lucky shot. Just enough to slow us and make good her escape.'

Smiling at this, Helford turned to face the court and said in deprecating tone, 'We have just heard Captain Van de Stadt testify to the expert handling and gunnery of *Restitution* and I'm sure the court will now accept that Mr Queen fired on the frigate to cripple her in order to allow his ship free passage: and only after making every endeavour for recognition as an English vessel.'

The Rear Admiral had plenty of detail to digest. With the sun already over the yardarm and, anticipating the brandy waiting in his chambers, he adjourned proceedings until the following morning. As he left the courtroom he said to one of his aides, 'There are only a couple more witnesses and we should have it all over by this time tomorrow.'

* * *

Margaret sat disconsolately at the dinner table. She had no appetite and left her food untouched.

'Can't we do anything, Papa? He must feel so all alone in that awful dock.'

Scowling, Sir James's face registered dismay and indignation. 'Like to get my hands on the mealy mouth idiots who set up this complaint against the lad,' he said in hard tone. 'Jason might have played the fool about the crew's money but what the hell does that matter against all his other achievements.' Gulping wine as though it might suddenly be taken away he then said in more thoughtful voice. 'Young McFie was the most damning witness for the prosecution though he tried his best to avoid hurting Jason. But his testimony: followed by the Dutch version of the fight between Jason and Hallmeyer?' Closely observing his daughter for reaction. 'You don't seem too perturbed about the native girl, yet this appears to be the main reason for his vendetta against *Zeevalk* and even more so against the man Hallmeyer?'

Maggie's mouth was set in a tight line. This thought had been in her mind all day, along with other more dominating, personal and intimate happenings, and as her father posed the question she looked him straight in the face. 'The true facts of the matter have yet to be revealed, and I must be content to wait, in the knowledge that he will tell me all in his own time.' She then said angrily. 'Could have put my foot behind the defence counsel! His performance makes me wonder just whose side he is on.'

Sir James was in agreement with this summary. 'Someone's been damned clever,' he said, 'even though I really enjoyed defence counsel's exposure of the impudent way Jason engaged the frigate we must realise that the Judge and his panel are Naval Officers and won't be at all impressed by the humiliation of one of His Majesty's proud warships. All of which confirms my suspicion that the whole thing has been very well stage-managed and there is no doubt that today's honours went with the prosecution.' Frowning as he concluded. 'The shareholders picked a good man for the job.'

'Think they picked two good men,' said Maggie.

After a miserable night in his cell he had an early morning visit from his solicitor whose face was long and mournful as he said, 'Mr Helford wants you to take the stand today.'

'Will it make any difference?' Queen asked with a shrug.

'We are in his hands, but I personally don't agree. The prosecutor will no doubt ask questions which will again have you viewed in the worst possible light. Just as he did with McFie.'

'Poor Billie: he certainly went out in a temper.'

The court reconvened at ten o'clock. As Queen and his escort marched in a sound of disturbance came from the foyer and through the open doorway he caught a sight of Martha Harper accosting the prosecuting counsel with her umbrella held in threatening position over his head. Mrs Harper wasn't allowed in after this skirmish and the courtroom seemed somehow drab without her colourful presence.

Toby Bonham-Jones was called. The last witness for the prosecution his educated voice rang confidently as he took the oath and identified himself.

Advocate Chapman approached the witness in casual pose.

'Mr Bonham-Jones,' he commenced, 'we are already in possession of the facts concerning the ravaging of the Dutch merchantman and now wish to learn about the many valuable items seized at this time.' Toby seemed relaxed and well in control as Chapman continued. 'After the sacking of *Zeevalk* did you resume the activities of piracy on the high seas?'

'In the first place,' drawled Toby, 'it hasn't yet been proved that we were pirates, privateers, or anything else for that matter. Yet we straightaway decided to sail the ship home before the adverse monsoon wind and foul weather combined to make conditions difficult for crossing the Indian Ocean.' His reply was couched in almost arrogant tone, which brought a narrowing to Chapman's eyes, also the malicious thought that he would take pleasure in destroying this one.

'Any ports of call?' he asked in deliberate, compliant tone.

'Malacca and Ascension Island.'

'Are these recognised ports for returning East Indiamen?'

'Recognised ports,' said Toby scathingly, 'were not available to *Restitution*.'

'Why stop at Malacca?'

'For provisions and water enough to take us on round Africa.'

'What else happened at Malacca?'

Toby seemed hesitant and his reluctance to reply obviously pleased Chapman. 'Don't be coy, Mr Bonham-Jones.' Counsel had grown weary of the witness's arrogant manner and, suddenly acid tongued, snapped. 'Let me refresh your memory! Because at Malacca you disposed of the many treasures acquired while pirating.' A further thought occurring, he looked at Toby with calculating eyes. 'Weren't you perhaps worried that you might not receive a fair exchange for your valuables in such a disreputable port?'

Laughing in counsel's face, Toby retorted, 'If you knew Abraham Verber you wouldn't ask such a damn fool question.'

'My God! Another midshipman! Is the Company run by, and for the sole benefit of midshipmen? I ask again, did you receive gold and silver coin for these treasures?'

'Yes.'

'And I suggest you called at Ascension rather

than face the enquiries that would have awaited you at Table Bay or St. Helena, which I believe are the recognised havens of East Indiamen and ships of the Royal Navy on passage to and from the Far East.'

Toby remained silent and the prosecutor regarded him with a sly smile.

'This business of seniority is somewhat confusing. As senior officer wouldn't it be normal for yourself to assume command?'

'Yes.'

'Why was it not so in this case?'

Looking at Queen, who acknowledged the look with a supportive nod, Toby took a deep breath and faced his tormentor. 'Because Mr Queen was better fitted than myself to take charge,' he said firmly. 'Not only this, he had our unqualified support in all decisions and he alone could command the loyalty of the ship's company.'

Having opened up his main line of attack, Chapman probed. 'Could one of the reasons for this loyalty be the fact they expected more than a fair share of the spoils? Even demanded this in return for their doubtful loyalty?'

The prosecutor had led his witness into deep water and Toby was slow to reply, then recovered to say tersely, 'Not so.'

'Come now, Mr Senior Midshipman. Didn't Queen ply his men with copious draughts of rum to keep them happy, much more than any normal crew would expect?' This question shattered Toby and Chapman went on to state with malice. 'It has been explained to me in detail by one of your seamen that before you went into every foul act of piracy the crew were encouraged into a drunken frenzy by their Captain.'

'No!' The shout echoed round the courtroom. Queen had lost all restraint and his eyes flamed outrage. 'This is completely untrue,' he cried, 'and casts defilement on the actions of brave and loyal men!'

Uproar in the court, public all on their feet, the Rear Admiral almost breaking his gavel as he hammered without effect, his officers locked in fierce dialogue, Queen wondering about the prosecuting counsel's knowledge and now thinking one of his crewmen must have been cornered and questioned for information: probably while being plied with strong liquor.

Regaining order, Lord Temple stated angrily, 'If I have one more outburst of hysteria I will clear the court forthwith.' He now directed his wrath towards Queen but before he could speak his mind the advocate for the defence approached the bench.

'My Lord,' he said respectfully, 'the only person qualified to reply to these accusations is Mr Queen himself and I now wish to call him to the stand as sole witness for the defence.'

His Lordship looked at Chapman, who nodded in quick agreement. He wanted nothing better than to have Queen at his mercy. With Toby dismissed, Queen took his place in the witness box. Oath administered.

'Do you swear to tell the truth, the whole truth and nothing but the truth?'

'I do.' Voice ringing through the courtroom . . . onlookers settling back in their seats with their attention caught and held by the bearing of the dishevelled but proud speaking young man. This trial was of consuming interest, the audience sharing, and revelling in the adventure unfolding before them. Up stepped defence counsel Helford?

Commotion erupted in the hallway outside. Double doors crashing open as in swept Fitzroy Probus in full uniform and wearing a sinister-looking black eye patch over his left eye and all in court were in astounded silence at the impressive and unexpected appearance of the Captain as he stalked up to the bench and growled at the Rear Admiral. 'What nonsense is this, Nathan?'

Lord Temple seemed to have shrunk in size but recovered composure to snap, 'Captain Probus: this is a Naval court of enquiry and you have no business here.'

'On the contrary,' Probus was fighting mad and it showed in the tone of his voice as he stated. 'I am the only person who can refute these ridiculous charges.' Glaring at the Rear Admiral he then moved to confront Queen. 'From what I hear from McFie you need a new defence counsel.'

Re-addressing his Lordship to announce. 'Nathan, I am appointing myself as counsel for Mr Queen.'

'He could certainly do with some help.' The judge was not entirely without sympathy, for the weakness of the appointed defence had caused controversy on the bench. Speaking to his officers and their heads closed together for a few minutes. 'Fitzroy Probus,' he then snapped, 'you are fined fifty guineas for contempt of court.'

'Thought as much.' Slapping down money, growling. 'Can we now get on with it?'

Lord Temple shrugged resignedly. The audience settled back, consumed with avid attention. Prosecutor on his feet about to object but fixing him with his good eye Probus said, 'Do you want the truth: or not?'

Looking to the judge for help but finding none the prosecutor sat down again. Probus turned to address the court. 'For your information I am Captain Fitzroy Probus of the late ship *Earl of Rothesay*...in sole command and responsible for each and every member of the ship's company.' When Probus spoke this way people listened and the courtroom took on an air of respectful attention. 'Now then, lad,' he said to Queen. 'I have learned enough of this affair from McFie and I give my word that I knew nothing at all until yesterday when he burst in on me like a rogue elephant.' Adding in sardonic tone. 'My little cottage seems far removed from the intrigues of the City.' Allowing this to be absorbed he gave Queen a glance of condemnation. 'I've seen you in some strange rigs, but never so shabby.'

In ecstatic turmoil at the appearance of his Captain, Queen explained, 'I was allowed no toilet facilities, sir.'

'Probably afraid your good looks might influence the hearing,' said Probus nodding his head grimly. His voice now rang out for all to hear. 'Mr Queen, I would like to know what happened to the money realised at Malacca?'

'It was held in my cabin until we came into the Thames then distributed evenly between officers and crew.'

'Evenly!' Probus exclaimed in startled voice. 'This is not traditional procedure. Why did you and your officers give up your recognised share? The sum must have been considerable.'

'For two reasons, sir, first because we shared the dangers evenly, and second because I had earlier made a promise to the men which I was unable to keep.'

'What kind of promise?'

'They were to receive a fair share of any prize money realised from the sale of *Restitution*.'

'You had reason to assume you might not be able to keep this promise?'

'I had to anticipate that we would be looked upon as buccaneers and our prize confiscated.'

'So you sold your booty for cash and distributed it to the men. Then, I suppose, as soon as you dropped your hook in the Thames they all scampered ashore safe and sound with sea bags over their shoulder and pockets bulging with gold and silver coin.' Smiling broadly as he went on with. 'Like it better all the time and begin to fully understand why men would follow you, Jason Queen, it's a wonder they're not here breaking down the door.'

'They had orders not to show themselves.'

'That's as may be,' countered Probus, 'but I counted a few familiar heads in the street outside and looking ready for boarding if need arose.' He then said briskly, 'Back to business. How much was each man's share?'

'Twelve hundred guineas.'

'And there were three officers and about forty men.'

Queen nodded and, after a quick calculation, Probus said, 'More than fifty thousand guineas. Not bad going for a youth and half a ship's company. But didn't you feel that the money belonged to the Company?'

'Under the circumstances no, sir, we had been sailing as privateers and I was reasonably sure the Company would deny any association with us.' Looking at Probus as if to justify. 'The men risked their lives, both in the taking, and sailing of *Restitution,* and I couldn't ask then to return home as penniless outcasts. Anyway, Captain,' he added, 'I believe the Company has already sold the ship and pocketed the proceeds: and a considerable cargo of goods still remained on board after we docked.'

The court heard this account with consuming interest, their eyes glued to the intense face of the midshipman . . . sensing the pride he felt for his ship and for his crew they could associate with his determination to keep faith with those who had served him so well.

Probus turned to the Rear Admiral. 'As for the charge of piracy,' he said, 'Mr Queen acted under my orders at all times, both when they took *Restitution* from the hands of Swally himself, Swally . . .' interrupting his narrative to repeat the name he then said in scornful tone, 'who had thumbed his nose at the Navies of the three most powerful seafaring nations ever to sail the great oceans, a monster who murdered and pillaged his way across the entire width of the South China Sea.' Prowling before them...voice commanding every ear. Prosecuting counsel shrinking in his seat as Probus passed, as if feeling the Captain's wrath directed at him personally.

'*Can you possibly imagine?*' Thundering every word as though underlined. 'How these three young officers and thirty shipwrecked seamen force-marched more than fifty miles over a volcanic island and then had the nerve: the sheer audacity to take Swally's ship from under him! I ask the court to also acknowledge the fact that *Restitution* was then sailed back to the relief of the original ship's company.' A note of compelling humility had crept into his voice and which communicated to the Naval Officers more than any cry of outrage.

'No,' declared Probus, 'there is no charge of piracy to answer here. For these men were acting under my orders at all times, including the taking of *Zeevalk,* and never overlook the relevant fact that Mr Ernest Harper and several of my crew were imprisoned aboard this Dutch vessel and subsequently recovered.' Bracing his shoulders and, with great authority, he stated. 'When Fitzroy Probus is in command orders are obeyed: and no one else is allowed to assume the mantle of responsibility.' Pausing. Allowing the court time to absorb this bold statement he then resumed his questions to ask. 'One thing puzzles me, Mr Queen. Why were you flying the black flag when you engaged *Zeevalk?*'

Looking straight at him, Queen said, 'I had to accept that I had a very personal motive to take her and couldn't violate the English ensign by an act which could be thought of as deliberate piracy.'

'This personal motive being the Dutchman Hallmeyer?'

Margaret Passendale's eyes were wide in the parched ivory of her face. All in the court entranced as Queen jerked upright and gripped the front of the witness box with an emotion and intensity that transformed his hands into white-knuckled talons.

'Hallmeyer!' The name was a sentence of death on the mouth of Jason Queen. His head came high and his eyes stabbed at them. He looked lethal! Then he said in growling voice. 'This man took someone both beautiful and innocent and ravaged her in the most vile manner . . . leaving her with a disease so foul her sensitive soul could not endure the shame.' Tall. Dominating. And with his eyes afire as the memory consumed yet again. 'Now hear this! And mark me well!' Words powering with deadly intent. 'If I were to meet this man yet again I would cut him down without mercy: and without the slightest remorse.'

Probus allowed a few moments for this awesome declaration to hover like a hangman's noose over the courtroom. Looking at Queen, and his look was one of compassion and affection. 'This maiden,' he asked in gentle voice, 'this Princess? How old was she?'

'Just sixteen.' He couldn't take anymore, and the words strangled into a sob and he slumped against the witness box, and Probus turned away to announce:

'There is your murderer and pirate.' Looking with disdain at the Judge and his officers, he said in biting voice. 'Who among you would condemn an officer for obeying the orders of his Captain? And also for following the most noble and challenging instincts known to man. Members of the court,' said Probus with moving eloquence, 'I ask you to look upon the face of chivalry in the person of one Jason Queen. A youth valiant! Cast in the mould of the early seafarers of our great nation. Men who carried the name of England into the far corners of the world with pride and determination . . . and to whom there is no hardship that cannot be endured and prevailed against in the cause of King and Country.' Pausing with dramatic effect, he then concluded. 'And in the pursuit of gallantry!'

Brief look exchanging between Lord Temple and his Officers, gavel crashing: once.

'Case dismissed!'

A great shout of approval blasted across the courtroom. She ran to him and he caught her with eager hands.

'Jason, Jason,' was all she could say. Brushing moisture from her eyes with a gentle finger and his arms tight around her, he murmured:

'No more tears, Maggie.' Turning to Probus. 'Thank you, Captain,' he said, 'all seemed hopeless before you came.' Looking around the courtroom where everyone was engaged in animated conversation and the place a hubbub of noise he said with a grin. 'You certainly changed the atmosphere in this court.' Then, in serious tone. 'I'm sorry about the loss of your eye, sir.'

Eyebrow lifting sardonically, Probus flicked up the patch to reveal a flawless left eye and said with a snide smile, 'Nothing like an eye patch to intimidate the enemy.' Amusement changing to concern, he added, 'You're not out of trouble yet. When word of your acquittal gets about the Excise Men will be hot on your trail. They're not going to appreciate the story of forty men sneaking ashore with a fortune in gold between them.' Barely restraining laughter as he announced. 'I've arranged for you, Bonham-Jones and McFie to join ship at Blackwall. Alan Sethman is taking the *Eastern Light* down the Thames as soon as the wind serves, and you three have officers berths aboard.' He was justly pleased with himself, and added, 'There are a few others joining who you might recognise.'

'Right away?' Maggie's voice came as a whisper of despair.

'It's either that or finding him in the dock again. Jason won't be safe until he puts some sea miles between himself and London.' Her distress was too obvious to ignore and, in an attempt to reassure, he said. 'It will only be a return trip to Java this time and he'll soon be back with everything forgotten.'

Maggie wouldn't be consoled. She thought he was talking about the other end of the world!

Chapter Thirty-two

Newly commissioned and ready to set forth on her maiden voyage *Eastern Light* swung to her mooring at Blackwall. The officers assembled in the aft stateroom, lining up in order of rank.

David Ashbury. First Officer.

Bonham-Jones. Second Officer.

Queen. McFie. Joint Third.

'Gentlemen,' said the Captain, 'let me say how pleased I am to have you sailing with me and that I'm confidently looking forward to a happy ship.' Sipping brandy, puffing on a cigar as befitting the Master, he asked. 'How is the leg, Mr McFie?'

'Doctors say I'll never walk properly again. What do they know?' Swinging his leg in emphasis. 'This leg will come alive when it feels the warmth of a tropic sun.'

'With you three aboard all the buccaneers in the South Seas will be running for cover,' said Sethman with a smile, before querying. 'Why so subdued, Mr Queen? None of my business I suspect.' Resuming his briefing to state. 'You are aware, of course, that the ship has been commissioned to trade direct with the Spice Islands.' The name conjured up a picture of coconut palms and pounding surf as he continued. 'We'll have a merchant venturer on board to no doubt instruct us in the proper conducting of ship's business. But we've played this game before and will be expected to cooperate wholeheartedly,' Drawing thoughtfully on his cigar before admitting. 'I'm sorry Fitz wouldn't resume his Captaincy but I know his reasons and must respect them.' Shrugging away regret. 'I trust you will give me the same support, and ask you to drink to the success and mutual prosperity of our voyage.' Topping up their glasses, he announced. 'Many of our old crew have rejoined, which I take as a great compliment to my officers. They even subscribed to a new lute for Vindo.'

'Heard him playing on the main deck as I came aboard,' said Bonham-Jones, 'hope he allows us to join in sometimes. Fancy a few choruses of "Spanish Town" would soon liven things up.'

'Don't think much of our new apprentices,' said McFie, 'three of them were green as grass at teatime and we haven't yet dropped the mooring.'

'Young lads all look alike when they first come aboard,' said Sethman blandly, 'but I'm sure they'll soon learn a trick or two before we get very far at sea . . . especially with such a model of propriety as yourself to observe.' Shedding his casual manner he then instructed. 'All hands on deck at first light, we anchor at Deptford to change pilots.'

Fine drizzle, mist, the river dark and quiet. No bird called. Even the wind was still. Lights from the shore jetty just visible through the clammy mist and the rigging dripped cold and wet . . . a gloomy atmosphere that matched the sombre state of his mind. 'It's no use, Billie,' said Queen, staying his restless pacing. 'I have to go to her!'

'For crying out loud! We sail on the morning tide. You'll never get back in time and the Captain won't wait: even for you?'

'I'm not coming back.'

'For God's sake, Jase! Why?'

'To prove her wrong! She recently said our biggest problem is my desire to selfishly hold on. That I couldn't let go! Of my need to command a tall ship, of my friends: and especially of herself.'

'I was once proud and grateful to be on the receiving end of such selfishness.' Sensing torment but devastated by the announcement, McFie asked in doleful tone. 'Are you sure this is what you want to do?'

'No,' replied Queen candidly, 'but I'll surely lose her if I sail away.'

'You don't have any choice then. Get yourself off the ship and go to her.' Reaching out his hand, large and warm, and the two clasped each other in a tight, emotional grip. 'Think of us sometimes,' entreated McFie.

'Keep away from dainty Chinese girls, Billie,' said Queen with a sob in his throat.

'Shut up! You'll have me in tears.' Breaking away McFie said in a distraught manner. 'Give me a few minutes to organise a boat's crew.'

Three men in the longboat as he scrambled down the netting, Vinderman at the tiller, Dooley and Abbot at the rowing thwarts . . . grim faced and silent as he came aboard.

'All gone.' McFie released the painter and stood clutching the rigging for support.

Helming towards the shore. With the longboat on course Vinderman commented:

'Finally made up your mind then?' receiving no response he added, 'about time because you were good to neither ship nor yourself in that state of mind.'

Dooley and Abbot rowing with little show of enthusiasm. 'Won't be the same without you, Mr Queen,' spoke up Dooley, 'most of us only signed up again at such short notice because you were aboard.'

The compliment was appreciated but served only to reinforce anguish as he looked at his men. 'She's a stout ship,' he said, 'and you'll have a fair Captain but better make sure you give of your best, for Billie McFie will be keeping a beady eye on you.'

'If we have to go over the side in action again, I hope he brings his crutch,' Jacko Abbot had them all smiling as he added, 'one of the greatest sights of my life at sea is Billie McFie wielding his crutch.' Jacko seemed unusually talkative and went on without pausing. 'My share of the money set the missus up in a little waterfront pub and, with my two lads to help keep order, I reckon she'll do very nicely.'

'Can't imagine you on the other side of a bar, Jacko?' Never picturing Abbot as a family man, Queen's comment reflected surprise.

'Just what the missus thought, she wasn't too unhappy to see my arse-end disappear out the door, said she might be able to show a profit with me out of the way.' Grinning in carefree manner. 'Seems a fair arrangement and at the same time gives me a comfortable berth to come home to.'

The big man seemed very sure of himself and Queen looked at him almost with envy as he said, 'I'm glad for you, Jacko.'

'Just thought you'd like to know how grateful we all are, sir,' responded Abbot, 'most of the lads blew the lot on a wild spree but my missus is a shrewd old bag and all she needed was a start. She's set up now though and seems to think more of me into the bargain.' Repeating in conclusion. ''Tis a fair arrangement.'

'Which is what you're seeking, Jase?' Vinderman said.

'Something of the sort.' He knew Vindo had

used most of his share to purchase a half ownership in a sloop trading out of his beloved Dartmouth. Aching with turmoil and indecision. Vindo. McFie. The crew? They had come a long way together . . . were part of him?

'What a waste of a great skipper!' Dooley had no ties ashore and was usually bored to frustration after a few weeks. 'Don't suppose we'll see the like of *Restitution* again,' he mused, 'wonder where she is now'?'

'Sailing under the Royal Navy ensign and on her way to the Mediterranean, ' answered Queen reluctantly.

'She was a beauty,' broke in Vinderman, 'lines like hers could seduce me more than any woman.'

'Enough, Vindo! You've made your point.'

Suddenly alert, Vinderman pushed the helm hard down. 'Boat ahead!'

A small ferry with just one man rowing had come chunking out of the gloom and swept alongside as Vinderman steered clear. His eyes met Queen's in an incredulous stare as they made out the tiny figure sat huddled into a sea coat with just her face showing.

'Maggie!' He couldn't believe it and his cry brought her surging round in shock. The boats swept apart and out of sight in the mist but her call echoed back:

'Jason, is that you?'

'Vinderman's voice held a mixture of amusement and conjecture as he said, 'Reckon we're going the wrong way, lads.' Easing the helm over and as the longboat came round in pursuit. 'Now put some muscle into it, you grinning sods.'

Dooley and Abbot didn't need prompting and the longboat soon closed on the ferry. *Eastern Light* loomed ahead and they came together alongside the black and yellow hull. Maggie stood up excitedly and the little craft took a sudden list to starboard as Queen brought her up against him and pulled the hood from her face. 'Maggie,' he exclaimed in bewilderment, 'how on earth?'

Her mouth stifled the question and they clung ecstatically to each other and in full view of the delighted seamen. 'I'll never let you go, my darling,' she whispered, 'and if you can't come to me? – 'Reaching for him again with the words unfinished.

'Mr McFie!'

Vinderman's call brought him running. His eyes nearly popped out of his head when he saw the embracing couple. Then, with a whoop of acclaim, he blurted. 'Never know whom you might bump into out here in the River Thames,' as she clambered up the boarding net, he greeted her with a very formal, 'welcome aboard, Miss Passendale, may I ask how long you intend to be with us?'

'As long as it takes to persuade your Captain to marry us, perhaps all the way to your South China Sea and back again?' Overwhelmed by McFie's delirious welcome she had no time for further comment as Queen appeared on deck, and dropping her trunk from his shoulder reached out, hungry for the touch of her. She came without inhibition into his arms and their bodies moulded as one and her mouth on his, though tremulous at first, seemed to draw him further into her and insist she would never allow anything to part her from him. Then with eyes afire, she asked. 'Where were you going at this time of night?'

'To find you.' McFie couldn't keep still in his excitement as he exclaimed. 'Jason Queen was jumping ship to be with his Maggie.' This announcement brought a surge of emotion and fulfilment and her eyes were deep and wondrous on Queen.

'You finally let go.' Almost sobbing the words. 'You would have given it all up? For me!'

'And for myself: for without you I have nothing.'

Quiet but convincing tone and she stood on tiptoe to kiss his mouth, then said, 'The very words I used to convince my father.' His head cocked as a diminishing rattle of coach and horses carried across the water, bringing confirmation from Maggie. 'He wanted me to go direct to Portsmouth, but I insisted that he drive me here.' Adding with a shy glance. 'I couldn't wait so long.'

'Just as well,' interrupted McFie, 'otherwise you two could have spent the rest of your lives chasing around the Seven Seas trying to catch up with each other.' The thought caused him to collapse helplessly against the rigging.

'You're hopeless, McFie.'

Picking up her trunk he began to lead her away and Vinderman, Dooley and Abbot, lined up by the rail, whipped off their caps in spontaneous salute as she came by and Vinderman bowed before her. 'May I say how glad we are to have you aboard, Miss Passendale,' he said in warm voice, 'and to have our Jason Queen returned to us.'

She looked at the three burly seamen with sudden tears clouding her eyes, and then returning his bow with a little curtsy she murmured, 'It seems I must share my love, not only with his ship but with his crew also.' Tears streaming unchecked now and, in a voice breaking with emotion, she said very huskily, 'I only hope I can prove worthy.'

'Margaret,' there was great dignity in the bearing of Daniel Vinderman as he spoke her name, then stated, 'your beauty is matched only by the understanding of a gentle heart.' Pausing, he then said in typical, sardonic manner. 'There is a chance that together we might make a man of Jason Queen.'

Smiling through the tears, Maggie said:

'He's man enough already.'

Chapter Thirty-three

Spithead. Bustling with colour and movement. Portsmouth wherries plying their trade between the town and Ryde on the Isle of Wight, tiny sloops and luggers dipping and heeling betwixt shore and anchorage. Naval frigates and immense three-deckers of the line lying quiet and dignified to their anchors. Commissioning pennants fluttering in the fitful breeze and the grey waters of Spithead Roads were still on this clear day. A convoy of East Indiamen swung to their cables impatient to feel blue water under their keels. Newly designed vessels . . . sleek of hull. Breathtakingly lovely: and romantic as any love story.

'Take over the foredeck watch, Mr Queen,' ordered David Ashbury. 'Captain is standing by the entry port to welcome aboard our new merchant venturer and others of importance. We have quite a number of passengers this time, more's the pity, but passenger carrying is something we'll have to accept because our ships are becoming vehicles for the transport of personnel as well as cargo. Trading empires need more and more staff and what more natural than for the Company to make full use of its ever growing fleet.' Grinning boyishly. 'How did I get started on such rubbish? We only have to sail 'em.'

Bonham-Jones had joined them and now interrupted to say, 'The advantage of having just a few passengers is that you soon get to know them.' Glancing around. 'Even now I expect to see Martha Harper swinging inboard on a rope's end. You know they have moved to the country because of Mr Harper's poor health?'

'Good to see her at the trial though, I thought she was going to belt the prosecutor with her umbrella.' Smiling in remembrance, Queen added, 'They offered to pay for my learned advocate but I had enough left from my prize money to cover the legal fees.'

'They were all there,' said Bonham-Jones, 'Martha, the Verbers, but when Old Probus came sailing in with his eye patch smoking hot the Rear Admiral nearly took off out the back door.' A thought occurred which caused him to query. 'You must have been left almost penniless afterwards?'

'A native Princess taught me there are values of more importance . . . values which have lately been in great evidence.' Queen's eyes levelled on Toby's face. 'If a man is deemed rich by the quality of his friends,' he stated, 'you are looking at a veritable treasure trove.'

Holding his gaze, Toby said, 'Isn't this because you get back from people in equal measure only what you are prepared to give of yourself?'

After delivering this gem of philosophy Toby thought it time to go about his business but paused as David Ashbury looked at Queen and said, 'What happened to your little half-caste interpreter and personal shadow?'

'Ramon Salvador! He was reluctant to leave us but the men kept telling him horrific stories of the weather back home, so he paid off in Malacca with a share that was riches beyond his wildest imaginings.' Queen was very content at this moment and, smiling in reminiscence, added, 'Said he would be waiting impatiently for our return.'

'Somehow see him with one of McFie's Chinese maidens,' said Toby, 'and a shoal of dusky children.'

'Aye,' said Queen.

'Remember the Captain has ordered us to pre-dinner drinks in his stateroom this evening.' Ashbury then casually suggested. 'But if your duties prevent you attending, I'll be most happy to entertain the captivating Maggie.'

'Better steer clear of McFie then. He's already made the same proposal.'

Clasping his arm as they approached the stateroom, she was dressed in a full-skirted gown of blue poplin cut daringly low to display the splendour of her shoulders and the full, revealing curve of her breasts and the cleavage between. She had greeted his gasp of admiration with a toss of her head and a pertinent. 'I don't see any reason to hide my womanhood, for after all, who better than you to know I am no longer a maiden?' Eluding his hungry arms. 'Later, my impetuous darling, for now we have some very important people to meet.'

A cabin steward attended the door. Maggie entered first, pulling Queen along with a firm hand. He had a momentary vision of Probus flash in his mind accompanied by regret that his Captain was not there to greet them. A thought quickly replaced by astonishment as a smiling Sir James came forward with his hands outstretched to them. Delighted but incredulous, Queen stammered, 'Are you sailing with us, sir?'

'I had a sudden urge to inspect our trading establishments at first hand.' Adding with a smile. 'Why should you young people have all the excitement?' Sir James was dressed in a burgundy velvet jacket and matching waistcoat. His breeches were white silk and showed to advantage the shapely calves of his legs. He wore no wig. His hair was long and tied behind his head with a black ribbon and just then his faces was all smiles.

'You look magnificent, sir,' said Queen, but there was question in his tone that brought a chuckle from Sir James.

'Bit too formal, am I? You haven't seen anything yet for I have some sailing gear with me that will really make your eyes pop.'

Fellow officers and male passengers soon converged on Maggie, the passengers seemed a mixed lot and several women were on colourful display. Sipping claret from a crystal goblet, Queen's eyes widened over the brim as he caught sight of a solitary figure with his back turned and looking out through the stern windows. Moving behind the elegantly dressed man. 'Abraham . . . I don't believe it!' Verber spun round and his face was alight. They clasped hands, then embraced: warmly.

'Saw you come in, Jase, and wondered how long before you recognised me.'

'What the hell are you doing aboard?' Standing back to take in the richly attired Verber, who appeared to have grown older and somehow more worldly. Then he nodded in enlightenment. 'Captain said we would have a merchant venturer with us, but obviously was keeping you for a surprise package.' Delighted, but sceptical. 'Thought seafaring was too restrictive for you,' he said, 'that you needed the cut and thrust of business life ashore?'

'So did I. Strange how colourless it all seemed and after a few restless days wandering the dusty streets of London I managed to persuade my father and some of his rich friends to commission *Eastern Light* and allow me to prove that money can be made in the Far East. But don't be fooled by the fancy clothes, Mr Third Officer, I can still do a trick aloft should need arise.' Exuberance fading. 'I almost bought *Restitution* when she was up for auction but I just couldn't see her as a merchantman and let her go to the Navy.' Looking for reaction as he quietly added, 'And I knew our buccaneering days were over.'

'She really was something,' said Queen forlornly. 'Sleek, fast . . . and deadly. But never less than beautiful.'

'You make it sound like a love affair,' said Verber with perception.

'Isn't that just what it is?' Melancholy tone of voice as he added, 'yet she was always a free spirit: and only happy when on the chase of a distant sail.'

'Fond memories, eh Jase.'

'Can we avoid them?'

'No,' replied Abraham, 'but we can try to remember the philosophy of enjoying each particular moment and letting the rest go.'

Queen's eyes met the searching gaze of Maggie from across the crowded stateroom. She was flushed and lovely and, noting the pride on his face, Abraham said:

'Why do you waste time with me talking of old ships when Maggie looks at you with love enough to turn a man to jelly? Count your blessings, Jason Queen, and go to her,' smiling fondly at him, Abraham added, 'and pay homage to the teachings of the natives of Semarund.'

Epilogue

'Heave short!' Familiar command. The anchor cable was hauled straight up and down.

'Make ready all plain sail.'

'Set foretopsails: and back mizzens.'

She hovered . . . eager to find blue water.

Jack Dooley was in Vinderman's old steering position. Vinderman was sailing master. Hawk faced. Formidable. 'The Navy is watching us, Jack,' he said.

'Aye, aye, Mr Vinderman.' There was need for no further comment. These two were as one at the helm.

'Break Out!'

Up came the anchor. Flukes clean. Dripping salt water.

'Set topsails and main courses!' The sails dropped and bellied into curving white wings. *Eastern Light* moved with stately grace through the anchored fleet. A bosun's whistle trilled salute from the flagship and a solitary cannon boomed farewell.

'All clear ahead,' said the Third Officer, 'keep her steady as she goes.'

'Wheel steady on, sir.'

The wind came free. She heeled to a gust. The wheel kicked in the sure hands of the helmsman. The bow wave growled. Vinderman closed one eye in an exaggerated wink.

'Here we go again, Mr Queen.'

THE END